When Lucifer Met Calamity

D. Alyce Domain

This book is an original novel self-publication by the credited author, D. Alyce Domain.

This is a work of creative fiction. Names, characters, places, and incidents are either a product of the author's imagination or are used fictitiously, and any resemblance to actual persons, living or dead, business establishments, events or locales is entirely coincidental.

1st Edition: April 2016
Cover Design by D. Alyce Domain
Cover Image/Photography by Pramadhita | Dreamstime.com

ISBN: 0996926739
ISBN-13: 978-0-9969267-3-7

DEDICATION

I dedicate this book to my big sister, Nicole, who helped
me eliminate all those pesky hard-to-find typos. She
provided an invaluable service in the road to publication.

CONTENTS

ACKNOWLEDGMENTS

I would like to acknowledge the unconditional love and undeserved blessings that I receive from God and his precious son Jesus Christ. Without his saving grace nothing in my life, not even my life itself would be possible.

I send a special thanks to my very supportive very patient parents, Charles and Eunice Domain who believed in me without fail.

I also thank all my long-time friends and family who have sent me positive thoughts, without which I would not have been able to focus and complete my writing goals.

CALAMITY JONES...THE RULES

Rule #1: Lie

Rule #2: Bait-n-Switch

Rule #3: Play the Female Card

Rule #4: Exhaust All Avenues

Rule #5: Shred the Evidence

Rule #6: Deny Everything

Rule #7: Lawyer up

Rule #8: Spare the Innocents

Rule #9: Always Have a Plan B

Rule #10: Face the Music

D. ALYCE DOMAIN

THE SET-UP

"You *what?*"

"I resigned, Mama."

"You quit your job. Just like that." Her coffee eyes went owlish.

"The man put his hands on my ass, Mama. What the hell was I supposed to do, bend over?"

"Calam, please say 'bottom' or 'rear'. Anything but 'ass'."

Her mother was always upset with her for one reason or another. True, Calamity tap danced to a slightly different beat than the rest of world but what perplexed her was why after twenty-seven years her mother hadn't gotten used to it.

"Weren't *you* the one who claimed that I was casting my pearls before swine by working as a–and I quote–'glorified receptionist'." Calam flittered her hand about with casual exasperation. "End quote. Well, I've quit…so, now, what's the problem?"

"Calam, you cannot just quit your job without lining up another one first. Did you even give them two week's notice? Will they give you a reference? Wait." Her mother turned her stock 'please-tell-me-you-didn't' expression on her. "Maybe we can fix this. How did you leave it?"

"Hmmm, how did I leave it? An excellent question." Calamity fidgeted with a kinky two-stranded twist, chocolate eyes rolling. She felt one of her mother's 'why can't you be more like your sister' lectures coming on like a split-level headache.

"Calamity, you haven't answered my question."

"Oh, right. Well, I submitted a formal notice of resignation, right after I tattooed my heel print into his forehead. Or, did I drop kick him first? I forget." She tapped a finger against her temple as if trying to decide. "Either way, I don't think we can fix it, unless you and daddy have one of those hot-tub time machines in the backyard. Mama, do you really want me working some place where the Boss sticks his hand up my skirt twenty times a day?"

"Heaven help me." Her mother groaned, throwing up a frustrated hand. "I should have never agreed to those Karate lessons, but like an idiot I listened to your father. 'Marian, it'll be good for the girls to have separate interests,' he said. 'Help them make friends outside of each other,' he said. 'Give them a sense of individuality', he said. BAH! I should have *made* you take ballet just like your sister."

Calamity mouthed the last four words, the four most popular words in her mother's vocabulary.

"Mama, we're identical twins." She reminded her in a caustic tone. "Right down to an embarrassingly situated birthmark...I don't see how we could get any *more* alike." Her mother continued her worry-fueled spew without registering the sarcasm. Not in the mood for an argument, Calamity allowed her mind and eyes to wander a bit as Marian droned on.

Her thoughts turned self-reflective. Exactly why *did* the most bizarre happenings befall *her*? All her life, Calamity had been prone to...well, *calamity*. She recalled the third-grade field trip to the zoo. She got her head wedged between the bars of the monkey cage and the teacher had to call the fire department to pry her loose. Her mind skipped forward to prom night...when her one-of-a-kind dress unraveled at the seams leaving her next to naked on the ballroom floor. In retrospect, learning to sew via a six-week correspondence course *was* a bit dicey. But still, things like that had never happened to Charisma.

"...of course, don't get me wrong, Sweetie. I wouldn't want you being groped at work, but couldn't you have filed a complaint or something? Try to get *him* fired instead of kicking the man in the teeth and quitting your job. Things are not like they were in my day, Calam. Sexual harassment is taken very seriously. Calamity? Are you listening to me?"

She snapped back to attention, to see her mother frowning. "Yes, of course, Mama. I'm listening and I am taking every word you say very seriously." Calamity tried for a reassuring smile.

Her mother gasped, "What have you done?"

"Mama, have you ever considered hardwood instead of this stuffy old carpet? Carpet holds heat. Remember, we live in Houston, home of eternal summer."

"Don't change the subject." She chastened, as only an overprotective mother could. "Out with it. Tell me what you did right now and maybe we can still fix it."

"What makes you think anything needs fixing?"

"Because I know you, young lady."

Calamity studied the woman before her. Marian Lowe. Caramel complexion, middling height with relaxed silver-streaked hair and laughing eyes. Meanwhile, Calamity was darker complected, more hazelnut than caramel and several inches shorter; however, overall, she and Charisma resembled their mother the most. While her twin had inherited a bit of their mother's apple-pie mentality, Calamity resided at the opposite end of the spectrum, sharing nary a personality trait with her mother. In fact, if not for the obvious familial resemblance, Calamity would have sworn she'd been left on her parent's doorstep by

Gypsies.

"Calam? I'm waiting." Her mother's pointed glare aroused her from her thoughts.

Again, she fidgeted with an inky coil of hair. "Eh, well, I didn't just resign, Mama. I have a plan."

Her mother rolled her eyes. "If I didn't already know drinking was a sin, I'd be knocking back a wet one right now."

Ever the comedian, Calam pointed out her mother's mistake. "Actually, Mama, drunkenness is a sin, not drinking."

"Don't split hairs with me, young lady. I was an English teacher. Noun, verb, or adjective, they all have the same root word, drunk."

"Semantics, Mama."

"Look, I'd much rather finish our first argument before we start a new one. What is this scheme of yours all about?"

"It's brilliant, a real masterpiece." Calamity beamed at her mother, marveling at her own genius. "And the best part is, I won't have to lift a finger. He'll hang himself. See—" She stopped short at the digitized James Bond theme music. She held up her hand to indicate that she'd only be a minute, then reached into her pocket to whip out her cell. "Hello?"

"Calam, it's me. The door's locked. Come open it, will ya." An ominous click followed her sister's breathless oration.

Calamity's brow arched as she slipped the cell back in her pocket. "Eh…That was Charisma. She's outside."

Calam noticed her mother's expression mirrored her confusion. Though neither she nor Chris still lived at home, they each retained a key in case of emergencies. "If she forgot her key, why didn't she just knock?"

Marian and Calamity opened the dark mahogany door to find Charisma sagging against the doorframe with an over-night bag in tow. Her usually feathered pageboy-bob clung sweaty and lank against her head like the 'before' picture in a hair-care ad.

"My goodness," Their mother exclaimed. "What happened to you?"

"Calam, help me with this will ya." She all but tossed the bag into her sister's hands without breaking stride. Calamity followed, bewildered.

"Charisma." Their mother trailed them into the living room, ringing her hands. "What's going on? Why are you toting a suitcase? Did you and Paul have a fight or something?"

"Ahhh..." Charisma plopped down on the hackneyed, but comfortable, couch and kicked off her navy block heels. She took great and obvious pleasure in rolling her ankles to get the kinks out of her joints, moaning contentedly as she wiggled each stocking-clad toe. "Eh, no of course not, Mama. Paul and I are fine, better than fine. We're great actually, but Calam I'm going to need to bunk with you for a week or so."

"You moved out?" Calamity gaped at her mirror image as if she'd just morphed into a three-headed hell hound. She dumped the baggage on the ruddy hued carpet. "And where is Manny, huh? Foster care? I thought you wanted me to keep him tonight. You're not due at my place for another—"

"Manny's got the measles." Charisma grimaced, the words themselves seemed to remind her of some irritating situation. Uh-oh. Calam recognized that tone. The vent was about to blow, any second now.

"So, eh, he's not—"

"Still at school, eh, *no*." She snapped, chopping off the end of Calam's sentence like a fish-head on the butcher's block. "Paul had to go pick him up early because the teacher didn't want him *infecting* any of the other children with his foreign germs. That's what she said, *foreign* germs. Like he's a world traveler, exposed to exotic diseases from around the globe. The only place he goes is *school.*"

"Chrissy, don't you think you're overreacting a tad." Calamity suggested, cautious not to poke the snake.

"Maybe, but you didn't *hear* her. She speaks in this posh little sneer. To let her tell it, he's *Typhoid* Manny, the scourge of pre-school. Just who exactly does she think gave it to Manny, anyway? His imaginary friend? Those diseased little brats infected my son, and now he's the one banished into quarantine."

Marian sighed and plopped down in the too-soft couch beside her daughter. "Is he ok? Poor baby, we should take him some soup."

"No!" She shrieked. "Mama, we can't. Paul will take care of Manny."

Calamity and Marian shrank away and stared at her, appalled.

"Relax Charisma, we both had measles in the fifth grade. Remember?"

"Listen to me okay, and try to keep up with the conversation." Charisma pulled her sister down to sit on the glass-top coffee table opposite her. "I've already talked to my Ob-Gyn and she said that it's possible to have measles more than once. The chance is slim but it's there. As much as I want to be at home taking care of Manny, I can't catch measles."

"Ob-Gyn?" Calamity repeated, eyeing her sister's flat midsection with suspicion. "Are you—"

"Pregnant, yes." She confirmed. "Worse case scenario…if I catch measles, your new little niece will be born with two heads and a negative IQ."

"Well, damn." Although a part of Calamity rejoiced at the news, a tiny little voice inside her heart railed against another reminder of her own unfulfilled longing. "Couldn't you have waited until I got married at least? I wanted our kids to grow up together. At this rate, you'll be looking at college brochures before I've even started breast-feeding."

"Yeah, Calam…family planning, *that's* what we were

discussing. Does your brain have detour signs or something?" She prattled on, excited. "But while we're on the subject, Paul knows this guy—old college buddy—perfect. I said I'd run it by you first."

Oh, please no! Calam cringed inwardly. She was still having night terrors from the last blind date she suffered through. "Eh, weren't we all in college together? I don't remember Paul having any date-able friends."

"Not *then*, but things change." Her sister nudged her, trying to conjure up some excitement where none existed. Calam had no wish to go on another dead-end date.

"Think about it at least, and let me know. We'll do dinner at our house."

"Would that be before or *after* the quarantine is lifted?" Calam reminded her.

Her sister gave her the side eye. "Well, we certainly can't have dinner at your place, not with that…*person*…in and outta there."

"Charisma please, be tolerant. *Shane* is a talented artist and a friend, who also just happens to be having a difficult time lately. Cheryl left him again."

Her sister's only answer was an exaggerated eye-roll.

"A little girl. Really?" Their mother murmured. "I didn't know the doctors could tell so early."

Calam smiled, shaking her head. Marian's one-track mind had glazed over, contemplating her future granddaughter. Talk about mental detour signs.

"Mama, please try to keep up. That was two conversations ago." Charisma chided. "But I *do* need to make it absolutely clear that *no one*, at any time during the next week and a half, is to go near my house, Paul, or Manny. Understand? Now, I'm going to stay with Calamity because I will need to borrow some clothes. I didn't get a chance to pack a whole lot before Paul drove up. I didn't want them to have to wait in the car with the heat and Manny being sick and all, so I just took a few things and left. Calam, we'll discuss the details of dinner later. And you had better call that He-beast squatter you got living with you and tell him there'll be none of that new age weirdness for at least ten days."

"Oh snap!" A light bulb poofed in Calamity's head. The epiphany corresponded with the mischievous gleam in her chocolate gaze. "This is great. You can help me with my project."

"There's a project?" Her sister echoed, leaning forward as if to begin the conspiracy at once. "What kind of project? Whatever it is, I'm all in."

"Ohh, I almost forgot." Marian mumbled wearily. "Your sister quit the firm today because Mr. Perkins pulled a fast-one."

"Translation…He waylaid me in the file room and grabbed my ass."

"Sweetie, please, is such graphic language really necessary?"

Both sisters ignored their mother. "He copped a feel? Oh, *hell* no, we have got to bust his ass. Just tell me what the plan is."

Marian groaned long and deep, shaking her head at the two of them. "Calamity, I really wish you wouldn't involve your sister in these ill-fated shenanigans of yours, especially in her delicate condition."

"The doctor says I'm fine." Charisma assured her. "No worries."

"See there, Mama. She said she's fine with it and besides there's no danger involved. I *promise*."

"That's what you said when you volunteered to be a live dummy for the CPR class." Her mother shot her a dubious glance. "Two weeks later, I'm signing DNR forms while an emergency room doctor is explaining to your father and I about how to take care of a fractured sternum patient, post-surgery."

"Ancient history. Quit being such a doomsayer." Calamity advised. "If this works, I could get on Good Morning, America. Gender inequality in the work place is big news lately."

"*WE* could get on Good Morning, America. *And*, I want Robin Roberts to interview us." Her sister stood and pulled her away. Charisma's strength seemed to be renewed with the possibility of something interesting to do during her ten-day quarantine, Calam noticed.

They rounded the corner, passing the dining area that lead into the kitchen. "Come on, Calam, I'm dying to hear the plan. I mean it, I'm down for whatever."

Calamity's business pumps click-clacks on the ceramic kitchen floor, as they passed through the swinging door. She hopped up bottom-first on the cubic island counter while her sister stood opposite, leaning against the rim of the dishwasher's handle. Calamity toyed with a chef's knife whose handle protruded from a sandy wood mount angled in her direction.

She eyed her sister, seized with last-minute guilt. "Chrissy, are you sure? I mean…if there's even the slightest chance that—"

Her twin's good-natured grimace cut her off. "Geez, I'm fine. Don't go soft on me."

Calam grinned, relieved, all reluctance forgotten at the prospect of dishing out some good old fashioned poetic justice with her twin by her side. "Ok, cool, so first you have to do my hair just like yours. You're not too tired, are you? Because there's a few other things we have to get if this is going to work." She ran it down, as she had in her mind earlier. "…So what do you think? It should be a cinch with the two of us working in tandem. Though we might need to pull in a third."

"Wait, what's a nanny-cam?"

"Good grief, Charisma. You have a four-year old, and you've never heard of a nanny-cam?"

"I don't even have a nanny." Charisma shot back, finger-combing her sweat-flattened hair. "I can't be expected to know their lingo, can I?"

"Well, it's one of those secret video cameras that's

dressed up to be something ordinary, like an alarm clock or stuffed animal or something. But really, it's a cool way for parents of young children, such as yourself…" She cracked, sarcastic. "…to make sure the 'sitter isn't getting slap-happy with the kids. I figure we set up some at Ross-Warner. In the file room, that's our in-house research law library we use for obscure legal—"

Charisma waved her off, anxious to hear the meaty details of the Perkins comeuppance. "Uh, that's not really need-to-know at this point."

Ignoring the attitude, Calamity continued. "It'll take us a day or so to get the cameras. Is Paul still friendly with that dude with the electronics franchise?"

Charisma nodded.

"Excellent, call him. We can get what we need from him and there won't be any official records to trace. After we get the goods, I need you to come to work with me. The office is key card access only since that little domestic dispute with the Rubin's divorce case spilled over into the lobby last year."

"It time-stamps everyone's arrival?"

She nodded. "Yes, unfortunately. And we don't want a record of us skulking around the office at weird hours. So, we'll dress alike and pull a bait and switch. You know the drill. Ok placement, we should concentrate on the hot zones—"

"Where he's attacked before, you mean?"

"Down girl." Calamity saw the wicked gleam in her sister's eye. "I think 'attacked' is a bit melodramatic, but yeah. Once we have some leverage, I will force him to cop to the harassment. It'll be on the record and he'll have to abide by whatever punishment Ross-Warner shells out. Probably every lady in the building will breathe a sigh of relief. I, of course, will then withdraw my resignation."

"Flawless." Charisma beamed, shuffling over to raid the refrigerator. She bowed low into the chilly atmosphere and came up with an apple.

"Not quite." Calam admitted. "There is *one* sticking point."

"Which is?"

"Well, receivers have a range limit…which I doubt my apartment lies within."

She paused, an apple half-way to her mouth. "Oh, yeah, that *is* kind of a problem."

"I'm conflicted. The only solution I could come up with involves a third party. And, I was trying to keep this thing as streamlined as possible." She bobbled, still undecided, but letting the idea roll around in her head. "The whole plan just blossomed on the drive home from work so give me some time. For now, let's just get the cameras set up."

"Ok. So, where are you going to put them exactly?" She tucked her shoulder-length hair behind her ears and bit into the apple.

"Toss me one of those, will you." Calamity was already armed with a cutting knife when Charisma turned back around and flipped her a Granny Smith. "Let me do the file room, the mail room, and Stella's cubical. You'll be there anyway, so you do mine and Perkins' office. If he's not in, then I'll give you the code. Eh, oh and the conference room. I'm still not sure what to do about it."

Her sister crunched on a bite of apple, garbling her words. "What's up with the conference room?"

"There's nowhere to hide. It's just a big empty space with a rectangular table in the center and chairs all around. Sure, there's a mounted projector and retractable screen built into the ceiling. But, that's it." Calamity groaned, frustrated. "No matter what the camera is disguised as, it will seem weird in *that* room…especially, if it just appears out of nowhere. We can't put anything under the table either. It'd have to be mounted. Hmm."

Charisma wiped a trickle of juice from her second bite just as Calamity popped a crisp crescent shaped slice of apple into her mouth. "Why not just bag it then."

"I don't know, maybe."

FLIPPING 'THE SWITCH'

With the sudden violent movement of the vehicle Calamity's head bobbed sharply to the side, jarring her awake. She glared to the driver's side.

"Watch it, Charisma. I don't want whiplash."

Her sister rammed the gearshift forward causing the open-air jeep to jerk once more before the engine killed dead. Then, and only then did she look over at her twin.

"Don't blame me. You're the one who insisted we take your car."

Calam turned to open the door and climb out, checking her new 'do in the side-view on the way down. She exhaled a resigned sigh. Nope, it still hadn't grown on her. A full two days hadn't pasted since she'd sacrificed her kinky two-stranded twists. But, the blown-out page-bob was a small price to pay if it meant the difference between getting her prick boss over a barrel and being put over one herself. And since it was blown out and not permed she could always go back to her own style later.

"Well, Charisma, since you're supposed to be imitating me, it seemed a good idea if you at least showed up with the right set of wheels. Everybody who's anybody knows I love my jeep. Besides, you need to learn how to handle a stick anyway. That Tonka toy knock-off you drive is an affront to adult cars everywhere."

"Oh, excuse me if I don't have four-wheel drive, Calam, but Paul and I have a responsibility to someone other than ourselves. What would you have us do, buy a Corvette and strap Manny to the roof?" Charisma slammed the driver's side door and made headway towards the sidewalk leading to their parent's black and white matchbox house. "I don't understand what we're doing here, anyway. Surely, no one will care if you key in just a few minutes early."

"Too risky. It's best not to vary the normal routine. Besides, I want to give the plan a run-through first. You be me and see if daddy catches on."

"We've never been able to fool daddy and you know it. Remember that time in college?"

"Merely a fluke." Calam disregarded her sister's snort and nudged her up their parent's drive.

Charisma ran her hands over the unfamiliar navy blue suit, Calamity's. The infamous pin-striped suit, with its long straight skirt and double-breasted jacket was so not Calamity's style, which was why she had suggested that Charisma wear it. Everyone knew the story, to Calamity's never-ending embarrassment.

In rare form, she purchased the two-hundred-dollar outfit she hated merely to provide a smooth way for the shy salesman to ask for her phone number. Then she'd conspicuously worn said suit twice as often as the rest of her clothes just to prove that misguided flirting wasn't the sole reason she'd purchased it. Calam shrugged at the memory. Live, learn, and laugh about it later. She gave herself props for at least not making the same mistake twice.

"Chrissy?"

"Huh?"

Calam shook her head as if to clear it. She came out of her thoughts to find their ebony-skinned father staring at her and Chris from the kitchen's threshold.

When Charisma didn't immediately follow him inside, his wiry eyebrows rose a centimeter. "Is something the matter?" Their father asked, looking to her sister.

Calamity grimaced inwardly at Charisma's obvious awkwardness.

"Of course not, Daddy." Calamity assured him, trying to give her twin time to recover in a manner befitting their role-playing experiment. "Everything's fine. She...*Calamity* and I just dropped by on the way to work to see if you liked her hair; I talked her into it last night. So what do you think?"

"Nix it." He gave a disapproving shake of his salt-and-peppered head as he turned. "You two look like the Doublemint twins added a chocolate flavor." He commented as they followed him back into the kitchen. "Coffee?"

Calamity nudged Charisma into accepting the proffered beverage. "Yeah, sure daddy. That's me, caffeine junkie Calamity."

Isaac bellied up to the cappuccino machine in the corner, under the bank of cabinets. "What's going on with you two? I vaguely remembered Marian having bent my ear about some harebrained scheme—your mother's words, not mine—of Calamity's. But, I didn't get all the gory details. The game was on." He came away from the counter with a steaming cup of cinnamon mocha something from the smell of it. Calamity felt her mouth water as he sat the offering on the island counter in the circle of her hesitant hands and eyed her expectantly. "So?"

Calamity's head shot up, "Daddy, *she* is Calamity." She assured him, reluctantly pushing the sweet-scented cup toward her twin. "I'm Charisma. Why do you think I'm not having coffee?"

"Oh."

Calamity squirmed at the keen look he aimed first at

her and then Charisma. The pregnant paused ended with his shrug. "Marian said something about Calam quitting her job."

Calamity grew suspicious. Surly, he couldn't be…playing along?

Charisma chimed in. "Well yeah, she…eh me, *I* did, but I need to leave properly or I can kiss a reference goodbye." 'Calamity' glanced down into the steaming mug between her hands, struggling to choke back a wave of nausea the pungent aroma caused.

Their father reached over to take the cup from her. "You know, Chrissy, if you're going to impersonate Calamity for the day you really should get in more practice."

Lovely. Calamity thought. This little field test of theirs was officially a flop.

Charisma's shoulders sagged as she stepped away, putting more distance between her and the offending aroma. "This'll never work, Calam. We need to come up with something else."

"Here, give me that." She took the cup, kissing her father's cheek in the process. "Its much too early to throw in the towel. Of course we can't fool Daddy." Calamity cajoled, undeterred. She made straight for the pink box next to the cappuccino machine which was sure to hold some form of bakery treat. En route, she sipped…oh yeah, cinnamon mocha. Most def.

"Sorry Daddy, but we needed the practice. Now Charisma, all you have to do is sit at my desk, pretend to be working, and look like me. That's it. Once I get everything set up, we're home free and you can get the heck outta Dodge. No one will know the difference. Perkins probably wouldn't care anyway." She pontificated, as she skimmed through the bakery box offerings. "Trust me, he's not that discerning. Felecia in accounting looks like Medusa's kid-sister, and I know for a fact he slid his hand up her thigh during the last departmental meeting."

Charisma turned up her nose at the horror of being a potential target of her boss's pervy advances. "Ewww! What if that creep tries something while I'm being you?"

"A knee to the groin works best." She garbled around the tasty bite of caramel mini-muffin. "I could show you a move or two if you want?"

Their father beamed with pride. "That's my Calamity, always a drop-step-kick ahead of the rest."

* * *

Calamity stood in the middle of the Ross-Warner's law library, contemplating her options. The spacious cylindrical room rivaled a football field in size and boasted a modest clearing in the center furnished with four tables, and several private cubicles off from the center. Now, *there* was an option, she thought. The most recent case references and files lined dirt-brown metal shelves along the adjacent walls of both entrances. She should put at least one camera at each end. Those were the most-used areas. Less travelled were the archived and bound serials stored in the central space.

But still, the periodicals entombed in several dozen rows of gray mobile shelves were an opportune place for the lecher to catch his prey in a tight, isolated place. The six-tiered rows of shelves ran the width of the room. They were on a rail system built into the floor that allowed them to condense together and conserve space. The perfect trap.

Her eyes went back to the shelves along the peripheral wall. Still, those were the materials most often referenced, researched, and requested. Of course, that was *a lot* of area to cover. Plus, the cameras only had a fifty-degree viewing angle off the horizontal, so she needed both a higher and a distant vantage-point in order to get a decent glimpse. Another issue, the near claustrophobic aisle between the outer and inner shelves narrowly afforded enough space to walk, much less produce a low budget skin flick starring

Charlie Perkins as Clarence Thomas and some poor unsuspecting paralegal as Anita Hill.

Vertically-challenged at five foot two, she had to crank her neck back to eye the top tier of the shelves.

"Ugh." She estimated it to be an easy three and a half feet above her head. "A bottle of miracle grow would come in handy right about now."

Not one to back down from a challenge, Calamity stepped out of her favorite blue-green sling-backs. "One small step for woman, one giant leap for womankind." She hiked up the hem of her silk-lined skirt, and moved cautiously toward the uppermost shelf of the looming towers.

* * *

"Calam, what have you done to your hair?! Looking good, but geez girl what's the idea leaving me hanging like that? Get over here and tell me what happened with you and Pervins Tuesday!"

Charisma choked on her box-drink upon hearing the infamous Mr. Perkins referred to as 'Perv'ins. How appropriate, she thought whilst she gagged painfully on the sweet pink liquid. In the end, she just forced the juice down the wrong leg of her esophagus so she could breath again.

"Boy, they didn't name you 'Calamity' for nothing, did they?" The wide-waisted woman grinned at her from the opposite side of the desk. She wore a lead gray pant suit with a blinding slime-green under blouse, matching slime pumps, and Ghostbuster Logo earrings dangling from her lobes. Charisma recognized her as Reese Martin, Calam's office BFF. Calam had introduced them one day when Charisma came to take her sister to lunch and she'd seen her briefly on two other occasions.

She lowered her voice to a loud whisper, as if there was a secret plot afoot. "Say, where the heck is Pervins? I want to see the shiner you gave him. Word around the water-cooler is that you weren't the only person he set off."

Reese was one of those folks whose image was difficult to sandblast from one's mental canvas. Her clothes only came in two colors, bright and brighter. She was buxom enough to put an eye out if she went braless, and blonde...well, technically anyway, Charisma corrected as she eyed dark-roots lurking beneath her Texas-sized hair. She didn't have A-list looks; On a good day, she resembled a poor man's Jessica Simpson...on a bad day, a twenty-something Bette Midler. But what she lacked in looks she made up for with style. Charisma reckoned the bangles jangling off her wrists could probably be melted down and re-cast to make chain-mail for the entire Roman Empire.

"Reese, nice timing." She quipped, "You will excuse me while I gasp for air?"

She was exactly the sort of friend Calamity would have, Charisma concluded as she leaned forward to snatch wildly at the tissue box on the corner of her sister's desk. She could feel the fruit punch drink seeping down her nasal cavity, and she aimed to soak it up before it rolled out her nostril.

"No worries." Reese fell in line with Charisma's sauciness. "Let me know if you need CPR or that Heimlich thing."

Charisma hid her petulant eye-roll behind the mound of tissues. She supposed she'd better converse with her sister's office crony or risk blowing her cover. It wasn't that she minded so much. She liked Reese...well, as much as it was possible to like someone she'd only met once or twice.

"I can see that you're just dying to impart some hot office tidbit so don't keep me in suspense. Spill."

Reese complied in a chirpy Texas twang. "Don't mind if I do. Well, it seems that fine devil of a man you've been drooling over for the past six months had a bone to pick with Pervins too. He—"

Before Charisma could think better of it she heard herself blurting out, "What man?!"

Reese's mischievous smile faltered a bit as she studied 'Calamity' askance.

Uh-oh! Cover's blown to bits, need back-up plan fast. But Calamity was the strategist. Charisma excelled more as a minion type. Sheesh, what had she been thinking...she hadn't been, of course. When Reese mentioned Calamity in reference to a man, shock and curiosity clouded her common sense. On a positive note, at least she could get the goods on Calamity's mystery man. Or, should she stay mum and keep trying to piece together a plausible lie?

"Eh—actually, funny story...uh—" Nope, still nothing. She came up empty.

In the end, Reese took the decision out of her hands. "You're not Calamity."

"Busted." Charisma sighed. Well, what's done is done. "We met a month ago when I came to take Calam to lunch."

"Yeah, yeah, I remember." The younger woman regarded her like a demolitions' expert did his next condemned building. Charisma squirmed.

"Alright you, out with it. Where the hell is Calamity? What the hell is she up to? And why the hell wasn't I included?!" She ended her tirade on a plaintive whine.

O...k...That was unexpected. But, Charisma decided in a flash to use it to her advantage. "Give me the dope on Calam's mystery man and I'll give you the 4-1-1 on her latest scheme du jour."

"Deal. His name's Lucifer Phoenix. Middle name, Damien. Just gives ya shivers, doesn't it?"

* * *

"So what. People in Hell want ice water! I will *not* apologize to that greasy little weasel." Luce knew he was over-reacting, but the knowledge did nothing to stay his temper. If anything, his frustration level mushroomed. At eighteen months out of law school, six months on the job, and four weeks pre-BAR exam, he considered himself above having to schmooze with the 'Haves'. He'd been playing by other people's rules all his life and now, poised on the brink of success, he refused to revert back to placating the boss man in the hopes of being thrown a bone.

"First off, I did *not* give him the shiner. But, even if I had, it would've been no more than he deserved. Second, I completely stand behind my assessment of the Wallace vs. McKenzie Inc. case. And one more thing, just so we're clear, I will gladly shine his other eye if he puts his hands back on Stella." Without waiting for a reply, he hurled the phone across his office. It smashed into the back of the door, and spewed fiber-optic shrapnel as it slid to the floor. Screw it. He needed an upgrade anyway. The new voice-activated smartphones had finally come out.

At six foot four inches and two hundred nineteen pounds of lean hard sinewy, he often didn't know his own strength…especially when he was angry. He examined his hands, seeing the deep red imprints from where he gripped his phone and the corner edge of the desk. He ran both hands over his shaven head, mentally counting down from ten. His mother tried to teach him to be slow to anger, but the lessons never truly sunk in.

Luce smiled as he stood up and eyed the tangled guts of the cell phone, and made a three-sixty inspection of his office. The desk was his. The light wood shelves lining two of the four walls. The books, notebooks, files, paperweights, and papers were his too. He felt liberated and ready to take on the world standing in *his* office surrounded by *his* accomplishments. He had his own room in his very own apartment and he'd be damned if he would let that jackass junior partner undermine his new-found success. Perkins might be a legal genius and in line to become full partner, but that didn't make him any less despicable. Luce made up his mind to try to preserve a working relationship with the man but he wasn't taking any crap off him, and he aimed to let Perkins know it first hand. With that in mind, he strode out of his office hell bent on setting some ground rules.

* * *

"Whew! That was a close call." She averted a nasty fall only owning to swift reflexes.

Her life flashed before her eyes when she felt her feet slip across a thin layer of dust on the shelf's edge. The ultra-sheer pantyhose were to blame, but she couldn't remove them in so public a place. As it was, she clung to an especially thick case file, feet dangling beneath her and skirt hacked up midways her thigh. Calamity let the nervous tension ease from her body.

"Just one more to go."

Relief was short-lived, however. Before she could gather her bearings and attempt another descent to the floor, someone bolted through the south entrance at the opposite end of the file room. Calamity winced at the pain of twisting her neck at an awkward viewing angle.

Lucifer! She'd know his long-limbed stride anywhere. He was probably taking the file room as a shortcut on his way to somewhere. Rarely did the lawyers and higher-ups lower themselves to doing their own case research. That dirty little job generally got relegated to paralegals, legal secretaries, and legal assistants, such as herself. She observed him from above. He seemed intent on his destination, so maybe he wouldn't notice her dangling precariously from the top tier just adjacent to the north entrance.

Oh please, don't let me make a fool of myself, Calamity begged. She so much wanted to make a positive impression. If she came tumbling down on top of him, no doubt that would squelch him seeing her as anything other than a kook. Who was she kidding? She *was* a kook! Why else would she go through so much hassle to get retribution and keep her job when she could just request a transfer or let her resignation stand? Too bad either option would limit, if not sever, her contact with the object of her affection, the man who was at present ten feet away and closing.

It looked as if he wasn't going to spot her, thank heavens. But just then, a tiny tearing noise marred the silence. The split of her skirt gave way under the pressure, and ripped upward a good three inches, exposing both her presence and her left thigh in the bargain.

"Ms. Lowe?"

Bull's eye. He zeroed in on her like a homing device. "Ms. Lowe, did you need some help getting down?"

Calamity winced at the rather bemused expression on his upturned face. And what a beautiful face it was…thick sensuous lips, dark sober eyes that did criminal things to her feminine sensibilities, molten gold skin flecked with just the right touch of shadowy stubble. Have mercy! She flicked her neck to dislodge the annoying flop of her newly straightened hair from obstructing her vision, going for a casual tone.

"Eh, no Mr. Phoenix. I have it under control. Thank you." The over-torqued angle of her neck lent a squeaky, harried quality to her words.

Luce wondered about the miniature woman above him. He often saw her around the office, talked to her briefly on the phone whenever he called Charlie's office, but they'd never officially met…until now. He'd heard the stories though, starring the infamous 'Calamity Jones' from his assistant. The sight of the pristine Ms. Lowe jack-knifed atop the archival files made him question if she really was the loopy ingénue Stella described.

One rumor he *could* confirm, ingénue or not, Calamity Lowe filled out a skirt better than he ever imagined a woman as small as she could. Shapely legs and a firm round bottom were traits he'd always appreciated in a woman, though proper up-bringing and company policy kept him silent on the finer points. Instead, he stepped nearer the shelf and put two steadying hands around her waist, nearly spanning it.

"Let go before you fall."

He gave the order in an authoritative tone, and Calamity obeyed as she had her third-grade teacher when she was eight years old. His hands tighten around her, etching fiery imprints she felt burning through to the skin. He lowered her to the floor with military efficiency and, to her disappointment, initiated no further body-contact.

"Next time use the latter, Ms. Lowe. There's no excuse for breaking your neck when Ross-Warner has set up measures to prevent work-place accidents."

Calamity flipped her feathered blow-out so that it fanned attractively atop her shoulders, hoping he'd notice the change. "I'll remember that, Mr. Phoenix." No such luck, he removed his hands from her waist and straightened to full height, gazing down at her with those searching obsidian eyes. How could anyone look into them and not be liquefied on the spot?

"Is Charlie in yet? I need a dime."

Eek! Must stay calm. But her heartbeat accelerated into panic mode. "I haven't seen him today. Either drop around the office later or I could pencil in a tentative ten minutes before lunch?"

Calam watched, shaky as a hairless cat, while he took the time to think on these options.

"Never mind all that. Have him call me on my office line when he arrives."

Ahhh, disaster averted. "First thing, Mr. Phoenix."

He nodded curtly and turned back towards the south door, talking as he retreated. "Stay out of trouble, Calamity. The odds aren't in your favor."

Excuse me, sonny? What on earth had prompted him to say *that*? She stared after him, speechless and not just because he'd used her first name.

The way he wore a business suit fascinated her. Even with an undershirt on, his chiseled muscles and washboard stomach, halfway peeked through the white dress shirt. His arms bulged slightly through the jacket's sleeves. Calamity stood transfixed, watching him retreat.

* * *

"Ok, so let me get this straight…Calamity's been mooning over this Lucifer guy for six whole months and she hasn't come up with a plan yet?" Charisma was stupefied. "That's amazing."

Reese snorted. "She claims she's turning over a new leaf, but I think it's just because she doesn't know how to approach him."

"So, what's he look like?"

"Like Vin Diesel and Denzel Washington hooked up and had a love child." She quipped. At Charisma's skeptical smirk, the taller blonde shook her head. "No joke. The dude is tall as an oak, bald as a baby, and built like a Mack-truck. He's quite literally the devil in a blue suit."

"Ok, a total badass." Charisma grew pensive. Her sister had been known to make major character misjudgments when it came to the men in her life. "But what sort of person is he? Decent, I hope."

"Who cares. He's fantasy-island for every woman in the building. Hell, probably some of the men too. Calamity is going to have to pull off a major coup to get this guy to give her a second glance."

Charisma pulled a face. "This is so typical Calamity. He could be a deranged lunatic. The man's name is *Lucifer* for the love of Mike. If that's not a sign of depravity, I don't know what is."

"Lucifer and Calamity." Reese shrugged, undaunted. "I think they sound cute together. And, its not like *her* name doesn't come with it's own bag of issues."

"I suppose."

It did make an odd sort of sense. Calamity just loved flirting with disaster. Of course her dream man would be named after the devil himself.

"How...poetic." Charisma muttered, mostly to herself.

"If only she could get his attention." Reese lamented. "She has the perfect opportunity, you know. He's involved with one of Perkins' cases."

The challenge somehow appealed to Charisma, but she didn't have her sister's flare for strategy so *her* idea would have to be elementary. She'd simply pretend to be Calamity and—no, she clearly had no flare for that trick if this morning's two-part fiasco was the standard by which she measured.

'LUCE' AFTER DARK

Luce lounged on the sofa of his two-room efficiency apartment. A velvety calico feline meowed near his be-socked feet. He hadn't even bothered to undress, just removed his jacket and shoes and loosened the necktie.

He'd decorated the place strictly with comfort in mind, that is, if buying bedraggled furniture from Goodwill and strewing it into empty space could be construed as decorating. He promised himself when he made his first hundred thousand, he'd hire a decorator...no, first he'd buy a *house* in a nicer neighborhood, *then* he'd hire a decorator.

He watched the muted TV screen, a dim flickering light source, with waning interest. An image of Calamity Lowe drifted into his mind. Of course, he knew she was lying. Her body language fairly screamed 'hidden agenda'. Impossible as it was, he tried to wrap his mind around a plausible explanation for the peculiar goings-on at the office earlier in the week. There wasn't a straight angle to her. The pristine Ms. Lowe was definitely up to something. Although, since he knew her to be otherwise upstanding and he knew her boss to be just the opposite, Luce wasn't compelled to warn Perkins of his assistant's recent mischief-making. What he *was* compelled to do was try to put the incident out of his mind. Too bad nothing on the tube offered him much distraction.

"Damn."

Disgusted, Luce tossed the remote to the other end of the worn tan couch upsetting Sasha to the point that she fled to the kitchen.

"I need cable."

* * *

Calamity stood in her bedroom, stretching into an inky form-fitting workout shirt to complete her cat burglar duds. Her sister lay on the nearby bed, similarly attired.

"He *saw* you? Dangling from the rafters with your skirt practically above your head…" Charisma trailed off into a fit of laughter.

"Its not funny." Calamity snapped, not enjoying being made a laughingstock. "If he mentions the incident to Perkins, we're screwed. You know that, right?"

Her sister sobered at the thought that their fun might come to an abrupt end. She sat up from deep crimson bedding. "Why would he rat you out? What does he know to tell anyway? So you were in the file room doing some case research, so what. There's nothing suspicious about that. And even if there were, from what you and Reese have told me about this Pervins dude, he sounds like a lecherous old creep. Who in their right mind would take *his* side over yours? Your Mr. Phoenix is no exception either; Reese told me that he and Perkins got into it the other day."

"That's true." Calamity considered her sister's words a moment, pacing around the room back and forth between the dresser on the far right and the computer table housing her laptop on the far left. "Mr. Perkins does tend to rub everyone the wrong way. I can name half a dozen people who wouldn't give a hoot if he got taken down a peg or two. But, that doesn't mean they would *knowingly* turn a blind eye to an illegal activity. It is a *law* firm, Charisma."

"Illegal?" She faltered, "You never said anything about the plan being *illegal*, Calamity."

"It's not…technically." Calam hedged, sheepish. "Unless you don't have permission from a judge, then yeah, it's illegal."

"I take it *we don't* have permission?"

"Of course not. I'd have had to file a complaint, then there'd be a formal inquiry, probably followed by a police report. In fact, I'm not exactly sure what the procedure—"

"Ok, I get it."

"See…" Calamity stopped pacing and smiled. "This way is much quicker and more efficient. I get Perkins on tape and then I get *him* to admit what he did and turn himself in."

Charisma nodded, not quite as enthusiastic as before. "Calam, aren't those camera batteries only good for six hours of running time?"

"Yeah, I know. I'm the one who told you. That's why I will be changing them first thing when I get to work in the morning. Right now we're going to finish setting up. I had to bale on the file room when Lucifer showed up. If anyone asks, I can say I'm working late…which is a little less conspicuous than coming in early. It's still risky, someone *actually* working late might be there but I don't want to lose another day without the file room being completely covered. Oh and Stella's cubical too. Then, its over to Reese's to set up the receivers and recording equipment. Speaking of which, I hope she's not still mad at me."

"And if nothing happens between now and two weeks from now, when your resignation becomes final, then what?"

"No problem. Since Reese knows what we're up to now, she can just keep changing the batteries. We can screen the tapes at her place, see if there's anything I can use."

"Well, you certainly have covered all the bases, haven't you."

"I'm the brains, Sweetheart." Calam reminded her, as she grabbed her keys off the hook mounted near the bedroom door. "Say, you still in or what?"

"Wouldn't miss it." Charisma stood to follow her sister, each decked out in sleek ebony spandex, and pony-tailed hair. "So, when were you going to let me in on your secret Satan crush?"

"*Lucifer*. The man's name is *Luce-ah-fur*."

"Whatever." Charisma pulled a face as she closed the door behind them. "Why all the secrecy? I'm literally your other half and I had to find out through the grapevine. That is soooo Sweet Valley High…"

* * *

Luce inhaled deep, letting the warm night air trickle out in a gentle rush from his mouth. A nice, soothing breeze was just what he needed to relax him, get his mind off his work…or more accurately, he troubles at work. He never thought he'd be the type of person who drove around just for the hell of it. But here he was, cruising north of seventy on the inner city loop in his sun-faded hoopty. He relaxed, head back, fingers tapping to the mellow groove of late night jazz while dim, intermittent road-lights cast shapes and shadows over him. The soft, unhurried night ambiance eased his tension away.

"Hmmm…" Even the ring of his car phone couldn't spoil his calm. He noted the sound, and reached for the receiver with a languid reluctance. "Yeah?"

"Luce, what the hell, man? I been tryin' to reach yo ass for two days. I left like three voice pages on the cell. You're turning me into a stalker over here. What, you got this new lawyer gig, and suddenly it's, Sly who? Yo, Luce, I'm talkin' here."

"Yeah Sly, I hear you." Luce grimaced. His cousin, Sly. Full-blood Italian on his father's side, complete with Sicilian flavor, and very high on drama.

"Where you been, man?"

"Nowhere, my cell died on me. What's up, why didn't you call me on the landline?"

"Couldn't remember the digits is all. You got like a million phone numbers—work, cell, car, home. All I got is a cell. *Consolidate.* Say, I thought we were gonna hang tonight."

"It's Wednesday, Sly. I got work tomorrow."

"Oh, is that why you're out driving around at what...eleven o'clock."

He had a point. "Alright listen, Friday...after work, you can help me pick out a new cell and then I'm all yours. Clubs, bars, strippers...I'm down for whatever."

The voice on the other end of the phone perked up like a kid in Candyland.

"For real?"

"*Joke*, Sly, joke. Bar-hopping Friday, that's it. The party's over at midnight and you better stay cool because I'm not driving yo drunk ass home."

Luce hung up the phone still shaking his head, a half grin on his lips. Ah, what the hell? While he was out, he might as well swing by the office. He'd mellowed enough for one night. Taking a second to glance in the rearview and seeing no close-range headlights, Luce swerved from the fast lane to the slow one and managed to make the exit. Twenty minutes later, he slowed his car and turned into the contract-parking garage behind the glassy edifice of Ross-Warner.

* * *

Calamity adjusted her black nylon tote to the opposite shoulder as she rounded a corner in the semi-darkened suites of Ross, Warner, and Lange Attorneys at Law. In daylight, the offices and cubicles all had a bright, antiseptic feel to them. The dark gray tone marble walls and corridors leading to and composing the permanent offices on the outer shell were corporate and upscale. Conversely, the dense scattering of collapsible, carpeted cubicle walls with their many intervening aisles in the inner area were mediocre but functional. The variance between the two working spaces, one for lawyers, accountants, and other elites, the other for secretaries, assistants and other subordinates, was as stark as the difference between a trailer home and the White House. Strangely, darkness divided the two even more. When veiled moonlight shined through the clear glass of the outer windows, it lent Ross-Warner an unsettling labyrinthine glint.

Calamity was one of the lucky elite legal assistants, with seniority, who had a glass enclosed outer office space. Hers also, unfortunately, held at its rear, the inner marbled and seven digit-coded office of her boss, Charlie Perkins. She'd sent Charisma to do the cams in hers and Perkins office while Calam herself changed out the batteries to the file room and break room cams...and of course, Stella's cubicle. She still hadn't decided what to do about the conference room. She was thinking about a smoke detector cam as she made her way to the cubicle preceding Mr. Phoenix's office.

Ahh, Stella, she thought to herself, the luckiest woman in the world. Calamity would kill to trade bosses with her. She'd heard a rumor that Stella had become the newest member of Perkins' harem of harassment victims. Made sense, Mr. Phoenix was second chair under him on the Wallace-McKenzie case, which meant Stella assisted with research and whatnot concerning the case. She too had the potential to become a subordinate subjected to his unwanted overtures, if she hadn't already. Calam shuddered at the remembrance of her own experience. She'd chosen a simple alarm clock design for Stella, having *accidentally* broken her normal clock the previous day. She strolled around the carpeted cubicle wall in question, traversing the open threshold to the desk area. She stopped in her tracks at the site of a small lamp-light. Uh-Oh.

Calamity crouched down behind Stella's desk so she could peer around it, which gave her a line of sight, however limited, into Mr. Phoenix's office. Crap! She saw a glimpse of him via the half-closed door.

"Lovely." She murmured to herself, voyeurism forgotten as she sat her bag of goodies on the floor, and reached up to grapple around on the top of the desk. "I'll have to do this the hard way."

* * *

Luce caught the silhouette out of the corner of his eye, a long time talent of his. He had two brothers to thank for his sharp eyes and quick reflexes. Careful not to make any sudden movements, he inched his way towards his assistant's domain as silent as a panther. It would be tricky because he'd have to leave the lamp on or else alert the intruder to his leaving. On the other hand, when he passed in front of the light he would cast a shadow, and the intruder would know he was moving to the door anyway. He took the chance and left it on, with the hope he'd be quicker than his opponent.

* * *

Calamity seized upon the clock, and brought it down to the floor face first and slid the batteries out of her bag. That was as far as she got before a towering shape loomed over her. She yelped just before arms of solid steel encircled her, and yanked her none too gently from her seat on the floor.

"Mr. Phoenix, please, it's me!" Calamity felt herself being slammed against the top of the desk and let out another involuntary yelp, this time of pain as her back connected squarely with solid wood. Several objects from the desk scattered to the floor. A moment later, the arms disappeared and a flood of light blinded her. She put up a deflecting hand to shield her eyes.

"Ms. Lowe?" She felt him move away from her a little. "You're like a bad penny that just keeps turning up."

Calamity removed her hand to squint up at him. He held the now broken clock as evidence, which under the present circumstances, she hoped he didn't examine too closely or he'd see it wasn't your average alarm clock.

"Mind telling me what the devil you're doing here?"

"Nothing." Generally, her first rule was: lie.

"Try again, Ms. Lowe."

"Don't you ever go home?" Second rule: distraction, or what she liked to call 'bait-n-switch'. Confusing the issue sometimes resulted in putting the other person on the defensive. "And another thing, I think we know each other well enough so that you should call me 'Calamity'."

He just gazed at her with a queer expression she couldn't quite define.

* * *

Luce stared at the tiny woman, now lying, in more ways than one, atop his assistant's desk: chocolate eyes, pert nose, and kissable, heart-shaped lips. He would kill to see that mouth in red lipstick, but Ms. Lowe never wore red lipstick, at least not that he'd ever seen. Still she–Dammit, why did the pretty ones always have to be nuts? Luce dropped the ruined clock. Without waiting for his rational mind to gainsay him, he stepped forward, leaned over the desk, forcing her flat on her back.

* * *

Calamity's eyes bugged even more when his hands

came down like prison bars on either side of her. Her breathing quickened as he inched even closer, and pinned her with those deep ebony peepers. She'd never seen him in casual attire before. The rugged jeans and wife-beater style T were definitely working...working overtime, in fact. She could feel the heat radiating off his sculptured chest and six-packed abs, which just did hover over her heaving bosom.

"Ms. Lowe, I'm an attorney." He spoke as if they were having any normal businesslike encounter at work. "Whatever you tell me—and make no mistake, you *are* going to tell me—it will stay just between the two of us. I prefer it that way, don't you?"

Calamity felt her throat go dry when his eyes flickered momentarily downward taking note of her erratic breathing, then back up to lock with her face. Unable to speak just yet, she nodded.

"Good." To her shock, he retreated in one smooth motion and let her up off the desk, helping her stand. "Nice outfit. Do you break and enter often?"

"Smart aleck." She murmured in a defiant voice, not quite meeting his eye. "I...Mr.... Look, I wasn't stealing or anything. I came to—"

He held up a hand for her to be silent. Calamity stood clueless for a moment, until he started to step further outside the cubicle, pan-scanning the darkness for movement. Yikes! Charisma. Drat the man. Did those cat senses of his miss nothing? It just wouldn't do for him to find Chrissy lurking around in the dark with her.

"Lucifer...Luce. You don't mind if I call you 'Luce', do you?" She didn't wait for his answer. "I have to tinkle. Can I just go to the restroom really quick? It's right around the corner."

He waved her off, "Stay here until I come back."

* * *

As soon as he was out of sight, Calamity high-tailed it back around the corner, rubber-soled shoes squeaking on the marble floors. She reached her office running and gripped the threshold to stop her momentum. Out of breath and off-kilter, she cast her eyes about for her sister, frantic.

"Charisma!"

A muffled bump followed her urgent whisper.

"Chris, is that you? We got problems, hurry up and come from under there."

Charisma emerged from the underside of her sister's desk, massaging the side of her head. "Geez, Calam, I thought you were security coming to arrest me." She gestured to her own disheveled ponytail, noticing that her sister exhibited a similar harried appearance. "Say, what happened to you?"

"Tell ya later, for right now, shut up and listen. Be me. Run to the file room, make as much fanfare as possible without it being too obvious that you want to be heard. Take the north entrance, climb up the nearest shelf…no wait, you might fall, don't climb up the shelf, just look like you're going to climb it. I'd go myself, but there is no way to get from his office to the file room without him seeing me, and by then he'd have passed by here and seen you."

Charisma peered out through the glass walls of her sister's office, confused. "Him who?"

"*HIM* …the guy, Lucifer. He's here, and he sort of caught me." Calamity flailed her hands, shooing her sister out into the hall. "Get going, and hurry, he's got Spidey sense or something. Go!"

"But won't he catch me?"

"That's the idea, silly. Let him catch you. Pretend you're me, and tell the truth. Only, say the ones in Stella's cubicle and the file room are the only ones. Got it?"

"Yeah."

"Go!"

* * *

Luce stopped to rethink his haste. A hunch led him to switch directions and head for Ms. Lowe's office. He wasn't disappointed to find her there, hanging about.

"Luce, hi." She greeted, skittish.

"Get lost on the way to the restroom?" He didn't bother waiting for her answer. It was clear to him that he'd have to piece together an explanation himself.

As he advanced on her, she took several shaky steps backward. Good. She should be scared, he thought. He was fast losing patience with her loopy antics.

"Mr. Phoenix, eh, there are laws against man-handling women." She glanced around her, a wary nervousness in her voice. "Ahhh, listen, maybe we could rewind and start over—"

She stumbled back a couple of steps before Luce locked an arm around her waist and hauled her off the floor in one fluid movement. "Oh no you don't...There are laws against breaking and entering too, Ms. Lowe." He menaced, not bothering to curb his rising temper. "And I'm making a citizen's arrest."

The mention of 'arrest' propelled her into action. She fought, kicking out sideways at the air, clawing at the taunt muscles in his arm, the arm clamping her stomach against the side of his torso. "You said we weren't going to tell anyone? That it would stay between us."

"I'm a lawyer, I lied." He taunted more to scare her, into maybe telling the truth for a change. "Who else is here?"

"No one."

"Now *you're* lying."

She started wiggling again. He adjusted his grip so that it brokered no resistance.

* * *

41

Frustrated, Calamity realized she'd never be able to wiggle away from his grip and ceased her struggles on a sigh. Even under the circumstances, it was rather nice, being carried by him. Wedged against his rib cage, she could feel the solid warmth of his body. If only he hadn't positioned her under his arm like a sack of feed. She felt like the class clown being hauled off for a spanking. "Alright, my sister's in the research library, north entrance."

He struck out in that direction devouring the floor with an equestrian gait. Amazing, his feet never faltered, even with the added weight and awkwardness of carrying her.

"Chrissy's pregnant so don't you dare snatch her up like a rag doll. I don't care how pissed you are." Calamity snapped as they reached the south end of the research library.

He paused to sit her down, but she was by no means free. Her left wrist he kept in an iron grip, hitting the main light switch with his other hand.

Calam became increasingly edgy as she spotted a Charisma-shaped shadow at the other end of the room. She'd never seen him so angry. His long strides forced Calam to jog alongside him to match his pace. He closed the last fifteen feet like a heat-seeking missile.

"I mean it. Leave my sister alone."

"Worry about yourself, Ms. Lowe."

He halted, without warning. Unprepared, she slammed into his side, bouncing off inelegantly and just did avoid a most embarrassing fall. Luce stiffened his arm, and tightened his hold on her hand, which helped her to regain her balance. He shook his head as if he thought he were seeing things...The same reaction most folks had when they met her sister, without prior knowledge of their twin status.

Calamity shrank away when he snapped around to glare down at her, then back to her mirror image. Charisma was no help either. She poked her thumb up at him with a loopy too-glad gleam.

"That's him, Calam? Sweet!"

"See, eh, we're twins." Calamity announced, sniffling back crocodile tears. Third rule: Play the female card.

"Hi, I'm Charisma." She stepped up, proffering a hand like they were meeting for drinks at Chili's. Calam rolled her eyes, geez, Chris.

Recovered from the jolt of seeing both sisters together, he addressed Charisma in a toneless professional voice. Was he still angry? Calam couldn't quite tell. Maybe he'd reached a plateau or something.

"Ms. …Lowe?"

"No, actually it's Tate. Charisma Lowe-Tate." She dropped her ignored hand, glancing to Calam, eagerness faltering. "Eh, Calam?"

"Look, leave her out of it. I started this and I'll finish it." Calam could almost feel her sister growing uneasy. For all the outward sex appeal he oozed, Mr. Phoenix could also be scary as hell in his silent-but-deadly lawyer mode.

"Mrs. Tate, go home. I'll take care of your sister."

Charisma locked eyes with hers, "Eh…Calam's upset. I think, I should take her home. Did you know that nasty Perkins put his hands on her the other day, which is how all this got started. Ok, so maybe the Nanny-cams aren't the best way to handle it, but come on, the guy's a jackass. Reese told me so." Her voice cracked as she pled her case. "Look, I know you're a lawyer and all, but please don't turn her in."

"Oh, Hell. Don't *you* start crying, too." Against his better judgment, and all common sense telling him not to get involved, Luce felt their obvious sisterly affection nagging at his softer side. And, Perkins *was* a jackass.

"Relax, Mrs. Tate. I won't turn her in. We're just going to take a drive and chat."

"It's ok, Chrissy. Go on. Don't worry, I'll be fine."

A DEAL WITH EL DIABLO

Calamity sat eating humble pie in the front seat of a car that seemed to her to be running on borrowed time. The exterior paint was faded a rainbow of shades from the original color. The once smooth beige leather seats were dingy, brittle and in certain spots cracked open to reveal spongy orange foam. Only a hardened pasty residue on the front windshield remained where the rearview mirror should have been. And of course, the ultimate nightmare, there was no CD player merely an AM/FM radio tuner. Amid suspicions of a crappy sound system to match the archaic style of everything else, Calam nevertheless wished he'd turn on the radio. They'd been driving around for at least twenty minutes in dead silence. Glancing out the open window glad for the rushing air, despite the accompanying humidity, she saw that they were still cruising down the freeway.

Luce used the opportunity to get a candid glimpse of a pensive Ms. Lowe. He wondered what went on in her mind. She was an enigma, a petite enigma with curvaceous hips and bosom enough to keep a man's interest. Her hair, he noticed, she'd changed. It made her more difficult to distinguish from her twin, probably some integral plot point having to do with tonight's bizarre goings-on. He groaned inwardly. Did he really want to involve himself with the infamous 'Calamity Jones'? On the other hand, she was an attractive woman and he was growing frustrated with his lack of social life. The bottom line, she intrigued him. Something about her compelled him to dig deeper.

"Ms. Lowe—"

"Call me 'Calamity'." She corrected, without turning around. "It's just better that way. *Ms. Lowe* makes me sound like I'm five years old and you're the principal about to call my parents."

"Calamity." He complied. "Tell me what happened."

* * *

She swiveled to face him, observing his profile, cast in dim shadows of the passing streetlights. She wished she could see his eyes.

"Perkins cornered me in the law library, pretending to help. I had an armful of case law research. He reached around me to take the bag off my shoulder. His hand slipped of course." Calamity paused in her story, surprised to feel Luce's hand massaging her shoulder. A gesture of comfort. Did he really care? "I ah dropped my load...stomped his foot. Then, I jabbed him in the eye with my elbow, which is the *real* reason Mr. Perkins wasn't in on Monday."

His baritone chuckle drifted between them. "That was *you*? Half the office thinks I'm the one who shined his eye."

"Yeah, it felt good at the time." She let out a deep sigh, leaning into his impromptu caress. "Only now I wish I hadn't."

"Why?"

"Because he's using it to his advantage. Says if I try to report the incident, he'll deny it and file formal assault charges against me. It's perfectly legal, and *true* in fact. I *did* assault him." She gestured, resigned. "But then, he's a lawyer, I should expect nothing less."

"Hey, we're not all like Perkins, you know. But I think, now, I understand the reason for tonight's bit of…lunacy." He gave her shoulder a reassuring squeeze. "Fighting fire with fire?"

Calamity nodded, giving in to his finger's divine stroke. She let her head rest on the top of the seatback when she felt his hand working around to the nape of her neck and into her hair. Her ponytail went the way of the dinosaur. "I set up Nanny-cams disguised as clocks and smoke detectors in all his favorite haunts. I figured if I could get him on tape with his hand up some poor woman's skirt then I'd have some leverage to force him to come clean. Once he fesses up, Ross-Warner can deal with him. I get to keep my job, and I can still be close to–" She stopped short, realizing she was about to say 'still be close to you'.

"Still be close to what?" He prompted, flashing her a quick glance.

Calamity scoured her mind frantically for an intelligent ending to the sentence…and coming up empty-headed…she settled on the one plausible, yet silly, ending she could think of. "*Reese*. We're friends, and she lives a few blocks away from Ross-Warner." It must be his heavenly hands addling her brain, Calamity realized. Abruptly, she sat up straight, breaking contact. "As a matter of fact why don't you drop me by there. Chris is probably getting worried."

He gave her the skeptical side-eye. "But we're not done."

* * *

"So, where do you think they are?" Reese asked, plopping down on the sofa beside her.

Charisma paused, bringing the hovering forkful of mac

and cheese back down to the plate in her lap. She pondered a moment. "Hard to say. He was seriously p.o.'d. I thought for sure I'd have to break my piggybank and bail Calam outta jail, but then he just...mellowed. Said they were going for a drive. Nothing's open this late except Walmart, so my guess is they're either driving around talking or parked somewhere talking."

Reese wagged an eyebrow, playful. "With any luck, maybe they're parked somewhere, *not talking*."

Charisma shrugged, and took up her fork again. Meanwhile, Reese grinned devilish, glancing around at the rented video surveillance equipment covering every usable surface in the living room, including the floor. Still-boxed gadgets made a circular trail from the door all around the perimeter walls traversing the odd piece of furniture. Plugs, extension cords, and accordion-folded instruction leaflets littered the floor in-between leading to the central couch where Reese and Charisma sat.

"So Chris, you think we'll still need any of this junk after tonight? I sure hope so. I can't wait to stick it to Pervins!"

To Charisma's mind, Reese was like a wind-up doll. Give her a good twist and she was good for hours of senseless chatter.

"Say, how the hell is Calam able to afford these elaborate schemes of hers anyway. She makes the same thing I make, not that I'm complaining mind you. Today and tonight is potentially the most fun I've had since...well, since Calam's last plan."

Charisma smiled. "My husband Paul's a computer program designer. He's got the 4-1-1 on lots of folks in the business. They let us use most of the stuff for free. This is their bottom-drawer junk. Security, like everything else, has gone digital."

"How can you be so calm? Aren't you dying to know what she's doing right now?"

Charisma considered this as she loaded another forkful.

"Well, you have to understand I've known my sister all her life. This is pretty much standard procedure. She's either *hatching* a plan, *initiating* a plan, or I'm helping her clean up *after* a plan." Charisma paused to pack the food in her mouth, then continued on with a dismissive wave of the empty fork, her words amusingly garbled. "Hell, Pike and I, we've been getting Calamity out of trouble for years. Ahh, it's a dirty job, but...you're right, it *is* fun, *isn't* it?!"

* * *

Working for a law firm, Luce knew she was well-acquainted with certain legalities and illegalities. Still, he felt compelled to point out the obvious. "You realize this plan of yours is breaking the law on about a hundred different levels? Starting with illicit surveillance and blackmail. If any of those cameras are discovered, you'd be looking at separate *cumulative* counts of privacy invasion for each and every employee at Ross-Warner compromised or reasonably expected to be compromised by their existence. The DA will probably toss in Perkins' assault charge just for giggles."

Dejected, Calamity nodded comprehension. "So, what's your advice, Counselor?" She asked, sending him a rueful smile. "Assuming you'd represent a hardened criminal like me, that is. Should I bite my tongue, grin and bear it every time that snake slithers up my thigh? Or should I let my resignation stand so he can go on slithering up some other woman's thigh?"

"Ditch this plan, report what happened, and let me help you nail him." He suggested evenly. "Perkins is a habitual. I may be able to secure a corroborating witness. My legal assistant, Stella, for one."

"And the assault charge?" She studied his profile as his drove, long lashes, prominent nose, full lips, strong jaw. He had an honest face, she realized. If it was at all possible, her crush on him enhanced threefold into full-fledged longing.

At that moment, he chose to look away from the road and lock on her face. "Under these circumstances, give me or any lawyer worth his salt five minutes of cross examination and the assault could be spun into justifiable moral outrage."

"Can you guarantee that?" He turned abruptly back to the dark road, she noticed. A dark road ahead, the perfect metaphor for her present situation, she thought.

"As much as I want to say 'yes', I can't *promise* you anything. Nothing's guaranteed, Calamity, not where the law is concerned. Its written to be...*interpretable.*"

"Don't you mean, *flexible?*... So certain people can slip through."

"No. That's not what I mean. Interpretable, so that it can apply to all possible illegal permutations."

She scoffed. It still sounded like double talk to her. "Well in that case, I'll think about it and get back to you."

He shook his head. She could tell that wasn't what he wanted to hear. Yeah, well, ditto buddy, she thought, acidly.

"Calamity, whether or not you accept my help, I'm going to have to insist on taking down the cameras. Ross-Warner is liable should their existence be discovered and any employees and/or clients decide to file a civil suit or worse, a *criminal* one."

"Now you sound like a lawyer." Humph, traitor. "Fine. I know when I'm licked."

Luce sighed, as he changed lanes on the freeway in preparation to exit.

* * *

They arrived back at Ross-Warner's parking garage just inside thirty minutes. Calamity was glad to be out of the car. The drive back, with its tense restrained silence, had been a chore. Considering how things stood, Calamity was surprised when he relieved her of the tote and swung it over his shoulder. She thought the gesture sweet and gentlemanly, until it occurred to her that he probably wanted the bag so he could be sure they took down each and every camera.

"After you." He moved to the side to let her lead the way.

Once in the building, Luce coded them in and they got down to the business of things. With a minimum of chatter and even less lighting, Calamity led him on a tour of each zone, the research library, Stella's cubicle, and her own office suite. Each time, he followed close behind her at an almost claustrophobic pace, and she handed off the offending Nanny-Cams into his charge. He removed the batteries, and tucked them within her tote bag. When they reached her office, he waved her ahead of him once again. She made quick work of collecting and turn to do the hand-off.

Luce watched Calamity swish inside to collect the stuffed animal-disguised nanny-cam strategically placed on a waist-high bookshelf behind her desk. They'd connected. He felt it, however tenuous, back there in the car...before he all but ordered her to remove the cameras. Now, less than an hour later, they were on opposite ends of the world or might as well be, judging from her measured aloofness. He'd been hoping to talk some sense into her, but having failed at that, he wasn't willing to give up yet. He fought for a reason, something to say or do to break the seal on the coffin of whatever delicate link they'd shared.

"Well, that's the last one...research library, Stella's cubicle, and my office."

"Good. I'm taking these with me for safe keeping, and the receiving equipment too as soon as we reach Ms. Martin's apartment...that *is* where you planned to set it up?"

"Killjoy." She murmured with childish malevolence.

"All this stuff is borrowed, you know. How am I supposed to take it back if you confiscate it?"

"Simple, Ms. Lowe. Write out the name and address of the rental shop and I'll return it for you." He continued to use her surname, trying to provoke a reaction ...any sort of an opening he could work with.

"My name is *Calamity*, dammit!" She snapped at him, eyes ablaze as she glared up at him from her diminutive height. "Write it down, take a picture, and remember to say it next time. Lawyers! You think you're so damn shrewd and savvy, but really you're all just a bunch of bloodsucking leeches feasting off everyone else's misfortune."

Luce didn't turn a hair, but with her unleash of fervor, he saw the opening he'd been hoping existed.

"Have lunch with me tomorrow, and give me a chance to prove myself." When she hesitated, he continued on, adding, "No one hates Perkins more than I do. It would be my pleasure to nail his slimy ass to the wall."

* * *

Calamity waffled, interested, but uncertain. On the one hand, she hadn't completely given up on her plan...though he was making it tough as nails. On the other hand, she so wanted to believe that the mind and heart underneath all that gorgeous body were trustworthy and stalwart. Did she dare put her faith in a man after whom she lusted, but wasn't quite sure she trusted?

"Noon, then." She dared.

* * *

The car's shock absorbers were shot to hell too Calamity realized as Luce turned into the inclined driveway of Reese's apartment complex. Every bump, pothole, and patch of gravel the tires encountered sent knots, sways, and twists pulsing throughout her body. She felt almost nauseous, when they finally turned into a parking square just in front of Reese's threshold. With the deadening of the engine came an onset of panic into Calamity's mind.

"Ah, do you think we could do this tomorrow?" She pleaded her case in a voice she hope mirrored sincerity. "I'm sure it's after midnight by now."

With a quick flick of his wrist, he confirmed the time. "One twenty-four actually."

"That late?" Calam grimaced. "Charisma is probably asleep. She's been so tired lately. I shouldn't have dragged her into this in the first place. Her little boy has the measles and she's been staying with me...you know, because of the pregnancy. Do you realize that if anyone else had caught us, I could have landed her in jail on top of everything else? I'm a terrible friend and an even worse sister."

It wasn't so much an act, as an exaggeration. She was exhausted, Calamity realized, rolling her shoulders to get the kinks out.

"Tomorrow is soon enough to collect the stuff, I suppose."

Have mercy, he's doing it again! She nearly moaned when his hand slipped over her shoulder and renewed the soft kneading to her nape. Calamity turned to face him, and saw a rawness in his eyes that struck her as desire. She recognized the feeling because it echoed her own emotions. Her breath ratcheted up when she felt the warm pressure of his palm on her nape urging her closer...just within range to touch soft lips to her temple in an affecting gesture which sent her senses reeling.

"Good night, Ms. Lowe." His smooth baritone voice tickled her toes, despite his use of the dreaded 'Ms. Lowe'. The realization that he'd done so didn't catch up to her brain until she stood inside of Reese's apartment, her back to the closed door, with her sister and her best friend beseeching her for a detailed account of the night's adventures…or rather *misadventures*. Calamity wasn't quite sure which category to file the night's activities under yet.

Charisma bounced up and down like a Ritalin addict in withdrawal. "Come on, Calam. Snap out of it and tell us what happened."

"Maybe Satan's still got her tongue." Reese suggested, cheeky.

"Oh, shut up, the both of you." Calamity snapped back into normal mode, dodged the prodding twosome with some difficulty, and came into the room with elongated looping steps to avoid tripping over the junk littering the floor. Reese and Charisma followed her into the muddled jumble of boxes, wires and equipment. Calam stood and observed the surveillance wares strewn about the living room, an intense purpose in mind. "Help me hide a few of these video gizmos in the bedroom."

"Ohhh, kinky…" Reese cooed. "Time enough for that later, sit down and tell us what went on with you and Satan."

"Yeah, Calam, spill." Charisma urged with equal enthusiasm. "Inquiring minds want to know."

As her co-conspirators, Calam supposed they were entitled to a proper progress report. "Well *we*, as in the three of *us* not including Luce, are going ahead with the plan…just on a slightly smaller scale."

"*Luce?*" Reese's eyes popped out of their sockets. "Since when did Mr. Phoenix become just 'Luce'?"

"He *lets* you call him *that?*" Her twin chimed in, an incredulous grin beginning to spread.

Calamity hunched up a shoulder, smug. "He didn't seem bothered by it when he asked me to lunch with him tomorrow."

"He asked you out?" Reese and Charisma gaped in unison.

Calam bobbled her head, screwing her mouth up. "Not exactly. Lunch is sorta business. I had to tell him the truth about the cameras. So, naturally he insisted I take them down, but since he has no idea exactly how many there are, I left a few of them up. This is why we have to hide three sets of this equipment tonight so tomorrow morning when he comes by to confiscate everything he'll think I'm cooperating in the fullest."

Charisma held up a hand. "Whoa Calamity, if he's coming in the morning to get the junk, then what will you two be doing at lunch?"

"Strategizing for our attack on Perkins, silly. Luce thinks I should take the direct, legal approach…and deal with Perkins' charges of assault when they come up. He's talking about rounding up corroborating witnesses and everything." Calam paused, remembering his words, his conviction, and the fire in his eyes as he pitched his solution to her problem. "He's confident he can help me, so I see no reason not to let him try. Meanwhile, we've still got a back-up plan waiting in the wings if and when Perkins decides to play dirty."

"And that's *all* that happened?" Reese implored, scanning her face like an x-ray machine. "A change of plans? That's what had you near catatonic for a full minute after you slipped through the door?"

"No, he…eh, Luce…kissed me." Calamity admitted on a sly smile, "And before anyone asks, it was platonic, but with definite non-platonic undertones."

SORRY, WRONG TWIN

Calam sat at her desk, drumming her clear-polished nails against the desktop. Having arrived home after two o'clock the previous morning to find a half-naked Shane painting disemboweled butterflies on plastic couch covers and gotten little sleep in the ensuing scuffle between him and her horrified sister, Calamity's mood wasn't the best. The clock hovering in the middle of the back wall read twelve fifteen and still no sign or word from Luce. In fact, she hadn't seen him all day. The only thing she knew for sure was that he had swung by Reese's place and picked up the equipment. There was a text message from Reese on her cell.

Her mind teemed with plausible explanations, ranging from the mundane to the ridiculous. Perchance he forgot about their lunch date? Or, maybe he had a sudden death in the family? What if he changed his mind about helping her, but then why didn't he call and tell her as much? Perhaps, a fender bender on the way to work side-tracked him? Recalling Luce's junkyard clunker, she could well believe that theory. Damn, but the waiting and wondering put her in an edgy mood. Calamity was a gun ready to go off. So much so, that she jerked when the inner door opened, to the mild protest of several vertebrae in her back. Her boss strolled forth like the King of England at his own coronation.

Perkins was a runt of a man, five eight tops. He did his best to keep in shape. Two maybe three nights a week, Calamity guessed he spent at the gym hitting on women half his age while he loped on the treadmill. What else was there for a degenerate prick just beginning to sag in the jowls to do in his spare time but run around on his wife and pretend his age wasn't catching up to him? Not that it mattered, his wife was in the process of divorcing him, according to the rumor-mill buzz anyway.

Calamity eyed the tufts of muddy gray hair that sprang up all around his head like vacuumed carpet. She stifled a grin as she visualized a crazed barber going at it with a weed-whacker. She could tell by the arrogant tilt of his head and leisurely glide in his step that he wasn't threatened by her. And why should he be, she thought sourly, he thinks he's got it made. Calamity shuddered when he turned that weak chin, bloodless complexion, and crocodile smile on her. Still, there was *one* facial feature she didn't mind seeing, and that was the fading bluish ring around his left eye from where she pummeled him with a combination heel-elbow maneuver.

"Care to join me, Ms. Lowe?" He leaned his hip against her desk corner and bent down to make his implication understood. "I'd love to *have* you...for lunch."

Ewww, so much for her appetite. "No, thank you, Mr. Perkins."

He shrugged and straightened, but she wasn't fooled. He'd been fishing for a reaction, and her failure to comply would probably cost her.

"Fine then, just make sure to finish typing and proofing the outgoing correspondence before you go gallivanting off to the break room. And be back in one hour, Ms. Lowe, I have some letters to dictate."

"Of course, Mr. Perkins." Watching him jaunt lazily

out of her office, Calamity let out a shaky breath. Where the hell was Luce?!

* * *

Charisma stepped lively on the shiny sable floors, clacking her shoes to the beat of a song stuck in her head from the drive. She stopped in front of the glass-enclosed suite directory mounted on the marble wall to get the office number and some idea as to where it was located. She was late, she knew. Calam's lunch date with the devil was scheduled for one o'clock. It wasn't her fault; she had an especially noxious bout of morning sickness when she awoke. Shane hogged the bathroom, then she had to stop and fuel up her car on the way. Still, she'd made a genuine effort to arrive on time. She even postponed her daily call home to check on Manny. If she were lucky, maybe Satan would be running late too and she'd still get the chance to execute *her* plan.

In the absence of something better, she decided to go with the old standby. Admittedly, Calamity didn't need any help landing the man, but it certainly would hurry things along a little. Temple-kisses were all well and good, but they were by anyone's terms, moving at glacial speed.

"Ah ha!" She rejoiced in triumphant.

"Found what you're looking for?"

Charisma leaped around and away from the directory. She paused to gather her wits, disguising the fact behind straightening the fly-a-way ruffle of her sister's blouse. She tucked the placid pink silk back beneath the jacket before glancing up to face the towering gold-skinned Adonis. He was drop-dead sexy in a killer business suit. She couldn't fault her sister's taste. "Eh, Mr....Luce, hi, I was just looking for you."

"On the suite directory?" He arched a brow. "You don't remember where my office is?"

Oops, mistake, Charisma waffled. "Oh...eh, no. I

mean, yes of course I remember where your office is. I was just checking my collar in the reflective surface. When I said looking for you I meant in the general sense."

Luce stood watching Mrs. Tate squirm, uncomfortable with the ruse. Her chemically-relaxed hair, he noticed, shone to sleek ebony perfection, whereas Ms. Lowe's once kinky twists were straightened using a heating element. The difference being that Calamity's tended to have tiny kinks at the scalps' edge, a testament to Houston's humidity no doubt. Her sister's hair showed no kinks.

He wasn't quite sure what she was up to, but he decided to play along until he found out. "I apologize, I know I'm late, but something came up with one of the cases. It's handled now. Shall we?"

Charisma had to think fast, not a strong talent in her queue. "No, wait. I need to go back to my office...for–" She fumbled for something...anything. She couldn't say purse because she had one on her shoulder. "–keys! I forgot my keys. Separate cars and all that jazz. Keeping it covert, you know." Looking up at his dubious expression, Charisma knew she sounded like an imbecile. Well, when in doubt, ask him out, she chanted to herself. Not a proverb for the ages, but it worked at the moment.

"Would you like to go out? Eh, with me. I mean, not to lunch obviously, we're already doing the business lunch thing. I was thinking more like dinner sometime. I mean, 'dinner and a movie' type dinner. A dinner *date*, is what I'm saying." She could have shot herself just then.

"Yes, Ms. Lowe, I believe I catch your meaning." Luce stuck his hands in his pockets and smiled despite himself. She was almost as cute as Ms. Lowe. He'd let her off the hook just this once. "Why don't we talk about it over lunch? I'll..." He paused to beat growing amusement from his voice. "...let you get your keys and meet you at La Madeleine. There's one in The Village."

It worked! Mission accomplished. "Good. That's good. I'll be there. Eh, gotta go." Charisma reiterated, as the sing of her cell phone pierced the air. Knowing the call was from Paul, she beat a hasty retreat, unaware of Luce's ensuing chuckle.

* * *

"Well, I declined, of course! But, I should've told his raunchy ass to stick it where the sun don't—" Calamity broke off in mid-sentence at the conspicuous arrival of her sister. Reese too cranked her neck around, from her lofty perch atop the desk's edge, to lay eyes on the brazen visitor.

Charisma, having yanked open the door to Calamity's office, breezed inside all aflutter, cell phone in hand and in use. "Paul, I have to...yeah honey, I have to go. Love you, too. Give Manny a kiss for me. Bye. Hey Reese."

"Hey you, what's cookin'?" Reese grinned, good-natured.

"Charisma? What on earth are you doing here, I thought you were sleeping in?"

She shrugged, "I *was*, but I had morning sickness and figured as long as I was up I might as well give you a hand. Satan's meeting you at that French place in The Village so you'd better hurry up and shimmy out of that suit."

Calamity groaned as she stood from her chair. "I take it you've been role-playing again. Come on to the restroom so we can change. While you're here would you be me a little longer. I might be late getting back and Perkins mentioned doing dictation later."

"Dictation?" Charisma screwed up mouth, repulsed. "Gross. That had better not be a euphemism for something sexual."

As an afterthought, Calamity called out over her shoulder. "Watch the phone until Chris gets back, Reese."

"Sure, but I want details about lunch."

Charisma followed her sister around the corner. "You'll have to take my purse too, otherwise he'll know."

ALYCE DOMAIN

Calamity groaned again, "Why on earth were you being me anyway? Luce knows pretty much everything. Geez, now I'll be nervous thinking *he's* thinking I'm *you*."

"Sorry, Calam, it was a reflex, ok. Don't worry. I'm wily as a coyote. No way he knew it was me."

"If I remember my cartoons correctly, Wile E. Coyote wasn't known for his mental prowess, Charisma."

* * *

La Madeleine's hailed as a coffee and dessert place where people came to relax, be social, and lap up the atmosphere. It boasted of sinful French sweets but only served a minuscule selection of non-filling entrees...in the background of exotic music infused with sitars and harpsichords. Not surprising, Madeleine's was mostly patronized by the neo-rich, who just loved to waste money and be seen doing so.

Luce was already seated at a table in the back when Calamity arrived. A pizza-faced hostess showed Calamity to her seat with zeal. The hostess' arms moved in exaggerated elegance as she produced two cream-colored menus out of thin air and placed them on the table's edge.

"Armand will be over shortly to take your order."

"Thank you." Calamity followed the departing waitress with her eyes. Avoidance wasn't her best tactic, but she needed a few extra seconds to get herself together.

"Glad you could make it." His spoke polite and business-like.

Calamity was somewhat relieved to find his eyes on the menu instead of her when she bit the bullet and faced him.

"Try the pasta, excellent flavor." He recommended.

"Yes, of course." She retrieved the second menu and flipped it open. Ordering was at least a task to distract her. Since she wasn't planning to eat anyway, she might as well take his advice. "I guess I'll have the—no wait, I think maybe I'll stick with something simple."

60

"Relax, Ms. Lowe, I don't bite." He faced her then, with ebony eyes and a hint of something wicked. "Unless you want me to."

Calamity flashed hot at the harmless innuendo, bumping ever-so-slightly into his tree-trunk legs under the table. Crap, didn't he realize what that smile in combination with those words did to her insides? She almost fanned herself with the menu, but squashed the urge at the last second.

"Eh, we should order. And, I thought we agreed that you would call me 'Calamity'?"

"So we did." He abandoned the menu and hailed for service. Armand appeared, a waif-thin vampire by the looks of him, and stood tall and erect with pencil poised over pad.

"Your order, sir?"

"Yeah, give me the house special, and regular coffee, black."

"And for the lady?"

"Right, yes, I'll have the three dessert sampler; éclairs, strawberry tart, and almond croissants. With café au lait, please."

The pen whirled as he jotted down their order. "Excellent choices, I assume you'll want the coffees first?"

"Yes, thank you." Calamity answered for them both.

* * *

Once the waiter removed the menus and departed for the kitchen, he nailed her down with a sedate yet serious expression, both palms face down on the table.

"Calamity, you're a sensible woman. I know this because Ross-Warner wouldn't have hired you otherwise. You've worked at the Firm for three years, which proves as much. But, it's not enough to *be* sensible. I also expect you to *act* sensibly. Which means, no more vigilante stunts like that lunacy I caught you and your sister at the other night. Before we start this legal crusade, before I become officially involved, I need your word on that. Agreed?"

* * *

Calamity did, at least, shift in her seat—bumping his knees—and finger-combed her hair behind her ears before she lied through her teeth. "No more midnight madness, I promise."

He gave a quick nod, pleased with her promise…making her feel guilty beyond what she thought herself capable.

"First thing, you need to go up to Employee Relations, report the incident, and file an official complaint. It's been less than a week so they shouldn't harangue you too much with 'delayed filing' questions. Tell them just what you told me. They'll take notes, ask lots of questions, look for details, and eventually assign one person to your complaint. The whole shebang will take an hour to an hour-and-a-half, tops. I want this done before the end of the day and then I want you to go back to your office and wait. Let them take it from there."

Calamity listened, the paradoxical rough-edged polish of his speech. The workings of that stubble-sprinkled jaw, and golden skin fascinated her. Only occasionally, did she listen to what he said, so much so that she was ten seconds late to react when he finished his spiel.

"You mean, I just have to wait it out? I can't. I'm not a sit-around-and-hope-for-the-best-type person. I'll go nuts, sitting there, taking dictation, thinking any minute Employee Relations is going to ram the door like gang-busters. Reese will have to pry me off the ceiling by five o'clock."

Luce reached a hand over to eclipse hers. "Don't go gettin' excited. It won't happen today. The investigator will need time to poke around first, question everyone around the office. When Charlie himself is questioned they'll most definitely call and ask him to come up to ER. So, in the meanwhile, just think about something else."

"Think about something else, just like that." She mocked. "How on earth can you be so...composed. And what'll you be doing while I'm fighting off a nervous collapse, huh?"

If it was at all possible his voice and mannerisms became even more sedate. "I'll be working on Stella. If I can get her to follow suit, that'll take the edge off, even if Perkins decides to go ahead with the assault charges. In either case, it'll look good that you beat him to the punch. Him alleging assault after the fact could be spun into 'sour grapes'."

"I guess." Calamity nodded, as the waiter re-emerged with their coffee. She took a sip. Humph, café au fait. This is just cinnamon-flavored steamed milk with a dash of caffeine, she thought. The sweet drink in conjunction with Luce's favorable legal prognosis mellowed her nerves a little. "Ok," she smiled, almost apologetic. Even *she* knew she could be a pain at times. "I can do it. I'll just order a second one of these to go."

* * *

"Good." He gave her fisted hands a final reassuring squeeze before he abandoned them in favor of his coffee cup. He took a long swig of the mild hot liquid, eyes never leaving hers over the lip of the cup. "So, Calamity, how's Friday night for you?"

She blinked at him, puzzled. He definitely had the right twin this time. Luce served up a half-smile, mostly because her expression amused him. Her lips, a delicious mauve, parted, begging to be kissed. He wagered with himself that he would do just that before long.

"How's Friday night for what?" She asked. "Are we going on stakeout or something?"

"Nope, just dinner...that's dinner-and-a-movie-type

dinner. You and me, tomorrow night. Game?"

Armand approached, pre-empting her response. He bore two large circular dishes one with a deep concave in the center, the other a shallow but wide saucer. Luce's deep dish held a marginal serving of creamy pasta and seafood while Calamity's was scattered with mouth-watering pastries. All talk ceased.

Back in the parking garage at Ross-Warner, Calamity walked over to Luce's four-wheeled nightmare with a La Madeleine's to-go cup warming her left hand and Charisma's purse over her shoulder...wondering why he'd beckoned her. They were thirty minutes late getting back, which meant she and Charisma would have to time their switch carefully. She'd go to the restroom, call Charisma on the cell, change clothes, switch purses, then walk back to her office, and that'd be all she wrote. Except, instead, she was standing in two-inch heels, nursing blisters, feeling foolish and nervous all at once. What-ifs swirled around in her head like a swarm of bees.

"Get in." He slid an arm across and popped the lock. He waited until she complied and closed the door behind her.

"So, eh, I thought we covered everything at lunch." Calam shifted in her seat under his unwavering gaze. "Its after two, I need to get back."

"I'm sure its under control. Your sister seems quite...versatile." He reached over, took the coffee from her twitchy hands and deposited it into the cup-holder on the dash. "Meanwhile, you didn't answer my question, Ms. Lowe."

"What question?" Miffed at the 'Ms. Lowe', Calamity looked sideways at him when he slid the purse off her shoulder and onto the floor. "Luce?"

"Dinner, Friday, you and me?"

Yeah, duh! "Oh. Yes...I meant to say 'yes'. And my name is—"

"*Calamity*." The roguish smile he flashed should have

tipped her off. It didn't. Like a shot, he cupped the back of her head. His fingers made mincemeat of her neatly-styled hair. But she didn't care and offered no resistance when he propelled her forward and silenced her with his mouth. The firm smack was brief, with a slow deliberate quality that left her dazed. He leaned to touch his forehead with hers while using the thumb of his free hand to wipe her lipstick from his mouth. "Thank your sister for me...and you be good."

* * *

"Calam, what on earth happened to your hair?" Charisma fussed, patting it down. "It's all pushed up in the back."

"Stop that." Calamity swatted her away as she buttoned the last button and turned to check herself in the central wall-mirror above the row of sinks in the restroom. "You asked him out, didn't you...while you were pretending to be me this morning."

"He told you?"

"Not in some many words, but it was pretty obvious."

"Are you mad?" Charisma asked, looking forlornly at her sister through the mirror. "I hate it when you're mad at me."

"Yes, I'm mad. Mad as hell. You could've at least told me...as it was, I–" Calamity sighed. She turned to face her sister, excitement in evidence. "Oh never mind already. I have a date with him tomorrow night! You have to help me pick out something to wear tonight...that is, if I can get through the end of today without having one of mama's conniptions."

Confused, "What's going on later?"

"I have to go file a report with Employee Relations about the harassment. Luce says I could be there up to an hour and a half. Then I'm to come back to my desk and resume my normal duties like nothing happened. That's what the extra coffee's for. My nerves are shot."

"Ohhh, sounds heinous." Charisma grimaced, grabbed her purse and made for the door. "Good luck with that. I'm outie."

* * *

Calamity trudged up to Employee Relations, two flights above hers and Perkins's digs. The ER folks verged on upscale with dignified frosted-glass cubicles. Tre' chic. She approached a circular workstation preceding the sea of frosty cubes. The station housed three women, one older lady parked in a swivel chair deep in a phone conversation. The woman to her right had marcelled hair and a frown tattooed across her forehead.

She bypassed the paper explosion atop the counter and the 'tude woman. Instead she stepped up to bachelorette number three, a bored yet pleasant-seeming twenty-something, who paused from texting and greeted her with a smile. They were almost eye to eye, with the younger woman on the short end of the stick.

"Hi, I need to report an incident to Employee Relations. Is this where I should be?"

"Yep. What's it got to do with?"

"Eh, sexual harassment."

"Sheila Heyes, third row, fifth cube on the left. If she's got a complaint in there already, anyone else free on that row can help you."

"Thanks." Not knowing anything, positive or negative, about this Sheila Heyes, Calamity didn't know whether to be grateful or wary to find the cube free. She plastered on a random, icebreaker smile for good measure.

"Ms. Heyes, the front desk directed me here. I need to file a formal complaint against my immediate supervisor, a…eh…harassment complaint."

The woman turned from her computer screen, opened the middle drawer of her desk and pulled out a legal-size carbon-back form. "Have a seat."

She asked a barrage of questions, ranging from general name, start date, job-title-type information to middle of the road inquires including immediate supervisor, time/date of incident and infraction description. From there she moved on to more specific details: which hand was used to do what, reaction times, and wording of threats. The woman was robotic almost. She showed an intense thoroughness, but exhibited no discernable emotion as she queried and questioned, back-tracked, double-checked details, noted and annotated every last crumb of information. By the time they'd finished and the bespectacled towhead informed Calamity that her complaint would be duly investigated and she was free to leave, Calamity felt like a skeletal carcass picked clean by cannibalistic natives.

On the way back to her office to endure what was sure to be a reprimand for her unexplained absence, Calamity wondered if Sheila Heyes' interrogative precision was designed to benefit the victim in pursue of vindication or to aid the perpetrator avoid punishment? Working for a law firm as she did, Calamity knew legal loopholes were bilateral. They cut both ways.

SATAN & THE SINGLE GIRL

Standing outside her apartment, purse on one shoulder, navy tote over the other, Calamity hesitated over the knob, not wanting to come home to another boxing match between Charisma and Shane in which she'd be cast as referee. She opened the door of her apartment careful as a cat burglar, and peeped inside. A pleasantly pungent swish of air back-drafted into her nostrils. Bless Charisma for cooking, spaghetti from the smell of things...and no sounds of physical warfare. Hallelujah! Fears assuaged, Calamity barreled inside, tossed her purse, tote, and keys in the general direction of the purple mohair couch and turned the corner. She bypassed the dining table off from the living room and shimmed up to the bar overlooking the kitchen. Across from the bar, the stove was littered with steaming pots. One particularly mouth-watering aroma came from an enchilada-red sauce boiling, with veggie chunks popping up through the air bubbles.

Charisma, bless her heart, juxtaposed the opposite counter, was leaning her hip into it while she tossed a very luscious-looking salad.

"Damn, that smells good. You're an angel, Chris." A thought suddenly occurred to her as she reached over and dipped a finger into the whipped dessert-looking thingy just over the bar. "Say, where's Shane?"

"Oh. Cheryl came by and accused him of cheating on her, with you no less. I think she actually thought *I* was you. Anyway, they got into a screaming fight. So, I told them that they either needed to kiss and make up or get the hell out of here before six o'clock rolled around because I figured you wouldn't be in the mood to referee after the day you've had." Charisma turned, sporting a kiss-the-cook apron, and walked out to the dining table adjacent the kitchen and deposited the salad bowl.

"Oh, by the way, Reese called. She wanted to know when we're coming over to scope the junk for evidence *and* she's bounce-off-the-walls impatient to hear how lunch with Satan went."

Calamity groaned, following Charisma. She seated herself in front of the salad. "Aw hell, I do *not* feel like fast-forwarding through hours of video footage tonight. What'd you tell her?"

Charisma grinned when a knock at the door precluded her answer. She tossed the apron, and smoothed out her jeans as she headed to answer it. "I told her to get her butt over here because dinner and story-telling start promptly at six-thirty. Voyeurism, we can put off until tomorrow."

"Hey Chris!" She called after her. "Did you ever know that you're my hero?"

Calamity heard Reese before she saw her. The ever-present bangles click-clacked like church bells, and to Reese they were like an American Express card, she never left home without them.

* * *

Forty minutes later, all three pushed back from empty sauce-stained plates and headed for the living room sofa. Calamity plopped down in the middle with Charisma and Reese on either side.

Reese took a moment to eye what she sat upon. "Did they skin Barney to make this couch or what?"

"Hey don't knock it. It's Shane's signature color. He snagged this puppy for fifty bucks at an estate sale."

"Whose estate...*Elvis*?"

"Ha, ha. It was a sweet gesture on his part. It saved me on decorating expenses, plus I kinda like Barney's purpleness." Upon seeing both Charisma's and Reese's dubious expressions, Calamity hastily added, "I *know* but cut me a break, ok. I lost the custody battle in my last roommate divorce."

"Might have helped with the negotiations if you hadn't gotten her brother deported." Charisma tossed out.

"*Almost.*" Calam groaned. No one ever remembered the positive things she did. "*Almost* got him deported. Geez, I was trying to do him a favor. How was I to know he had open warrants in another country? And since when are poetry contestants subjected to background checks anyway? He did *win*. Can't a girl get props for good intentions. Look, we're getting off track. My original point was...This is my first solo place and I'm not a trust-fund baby, so quit giving me grief about Barney."

"Solo, huh?" Reese jacked a brow northward. "You do realize that Shane is living here, right?"

"Another vicious rumor." She corrected. "He's *crashing* here temporarily after an intergalactic fight with his wife."

"Not my favorite person, peeps...*Sooooo*, subject change..." Charisma elongated the segue, glancing between the friends. "You want to tell her or shall I?"

"Allow me." Calamity shifted to face her friend, grinning uncontrollably.

"Ooo, dinner *and* a story." Reese's sea-green eyes all but popped out of their sockets. "What?! Tell me. I'm drooling over here."

"Luce and I have a date tomorrow night!"

Reese let out a squeal the sounds of which triggered sonar scales in the Gulf of Mexico. "He asked you out?!"

"Well, no, not exactly. I kinda asked *him* out. Technically, anyway. It's a you-had-to-be-there kinda thing."

"No, its not. *I* asked him out pretending to be *her*." Charisma announced, smug.

Reese looked from one twin to the other. Glee spread like wildfire over her face. "You two should be on reality T.V. Seriously, think about it, 'The *Lowe* Down'. Or no, no… 'She said, *She said*'."

"Pul-ease." Charisma humph-ed. "There was no glitz or glory. I bumped into him on his way to meet Calam and he mistook me for her. The idea popped into my head, so I ran with it. Poof! Insta-date. No drama."

"Calam?" Reese pressed for more details.

She obliged. "At lunch he suggested we go out on Friday night. It took me a moment to get a clue because genius over here didn't bother to tell me she'd procured me a date by proxy."

Charisma rolled her eyes. "She must really have it bad, Reese. She's started using that lawyer jargon in everyday conversation."

"Don't tease me, Charisma…or I won't tell you about the kiss."

"What kiss?" She snapped back, "Why you sneaky little heifer! You didn't tell me he kissed you again."

Reese squealed anew, signaling dolphins world-wide.

"Hear, hear…I'll have order in my court!" Calamity rose from the couch with distorted regal elegance. "And now ladies of the jury, let us retire to the bed chamber, for the outfit-judging portion of the evening. Be forewarned, all voting must be unanimous."

* * *

The next day at work passed like a vague dream that she couldn't quite remember in the morning. She was on autopilot, typing, pulling research, and corresponding with clients or sometimes their legal liaisons. No Perkins come-ons to sidestep. No Employee Relations ramming her door.

At that moment, Calamity's reality consisted only of dinner, a six-foot-four lawyer with phone-sex vocals, and a certain little red number the natives helped her settle on the previous evening. She hopped in her car and zipped out of the parking garage. All she had to do was pop back to her apartment, shower, dress, do something with her hair, then drive to the restaurant. Every day should be so low-stress.

* * *

Meanwhile all the balls in Luce's world were colliding in mid-air. The bar exam loomed in just under three weeks. His heavy case-auditing load at work was fast becoming a major energy drain. The hands-on training meant to aid him after he passed the bar and acquired his own clients, had instead taken on a life of it's own. That afternoon, he endured a particularly grueling mediation session with Perkins, a former MacKenzie-Inc employee Lawrence Vallin, and MacKenzie Inc's representatives. And now with the added case-work for Ms. Lowe's defense to squeeze into his schedule, he felt the first scorching hot flames of burnout licking at his heels. And then came his research assistant, Stella. She hadn't responded well to his first attempt to convince her that reporting Charlie's behavior would be in everyone's best interest.

Not surprising, his after-hour diversions, like dating and hanging with Sly were beginning to blur into each other. Luce found himself double-booked for the night. He could shop for a newfangled cell phone and bar-hop with Sly on Saturday just as easily as he could on Friday, though he grimaced as he imagined the promise-breaking drama sure to ensue. Still, Sly he could put off. Calamity, however, was not so easily shoved aside. He couldn't bring himself to shuffle her back a day on his calendar. He wanted to see her...*tonight*. Being cooped up in mediation most of the day, he hadn't seen her, even in passing. Hell, he *missed* her. He never missed Sly. That's the part that scared him.

Tie and briefcase in hand, he keyed the lock and found his apartment not quite as empty as he'd left it. On his bedraggled sofa lounged a lanky Italian decked out in baggy yellow Old Navy garb...stroking a purring Sasha who was nestled against his hip. The surround sound TV cattycorner from the sofa, hummed noisily, brain-dead action flick in evidence. The black-eyed couch potato with slicked-back hair curling on the ends was his dubiously-employed cousin.

"Sly." He stilled himself against the urge to yank him up and shove him out the door.

"Hey Luce, hope you don't mind. Me and Sash was just catching a movie, and well, this high-def plasma screen gets off-the-hook reception."

Luce swung the door closed behind him and never broke stride to his bedroom, tossing the tie and sitting the briefcase next to the bed. "How'd you get in here?" He'd changed the bloody locks twice already.

Sly, flippant as if stating the obvious, "The same way I always get in. I jimmied the lock, no problem. Luce, man, you really need to think about gettin' a place with better security..." He paused a moment to eyeball the Spartan surroundings. "Not that you got shit to steal, except the TV. Man, it's like a thrift shop nightmare up in 'ere. Me and Sean V might need to get Martha Stewart to stage an intervention...or somethin'."

"You don't like it, there's the door." Luce revisited the living room barefoot and minus a shirt. His washboard abs, and smooth broad chest were as well-sculptured as any Greek statue, easy. "Listen, you should probably get going anyway. I'll have to take a rain check on tonight. Call me tomorrow 'round eight, we'll hang."

This brought his cousin out of repose and up off the couch. "Ah come on, Luce! Mike, Tony, and the whole gang's meetin' us at The Underground. Two-dollar drinks 'til eleven."

"Great, the guys will be so drunk by midnight that tomorrow no one'll remember I wasn't there."

"What the hell's so urgent—" Sly followed him into the bedroom, hearing the shower running in the adjacent bathroom. "Ah-ha! You're ditching me and the guys for some skank. No man takes a bath and changes clothes to go out unless there's a D-cup and a garter belt involved. Tell me I'm wrong, it's a skank, isn't it?"

"Language, Sly." Luce kept a tight reign on his temper, the boundaries of which were stretched to the limit. "I prefer to think of her as a date, not a skank."

"Figure of speech, you know what I mean."

"Goodnight, Sly." Luce, now wrapped only in a white towel, strolled to the bathroom. "I trust you'll jimmy the lock back into place on your way out."

* * *

Traffic proved a wicked nuisance, made worse by citywide construction projects. Luce arrived fifteen minutes late; an air-conditioned draft greeted him when he traversed the threshold. Houston's humidity had, sometime during the forty-five-minute commute, dampened and molded the snow-white shirt to his torso like a second skin. His cream linen pants showed crinkles, but linen was linen, after all. The dim inner restaurant lighting forced him to remove his shades, which he hung from the lip of his shirt.

A short, stocky man in his late fifties with a smiling if not attractive face, stepped lively to meet him. "Ahh, Mr. Phoenix, good evening. The young lady is waiting for you. We've seated her in a most charming nook. Jaclyn will escort you."

"This way, Mr. Phoenix." Before Luce could thank the man, a statuesque blond goddess appeared. She led him around a dusky wall crawling with ivy vines and into an inner sanctuary with an arched threshold lined with lush green garlands. A gentle trickling of water, as if from a stone fountain, added to the ambiance.

The attentive, and obvious preferential, treatment puzzled him. Certainly he'd patronized the restaurant on previous occasions, but not in any extraordinary way. Such superior service was Ms. Lowe's doing, no doubt. The woman had a way about her. Everything she did, she managed to accomplish with a peerless and conspicuous flare.

Sure enough, the waitress led him to a secluded niche– the likes of which he didn't even know existed. Mellow romantic paper lanterns hung from above. Below, Calamity lounged in the center of a half-moon shaped booth, sipping pinkish liquid from fluted crystal. A larger crystal decanter filled with more of the same sat as the table's centerpiece. Her dress, obscured but for the bodice, was a tomato red, with longish bell-sleeves and a cleavage-baring neckline. Something silvery and dainty-looking caught the light and glittered against her throat, while matching glitters dangled from her ears.

Ahh, he'd been right to fantasize. Her impish smile, executed with ruby red lips, was a thing of beauty. Her hair, he noticed, she'd swept up in a twist in the front while the back bounced with curls, the tips of which just did tickle the line of her jaw.

"Here we are, Mr. Phoenix." The waitress presented menus and smiled down at the two as Luce slid in next to his date. "Help yourself to the Sangria or feel free to request another wine of your choice. Dinner is on the house tonight, compliments of Mr. Leonardo." She inclined her head and strolled away, leaving them alone.

Luce rested an arm along the top of the mint-green seat back, settling Calamity under his wing. He smiled down at her, a warm, but questioning gesture. "Dinner on the house…what's up with that?"

Calamity took another small sip before she sat the glass down. "Family friend. Leo's grandson was one of my mother's students a few years back, before she retired. The parents died in a car accident, you may have seen it on the news. Sensationalized hit-n-run. Anyway, poor kid didn't take it too well. He became a problem at school, was even caught shoplifting at the museum while the class was on a field trip. Moms talked HPD out of an arrest and worked with him after school during the semester. Turned Jason's life around let Leo tell it."

"Who are Leo and Jason again?"

"Mr. Leonardo's the maître d', short stumpy man who greets everyone at the door. Jason's the grandson." Calamity scooted closer so her left side leaned against his right, and tilted her head up to look square at him. "He sends my parents a Christmas card every year."

"So your mother was the 'mind-is-a-terrible-thing-to-waste' type, huh?"

"More like a traditionalist who just loved kids."

"I didn't know teachers like that still existed." Luce tore his eyes away from Calamity's sinful crimson lips to face the newly returned Jaclyn.

"Ready with your drink order?"

"Yeah, give me the Chianti…and five more minutes to decide on an entrée."

"Of course." Jaclyn floated noiselessly away.

Luce turned back to Calamity, letting his hand wander from the seat back to rest on her nape, toying with her hair. "Did I mention how edible you look tonight?"

Calamity smiled, pleased. The words were menial, but the heat in his eyes spoke volumes of passionate love poems. His bold, hot-ink gaze electrified her senses, as it roamed over her like a lover's caress. "Thank you, Luce."

He dipped and dropped a quick kiss on her mouth.

Calamity felt her heart flutter at the simple touching of

lips. Have mercy if those lips ever touched any other part of her body. Enjoying herself, yet still jittery, she stared up at him, eyes wide and inviting, striving for something clever to say. "I didn't see you at work. Busy day?"

"Yeah, mediation with Charlie in the Wallace-MacKenzie dispute ran way over. It's progressing, but at a glacial pace. Every compromise is like pulling teeth from the jaws of death."

"That explains where he was all day...not that I'm complaining." Calamity grimaced at the thought, and reached for her drink. "Sheesh, cooped up with Perkins for hours on end, better you than me. I'd have shot myself by noon. Do you know that creep made another pass at me yesterday? Claimed he wanted to *have me* for lunch."

Luce watched her down half the contents of her glass, and frowned. He sensed the tone of the evening shifting, and not for the better in his opinion. "Shhhh... nobody's *having* anybody for lunch. Although, if you don't take it easy, we may be having your stomach pumped after dinner." He reached with his free hand, took the crystal from her and sat it down, then tipped her chin back around to face him. "In the interest of keeping you sober and preserving everyone's good mood, let's *not* talk shop tonight. No Perkins, no lawsuit, no ranting...just dinner, flirting, and intermittent conversation... maybe a 'lil reckless abandon on the side." To illustrate his point, he dipped again and nipped her lips with his own.

Breathless and flushing, Calamity agreed.

He gave her a quick chaser on the tip of her nose, and then turned to take up the forgotten menus that still hung off the opposite edge of the table. "We better pick something before Aphrodite returns. Wouldn't want her gettin' leg cramps running back and forth on our whims."

She giggled, a bit tipsy already, Luce noted. The present glass of Sicilian Sangria poised at her fingertips was definitely not her first. "It's Jaclyn, not Aphrodite, but I do see the resemblance. Hmm, I've always wanted to be that tall."

Luce handed her a menu, while perusing his own. "Tall? Why?"

"I don't know." She flipped open the green-tinted lamination, examining it with vague disinterest. What she was hungry for wasn't on the menu. "I guess because I'm so short. Poor Jaclyn probably wishes to be shorter. Then, the ratio of men she could date would be greater."

Her eyes soon wandered back up to his face, now in profile. "Luce?"

"Hmm?"

"What's it like being tall?"

"Nice." He replied, teasing, "I can date anyone I want."

Calamity chuckled at this. She glanced back at her menu choices, perusing them almost as an afterthought. "I guess I'll have the lasagna...or the fettuccine alfredo. No wait, *this* looks good too."

Luce noted with some amusement that when it came to food, she seemed to have a decision-making disorder. He'd been out with her twice and already noticed the pattern. If she held true to form, she'd order a sampler type platter, to avoid making a definitive choice.

He was right. In the end, she settled on the Tour de Italy, which came with portions of three different entrées, lasagna, chicken parmesan, and fettuccine. Meanwhile, he chose the Tuscan T-Bone which arrived at the table steaming and sizzling, next to a side of roasted potatoes and bell peppers.

They shared a layered chocolate tart for dessert. Luce had resumed his relaxed position, with one arm resting along the seat-back, hand at her nape. He was such an old-fashioned gentleman, Calam thought. The last miscreant she'd had dinner with hadn't been content to simply caress her baby hairs. The weasel started at the nape of her neck and during the course of the evening slithered lower until he dared to slip his hand into her cleavage. Shameless, the things some guys thought they could get away with on a first date!

"So, is it just you and your sister?" Luce asked, before taking a generous swallow of smooth red Chianti.

"No, we have a younger brother, Pike. His real name's Krystopher, but what with me calling Charisma 'Chris' half the time, we had to come up with a more unique nickname when Pike came along. How about you, any siblings?"

He sighed, the deep, long-suffering kind. "Yeah, two brothers. One older, Sean Vincent, and one younger, Giovanni. Gio died seven years ago. Leukemia."

"Geez, I'm sorry. That must have been hard on your parents."

He gave her neck a punctuating rub. "It was hard on all of us."

Calamity watched him turn to their shared saucer and fork off a piece of semi-sweet chocolate with his free hand. "I get the feeling there's a story behind that, but I won't ask and have you think I'm morbidly curious...even though I am."

Luce snorted a laugh despite himself. Only Calamity could get him—in the space of one flippant comment—to talk about a subject he absolutely loathed discussing even with his remaining brother. He gazed sideways at her, obsidian eyes ablaze with suppressed emotion.

"If Gio hadn't died, I'd be a different person." He admitted. "I used to be idealistic and naïve, thinking everyone had a fair shake, and I could save the world if only I tried hard enough. Kinda like you."

"Hey! Don't disparage us optimists." She chastised, smacking his hand playfully.

He apologized with a kiss to her temple. "Gio was sixteen when he first got sick. I was at the beginning of my sophomore year in college. My parents, my father in particular, were completely unprepared. No steady job, no health insurance, minimal savings, no rainy day plans whatsoever. Mama had to take on extra work wherever she could get it, which meant back-breaking janitorial and housekeeping gigs. You'd think Gio's illness alone would be a wake-up call to my pops, but no, it was business as usual. Oh, he'd pray diligently to the Virgin Mary and the Almighty Dio, then get up off his knees, bury his head in the sand and his money in one ridiculous scheme after another. Mama's killing herself trying to keep ahead of the mounting bills—prescriptions, procedures, chemo–and what's he doing? Working part-time as a cook, writing plays and movie scripts on the side…fairy tales, all with better endings than Gio got. There was always a friend of a friend of a friend who would read his shit, go hog wild, and make him a star. Then his son…his *Gio* would get the best of everything. They both died before that ever happened, Gio from cancer and him from heart disease."

Wow, that's a whole lot of unresolved anger there, buddy. Tentative, Calamity commented. "I gather you took a leave of absence from college, since I know you only finished law school last year."

"Somebody had to work and help pay the bills. Pops didn't. So, Vee and I took up the slack, him more so than me because he'd finished his Bachelors' and could get a higher-paying job. Later, he went back to medical school and became a radiologist. After we buried Gio, I was done with childish dreams, and concentrated on school and getting a degree in a lucrative field. My ultimate goal was a solid dependable career, with salary, benefits, stability, and dignity. I want to be able to step up to the plate like my father didn't…or couldn't."

Calamity's eyes widened. She wasn't so much surprised by what he said as she was unnerved by it. The two of them were such a stark contrast, until it was almost ironic. "Is that really how you see yourself?" At his answering nod, she sighed. "Boy, it must be true what they say. Opposites attract. I had six different majors before I finally settled on liberal arts, which is really just an amalgamation of all the other majors. And I still haven't a clue what I want to do with my life, career-wise. I know I want to get married and have kids, but that's about it. I thought for a second about…but never mind." Sheepish, she ducked her head.

"You thought for a second about what?" When she chanced a peek back at him, his expression held such genuine interest, until she shed her embarrassment.

"Being a lawyer, if you can believe that, but after two attempts at admission, this job at Ross-Warner, and Perkins, I think maybe I'm not cut out for it. I certainly don't possess the focus and single-mindedness that you have in spades."

He tipped her chin up, as had become a custom, caught and held her eyes before he spoke. "You can do anything you really want to do. It just takes hard work and discipline."

* * *

They strolled out into the darkness of a half-empty parking lot, wistful, holding hands. Neither wanted the night to end, but both knew it was time.

"That yours over there?"

"Yeah."

As they neared her jeep, and the official end of date number one, Calamity wondered if he'd ever ask her out again. She so hoped he would. She hadn't felt such a promising bond on a first date in a long time…if ever.

Somehow, the ball seemed in his court. She'd already made up her mind that he was the cat's meow. The only variable was whether or not he reciprocated her enthusiasm.

Reaching their destination, he untwined his fingers from hers and rested his hands at her waist. "I had a nice time."

"Me too."

"Goodnight, Calamity."

"'Night Lucifer."

For a split second, she thought that was it. She even went so far as to pivot the beginnings of a turn before she felt his grip tighten. He stepped forward, pushing her gently against the side of the jeep. She retreated to face him, grabbing a handful of his shirt, and tip-toeing on impulse. He stooped and met her midways in a fiery meeting of the mouths. This was nothing like the chaste little smacks of before. His tongue slid in and out of her mouth in a gradual but heated exploration. One palm stayed at her waist, steadying, while the other burrowed deep in her hair...he was in no hurry. There was no pressure to move past a certain point, no molesting hands or grinding hips. He simply kissed her...open-mouthed, leisurely, sensual, arousing even, but never sleazy or pawing. The movement of his lips over hers was soft, moist, hot, and addictive. Her stomach flittered in response and she felt herself whimper, saddened when he brought the pleasure to its natural close, giving her a parting little smooch.

He put a palm to her cheek, and she felt cherished when she heard the words he whispered.

"Call me when you get home so I know you're safe. And get some rest this weekend, the real fight starts Monday."

CREEP SHOW

The mid-August sun hung in the sky like a rotisserie disco ball slow-roasting the inhabitants below. Calamity grimaced at her reflection as she passed the mirror in her hallway. Houston's summer heat rendered her pathetic apartment air conditioner ineffective, leaving her hair in puffy, sweat-dampened tufts. It stood up all over her head like a charcoal-colored lion's mane. She'd be forced to wash and re-straighten it before the weekend ended. Despite the weather and her riotous hair, Calamity floated at altitudes above the stratosphere.

Charisma stared at her sister across the breakfast table, shaking her head, wry amusement apparent. "Why is it that you always come back from seeing Satan with your hair all jacked up? Is that his trademark or something...like, the mark of the beast?"

"Don't be a buzz-kill, Charisma." Calamity glared at her sister over a forkful of eggs.

The phone preempted her reply. Charisma stood to nab it off the kitchen counter. "For whom does the bell toll—Hello?"

Calamity mouthed an eggy, "Who is it?"

"Reese, hey. She's eating. What's up with you?

Nothing, why? No. Anything useful? Bummer. I don't know. But why—"

The dialogue continued for several minutes, but Calamity couldn't make heads nor tails of the conversation from listening to her sister's end.

Just when Calam feared the monosyllabic exchange interminable, Charisma hung up.

"She wants us to come over right away. One of the cameras caught something. She wouldn't say what, but the term 'creep-show' was mentioned. By the way, she asked if you'd ever had the pleasure of meeting Mrs. Perkins."

Calamity frowned, bemused.

* * *

Forty minutes later, they pulled into a parking space in her friend's apartment complex. Calam adjusted her red and yellow Rockets cap so the bill covered her nape and thankfully most of her humility-frizzed hair. She'd deal with it properly when they got back home. For now, the cap would have to suffice.

Reese opened the door in skinny jeans and an asymmetry off-the-shoulder tunic with 'Real Blonde' embroidered across the bosom in shiny neon thread. A smallish arrow hovered below, inserting a glittery 'dirty' between 'Real' and 'Blonde'. Her nose twitched with amusement as she eyed Calam's conspicuous headgear, while her twin sported a near-perfect-feathered coif.

Oh hell no, Calam thought, she would *not* be needled by a bathtub blonde. "Don't even think about airing whatever amusing little jibe I see forming in that demented brain of yours. Remember, we met *before* you became a real blonde."

"Touché. My lips are sealed." Reese ushered them inside, gesturing towards the couch. "Come on, I already have the tape cued up. You two are going to love this. Uh, by the way, neither of you is against porn…in theory, are you?"

Charisma turned to give her sister's friend a questioning glance before she plopped down in front of the TV. "If either of us had any high level moral standards we probably wouldn't be viewing illegal surveillance tapes in the first place, but that's just my take."

"Yeah, what she said." Calamity adjusted the volume and tuned the picture on the small screen dwarfed by Reese's family-sized flat screen sitting adjacent. Adjustments done, she hit the play button.

"Say, why can't we watch it on the flat screen?" Charisma gestured to the more modern TV.

"Impossible. That would be like trying to interface an old-school Walkman with the latest iPod gear." Calam explained as the mini-screen brightened.

A snowy, distorted image flipped in several rapid successions before it cleared somewhat into a grainy but color likeness of Perkins' office. The aerial view looked down from the ceiling, just adjacent to the main light fixture. The sound was muffled, a tad distorted, and a mere rush of silence at first. Calamity nodded her approval as she backed up to take a seat beside Reese on the couch. She'd known that a ceiling model smoke detector would be the best thing for Perkins' office. The image and sound, while not the most avant-garde, served well enough to ensure a good peep into the goings-on in Pervin's world.

The screen showed nothing, just a chestnut-stained desk, surrounding space, and the matching chestnut bookcases along one of two non-glass walls at the back.

"What exactly are we supposed to see?" Calamity frowned. Patience did not appear among her list of virtues. "Reese?"

Reese just pointed back to the screen, with an inscrutable smirk. Almost the next instant, the back of a head bobbed just inside the viewing frame. Calam recognized Perkins' perpetual, rucked-up hair as he backed into view from somewhere off screen. His hands were outstretched as if beckoning or drawing some unseen object to him. Turned out, that unseen something took the form of a woman, who appeared from the angle of the camera to be, several inches taller than Perkins himself. The woman was visible only from the top of her head and a side profile when she swayed a certain way. Her wall of darkish hair obscured most of her face. She followed the lure of arms and when she reached him she shoved him in the chest. The resulting flail of limbs fell backward against the desk, with the woman in the superior position.

"That's right, Darlin', come be Charlie's Angel…"

"Good grief!" Calamity gasped as a familiar flow of events took shape on the screen. "They're not going to—you know—do it, are they?"

Almost in answer, the woman spoke in a muffled, throaty voice. "Aahhhh Charlie…yesss, fill me!" Perkins gave off a chorus of guttural moans, ever increasing in volume and rhythm.

"Good Lawd, Calam—" Charisma wailed, "—turn the sound down before I lose my breakfast."

"Yeah, ok." At the frantic urgings of her sister, Calam surged forward to mute the screen. Sitting back down, she couldn't help but giggle. The silent image of the two-backed beast gyrating atop the desk seemed comical all of a sudden, an odd reminiscence of silent Hollywood and Charlie Chaplin sketches.

"This is *soooo* not funny, Calamity. I had to *touch* that desk not twenty-four hours ago. Ewww!" As if realizing the full implication of what she'd just said, Charisma leaped up and rushed towards the shallow hallway. "Reese, where's your bathroom please?!"

"Through the bedroom, the door off the foot of the bed." Reese tittered to the floor in a fit of helpless laughter, elf green eyes shining like emeralds. "I warned her it wasn't for the faint of heart."

"Stop that. You know she's pregnant." Calamity chastened half-hearted, kicking her friend playfully on the tush. "Poor Chrissy. I may have to run to the store for some pepto or something."

"Wait, you can't leave yet. They're getting ready for the big finish."

Calamity snorted, "Reese, I'm familiar with the eh...script. I know how it ends."

The big-haired blonde sobered and climbed back on the couch. "No, seriously, there's something I want your opinion about."

"I'm almost afraid to ask–" She glanced at the disheveled rutting twosome, now minus a few essential items of clothing. "What on earth is going to happened in the next, oh I'd say...thirty seconds, could you possibly want *my opinion* about?"

"Shut up and watch. Here it comes."

"Ooh, looks like the carpet matches the drapes." Calamity noted, dryly.

Reese humphed. "Don't believe everything you see. At The Pretty Kitty, if you slip Ramona a twenty, you can get the carpet dyed any color in the rainbow."

Huh? Calam glanced from the TV to her friend, incredulous. "Are you telling me that you get your eh...*carpet* dyed?" That must be a white girl thing.

Green eyes glistening, Calam watched her 'zip' her lips with a playful gesture. "Its like Jack Nicholson said...'Only the undertaker knows for sure'. Now, watch, its just coming up."

"Bad pun." Calam grimaced, turning back to the screen.

At the climax, or so she assumed it was, the woman again in the superior position, flung back her head, longish hair whirled around to land in a plop on her back. Reese and Calamity were then treated to the first and only clear view of the woman's face, mouth gaped, eyes wide, and brow furrowed in a perfect etching of female passion.

"That's not his wife."

Calamity reached quickly to pause the playback, then

sat back a minute to study the face. "Nope, not that it matters much. Their little romp is obviously consensual and he and his wife are in the process of untying the knot anyway. As much fun as this has been," She snickered despite herself. "There's nothing here I can use."

"Yeah, I know. Bummer."

"Sheesh, you'd think if he's getting lubed like this on the regular, he wouldn't be so randy at work."

Reese shrugged. "Probably a nympho."

"Figures."

* * *

Monday came much too soon for Calamity's peace of mind. She'd been hoping for one of those infinite time-loop anomalies like what always happened in cheesy low-budget science fiction shows. Then maybe she'd be trapped repeating the same day over and over again, and never have to face reality. Preferably Friday, so she could relive the perfection forever. She'd have the perfect hair, the perfect man, and the perfect kiss for all eternity.

Alas, she didn't get her wish. The weekend ended with all the usual pall of a looming workweek ahead. Only this particular week, she was in for the special torture of being the center attraction in a formal inquiry. Oh joy.

Calamity sat, tense, at her desk; her back ached from holding the rigid position too long. Lunch came and went, with no phone call, visit, or word from Employee Relations. Mid-afternoon saw her cleaning her computer files, deleting junk and clearing outdated information off the hard-drive as well as up-dating the status of current cases. During the course of the day, every client, opposing attorney, and business liaison of Perkins' telephoned her office. In addition, her mother rang to ask for Charisma's work number. Reese blew up her cell every other minute demanding a progress report. Hell, even Luce called to check up on her; his was the most gratifying of the lot by far.

As the day wore on she relaxed, letting her guard down little by little, satisfied that it just wouldn't happen that day. With each successive ring of the telephone, her tension eased. By three forty-five, she'd mellowed back into her normal office routine. So, twenty minutes later when she answered the phone to an aloof female voice requesting to speak with her boss she waffled.

"Eh, sure, Ms....eh? Please state the nature of your business. Mr. Perkins likes to be appraised beforehand."

"My business is for his ears only." Came the cool response.

No one called Perkins office without stating his or her business. Everyone knew by now that full disclosure was one in a complicated list of conditions callers had to satisfy if he or she wanted telephone access to the self-important Charlie Perkins. Keeping her hands as steady as possible considering the delicate situation, Calamity buzzed the inner office with news of a caller on hold.

"Mr. Perkins, you have a call on line three. Employee Relations wishes to have a word."

"Fine." A flat, decisive 'fine' was the answer she always received whenever Perkins chose to respond to something in the affirmative. To the untrained ear one couldn't tell the 'fines' apart, but over her three-year tenure at Ross-Warner, Calamity learned the 'fine' language quite well. There was the exasperated 'fine', which meant he'd talked to this person a dozen times already and didn't really wish to speak to them again about the same topic. There was the anxious 'fine' which generally cut off the end of her sentence and meant that he'd been waiting an inordinate amount of time for said phone call and was eager to get to it. Then, there was the confused 'fine', which was always preceded by a slight pause, and meant that he didn't understand why this person could possibly wish to speak with him. There was a wealth of other 'fines' each with its own unique meaning, but it was the confused 'fine' that greeted her today.

Calamity sweated it out for five excruciating minutes. She forgot her computer files in favor of straightening the photo frames and decorative knickknacks on her desktop. She picked up the phone twice, her first impulse to call Luce, but then she changed her mind. Her next inclination was Reese, which she also talked herself out of. Charisma had a doctor's appointment so calling her was out of the question. She'd have to stick it out alone, at least until Perkins left his office and she could have a full-on meltdown without fear of him walking in and/or wanting her for some menial task.

She didn't have long to wait. Perkins stalked out of the inner sanctuary at a brisk purposeful pace, giving her a glare that promised proper retribution upon his return. So, the other shoe had finally dropped. He shoved off through the outer door to take a meeting with the adept Ms. Heyes. The waiting was over, giving way to relief.

For about sixty seconds anyway. Then she realized that the opening bell of the first major skirmish in what promised to be a no-hold-barred brawl had just rung...causing her to break out in hives. Guerrilla warfare she could handle, but dueling by society's standards, rules she knew were stacked against her...*that* rattled her to the point where she exited the office in search of reinforcements. She reached Reese's cubicle in record time.

"Its happening. They called him up to E.R. about five minutes ago." She announced pacing the five feet or so of free space between her friend's desk and the two visitor's chairs facing the desk. "He gave me this glare. It was the sort of expression that says, 'You won't get away with this.' He was declaring *war* with that look. It's no holds barred now."

"Alright, calm down, Calam...better yet, *sit* down first, then calm down. Have you talked to Satan yet? What did he say? Is this the normal way of things?"

The knowledge that Charisma's ridiculous moniker for Luce had caught fire didn't break through the panic gripping her mind. "Well, I haven't talked to him yet. That's my next stop, it's just, you were on the way to his office and I needed reassurance that I'm doing the right thing by trusting him." She plopped down, fidgeting this way and that. "What if he's playin' me? He's a lawyer, a *colleague* of the enemy. This could be a *huge* mistake."

"Shhhh, no hyperventilating in my cube. Ok, let's do this…take long cleansing breaths and don't think of him as 'Mr. Phoenix', collaborator and bosom-buddy lawyer to Perkins." Reese flashed her hands out in front of her, bangles jingling at the wrists, using her spread-eagled fingers as a visual aid. "Think of him as 'Luce' from Friday night, old-school gentleman with Ward Cleaver manners, a liquid-sex voice…and a kiss hotter than a cattle rustler's branding iron."

Calam paused in her panic to frown. "Huh?"

"Ok, sorry, way too many late-night westerns. Worse case scenarios, Satan's plan doesn't work. Or, maybe it turns out he lives up to his name, in either case we still have plan B, remember? Perkins is bound to harass someone else, then we've got him by the 'nads…if you'll pardon the image that expression evokes."

"True." Calamity nodded, relaxing a bit. "You're right, of course. There's no need to get all worked-up. We always have plan B."

"Good, you're down off the ledge. We're making progress here. You need to consult the expert at once for some new strategy."

What she needed was her head examined, Calam mentally kicked herself. Why had she let him talk her into this? "Yes, I should talk to Luce, tell him what's going on." She stood again. "He'll know what I should, or shouldn't do. Man, I hate this. If we were doing it my way, I wouldn't feel so out-matched…and *powerless*."

"Go talk to Satan." Reese ordered. "He'll put you back

on the straight and narrow…eh, as weird as that sounds."

* * *

Calamity arrived at Luce's office door, having bypassed Stella's empty cube with no hassles. She tapped at the door and waited. Somewhere in her chaotic mind she still possessed the capacity to observe proper business etiquette. He opened the door, bedecked in his usual corporate attire, minus a jacket, which she guessed was hanging from a hook somewhere. How Luce maintained his ubiquitous image of professional brilliance and irresistible sex appeal was beyond her. Her appearance, she was sure, suffered her every mood swing.

He stepped back. Without breaking the tone or inflection of his phone conversation, he beckoned for her to enter, and closed the door behind her. Calamity was left to stand mute, nursing fragile nerves as he wound the exchange to a natural breaking point and began making preparations to speak to the person at a later date. She bristled in shock when she felt his hand at the small of her back, guiding her firmly into a chair opposite his. As he came round to the desk, she watched him hold up his index finger, she assumed to signal that he'd be with her in a minute. As he sat, the phone found a home on its cradle at the corner of his desk.

"What can I do for you, Ms. Lowe?" This he asked with all the articulation and interest of a lobotomized Vulcan.

"For one thing, you can drop the formality and that lawyer poker face. It's going down exactly how you said it would. Employee Relations called him up there. Sheila Heyes, that's her name, is she any good? Please tell me she's good."

"I don't know her personally, but I'm sure she's more than proficient at her job."

"Stop it." Calamity snapped, a little freaked out by his

lack of reaction. All the ground Reese won was lost again as Luce's blasé attitude pushed her back to the edge. Watching him sit across the desk with his hands folded, businesslike, impartial, as if she were any other client...like Friday night never happened. She felt the delicate threads of her control slip.

"Stop it right now! I hate it when you talk to me like a robot spitting out pre-recorded gibberish." To Calamity's horror, her voice cracked at her next words. "I'm scared. They're up there right now talking about me. There's no telling what kind of lies that creep is tossing around. How can you just sit there like Blind Justice and bury your head in logic and the legal process?"

"Dial it down an octave, Ms. Lowe—"

"*Calamity.*" Her name came out a hiss between her teeth.

"Don't be irrational." Luce put more emotion into the command than he meant to, but caught himself before he continued in the same vein. It wouldn't do to let her obvious panic rub off on him. "I think of you as 'Calamity', but I say 'Ms. Lowe' for propriety's sake. It's better to maintain a professional atmosphere here at Ross-Warner. Rumors of an illicit relationship or any other boundary-crossing behavior between you and I, or you and anyone for that matter is not going to have a positive effect on your harassment complaint. He'll say that if you're sleeping with me, your superior, you're obviously open to interoffice *dalliances* and perhaps not above *initiating* dalliances that would say, propel your career. Do you see where I'm going with this, Ms. Lowe?"

She winced at the ugly insinuations, closing her eyes to get a hold of the frustrated tears threatening to emerge. Anger at the unfairness of it all gnawing at her self-control. "Oh hell, he's going to make me out to be a—"

"Don't." Luce cut off any further discussion on the topic. "Just ease off the panic button a little. I'm still working on Stella. Go back to your office. I'll meet you at

The Coffee Bar on Richmond after work. And Ms. Lowe?"

She searched his stoic features for some sort of solace, not bothering to hide her desperate need for reassurance. He must have sensed her desperation. The ice thawed a little. Those beautiful sable eyes melted into hers, his voice lowered to a lover's caress.

"Don't let him see you sweat. He'll probably try something when he gets back to the office. Understand this, it's all for show. He's the one on the defensive and he knows it. You've got to stand your ground and not let him intimidate you. No matter what he says, what threats he makes, even if he brings up the assault charges, you *cannot* crack. Show him a weakness and he'll exploit it. In any war, the enemy always goes for the weakest link in their opponent's chain. Remember that."

Some of her apprehension drained away. She caught her bottom lip with her teeth and gave him a wobbly smile. "Thank you, Mr. Phoenix, I appreciate the advice."

* * *

Luce was nothing if not uncanny in his predictions. The second Perkins returned, as he traversed the threshold, in fact, he dictated she follow him into his office. She obeyed with renewed inner poise. Thanks to Luce and Reese she knew an attack was coming, perhaps not the exact threats or what shape it would take, but inkling enough to sidestep whatever land mine that awaited her. She stood straight opposite him sitting at his desk. She planted her feet, readying herself for the onslaught.

"You wanted to see me, Mr. Perkins?"

"Yes, Ms. Lowe." He fiddled with a silver fountain pen, twirling it counterclockwise on the desktop, while drumming his fingers with his other hand. An elaborate way of fidgeting, Calamity noted. "I want to know what you hoped to accomplish by hurling these unfounded accusations at me."

Calamity decided to play by her usual rules. "Come again?"

"As I'm sure you're aware, Employee Relations is under the mistaken assumption that I have acted inappropriately towards one of my subordinates."

"I'm aware of no such thing." It was difficult to keep her voice level. She found his interrogation pitiful, amusing almost.

"Are you denying that you filed a sexual harassment complaint against me, Ms. Lowe."

"Not at all, Mr. Perkins. I'm denying that my accusations are unfounded. You *did* harass me with unwanted and unprovoked sexual overtures."

"And you assaulted me, Ms. Lowe." He tapped the silver pen to his left temple. "An eye for an eye."

She shrugged, uncaring. "That's my usual reaction to unsolicited advances from pathetic middle-aged married men. A feminist reflex, so sue me."

"What a lovely idea." There it was, his one and only point of leverage, the threat of assault charges. "Unless of course, you can think of some mutually beneficial arrangement that would save us both the time and embarrassment of *two* formal investigations."

"The *truth*," Calamity put a sardonic emphasis on that pivotal word, "–however it may come to light, is not an embarrassment to *me*."

Perkins narrowed his eyes at her ubiquitous poise. Ha! Tactics not having the desired effect? Calam gloated with relish.

"Very well, Ms. Lowe, have it your way. I'm sure there will be plenty of time to regret your mistakes in the unemployment line."

"Are you firing me, Mr. Perkins?" She challenged, lifting a brow to double dare him. "Won't the hasty dismissal of your assistant mere days after she's filed a complaint against you give the appearance of impropriety?"

"This meeting is to be continued." His fingers ceased to drum, and the pen flew across the room, met noisily with a pane of frosted glass and ricocheted off in two pieces. "Now, Get out!"

He didn't let it go at that, heck no...Perkins was not a gracious loser, and he wasn't about to start now. Livid that she'd one-upped him in their first major scrape, he thundered up from the chair, pelting her retreating back with more threats.

"Stay on your toes, Ms. Lowe. One *hair* out of place, one typo, one *hint* of misconduct... That's all I need, one little excuse and your ass is *past tense*! You don't have the staying power. I give it two weeks, and I'll be breaking in a new assistant. *Two* weeks!!"

Calamity stepped gingerly back into her office, only when the connecting door slammed closed behind her did she allow herself the luxury of a deep breath...and a shaky one at that. Going back over the confrontation in her head, Calamity had one uplifting thought...besides her after-work get together with Luce, that is. Perkins cracked like an eggshell when she turned the tables on him, so maybe she wouldn't need the nanny-cams after all.

"Reese and Chrissy are going to go hog wild at the instant replay on this one."

THE REAL LOWDOWN

As much as Perkins wasn't a gracious loser, Calamity was an equally ungracious winner. She arrived at the Coffee Bar bubbling over with mirth and excitement. An impulse struck her to skip through the jumble of crowded tables to where she'd spotted Luce already seated. He stood and waved her over, as if she couldn't spot the six-foot four Afro-Italian Adonis on her own. Good grief, did the man even realize how magnetic his appeal was on the fairer sex? She was a predator scenting prey where he was concerned. She could probably spot him from a hundred yards on a foggy day, through tinted windshields and a pair of shades.

Handicapped by two-inch square pumps, she abandoned the skipping idea. Instead she made a careful path through the maze of bust-high tables, jammed with hordes of noisy caffeine junkies chatting in cliquish groups. Some were corporate, entrepreneurial types boasting of polished suits and square cut hair. Others were the college coffeehouse breed, with dreads, goatees, and oversized logo-ed T-shirts. There was even a table of giggly, high school-ish girls, struggling to affect an image of cool. Calamity traversed the last sprawling group and launched herself at the object of her adoration. Luce caught her in his arms and held her close against him lower torso.

"Whoa…"

"Luce! It worked! We've got him by the short-hairs now!" Her words were somewhat garbled by the hug; her cheek pressed into his rock hard chest. "Thank you so much for helping me earlier. I cringe to think what would've happened if I hadn't come to see you first. I was so freaked out, but all I really had to do was not let him… Oh, I…I'm sorry—"

Calamity came to her senses, stepping back a pace. She peered upward, sheepish and apologetic. If she didn't know better, she'd vow she felt crimson color creeping over her. But the thought was ridiculous; she did *not* blush.

"I didn't mean to tackle you. Not that it hurt or anything…you being a tree trunk and me a twig but…uh, sorry, tangent. I'm just a little juiced up."

He grinned down at her, a bit devilish, "Well, I guess this means a *decaf* latte for you." He dropped one hand while the other came up to briefly cup her cheek. "Come on, sit down before I kiss that pretty little mouth of yours and make a *real* spectacle of us."

As exhilarated and impetuous as Calamity felt, she couldn't help giving in to a little reckless abandon.

"Ah, to hell with *them*…" What did she care what a room full of people she'd never seen before and probably never would again thought of her? With a flick of her wrist she tossed the proverbial wine glass at the hearth. "Kiss me!"

"As you wish…"

And he did, with a seductive eyebrow arch a lá James Bond. Luce wasn't a general advocate of PDA, but her buoyant mood was infectious and dangerously intoxicating. She made him feel alive again, like he'd thawed out after a long winter hibernation. That's why, standing there in the middle of an unsuspecting crowd, Luce kicked caution to the curb and dragged her back into full-frontal contact with his powerful sinewy frame. He dove downward to capture her lips like a heat-seeking missile...snapping her head back. He kissed her long and deep, invading her mouth with a searing possession, easing off only to nab her bottom lip gently between his teeth.

Her heartbeat went into rabid conniptions. Good Lawd...

Luce couldn't keep his hands from stroking her face, thumbs on each cheek, while his other fingers messed her hair. He needed to rein himself in, instead he tilted her head to one side, kissing her more playful. His attentions soft, teasing, and caressing. He brushed her closed eyelids with quick feathery touches, likewise the tip of her nose, and nipped mischievously at the corners of her mouth.

"Hmmm, had enough? Or shall we hold out until people start clapping?" He made a thick guttural sound somewhere deep in his throat, and kissed her again, planting his mouth firmly on hers in a serious lip lock, urging her lips apart.

Oh...uh...overload, Calamity's mind flashed warning signs as her body shifted into overdrive. Got to stop, she ordered herself, heartbeat pounding in her ears, struggling to catch her breath.

"Alright enough!" She tore herself away, out of his arms, turning sideways to touch her fingertips to her scorched mouth with belated embarrassment. If, in fact, it was possible for her to blush, Calamity imagined that right about then she'd be a flaming hue from the roots of her hair to soles of her feet. "We don't want to get cited for lewd PDA."

* * *

Charisma lay sprawled atop her sister's hideous purple love seat, cell phone pressed to her ear. The continuous mechanized buzz of the air conditioner forced her to inch up the volume on the TV. The weather gods had seen fit to bless Houston with a brief but cooling rain-shower so the night air felt less sweltering than usual.

"...watching TV, how's Manny?" She allowed her head to lull to one side, whilst she aimed the remote to begin her nocturnal bout of channeling surfing. "Have you tried calamine lotion? Calam and I used it when we suffered through the chicken pox. It should lessen the itching and keep the sores from scarring too much. Well, just wait until he falls asleep and then rub it on. I think they have the clear kind now."

Twilight crept through the blinds of the air conditioner-laden living room window. The waning light reminded Charisma how late it was. Another reminder, the ever-present and annoying glare of her sister's nudist, vegan, and all around weirdo squatter, Shane. The miniature male diva, all of five foot seven she guessed, was brown-skinned, purple-haired and pierced in every conceivable place...and probably a place or two she didn't want to conceive. He hovered in the threshold between the kitchen and the dining area, hand on pivoted hip, foot a' tap with irritation. The pose reminded her of a bitchy Lauren Bacall giving Bogie rich-girl attitude in The Big Sleep. Charisma rolled her eyes as his exaggerated sigh escalated into an outburst.

"This is just *TOO* much!" His voice was smooth but pitched higher than normal, for dramatic effect, no doubt. "She knows Cheryl is coming at eight. I can't have uninitiated guests for yoga. Proper meditation and harmonious balance requires quiet, ambiance, soft lighting... *at*mosphere. Not–" His brown globe eyes and freakishly-arched multiple-pierced brows shot around the apartment, "–Miami Vice re-runs, cancer-causing cellular emissions, and...good *night*, hundred-watt bulbs."

Charisma groaned, muting the TV, "Hold on a minute Paul." She clamped a hand over the mouthpiece, and raised up on an elbow. "Let's get something straight. *You're* the guest here, pal, so don't imagine you can run me off.

I'm not leaving until Calam gets home. Take Shelly and play yogi in that demon-den room of yours…that is, if the neurotic nitwit herself ever decides to show."

He narrowed an eye at her, "Stones cast from a glass house do not carry much weight." And with that, stomped off in a theatrical huff to his sometimes domicile, a door down from Calamity's in the shallow hallway.

"*Whatever.* Hey, you better not be making another voodoo doll of me either. I've got mace!" Charisma yelled after him, turning back to resume her conversation only after she heard the emphatic slam of the door. "Sorry Paul, I'm back. Yeah, no, it's nothing, just Shane in the throws of a karmic hissy fit. No biggie. No, Calam's not home yet. But, hey, I don't think we'll have to set her up with that friend of yours after all. Well, just that, she's sorta seeing someone…at the office." Charisma was back into the full swing of the conversation, remote once again in hand, when a sharp knock stalled her.

"Hold up, honey, there's someone at the door, probably Shane's worrisome wife." Again, her hand went over the receiver and she jack up on elbows to face the hall. "*SHANE!* Don't make me come back there. Shelly's at the door, and I'm not the maid."

A minor, yet eloquent clamor preceded Shane's reappearance in the living room. He stalked rather than walked, kinky chest-hair bared, wearing floral spandex leggings with matching headband, and ashy feet. He didn't spare her a glance at his semi-sprint speed. "Shelly! I mean *Cheryl,* babe–" Surprise cut short his enthusiasm.

Charisma sat up, wondering what could've possibly thwarted Shane in mid-flowery greeting to his precious Shelly. This time she hit the off button on the remote and shot to her feet.

"Paul, I'll have to call you back." She flipped the phone off without waiting for a response.

"–with the Houston Police Department, sir. Is there a Ms. Calamity Jones Lowe residing here?"

Charisma bolted to the door, nudging her sister's roomie aside. She came face to shoulder with two, uniform-clad officers. The first one young, brawny, and blue-eyed, while the second came in the form of a pear-shaped black man sporting a close-cut fro. The latter man's age was difficult to determine, and Charisma didn't waste much time trying.

"What's happened?"

The youngster put out a steadying hand, as if to squash any rising histrionics. "Calm down, ma'am. We're here to speak to you about some—"

The other officer stepped forward, quelling his partner. "Burton, first we identify the person of interest."

"Yes, of course." He fumbled over his words a little as Shane and Charisma stood waiting, Charisma anxious, Shane confused. "Eh, Ms. Lowe?"

"Yes," she answered on instinct before realizing. "Well, actually no…uh, yes and no."

The seasoned officer frowned downward. "You fit the description pretty close. So, which is it, Miss?"

"I'm Charisma Lowe-Tate, you're looking for my sister Calamity. We're twins, you see, but this is *her* apartment."

The younger officer glanced between the shirtless, still-gaping Shane and a flustered Charisma, choosing to address the 'man of the house'. "Well, Mr. Tate we're sorry to disturb you and your wife—"

"Don't *even* finish that sentence. I'm pregnant and I could hurl at any moment." She didn't bother to suppress the horror his mistaken identity caused. "This missing-link person is *not* my husband. Shane, your darlin' Shelly's arrival is eminent so do go put on some clothes…*please*."

Oddly enough, he obliged, but not without a parting quip, "Officer, you have my permission to shoot her if she steps out of line."

Charisma pulled a face over her shoulder before turning back to handle the situation at hand. "Ok, now, he's gone. What is this about?"

"We need to talk with your sister, Mrs. Tate." The seasoned one gestured behind her. "Is she here?"

"Uh, no, not at the moment. What do you need to see Calamity about?"

It was like they were playing at some bizarre tag-team game. First, one answered then the other one. "Sorry ma'am," replied the youngster, "—we're not at liberty to give details. Can you tell us where to find your sister?"

"No, she's out. Hey listen, she's not under arrest or anything, is she?"

"No, ma'am. We just need to speak with her. Do you have any idea of when she'll be back?"

"Eh, no, not really."

"Thank you for your time, and again, we apologize for the inconvenience." With that, the twosome tipped their nonexistent hats and eased back.

* * *

"Good, you handled him just right."

Calamity cast her third cup of coffee aside, and leaned forward, elbows on the table, chin resting on interlaced fingers. "Ok, so now he's on the run, what's our next move?"

"Well, I'll have another crack at Stella. Other than that, all we can do is wait. Employee Relations will take it from here. When they're done, they will inform you what they've decided and suggest a course of action. Be prepared. First time offenders, in a standard his-word-against-her-word scenario, will get off fairly easy."

"WHAT?!" Her chin came off the comfortable perch.

"Relax, we're just exploring a very unlikely 'if.'" Luce paused to take her still intertwined hands in one of his. "The incident will go on record and both parties will be obliged to attend in-house *etiquette training*. Its just to re-educate everyone on the guidelines of proper behavior and social conduct in a professional environment. We have no way of knowing *if* this is Perkins' first official offense. I suspect it isn't, otherwise he wouldn't be quite so bent out of shape about it, but I'm telling you what to expect just in case."

"And if I'm *not* the first complainant? What happens then?" She radiated the kind of unrestrained optimism that proved devastating when the blunt trauma of reality hit home.

Damn. It was pure torture to see her rose-colored expectations trained on him when Luce knew he could guarantee her nothing.

"These are possibilities, not promises." He reminded her. "If Stella pans out, or if Charlie has other peccadillos on record or if we're *really* lucky, both, then he'll be facing a formal reprimand, possibly a suspension punctuated with mandatory counseling. They'll never fire him and Charlie knows it. He's an ass, but he's also a brilliant attorney and has an uncanny knack for attracting high profile clients."

"Why am I not surprised..." She sighed, still hopeful but the wind in her sails was fast deflating. Nevertheless, she tried her level best to be practical and maintain a certain amount of dignity. "As much as I hate to lose my office and my tenure, I really don't think I could continue working for him if things go as you say. I thought I could but I think now I'll transfer out or maybe even resign after all."

Luce sympathized with her. He knew from painful experience that the system didn't always serve the needs of the innocent. "Under the circumstances, no one would object to a transfer. Ross-Warner might even give you an office in your new department, to assuage their conscience."

"This is so unfair." She flinched, knowing how childish her outbursts must sound. So much for maturity and stone-faced martyrdom.

Luce didn't make the rules, her angelic mind pointed out...but he *did* insist on following them, her devilish heart

104

countered. Either way, she felt betrayed.

"You know, I should go. Chrissy's there, waiting for me—" Calamity found herself rambling on so he wouldn't notice the deterioration of her mood. It seemed rather petty to take it out of him, but the response was so natural and visceral until Calamity dared not spoil it with common sense. "She had a doctor's appointment today, plus Manny's still sick, and I just…"

"No need to explain. I'll see you tomorrow." Luce could feel her extricating herself, first sliding back to her side of the table, detangling her fingers from under his much-larger hands. He didn't like it, but knew she needed time to acclimate herself to the idea that justice was seldom blind or absolute.

* * *

Her mood did not improve on the drive home. By the time she stepped over the threshold of her apartment, both her spirits and her shoulders sagged.

"Calam!" Charisma stilled from pacing, about to spring at her sister and launch into the spiel she'd been composing over the last twenty minutes. Until, she noted her sister's slumped shoulders and blasé expression. Her hair, she noted, was its usual post-Satan mess, so the meeting couldn't have been a total bust. "Something the matter? You seem a little down."

Calam shrugged, exhaling a dejected breath as she relocked the door behind her. "Oh, it's nothing. What's up with you? Where's Shane?"

She grimaced. "I sent him to his room. Listen, I don't know how to tell you this, but while you were gone—" Calam sensed her sister's hesitation, almost as if she were afraid to tell her something. "I thought about calling but, well, I didn't want to ruin your date and its not like it couldn't wait until you got home. Bad news keeps forever."

She stiffened, on alert. "What happened, Charisma!? Are Paul and Manny ok?" Nothing like a good old-fashion family tragedy to bring one's priorities back into focus and dam the stream of self-pity.

"Oh yeah, no, it's not about them. They're fine, well, except Manny still has the measles of course, but other than that they're fine." She waved off her worries with a quelling gesture. "I was just going to tell you that the police came by. They wouldn't say what about, but I think maybe Perkins called your bluff, Calam."

Crack! The proverbial straw that broke the camel's back.

"*Lovely.*" Calamity hurled the keys at the couch and ran frustrated hands through her hair, leaving it in even more random disarray. "What on earth am I going to do now? This is a nightmare. In the space of one week I've gone from wronged victim to wanted criminal. Next week, they'll be reading my rap-sheet bio on the special white-collar episode of 'Snapped'!"

"Come on, it's not *that* bad." Her sister drew her to the chair to sit down. "The older one definitely said you weren't under arrest. They just wanted to talk and ask questions. If you're not under arrest, they can't *make* you do anything. In fact, you're not even obligated to say anything. Just plead the fifth. I think we should still call Satan, though. To be on the safe side. He'll know exactly what to do."

Calamity turned on her like a pit bull. "Oh, don't mention *him*! First Reese, now you. Is *he* the only solution the two of you can drum up? Recall, Lucifer is the one who got me into this mess in the first place."

"Who better then to get you out of it? Satan *is*, after all, a lawyer." She reasoned, reaching in the purse, which still hung limp from Calam's shoulder. "You've got him on speed dial, right?"

"Yeah." Calamity let out a sigh, anger and self-derision spent. Who was she kidding? Her first impulse upon hearing the words 'police came by' had been to run, break-neck speed, to Luce if for no other reason than to apologize. She wasn't being honest with herself. He *had* helped her—and was still doing so—just not in a way that felt familiar or comfortable to her. Calam prided herself on being a rule-breaker and a risk-taker. It was the only way she knew.

Adding to her unease...Luce differed, considerably, from the comical collection of Mr. Wrongs that had entered and exited her life over the years. His old-world charm spoke to some long-buried little girl fantasy. His honed intelligence intrigued her, and had her itching to ask his opinion on a barrage of different topics. That hint of something dangerous she sensed, it lured her most of all. The bad-boy he kept caged-up behind those intense sable eyes sent thrills down her spine. And it didn't hurt that he exuded erotic appeal with all that gorgeous body. A living-embodiment of sin...and yet, he also had this fifties straight-arrow thing going on. To be blunt, Lucifer just wasn't her type of man. And, she'd just bet she wasn't the sort of girl that usually populated his dance card either. Geez, had she been dating creeps so long until she hesitated to trust a real gentleman? How twisted was that? Disgusted with herself, she shook off her thoughts.

"Ok, call him, but don't tell him I panicked. He's liable to think I don't have a stable bone in my body."

* * *

Luce leaned a hip against his kitchen counter while Sasha trilled up at him with luminous saffron eyes. Typical male bachelor, he didn't bother to heat up the plate of congealed food in his hand, but devoured the leftovers straight from the fridge. Sly hovered nearby, swigging on a wine cooler.

"So let me get this straight. You're taking time out to help the bitc–chick–free of charge and she's still giving you grief? Are you at least getting some play off this girl? 'Cause from what you tell me, she ain't got nothin' going for her, personality-wise."

"Elaborate." He requested between chews.

"Well, let's see…she's making you neglect yo boyz. She's nagging you about legal maneuvers. Plus, she's a time drain. You been out with her–what? – three days in one week?" Sly knocked back the rest of the bottle in a single, massive gulp.

"Spending time together is an essential ingredient in dating."

"Face it, Luce. The woman's a shrew. I say ditch her and get with somebody less demanding."

Luce took another hefty bite of congealed pasta, and shook his head. Meanwhile, Sasha deigned to scale his jean-ed leg in desperate plea of sustenance. "Thanks Sly. Did you read that in *Relationship Therapy for Dummies*?"

"Hey man, *you* started this conversation." He accused, pointing the empty bottle to underscore his words.

"Yeah, there goes ten minutes of my life that I'll never get back." The phone rang, getting both men's attention. "Make yourself useful and snag that. I'm indisposed at the moment."

"I ain't yo secretary, you know." Sly dropped the empty cooler in the garbage in stride to the living room. A minute later, he returned. "Eh, its Carissa or Calista or something like that. I told her to take a hike but she threatened to blow up the phone if I didn't let her speak to you."

Luce abandoned his plate on the countertop, to the rapturous elation of a hungry yellow-eyed feline who bounded upward to take advantage.

In the living room, Luce retrieved the phone, "Mrs. Tate, to what do I owe the pleasure?"

He was greeted by Charisma's harried voice. "Oh, good, I was afraid I'd have to do something drastic just to—"

"Thankfully not." Luce made himself comfortable on

the couch. "So, is there a problem or are you calling to ask me out on a second date?"

Charisma chose to ignore his insolence and get straight to the point. "Calamity's upset."

"Yes, I know." His tone amended from vague sarcasm to polite indifference.

"No, I mean more upset than when you last saw her. While she was gone, the police came by looking for her. The officers wouldn't say why but it has to be that lecher Perkins. He's filed charges after all."

Luce sat up rigid, his tone still polite, but no longer indifferent. "What did they say, exactly?"

"Just that she wasn't under arrest, but that they needed to speak with her. They called her a 'person of interest' so, I'm sure they'll be back. We didn't know what else to do besides call you."

"It's fine, I'm glad you called. I gather Ms. Lowe is pretty worried." Luce stood, carrying the phone's base with him to the kitchen counter where he hurriedly found a pad and pen. "Give me the address there, I'll come over."

Charisma resisted that idea, the infamous Cheryl had finally arrived and Shane was in a tizzy to get her and Calam gone so they could do their I-Cheng Zen chant thing. "Uh, no, Calam's weirdo roommate and his wife are here and well—"

"Ok, find something to write with and I'll give you directions to my place."

Sly, having overheard his cousin's intentions, snapped up from the open fridge with a fresh cooler in his hand. He came around to Luce's side of the counter and pantomimed his displeasure. Luce eyed him briefly, pointing to indicate it was time for him to go.

"–It's apartment number twenty-six. Ok, call if you get lost."

Sly was on him an instant after the receiver touched base. "Luce, come *on!*"

"'Night, Sly."

"She snaps her fingers and that's it. Move over Sly, make room for Calista?"

"Yeah, ain't life a bitch?" Luce's flip words contrasted with the powerful forward glide of his rock solid frame. His movements like that of a jungle cat. Intimidated, Sly took a hasty step back for every one his cousin took forward, and soon found himself pressed against the front door.

"Luce, be reasonable–this girl ain't right for you. I know this fine-as-hell chick, Ginger, knockers that defy gravity, and not too bright, if you know what I mean…"

"Goodbye, Sly." He opened the door, tipping a gangly off-balance Sly into the back wall.

Sly straightened and shrugged off defeat. "No Ginger?"

"No Ginger." Luce confirmed.

"Alright, how's about Violet then?"

Luce grabbed a handful of his cousin's shirt and bodily shoved him out the door.

* * *

The twins arrived within the hour. Charisma relieved, Calamity apprehensive. Luce held the door as they entered. He watched as they came to a halt at the living room. Her sister seemed more relaxed than he would have expected. Calamity, on the other hand, was a ticking bomb of anxiety. Her chocolate eyes darted around the room, looking everywhere but at him.

"Nice place." She offered. Décor was always a safe, segue topic, even if his shotgun style apartment possessed none. Everything was functional enough; ratty couch, dull unvarnished coffee table, dining room table with no centerpiece, naked beige walls, spotted brown carpet unraveling in certain places, decent TV though. Perhaps the most bizarre sight in the apartment was a multi-hued cat staring at them from atop the kitchen counter, with, what seemed to Calam to be spaghetti noodles dangling from its mouth. The one saving grace, central air. The room temperature was perfectly comfortable, not over warm or over cool.

"Ladies, have a seat." Luce gestured them further inside.

Charisma opened her mouth, but came up short at the sound of a cell phone. Both sisters reached for her purse to check.

"Mine." Calamity hit the talk button and flinched at her mother's shrill voice. Pleading eyes, snapped straight to her sister. "Oh, great...Mama, hi, I've been meaning to— Chrissy's right here. No, what makes you think I'm in some sort of trouble, Mama? Is that Daddy in the background? The police, you don't say. No—I—uh...Mama please, it's not like that." Calam grimaced as she put a hand over the mouthpiece, "HPD just left the house. Mama's hysterical, and daddy's trying to calm her down. She thinks I'm a fugitive from the law."

Luce came forward, a mountain of calm. His strong hand closed over hers with an air of authority. The next thing she knew; he had assumed control of the situation. "Mrs. Lowe, yes, I am a friend of Calamity's. No, everything is under control. May I speak with your husband please?" A beat pasted. "Mr. Lowe, my name is Lucifer Phoenix. I'm your daughter's legal counsel. She's told you about her troubles at work? Yes, well I'm helping her pursue a strategic course of action against the immediate supervisor, Charlie Perkins. Understand, Mr. Perkins is not a very nice man, and as such he has chosen to pursue somewhat unsavory countermeasures. No, not at all. HPD's involvement is minimal at best and will soon be altogether negligible. Good, yes, I'm glad we agree, Ms. Lowe is upset enough by these events. There's no need to elevate her anxiety. By all means, call me directly if you have any questions. Let me give you my work and my home number..."

Calamity gawked in amazement as Luce worked his magic. He had *skills*. He handled Marian and Isaac like a professional; cool, confident, and down right sexy acumen. He was reassuring and logical, dialing down her panic-prone mother and appealing to her father's protective instincts. She'd been dreading the prospect of dealing with her parents and was more than happy to dish that particular duty off to someone obviously more capable.

Luce turned to hand the cell back to Calamity and came up against two pairs of grateful eyes.

"Thank you, Luce. I don't think I could've—"

"No problem. I need you at your best for our trip to the police station." His announcement was not received well.

Calamity groaned loud and doleful. Charisma shot up, chocolate eyes flashing, and stepped firmly in front of her twin. "What *trip* to the police station?! You're not taking my sister anywhere."

"She'll have to go in and make a statement. The sooner, the better."

"A statement about what? These charges are bogus and you know it."

Calamity stood, reluctant but determined, removing her human shield with scraped-together poise. "Charisma, take a pill. You sound just like Mama. Lucifer's right. I can't have HPD rolling around town harassing everyone I know. No doubt their next stop is either Pike or Reese."

Luce nodded his approval of her decision. For once, they agreed on something. He seemed as shocked as she. Somebody call Guinness, she thought.

"You *said* he was bluffing." Calamity accused, only half-joking.

"Yeah and you *said* you weren't going to dive for the panic button at the first sign of trouble." He tossed back.

"Ok, so we're even. Let's go."

"Just follow my lead." He came forward, put a palm to the small of her back, leading her towards the door as he spoke. "Keep your cool, do as I say, and this should be quick and painless."

Charisma scoffed at the both of them, "I've heard *that* before..."

BEDTIME WORRIES

They took her jeep, with Luce driving, Calamity riding shotgun, and Charisma fuming in the back seat. Calamity didn't have the stamina to endure another turn in his four-wheeled deathtrap. Wasn't it enough that her life had become like a freakish carnival ride? She refused to give up the guilty pleasure of riding high, looking pretty, and driving fast. And Luce didn't seemed to mind obliging her.

Silence prevailed. The humidity-heavy air whipped all around them, roaring in her ears, making conversation, polite or otherwise, impossible. Charisma sat, arms folded over her chest in childish petulance. Calam, relaxed, as much as she could manage considering the police were after her. She sneaked periodic glances at Luce's night-eclipsed profile behind the wheel. The moon and streetlights slid over the planes of his face. A vague thought drifted into Calamity's head…she hoped the police wouldn't take mug shots. Wind and moisture had long since shot her hair to hell. She forced a hand through it, trying to gauge the overall frizz-factor as Luce slowed to residential speed leaving the freeway.

"Shouldn't we be there by now?" Charisma spewed weary petulance. "I think my water just broke."

"It's not far now." Luce stated to no one in particular.

"We've probably bypassed a million police stations. What's so special about this one?"

Luce studied her in the rear view. In spite of the peevish undertone, her query was an intelligent one. "The charges must be addressed and tried, if it comes to that, in the precinct where the offense was committed."

"Oh."

Ten minutes later, Luce pulled into a parking space in the visitor's lot of the police station. He opened the door for her sister and helped her down, then came around to the passenger's side to do the same for Calamity. Seeing her hands tremble, he realized that she was more apprehensive than she let on. Luce gave her shoulders a reassuring squeeze.

"Relax, this'll be quick and painless."

"Unless that's a promise I think I'll stay on my toes."

Luce didn't bother to lie. It was good she knew the score. Nothing was promised.

They trekked over a wide median of poorly-lit landscaped grass, traversed the main driveway and a stretch of cement steps. This led them to the automatic glass double-doors monogrammed with a blue and black police emblem. Calamity swallowed, inexplicable dread consumed her when the doors, like cage-bars, closed behind them.

To their immediate left was a room, Calamity angled her head to peer through the ajar door. She spied what gave the appearance of being a conference or meeting room with lots of rows of blue-cushioned chairs, podium and retractable viewing screen at the head. Able to put it off no longer, Calamity faced the front. They were standing in a wide but shallow foyer, which ended with a glass-enclosed front desk housing two attendants, one uniformed, the other in plain clothes. The thirty-ish uniformed man eyed the threesome.

"May I help you?"

Calamity opened her mouth to explain, but closed it when she felt Luce squeeze her hand, a cue that she should let him handle it. Grateful, she remained silent, while he explained the exact situation and the reason for their 'visit' in a calm, rational...almost blasé manner, she noted. The officer ushered them in by buzzing the door on the far right.

"That's under the Assaults Unit." He asked Calamity for her driver's license, and then typed in the information from it. "You'll need to see Sergeant Willis." He pointed down a short corridor that opened into a voluminous space.

Calamity was surprised, and oddly comforted by the interior appearance of the station. It seemed very much like any normal office building to her, very modern, enclosed offices with shuttered windows and frosty-glass doors, a sea of cubicle-sized open-air desk stations, some with computers some without, and the occasional trio of file cabinets. The atmosphere bustled with movement and activity. The opening and closing of file cabinet drawers, click-clack of fingers on keyboards, the periodic ring of telephones and the buzz of telephone chatter. Uniformed and un-uniformed officers sat at desks, in offices, and milled around. The interior boasted two water-cooler stations, one on each end of the enormous rectangular space, a bay of elevators, and a corridor which Calamity presumed lead to another workspace, string of offices, and sea of desk stations.

"That's him. Over there." She and Luce turned in the direction of Charisma's zealous declaration. Willis came in the form of a pear-shaped black man of indeterminate age. "That's the officer who came 'round looking for you. One of them anyway."

"How do you know he's Willis if there were two of them?" Calamity mused.

"Well, because *he* called the other one's name and it wasn't Willis, it was...well, I don't remember what it was, but it wasn't Willis, ok."

Luce ushered Calamity along side him while he gestured for Charisma to hang back. "Sergeant Willis?" He greeted the man in question.

Willis, in uniform, was seated behind a desk in mild disarray, jotting down something on a half-size yellow notepad. He swiveled around at the sound of his name, and looked up, first at Luce…expectantly. "May I help you?"

"Yes, I'm here as legal advisor to Calamity Lowe, who has been implicated in a minor assault." Luce's explanation lost none of its eloquence on the second telling. "She's come in to address the charges filed against her and make a statement. I believe you were by her apartment earlier this evening."

Willis leaned back further in the chair to eye first Calamity and then her double. "Oh yeah, I remember…eh?" He paused momentarily, as if he thought his vision was blurred. "Which one of you is Calamity Lowe?"

"I am." Calamity raised her hand, like the teacher had called her name in homeroom. Oh, Geez. She caught herself and snapped it back down.

"Well, I appreciate your responding both promptly and willingly in this matter, Ms. Lowe." Willis straightened in his chair and stood, taking a moment to delve on his desk for a file folder to bring along with the pad and pen. "I'll need you to come with me, you and Mr.….eh…"

"Phoenix."

"Mr. Phoenix. This is of course, an official interview, so your sister will not be allowed to accompany you."

Charisma wasn't thrilled, Calam could tell, but she didn't launch a protest when the Sergeant turned an apologetic smile on her. "Have a seat in the waiting room, it's around the corner from the water-cooler. Second door on the left. This could take an hour or two. There's vending machines up on the second floor."

The Sergeant lead them into a room further down the same hall as the waiting area, calling out to no one in particular to 'flag down' Burton for him. It seemed more like a holding chamber than a room, one door, institutional white walls, a conspicuous mirror built into the wall like a window, and a table bolted to the floor with four chairs at opposing sides. Willis took a chair and sat with his back to the mirror, while he gestured Luce and Calamity to sit opposite him.

The sergeant made a perfunctory show of reading Calamity her rights before he flipped the file open and began.

"Calamity Jones Lowe, in case you are unaware of the full measure of these allegations, I am advised to inform you that you stand accused by one Charles Samuel Perkins of a minor physical assault which carries a maximum sentence of two years in a minimum security correctional facility. Mr. Perkins claims that you struck him without provocation and is seeking a restraining order as insurance against further incident. The order, should it be granted, will require that you maintain a distance of not-less-than a hundred feet between yourself and Mr. Perkins at all times."

"A hundred feet?!" Calamity gaped like a beached trout. "He's my immediate boss! How on earth am I supposed to go to work and stay a football-field away from him all day long?"

"Actually, a football field is a hundred *yards*." Luce corrected, matter-of-factly.

"Not helpful." Calam shot him a scowl. He laid a hand at the back of her nape; a familiar gesture by now that calmed her nerves somewhat.

The Sergeant continued, in the throws of duty that held no room for compassion. "The restraining order is not a foregone conclusion...yet. Right now, I need to hear your account of what happened. That, together with any pre-existing history of similar incidents will ultimately decide whether the order is granted."

Calamity shifted in her seat, uncomfortable at the mention of her previous record. She sought out Luce for guidance. Except for his useless football commentary, he'd been as quiet as a mouse. He nodded his permission for her to give her account of the assault. Calamity didn't hesitate. If Luce wasn't intimidated, then she told herself there was no reason for her to be either. She launched into the now familiar story in a bored recitation that leaned more toward tedium than furor.

The police interview went much like her session with Employee Relations. Willis fired an endless and idiotic string of questions at her regarding her account of the facts. Everything from her attire to what color her fingernails were painted at the time of the incident.

"Now, Ms. Lowe, you say Mr. Perkins was in the very act of sexually harassing you at the moment you struck him. Have you reported the alleged harassment to anyone?"

"Yes, as a matter of fact I have." Calamity began to relax a little as the questions took a friendlier tone. "I filed a formal complaint with the department of Employee Relations at Ross-Warner. You can check with Sheila Heyes if you want verification."

Willis' brows perked up at this news. "When did you make the complaint?"

"Thursday of last week."

Willis nodded as he made a note of the fact on his pad. "Anything of significance happen between then and now?"

"Well, Employee Relations called Mr. Perkins into their office."

"And?" The sergeant nudged her to continue.

At that moment, Lucifer stirred in the seat next to her like a wolf scenting danger. "Ms. Lowe would have no way of knowing what was discussed in a private meeting between Mr. Perkins and another department."

"Alright, fair enough." The officer conceded. "Have

you been bothered by your boss' *attentions* before? And if so, is this the first complaint you've filed?"

Luce gave the go-ahead, and Calamity continued. "Yes, he's been harassing me for a while, but I didn't file a complaint at first."

"How long? And why complain now, Ms. Lowe?"

"Over a year. Ignoring him just sorta became another part of the job. But then…the thing is, he'd never actually *touched* me before now. It was just nasty talk and innuendoes." She explained. "Easier to ignore than a hand up my skirt."

"Why didn't you quit or request a transfer? It's not like you're married with a mortgage to pay and children to support. Wouldn't it be easier to just remove yourself from a bad work situation?"

"Why should *I* have to do that?" Calamity felt her blood begin to boil at the mere idea. "If anyone should lose their job it's *him*, not me."

The officer nodded, a strange expression on his face. Luce watched him, measuring his character with increasing assurance. He'd already concluded that Sergeant Willis was an intelligent man, and seemed to have a fair and impartial grip on the investigation. Luce was further convinced of the officer's integrity when he squared a sympathetic, if not overly-confident, expression on them.

"Ms. Lowe, Mr. Phoenix, let me tell you what I think." He flipped his notebook shut, and entwined his fingers to rest atop it. "The boss man puts a hand out of place. Secretary decks him one good, then cries foul. Boss man gets ticked that some underling, a woman ta boot, has the gall to challenge him so he takes a potshot by claiming assault. I don't see these charges sticking, not under the circumstances…and I certainly can't imagine this ever getting before a jury. But, unfortunately, I still have to go through the customary arrest procedure. It'll be unpleasant, perhaps embarrassing, nothing more."

"What about the restraining order?" Luce inquired as

he plied Calamity's nape with soothing strokes until he felt the tension in her body slacken.

"Normally there wouldn't be a snowball's chance in hell of him obtaining one based on a single incident, but given *her* past record." The officer eyed Calam, pointedly.

Confronted with her prior hijinks, Luce exhaled long and eyed the woman beside him. "Do I even want to know?"

"All petty juvie stuff." She assured him, but still ducked her head while Willis enumerated.

"Two previous assaults, three counts of disturbing the peace, trespassing, criminal mischief, joyriding, *and* vandalism. The original rebel without a cause, weren't we Ms. Lowe?"

* * *

Charisma sat in the waiting room on a fiberglass chair she suspected was only slightly more comfortable than the electric chair. She'd long ago cease to be distracted by the hodgepodge of outdated magazines littering the low-lying tables running the length of the room. Ninety minutes rolled by. Restless, she shifted her feet just to keep the circulation flowing. She was contemplating a trip to the snack bar when a tallish female officer with dyed auburn hair and a sour face appeared in the doorframe.

"Is there a Charisma Tate present?" She inquired in a bullhorn voice.

Chris launched herself up from the chair, grateful for a reprieve from mindless waiting.

The woman's steely glare zipped to her quarry. She closed the distance between them. Her voice lowered in volume and doubled in vehemence. "Mrs. Tate, please come with me. We have a minor disturbance at the front desk. There's an individual…"

* * *

"So, what does that mean exactly?" Calamity asked, chocolate eyes shifted first to the sergeant and then to Luce and back again. "Am I free to go home or not?"

"Yes and no." Willis glanced at Lucifer before he returned his gaze to Calamity's anxious face. "There's a choice. I can go through the arrest procedure right now, which means booking you and putting you in a holding cell downtown until a judge can set bail. You'll have to spend a night, perhaps two in lock-up. *Or*, we postpone procedure. I send you home in the custody of and under the watchful eye of Mr. Phoenix here. He'd be legally responsible for you. In the meanwhile, I'll call a judge friend of mine. Mr. Phoenix promises to have you downtown bright and early tomorrow morning so we can run through the arrest procedure, get the judge to set an affordable bail and have you out by afternoon."

Calamity crinkled her brow as she considered her options. "I'd have to stay with Lu–Mr. Phoenix at his apartment?"

"Yes, otherwise..." He trailed off. "Why don't I give you two some time. I'll be back in ten minutes for the decision."

As soon as the door closed behind him, Calamity blew out a breath of frustrated relief. She stood and paced the room, presumably to calm her nerves, although from watching her Luce surmised the movement had just the opposite effect.

"This is ludicrous. I can't shack up with you!"

Luce stood, languid, trying hard not to show his surprise at her abrupt exclamation. "It's either me or jail."

"Think about it. What would my parents think of me living with some strange man?"

"Correct me if I'm wrong, but aren't you already living with a strange man?"

Calam stilled from her brisk pace, and rounded on him like a kitten hissing at an elephant. "Ok, first off, Shane is not *strange*. He's *unique*."

Luce crossed his arms as he continued his never-ending vigil of trying to understand her skewed logic. "My point is… he's a man and you're living with him."

"No, I am *not* living with Shane. *Shane* is temporarily chilling at my place…and I'm not sleeping with him!"

He arched a sable brow at her, amused at her pique. "I fail to see a difference. You're not sleeping with me either." Only Calamity would take an even more ridiculous stance on an already ludicrous…issue? Argument? Debate? He didn't even know what the heck to call it.

"Oh, get real." She snapped, pacing again. "If we were sharing space, who in their right mind would believe that we weren't getting our groove on? Hell, *I* wouldn't believe it."

"You're not *moving-in* with me. Its just for one night. Besides, why do you care *what* they believe?" Luce pinned her with a dark stare, wondering for the first time why she seemed so averse to bunking with him overnight. He rather liked the idea of having her in his apartment. The place was a tomb whenever his cousin wasn't making a nuisance of himself, and Calamity's personality was affecting…her presence, addictive. He found he *wanted* her there.

"This isn't medieval Jerusalem, Calamity. No one's going to stone you in the village square."

"Eh, hell-o. Wasn't it *you* who expressed to *me* the importance of refraining from illicit office relationships and boundary-crossing behavior?"

Luce relaxed his crinkled brow, glad to know that it was not *him* she was wary of. "On company time, yes. Anything you do or don't do when you're not at work is inadmissible and therefore irrelevant."

"Oh."

Calam's ire deflated, thinking how silly her protests were. One glance at his expression told her he thought so too. Why was she being so ridiculous anyway? The mere thought of spending the night at Luce's, however chaste it might be, sent thrills of desire down her spine. Brazen images of Luce cooking breakfast in a towel, twirled through her mind. In the end, she effected what she hoped was a cavalier expression and shrugged. "Well, in that case I'm good to go. Let's share some space."

That decided, Calamity found herself noticing the mirrored window for the umpteenth time. "Hey Luce, do you suppose there's somebody behind there watching us?"

"Uh, I don't know. Maybe."

"Wanna do something shocking and find out?"

He laughed...almost. The kamikaze glint in her eye sobered him. "As your lawyer, I have to advise against it."

* * *

Charisma arrived back in the main lobby, escorted by the dour-faced officer, to find her brother in a– 'frenzied' was the nearest word that came to mind–exchange with the two front desk officers. Pike, as tall as the twins were short, dwarfed any and everything around him. Charisma winced at the ire she heard in his normally teasing voice.

"Eh, Pike?" So absorbed was he in wrangling information out of the desk officers that it took two tries for her to gain his attention. "*PIKE!*"

He whirled his head around to face her as she emerged through the door into the lobby.

"Relax. Calam is fine." She reassumed him, gesturing to her escort that she wouldn't need any further assistance. "She's not under arrest. She's just here to make a statement. Let us handle this—"

"Whoa Chris, what is Calam making a statement about, exactly? And who is this Phoenix character?" Pike demanded. "What the devil is going on?! The police came around looking for Calam. I called your house. Paul had no clue what I was talking about, and Calam's not answering her cell phone. Dad and mama gave me some disjointed story about her boss attacking her and a lawyer named Phoenix."

"Calamity's boss *sexually-harassed* her. He didn't attack her."

Her brother stared down at her as if she'd lost her mind. "Wow. I'm so relieved you made that distinction because *sexually-harassed* is so much better than *attacked*."

Charisma grimaced, gesturing for him to chillax. "Ok, no problem, I can see you're going to need a few more background details. Maybe we should–" She was forestalled by the opening of the door.

Calamity emerged, with Luce pulling up the rear. His hands rested protectively on her shoulders as he eyed the unknown man who had assumed a similar position behind Charisma.

"Eh...oh." Calam's eyes widened on her brother. "What are you doing here? Did daddy send you to check on me?"

His eyes lowered to his 'big' sis, shaking his head. "I was in the middle of unpacking when the police came knocking at my door. What's this I hear about you getting sexually-harassed? I've been back in town two days and the first I see of you is in the big-house." He grinned, good-natured, despite the situation. "Chris was just about to give me a rundown but since you're here I might as well get it from the source. By the way, who's your friend?"

Calamity cleared her throat and half-turned. "Lucifer Phoenix, this is our brother, Krystopher Lowe. Pike, this is Luce, my...eh–" She faltered a bit, before she settled on, 'representative'.

The men eyed each other warily over a tense handshake as they exchanged the briefest of words. Calam was loathed to go into further detail, given her current living circumstances and the pending charges. She tried to give Charisma a warning eye while Pike was distracted with Luce but from her sister's confused expression she wasn't sure her S.O.S. got through.

Again her brother addressed her. "Eh, so, are we done here? I can follow you and Chris back to your place. Then, I want the whole story."

Calamity shrank closer to Luce, suspecting that her next comment would not go over well. "Uh, actually Pike, we'll have to catch up tomorrow. See, I'm...well, Sergeant Willis, he cut me a deal and..."

Both her bother and sister wore matching frowns as her fumbled around for an explanation and came up short, each eyeballing Luce for clarity. He didn't disappoint.

"What Ms. Lowe means is that she's not going back to her apartment. She's coming home with me."

Calamity spared a moment to glare at him over her shoulder. "Geez, did you have to drop the news like a carpet bomb?"

"Better a blunt truth, than a tactful lie." Luce shrugged, unmoved, leaving her to mop up the damage. She turned back to face a gaping, slack-jawed Charisma and a stiff, unhappy Pike.

Her brother's chocolate eyes flashed red. "Eh, you wanna run that by me again?"

"It's not what you think." Calam rushed to explain, winking at her sister in silent plea for a distraction. "If I don't go home with Luce, they'll arrest me and I'll have to spend the night in lock up."

Pike's face, a male version of her own, held comic horror.

Calam cringed. "Oh, eh, that didn't come out right. Would you believe, it's not as bad as it sounds—"

"It doesn't sound like it can get much worse." He flung back.

Charisma snapped her mouth shut as inspiration must have hit her like a bolt of lightening. She put her hand to her temple and swayed, leaning back heavily.

"About time." Calam murmured under her breath.

"Chris!" Pike caught her and carried her over to a chair in the corner.

Meanwhile, Calamity tugged at Luce's sleeve. "Come on. Pike will take care of her."

He hesitated, frowning in Charisma's direction. "What about your sister, is she—"

"No, no, no…she's just wagging the dog so we could slip away. It's a trick we used to pull when we were kids." Calam spoke in a harried whisper as she propelled him towards the exit. "Now, let's go. Go, go!"

In the car, Luce drove, taking fleeting glances at the woman beside him when traffic permitted. "I'm beginning to think your name suits you very well."

Calam chuckled, "Oh, this is nothing. You should have seen us when we were growing up: me, Chrissy, and Pike. We were a reign of terror at school and in the neighborhood." She sobered a little, feeling the need to make him understand the Lowe family dynamic. "You should know…Pike's used to pulling me outta the fire, so is Charisma for that matter. They can be rather territorial when it comes to protecting me."

"Yeah, I get that. You ever think about maybe, not getting into so much trouble? Then people wouldn't have to fight for the privilege of rescuing you."

Easier said than done, Calamity thought. Trouble seemed to follow her like an obsessed fan.

"Tomorrow, as soon as we get you squared with HPD, I'll try to convince Perkins to drop the charges and revoke this idiotic restraining order."

"And how are you going to do that? The man doesn't have a decent bone in his body."

"I'm hoping he'll agree to mediation and then maybe a compromise."

Calamity bristled at the idea. "I think I've been compromised enough already thank you very much."

"Simmer down. Mediation is a tried and true legal strategy. Saves time and legal fees. Also gives the opposing sides the opportunity to size up the competition."

She liked the sounds of that. "Ohhh…So, you're

playing it like recon? Or, no, wait…Prizefighters circling each other in the first round?"

"Yeah, something like that." The analogy seemed to relax her, so Luce didn't bother to tune her up on the finer, less optimistic points of this particular legal maneuver.

"But, what if it doesn't work?" She pulled a face. "Of course it won't work. I honestly can't imagine Perkins and I agreeing on much of anything."

For once, they agreed. "If nothing else it'll give me more time to work on Stella. If we can get the harassment complaint to reflect good on you and badly on him, that will pave the way to having the charges and the restraining order dismissed." He drew out his breath, glancing at her. "In the meantime, you'll probably have to take some time off to avoid breaching the distance mandate."

Expecting her to pitch a fit, he chuckled when she quipped, "Oh Luce darling, will you still love me when I'm jobless?" in a phony posh accent.

ARRESTED DEVELOPMENTS

Calam awoke with a headache and a confused void where her mind used to be. Propping herself up on her elbows, she squinted in the morning light as she eyeballed her surroundings. After a full minute and several pan-scans of the room Calam hunched her shoulders. She had no clue where she was. Geez, was it possible to be hung-over without actually getting drunk the night before? The question was second only to her wild curiosity as to whose bed she occupied. Good Lawd, had she been roofied or what? A quick glance to her chest. Nope. She still had her clothes on...or someone's clothes, anyway. Something furry moved against her leg, and she jerked away and nearly screamed...until she heard an annoyed meow. Sasha stretched in a deep yawn at the foot of the bed.

Sasha...Luce's pervy pet. Her mind cranked back up like a long-dead stalled car. She was in Luce's apartment, in his palatial king-sized bed, wearing his spice-scented t-shirt that dangled down around her knees when she eventually stumbled from the bed onto her feet. Luce, ever the gentleman, slept on the convertible couch in the front room. Had Calamity been in the exact same position but under different circumstances, she'd be ecstatic. But, her impending arrest cast a wee pall over her euphoria. Still, she preened with wicked satisfaction at having spent the night in his bedroom...Satan's Lair, she dubbed, as an impish smile twitched at her lips. Hmm, might as well have a quick lookie-loo. The chance may not arise again, she reasoned.

Luce's private domain dripped with personality as compared to the more Spartan décor of the rest of his apartment. Several framed family snapshots littered the nightstand along with a cordless telephone and touch sensitive lamp, which shockingly emitted a warm crimson glow when she brushed it with her fingertips. Two impressionistic prints adorned the walls. Each depicted vague anthropomorphic forms cavorting about against a pastel-blended background. They reminded her of something naughty she once glimpsed when she'd accidentally flipped to the Spice Channel on her pay-per-view.

The corner off the edge of the bed housed a dark mahogany desk topped with a matching bookshelf that ran up the wall. The books she discovered beneath one of the pillows and under the edge of the bed outed Luce as a late-night reader. Hmm, *The Count of Monte Cristo*. He likes the classics. Her eyes bucked as she skimmed across *Master: An Erotic Novel of the Count of Monte Cristo* riding shotgun next to Dumas' version. Likewise, she spied *Phantom of the Opera* paired with its erotic twin. Skimming further...*Pride, Prejudice and Zombies?* The titles were endless. Fascinated, she pulled *Robin Hood: Unmasqued After Dark* from the shelf and flipped through the pages. Good night! Is *this* what he reads?! Classic literature corrupted as modern erotica and horror tales? The thought curled her toes. So, Lucifer wasn't quite the choir boy he pretended. There might be hope for them yet, she mused.

Shaking off her fantasies, Calamity put the book down. She ran a hand through her hair and grimaced. It had, of course, gone into kinky snarls during the night. There wasn't time for a wash and press even if she had a hot-comb or flat iron with her, which she didn't. She'd have to French braid it if she didn't want to mirror Leo the Lion when she took her mug shot. First things first, though. She padded to the living room on bare feet to sneak a peek at the object of her affection.

He lay atop the covers, one solid sinewy arm flung out over the empty side of the bed while the other was bent at the elbow and pillowed behind his head. His torso was a study in Italian sculpture. Smooth tawny-gold chest as broad as the Atlantic tapered downward into a rippling six-pack of muscles. Her gaze wondered lower. The suggestive spiral of coarse dark hairs disappeared beneath the drawstring pajama bottoms. Oy! Calam stepped closer so that she cast the sunlight from the window in a shadow over his face. Lashes like paint-brush bristles fluttered open. Curious inky slits regarded her…with groggy interest, she noted.

"Yeah, I'm not a morning person either." She admitted.

"Hmmm, C'mere."

Before she could respond, his hand shot out from behind his head and Calamity found herself sprawled torso to torso atop him, enveloped in a loose embrace. She popped herself up on her elbows to spy two intense pools of ink impaling her…unable to resist, her gaze drifted downward to his mouth.

"Did you sleep well?" His voice reverberated deeper than his usual baritone.

Lusty thoughts a' jumble in her brain, Calamity could only nod. Have mercy! He might think her a presumptuous tart but at the moment, the sensual lure of his lips was too powerful to ignore. Calam shimmed up to close the distance between them before she lost her nerve. His bottomless-pit black orbs stalked her, seeming to guess her intent…but he made no move to help or to hinder. So she brushed his mouth with a light, lingering kiss, giving him the choice to put an end to it if he wanted.

A deep rumble in his chest vibrated through her, stoking the fires of her confidence. She smiled against his mouth when she felt his lips part, inviting her in. Encouraged, Calam deepened the kiss. For the sake of balance, she flattened her palms on either side of his head.

Meanwhile, Luce lost a hand in the kinky tufts of her hair. The other roamed up and down her t-shirted back. Heaven help him, but her small warm form felt sinful atop his body. The knowledge that she wore his shirt, and judging by her simmering body heat, nothing underneath, intrigued him all the more. The soft feminine feel of her ignited his lower regions and sent them into a slow burn. He derived an almost perverse pleasure from letting her set the pace of their interlude. That this woman, whom he out-weighed by at least a hundred pounds, could produce such a quicksilver reaction in him with a chaste little smooch amazed him, hooked him, cementing his fascination with her.

She caught his lower lip between her teeth, teasing at first but then with purpose, she inched away...upward, pulling him along for the ride. He knew what she wanted and complied, rising to follow her into a sitting position. Her rear slid snugly into his lap. Her bent knees rested on either side of his hips, while her hands crept around his neck.

Unable to curb his appetite for her, Luce slid his hands down to her compact yet delectably curved bottom, tilting her closer, molding her against his body. He wanted her to feel him...see her expression, gauge her reaction to the telltale—He felt her tense, and chuckled as she broke off their playful-turned-explosive kiss. She squirmed against his blossoming 'affection'. Ah hell...he grimaced as a pleasurable pain ripped through him.

"Shorty, uh..." He pulled back a ways. Inky black eyes met her chocolate brown orbs... checking for approval or revulsion. She broke off first.

"I only meant to kiss you." She explained in a squeaky

voice strangled with embarrassment. "I'm…eh, sorry."

"Don't be. I'm not." Luce grinned despite himself. Damn, did the woman know how adorable she was? "Although, it's probably better if you get up now."

"Oh! Of course, my bad." She clumsily disentangled herself from him and got off the bed. He watched her meander over to the kitchen, fidgety, with his ginormous t-shirt dangling teasingly off one shoulder.

"I could fix us something to eat while you take a shower? I mean, if you don't mind my invading your kitchen."

Luce stood, heading toward the bedroom. A *cold* shower, he thought. "Yeah, sure, make yourself at home."

* * *

As if Monday hadn't been a staunch enough test of her endurance, Tuesday was exhausting on a whole new level. Her and Luce arrived at the central police station at nine o'clock, having to make a slight detour by Calam's apartment so she could procure a suitable outfit to wear. She checked the voicemail on her landline and found thirteen messages waiting for her. She'd turned her cell phone off the night before, anticipating the blitz. After all, a girl could only handle one thing at a time, couldn't she?

As it so happened, her arrest, subsequent bail-posting, and release went off without a hitch. Officer Willis was solicitous and helpful. The judge was polite and timely, and Luce stayed close by her the entire time, reassuring her with calm words and wise advice. Thankfully, she'd amassed just enough in her emergence fund to cover the two-thousand-dollar bond. No need to call pleading to Charisma or Pike or even her parents for money. Of course Calam knew she couldn't avoid them forever. Luckily, or unluckily Calam wasn't sure which, she'd have plenty of time to dial around and assuage everyone's fears. A two-week leave of absence from Ross-Warner had quite freed up her schedule.

By two o'clock, they were back at his apartment. Luce stood in the door's threshold, his eyes skimming over the woman before him. Bedecked in a casual and conservative black pants suit, with two thick braids, the ends of which just did catch her shoulders, she seemed to have it all together. He caught the two braids in his hands, searching her face.

"You sure you're alright? This morning went easier than I'd imagined...except for that one thing. If you need me to stay, I could help you explain."

Calam almost rolled her eyes. Yeah, like you *explained* things last night? No thanks, she thought. "No, no, I'm fine, really." She assured him, shooing him with her hands. "You go to work. I'll do the explaining. After that, I'll have plenty to keep my mind occupied, *believe* me. And, I have my car to get around. Seriously, I'll be ok."

He bent and kissed her temple. "You have my office number. I'll probably have to work late."

* * *

"I'm fine, Reese, really. Look, I don't know how Perkins explained my absence but—" Calam switched the phone to the opposite ear.

"He didn't, just said you took a few days off." She could almost *hear* the bubbly blonde fuming. "Personal time, he said. Made it seem like you were having a nasty bout of PMS or something. When all the time, he'd gone and had you arrested. That rat bastard."

"Yeah, well, I'm just grateful that the police aren't taking the charges too seriously or I really would be screwed. But no more feeling sorry for myself. It's time to take action. Which is the other reason why I called." Calam paused to take a breath. "Reese, I need you to do me a big favor."

"Name it, girl. You know I got yo back."

"Been watching a 'lil too much BET, have we?" She couldn't help but tease her Caucasian friend about her newfound ethnic colloquialisms.

"I do try. So, what's cookin'?"

"Sit down if you're not already."

"I'm primed, hit me."

"Reese, I won't be back for at least a couple of weeks. Its not *just* the arrest. Perkins took out a restraining order against me. I can't be within a hundred feet of him, his house or his place of business. I had to take a leave of absence to avoid violating the order."

"Get out?!"

"No joke. And I sorta have a record of less that orderly behavior so that didn't help either. I mean, nothing recent, but still, you know. The only saving grace—"

"Wait, there's more?"

"Yeah. The only way they'd let me out on such a low bail was if Luce agreed to take legal custody and responsibility for me. So I'm...eh, living with him temporarily. It was either that...or wear one of those electronic anklet things." Calam shudder at the thought.

"But, this is great! House or apartment?" Reese asked with the eagerness of a child at Christmas.

"Apartment, why?"

"Apartments have less space and no privacy. More chances for a...eh, close encounter. Hell, this is better than Daytime."

"Down girl." Calamity could almost see the lecherous gleam in her friend's elfish green eyes. "No one's jumping anyone's bones just yet. This little detour is causing some serious ripples in my pond. The police went looking for me at my parent's house and Pike's place. So, my business is in the street. Matter-fact, as soon as I get off the phone I'm headed over there to clear up whatever wild assumptions are going around before Pike hires a hitman to hunt down Luce or Moms has another dramatic episode. I'm hoping Daddy and Chris can keep them both in check until I get there. Oh, I almost forgot…Shelia Heyes left me a message, Employee Relations wants to talk to me. To tell you the truth, I've got a little too much on my plate to be seducing my legal advisor out of his pants." Calam paused on a wicked thought. "Although I did kiss him silly this morning, details later I promise."

"Fair enough. Now, what's this favor you wanted to ask?"

"Oh, yeah. I need you to take over changing out the nanny-cam batteries for me. I'd been doing it every evening before I leave work, but I can't anymore for obvious reasons. Charisma can't either because…well, she looks just like me. So—"

"Say no more. I'm your girl."

"Sweet! I can get Charisma to bring you the re-chargeables and the battery-charger. And I'll try to get by there in a day or so to screen for anything useful, but being at Luce's introduces a new, even riskier element to the plan. We *have* to be careful."

"No problem. I got this."

"Thanks a million, you're a lifesaver. Talk to you later."

"Count on it!"

* * *

"May I ask who's speaking, sir?"

For the briefest second, Luce thought he dialed the wrong number. He was so accustomed to hearing her greet him when he called Perkins' office. Calamity would've recognized his voice and put him through directly, whereas the Stepford temp had no such familiarity thus she subjected him to the usual screening process.

"Lucifer Phoenix."

"What is the nature of your call, Mr. Phoenix?"

"Certain legal matters pertaining to a minor assault case. He'll know."

"One moment please." Her toneless voice reminded

him of the recording used to inform callers that a line was disconnected or no longer in service.

A moment later, Perkins came on the line. A good sign in Luce's estimate. Perkins wouldn't have taken the call if he was sure of a victory. "Phoenix, since when did you decide to champion that defaming little nitwit? Really, I'm disappointed. There are other charity cases so much more worthy of your legal expertise...however rough and unpolished. I could throw some pro-bono work your way, that is, if you're not too busy cramming for the Bar?"

Luce did his best to tune out the static. Perkins being Perkins just couldn't resist taking a cheap shot or two. Arrogant, callous, and opportunistic, all traits that made him a good lawyer were ironically the same traits that made him a despicable person.

"Charlie, we need to talk mediation." He ground his teeth to keep any annoyance or inflection from projecting. "I've got time after work for a dinner meeting, strictly exploratory."

"Sure, why not. I got nothing better to do. The Houston Club downtown, I have a standing table."

"Six-thirty then?"

"Fine."

"Good deal."

Luce hung up the phone with unexpected satisfaction. Now, Luce *knew* Perkins' confidence was a farce. He considered it beneath him to defeat his opponent graciously. The only way he knew how to win was to crush the lesser man under his boot heel. A willingness to mediate betrayed a weakness in his position. Luce smiled at this revelation. Next up...

Sitting at his desk, Luce depressed the intercom button on the telephone. "Stella?"

The reply was immediate. "Yes, Mr. Phoenix?"

"Could you come in for a moment please?"

"Sure."

His legal secretary, Estella was just on the wrong side

of forty, but her skin looked fifty. She had a wide body the consistency of Jell-O and harsh-dyed hair that stood stiff off her head. Not attractive, but Luce liked her calm manner and willingness to adapt to each new situation with minimal fuss. She wasn't much taller than Ms. Lowe, though her hair gave the illusion of a few extra inches. Luce gestured for her to take the seat opposite him across the desk. He noticed that she'd brought her note pad and pen in with her, anticipating shorthand.

"I know that we have discussed this once before, but I was hoping to change your mind." No sense beating about the bush, he decided. "I want you to reconsider filing a complaint."

"Yes, I know." She gave him a sad, apologetic smile. "I'm sorry, Mr. Phoenix. But I can't rock the boat, not while I'm sitting in it. My work hours are good. My salary is even better. My eldest, Roberto, he's in college now. The younger ones, Maria and Isobel, they like having their mama pick them up from school. Eli, we're separated. He helps, but...If I go up against Mr. Perkins and lose, what are the odds of my finding another job like this one? Me against him, I can't. I'd lose."

Luce understood her point all too well. He'd come from a struggling working class family himself. Hell, he even sympathized with her, but he couldn't let her play it safe, not when there was an excellent opportunity to nail Perkins to the wall.

"What if I told you, there's another woman?" This revelation, he noted, captured her undivided attention. "Yours, should you choose to file it, would not be the only complaint. I can't divulge her name yet but I can promise that you won't be alone."

"Someone else has already filed with Employee Relations?"

"Yes. She's single, no kids so she can afford to be brave. And she has some of the same reservations as you. She's worried no one will believe her, that her moral character will be questioned. That it'll be his word against hers. Charlie will play dirty, and ultimately if she loses, she'll lose big." Luce watched Stella unflinching as she shifted in the seat. Good, he thought, he'd made her think about it. Second thoughts were the first symptom of a change of heart.

"He shouldn't get away with it..." She trailed off, caught up in some silent pondering of her own. "It's not right but—"

"Will you at least think about it, Stella?"

She eyed him like one would a stranger baring gifts, but nodded her head in agreement. "Yes, I think maybe I will give it a second thought."

"Thank you." He stood as she did and came around to open the door for her. "Call me anytime and let me know what you decide."

* * *

Calam sat in her parents' kitchen clad in jeans and a tie-dyed mullet top.

"Honey, are you sure the avenue you've chosen is the best road to travel? I know I was upset with you for not going through proper channels and filing a complaint, but now that you have it just seems that the problem has gotten worse not better." Calam felt her mother studying her across the kitchen table, worry knitting her brow. "Who exactly is this Satan creature and how do you know you can trust him?"

"Mama has a point, Calam." Pike, leaning his six foot four frame against the counter next to the sink, tossed in his two cents. "What if he expects some form of lurid *payment* for his legal services? At his apartment, you're isolated and vulnerable. He's twice *my* size. How are you planning to fend him off if it comes down to that? Huh?"

She puffed up to her full five-foot two-inch height. "You forget, Pike, you're looking at a brown belt in karate.

I can take Lucifer anytime I want."

Charisma deigned to clear her throat conspicuously, "I recall a certain night a week ago when Satan not only overpowered you, but he also reduced you to crocodile tears. And isn't that number three on your list?"

"Charisma!" She snapped. "Whose side are you on?"

She threw up her hands in surrender. "Yours, geez! I'm just playing devil's advocate here...eh, in a manner of speaking."

My sister, the traitor, she fumed. "Luce has been a perfect gentleman. How can you even *suggest*–"

"I'm not *suggesting* anything. Its just...Well, the man *is* built like a Mack-truck, Calamity. There's no denying who would win a fight between the two of you. That doesn't mean I think he's a rapist-in-waiting."

"Humph! A ringing endorsement if ever I heard one." Rolling her eyes, Calam turned to her last port. "Daddy, what do you think? You spoke to him on the phone. He must have made an impression. Tell them, Luce is a perfect gentleman."

Her father sighed, before coming over to drop an arm around her shoulders. "Calam, as much as I want to believe him to be the honorable sort, it just isn't possible to make that kind of judgment without meeting the man first. What I suggest is that you bring your new friend, Mr. Phoenix, around for dinner so we can *all* have a chance to form a decent opinion of him." He eyed the others in the room as if to solicit their support of the idea.

"Yeah, jump right into my nightmare, the water's still warm..." She murmured under her breath as she spied, Pike and her mother perk up at the prospect of raking Luce over the coals. Oh geez, this is *bad.*

"What a lovely idea, Isaac. I wish I'd thought of it myself." A dazzling smile passed between husband and wife before her mother refocused on her. "What day is good for you, honey?"

"Tomorrow night works." Pike announced to no one

in particular.

"I think she was talking to *me*." Calamity retorted, scowling at him.

* * *

"A dinner party?!" Calam fumed an hour later as she wore out the living room carpet in her apartment. "I could shoot you for this Charisma! As if it's not bad enough I've got criminal charges pending and I'm half out of my job. Now, mama, daddy *and* Pike are hip-deep in my love life. Sisterhood 101…You're *supposed* to have my back."

"Get over it. They were going to have to meet him eventually. Why not now?"

Gawd, she didn't even know how to explain it. "*Because*, with Luce, its special…and still very delicate. I really like him, Chris. How the heck am I supposed to explain that my parents and my brother have demanded he come to dinner so they can read him the riot act about—of all things—encroaching upon my honor when the truth is…I have no honor! I lied to him about the nanny-cams. I perjured myself in front of a judge today. I've conspired with my sister and my best friend to blackmail my boss." She flinched at the thought of his finding out. "If he knew the truth he'd probably take one look at the lot of us and run from the room screaming."

Charisma laughed outright. "Oh please. He's already gotten a whiff of the Lowe family madness. If he hasn't already washed his hand of us than I think you're safe."

Ok, maybe she had a tiny little point. "True, but it's not just that. It's everything! Reese is supposed to be coming over here to pick up the battery stuff for the nanny-cams so she can continue to change them…no wait, I told her you would drop them off at her place. Argh! I'm supposed to go over there and screen the footage sometime this week. And I still haven't had a chance to get together more clothes to take back to Luce's. Sheila Heyes left me a message, and I haven't returned her call—What if Luce finds out what we're doing behind his back? You know how he is. He'll hate me for lying to him."

"Whoa, slow down…you're making *me* nervous." Charisma pulled her towards the couch, where they both plopped down on the deep purple cushions. "Satan's not going to find out anything. We just need to keep everything organized. Here's what you do…Go back to his place and relax. Figure out how to put a positive spin on the family dinner thing. I'll drop off the junk with Reese, and do the screening for yesterday and today. It's after six o'clock now so she should be home. The clothes can wait until tomorrow morning and so can Sheila Heyes."

"Are you sure you don't mind?" She hoped she came off as grateful and not pleading and desperate like she felt.

"Mind? My house is still under quarantine, remember. I work part-time. I *literally* have nothing better to do."

The mention of her nephew and brother-in-law generated new waves of guilt. "Oh hell, I haven't even asked you how Manny is doing."

"He's fine. I told Paul to rub calamine on him at night to help with the itching. Get going and don't worry. Everything will work out."

* * *

Calamity had her doubts, but decided to think positive for the time being. After all, having a panic attack every five minutes wouldn't help anyone. She needed to chillax and think about something else for a while, maybe watch a movie on TV. With just that idea in mind she turned Luce's spare key in the lock and glided, mentally haggard, across the threshold.

"Yo, who the hell are you?" An unmistakably male voice brought Calamity up short. Her purse flew forward and emptied on the nut-brown carpet, exposing a half-eaten candy bar which Sasha meandered over to sniff at.

"Well?"

Calam stared gape-mouthed at the dark-haired, jean and jersey-clad stranger lazing comfortably on the couch, remote in hand. "Oh...Luce didn't mention he had a roommate, I mean, there's just the one bedroom so I assumed—You *are* his roommate, aren't you?"

"No, I'm his cousin, Sly."

She got a hostile vibe from him. The body language, his tone of voice, not to mention the disdain tattooed all over his face. The combination was enough to make her hackles rise. "I'm a friend of Luce's. Calamity."

Her statement brought him up to his feet. From what she could see, Sly was definitely a relative of Lucifer's. His height alone was proof. The similar coal black eyes confirmed it. But instead of a solid frame rippling with muscles, his cousin was all spindly legs and floppy hair.

"Ahh, so you're the office-shrew who's been hounding him all week?" He circled her, inspecting the goods with a critical eye. *"Nice.* Vertically-challenged, but hey I can see why Luce would be willing to jump through a few hoops for you."

"Excuse me, Mr.—"

"Oh yo, call me 'Sly'."

"That remains to be seen." Calamity hissed under her breath. The man had the nerve to insult her with his Neanderthal behavior. "Look, I'm not in the mood to mince words. Luce invited me to stay with him." She held out the key as proof. "And since you're not his roommate, and we obviously haven't hit it off, would you please leave so I can fix myself something to eat."

"I ain't going nowhere. I was here first. And how do I know you ain't gonna make off with the TV? You could be a crazed ex-girlfriend or an obsessed fan or somethin'."

Since when did lawyers have fans? Calamity rolled her eyes at the imbecile apparent in front of her. It grated on her nerves that she was forced to look up at him. "I realize that you're severely handicapped by stupidity, but do try to read my lips. *Luce. Gave. Me. His. Key.* So, *he's* not worried that I'll make off with the TV. Now, go away before I swat you like a fly."

"Try it, Cupcake." He crossed his arms over his chest and cocked a skeptical gaze down her frame. "In fact, I dare you."

So, he wasn't impressed by a threat of physical violence from someone her size, was he? She grinned, wicked.

"Come on, hit me with your best shot—"

"Don't mind if I do…" Calamity kicked the door closed behind her and whirled around with a quickness. Sasha scurried away into the kitchen at the flurry of movement. "Hi–YA!"

* * *

The Neanderthal lay sprawled out on the living room floor, one hand massaging the 'family jewels' while the fingers of his other hand pinched off his nasal cavity. He scooted back to prop himself between the couch and the coffee table, nursing injured pride, along with a bloody nose, swollen lip, and very soar crotch. She kicked the crap out of him in three strokes, then stepped over his prone body without a second glance. That'll teach him never to underestimate the short in stature.

"Hey!" His voice came out an over-torqued grunt of pain. "Yo, Insanity, get me some ice, will ya?!"

Calamity watched him from the kitchen. He leaned his head back in an effort to stanch the flow of blood from his nostrils. She supposed she should try to be gracious about the whole thing. She'd bested him…no need to further injure his pride. Getting beat down by a girl was humiliating enough…*and* he was Luce's *cousin*, after all. She shrugged, and crossed back towards the frig to make an ice pack.

Five minutes later, she stood with her peace offering in hand, undecided. When he lifted his head, he saw her in the doorway leading from the kitchen. Ah, what the hell, she thought and tossed the zip-locked bag of ice at him. Disoriented as he was, the offering bounced painfully off his noggin and fell to the floor a few inches away.

"Watch it, huh. I'm bleedin' over 'ere."

"My name is *Calamity*."

"Insanity...Calamity...*whatever.*"

Calamity toyed with the end of her left plait as she glared down at her quarry. "Get it straight or I'll give you a black eye to match that bloody nose."

"Hey, hey, hey...You best back off. I'm not yo punching bag." He snatched the ice pack from the floor and pressed it, careful like, against his lip and nose. "Matter fact, stay yo insane ass over there...on *that* side of the room."

Calam humph-ed as she pivoted towards the kitchen. "Crybaby."

She heard the 'Sly' one mutter under his breath, "Loose screw."

PRIMA DRAMA

Luce paused at the door of his apartment, burdened with good news that wasn't nearly as good as he'd hoped, and bad news that at least wasn't as dire as he'd anticipated. He shifted his briefcase from left hand to right trying not to dislodge the jacket he'd shed and slung over his shoulder. His dress shirt, gapped open at the neck and damp with sweat, was half out of his pants while the two ends of the tie fluttered about freely in the thick humid breeze.

Nothing definite yet from Stella, and Charlie had played hardball exactly as he'd suspected. There was a deal on the table, not the one Luce had lobbied hard for and certainly not one that Calamity wanted to hear, but a deal nonetheless. Luce couldn't help but ponder how she'd react. Would she be disillusioned, angry, tearful?

"What the—" Luce tensed when he realized his apartment door wasn't closed. His immediate thought was that someone had broken in, but then he remembered Sly's general habit of entry. Although that still begged the question of why his cousin hadn't closed the door behind him as he usually did. The bizarre scene in his living room made him forget his quandary.

A blue jean-ed figure he assumed was his cousin lay

146

spread-eagled on the floor beside the upended contents of a purse. Ms. Lowe hunched over the body's torso, her head leaning in. The two hadn't heard him enter because neither turned or broke from their conversation. In the background, the TV flashed images and dialogue of some long-cancelled sitcom.

"Quit whining. It's not broken." She straightened and sat back on the heels of her feet, fondling a bloody cloth in her hands.

"I thought I told you to keep away from me."

Now privy to a view of the prone figure Luce saw ire on his cousin's face, as well as a swollen lip and the remains of a bloodied nose.

"Luce!" Sly bolted around Calamity, rising to his feet, an awkward palm cradling his privates. "Say, what's the idea leaving me at the mercy of that—" He pointed at Calam, who smiled innocently as she too rose to a standing position. "—crazed ninja woman!"

Calam glanced up at Luce, unmoved by Sly's ranting. "For the record, I'm a brown belt and I was provoked."

Lucifer eyed the pair of them, askance, not certain what to make of the situation. "I take it *this*...wasn't a meeting of the minds?"

"You need to put yo woman in check, man."

"Hey Porky, I've about had my fill of sexist pigs for the week so don't mess with me...unless you're itching for another smackdown."

So much for the 'Honey, I'm home' reverie he'd been nursing all day wherein Calamity met him at the door with a smile, a kiss, and a plateful of piping hot pasta. Luce, clear now that he would be forced to play parent to the 'kiddies', expelled a sigh bespeaking a long day and a limited reserve of patience. "Ok, who started it?"

It attested to the silliness of the twosome that neither noticed his blaring sarcasm. They both spoke at once, each increasing in volume, in an effort to drown out the other's side of the story. The fuse to Luce's temper ignited like kindling, and his face darkened at their childish squabbling.

* * *

Charisma hit the power button on the remote to shut off the small screen, before she reclined back into one corner of the couch. "Well that was a complete waste of time."

"Yeah," Reese flopped back against the opposite end of the couch. Her signature bangles lay resting their cockles on the coffee table. Her toes toyed with them, absently. "Too bad Perkins was too busy filing bogus charges on Calamity to pull his usual brand of slap and tickle on the temp. Speaking of which, I just can't get used to her. The woman has a personality akin to over-chewed gum. She inflates only so much before the strain of being interesting pops her bubble and leaves a flatten mass of goo."

"That bad, huh?"

"Well, let's face it, who *isn't* boring in comparison to Calamity?"

Being the proud holder of front-row tickets to all of her sister's madcap antics, Charisma bobbled her head. "I can't disagree with you there. Although, I think it's probably best that Calam is on leave during this whole thing." She reached to the center of the couch, grabbed a handful of caramel popcorn from the half-eaten bowl, and took to nibbling. "She's totally stressed out. Says it's like everything is happening all at once: the charges, the complaint, the nanny-cams, her and Satan. And to add insult to injury, thanks to me and Pike, she's being forced to bring him home for dinner...you know so the Lowe family herd can give him the once-over, and make sure he's a worthy specimen for Mr. Right."

"Yikes." Reese screwed up her face.

"Yeah, well..." Charisma sighed, guilt-ridden. "If I'd known her nerves were so threadbare I'd have lobbied harder against it. But twenty-twenty hindsight and all that."

"What is she going to do? I mean, there has to be a way to get these ridiculous charges dropped. Then at least she wouldn't have that to antagonize over while her complaint is processed."

"Well, she told me earlier that Satan had a mediation session with Perkins after work today to try to reach a compromise. So maybe if we're lucky they can hash out a deal that'll bring everything to a quick close."

"Compromise?" Reese shot her a jaded glance, "You *clearly* have never met Mr. Perkins."

* * *

Luce's feeble hold on his irritation broke loose as he watched Calamity and Sly trade verbal snipes like a Pekinese beefing with a Doberman.

"E-NOUGH!"

They stilled at the brusque command.

"*You.*" Luce pivoted, menacing, toward his cousin. "Make yourself scarce."

"Oh sure, take *her* side."

"Out, Sly. NOW!"

"Ok, but don't say I didn't warn you." With this dire prediction, the younger Italian hobbled to the door, privates in one palm, ice pack in the other. "Hang around with Insanity, see if I care…but don't come running to me when she bottles yo manhood like cheap wine and all her girlfriends are getting drunk off *yo* humiliation."

Calam rolled her eyes, and tossed out a parting barb just as the door closed behind him. "Wow, a complex analogy. Should we alert the media? Luce, look, I know he's family and all but why do you put up with that guy?"

Luce exhaled a long guttural sigh, born of frustration and worry. "Because he reminds me of my brother. Gio favored our Italian side much more so than Vee and I. Plus, Sly is the same age he would be if he hadn't…" He trailed off. Not sure why he'd admitted as much to her…he barely admitted it to himself most of the time.

He dropped his briefcase along side Calamity's purse and trekked mindless to the kitchen, oblivious of his jacket and tie slipping off to join the other accoutrements on the living room floor. Sasha, at least, was her affectionate trilling self as she looped around his legs meowing for all she was worth. Luce bent and picked her up. A shameless attention-ho, this was all the encouragement Sash needed to curl up in the crook of his arm, purring like a buzz saw, tail swishing along his ribcage.

"That's my girl." It was nice to be welcomed home, even if it wasn't the warm body he'd been hoping for. "Let's go see what's for dinner."

Calamity hovered in the kitchen threshold, feeling a bit like the fifth wheel. Luce hadn't said a word to her since his odious cousin's departure. His odious cousin who reminded him of his dead brother…Geez, she'd really put her foot in it this time. But surely he couldn't be *mad* at her? How could she have known? Granted, she hadn't been particularly welcoming at the end of what she knew had been a long exhausting day for him but he didn't have to ignore her like she was invisible or something. Well, one thing was for sure, now definitely wasn't the time to bring up the whole family dinner slash Gitmo-esque interrogation tomorrow night.

As he studied the contents of the frig, Calam got treated to a view of his broad back, taut muscles not quite concealed beneath his white dress shirt. The longer the silence stretched out the more awkward it would be to break. So, after five minutes of him neglecting her to flirt with Sasha and her staring at his unsympathetic back hatching slow and torturous methods to do away with the feline hussy bent on stealing her man, Calam bit the bullet.

"I could fix us something…since, you've been at work all day and I'm basically living off you now." She tested the waters in a meek voice reserved for animals (other than that skank Sasha) and the elderly. "Or if the thought of me cooking sends chills down your spine, we could order pizza? Though I might add that you liked my pancakes this morning...unless, of course, that was all a sham to spare my feelings and you were really hiding them in your napkin whenever I looked away."

Realizing that she was rambling maniacally, Calamity clamped her mouth shut. An infinitesimal second passed, during which she went through the whole range of human suffering thinking he would continue scanning for food in stoic silence.

"Pizza sounds good." Luce stood to face her, closing the refrigerator in the process. "Here, take Sasha while I get the number."

Not altogether happy to be left holding the cat, Calamity disentangled overeager claws from the mesh of her shirt, hoisted the calico man-eater to eye-level and fixed her with a no-nonsense expression. "Paws off the Phoenix, furball. He's mine. Comprendes?"

Sasha gave a disgruntled meow and twisted sideways to hop onto the kitchen counter.

Forty minutes later, a ruddy-faced teenager arrived with two large pizzas, a complimentary bag of breadsticks and several small Styrofoam saucers of marinara for dipping. Calamity paid him, feeling that it was her duty not to become a financial burden, while Luce carried the piping hot loot to the table. By the time she shoved the change into her jean pocket and joined him, Luce was on the second slice of his cheesy meat-lovers special. Calamity plopped down in the chair opposite, where he'd put her thick-crust veggie primavera. The breadsticks and sauce, she noticed, were positioned neutrally in the center of the table. Did that mean she wouldn't be allowed a slice of his? She decided not to press her luck, so she flipped open the cardboard and inhaled her first slice.

She got through two successive slices before she subsided to breadsticks and marinara, deciding at last to risk conversation. "So, eh, are you going to tell me what happened with Perkins or do I have to guess?"

These were the first words she'd chanced to speak since he agreed to order pizza. After ten minutes of haggling with the Collinas people, he used the intervening delivery time to have a shower and change clothes, neither of which Calamity could attend with him. She was forced to hang out in the living room, alternating between watching TV and playfully threatening each of Sasha's nine lives. Not that the results of his stint of freshening up weren't enticing as hell. Woo boy, if it weren't for the distraction of eating she'd be ogling him full-time. At the moment her focus was split between dipping, chewing, and wondering how he managed to make a wife-beater tank and five o'clock shadow come off quite so G.Q.

Luce stood, taking the half-eaten bag of breadstick with him. He inclined his head towards the sauce, as he abandoned the table for the living room couch. He was stalling, he knew. She had a right to know, but for reasons too uneasy to examine up close, he hesitated to convey news that would cause her upset and likely dampen her spirit. Luce found that's what he admired most about Calamity, her vivacious spirit.

She was effervescing with excitement and utopian ideas, clever and witty, sometimes to the point of zaniness. But he needed a little silliness in his life to lighten the dirge of everyday reality. He'd always been a straight-laced type person, but in the past few years, he felt himself hardening into a humorless cynic who'd forgotten how to lighten up, or worse yet, a number-cruncher who acknowledged only the bottom line and made all his major decisions based on the 'worse-case scenario'.

"C'mere."

Drawn like a moth to his soft sexy command, Calamity took up the sauce and followed him to the couch. Seated on the coffee table facing him, with sauce and bread sticks out of the way, she found him regarding her with an impassive gaze. Uh-Oh. She was in for a cruel kick in the teeth. She willed herself not to shoot the messenger.

"Alrighty then...let's start with the good news shall we...that is, if there *is* any." In Calam's experience, it always helped to cushion the blow.

"I talked to Stella again. Nothing's definite yet, but I got her to think about it."

"She's considering filing a complaint?" She grasped his drawstring pant legs as she sat forward. "Really?"

Damn. He promised himself he wouldn't get her hopes up with half-truths and sweeping statements, but he couldn't help flashing a smile imbibed with more confidence than he felt. "Yeah, it's a good possibility. When I told her that she wouldn't have to go up against Perkins alone, she wafted and agreed to consider it."

"This is great! She'll lend me credibility, right?" Without much thought to propriety and with even less to the still unspoken bad news, he suspected, she launched herself into his arms *and* his lap. "I mean, not that I'm not *already* credible but two complaints prove he's a habitual perv and I'm not just some disgruntled office tramp out to spite the boss."

Luce held her to him. Their embrace was an awkward jumble of limbs, but he nevertheless savored the feel of her soft warm body against him. "Hold the phone, there's still the manner of Charlie."

She pulled back, taking a moment to situate herself comfortably, her bottom resting on one thigh while her legs stretch across his lap and her socked feet thumping up and down on the couch cushion beside his other thigh. "Well? What'd he say?"

Luce studied her upturned face. Dauntless eyes filled with idealistic expectations beseeching him not to ruin her illusions of vindication. It troubled him more than it ought to lower the boom on those illusions. "He's bargaining with the charges. Basically, its 'you drop yours, I'll drop mine' politics."

The wail that ripped from her plucked right at his heartstrings.

"Nooo! He *can't* do that! That's not a fair compromise!"

Luce refrained from pointing out that often times life was unfair. In truth, each party lost a little leverage in any mediation agreement otherwise it wouldn't be possible to find a middle ground upon which both sides could stand.

"I could go to prison for two years if his charges stick. If the harassment complaint goes in my favor, all he'll get is a slap on the wrist and sensitivity training." Agitated beyond the point where she could sit still and think rationally at the same time, Calamity extricated herself from Luce's lap, stepped around the coffee table to find an open stretch of carpet to pace.

"If I retract the complaint, won't they assume I contrived the whole thing and then thought better of it when things got too serious? I won't be able to get a decent transfer. After all, who wants a woman of ill-repute for an assistant? And what happens the next time Perkins puts a hand outta place? Huh? Employee Relations will think I'm a lying flake—"

Calamity wound down as the misery of being stuck between a rock and a hard place settled on her. She stilled from breakneck pacing, rounding on Luce to divine what she could from his expression. His face, apart from being a study in gold-skinned magnificence, held little to encourage her of future success. She glimpsed, not pity, but a disturbing hint of resignation in his dark eyes.

"I can't win, can I? I'm screwed either way. I hate this. Now, what the hell am I supposed to do..." Calamity resumed pacing, but at a more subdued calculated gait. Outrage and frustration cease to be the name of the game. Cunning and strategy took over.

What she needed was to talk to Reese. The time had come to pull out their ace in the hole. No more Mrs. Nice Guy! Granted, at present, all they had was a useless bit of after-hours hanky-panky starring Perkins and an unknown Lady Godiva riding him like a triple-crown stallion. But, surely it wouldn't be too much longer before her boss's licentious nature got the better of him and he compromised an unwilling female.

These thoughts and more were swirling around unbridled in her mind like tornado debris when the touch of hands caressing her face, and the soft pressure of lips to her forehead startled her back to the present. Calamity looked up in slow motion, to see her prince charming smiling a crooked grin she was sure meant to reassure her of his support. She also detected concern swirling around in the inky depths of his eyes. Luce must think that she'd given up. Little did he know, she was now more determined than ever to hit her boss where it hurt.

"So, what do you think I should do?" Curiosity alone forced the question from her. She'd already made her decision.

"Calamity, I feel compelled to outline your legal options, but I can't tell you what to do." This time his hands migrated into her hair, tracing the two thick French braids down to their ends flush with her shoulders. "Take the deal, retract your complaint and you'll lose not only any chance of getting even the smallest measure of satisfaction for your trouble but you'll also be tossing your credibility to the wind."

Calamity supposed now wasn't the proper time to confide that his sexy lawyer jargon was turning up the heat on her already raging libido.

"...If you continue to pursue the present course of action, with help from Stella's corroborating complaint it might put a major dent in Perkins' charges and quite probably result in his receiving a formal citation and reprimand. I'm on your side no matter what, but if it comes to trial I can't promise I'll be able to represent you."

"Why the hell not?" What should have been a cry of righteous indignation ended up being a breathless toss-away-line as she swayed forward into his beckoning warmth. Had his voice lowered two octaves? "I've made up my mind. I'm going to fight him. Why won't you help me?"

"For one, I haven't passed the Bar, and I need to study…" He hoisted her up against him so her feet hovered a good five inches off the floor. He spoke huskily between nibbles at her lips and throat. "Perkins might claim it's a conflict of interest…and…eh, did I mention that I like your hair this way?"

"What about the food? Shouldn't we tidy up…" Calamity trailed off not caring if the roaches—or more likely Sasha—feasted all night on their forgotten Italian repast.

She hardly noticed being carried, but in the next several seconds she found herself laying on his bed in pitch blackness—as it was nighttime and the shades were drawn over the window off from the headboard. Luce was nowhere to be seen. Of course since she couldn't actually *see* anything, he might have been right in front of her. His unnerving talent for mute motion rendered her helpless to pick up a trace. How the devil was he able to see? Not that she wished him ill but couldn't he at least trip over the nightstand or something so she could get an inkling of his whereabouts? She considered sliding off the bed to institute a blind search, but with a name like 'Calamity'…no sense in taking unnecessary chances.

"Lucifer?"

Disembodied hands appeared next to her bathed in an eerie blood-red luminescence. The weird glow and reaching hands made her think of 'The Shining' and the little kid chanting 'redrum' as Jack Nicholson hacked away at the bathroom door. A Victorian scream rose in Calam's throat, the likes of which would put Neve Campbell to shame. Luckily, Luce appeared in full form and Calam's vision adjusted to the strange crimson light the last second before she let her rip.

"Relax, Ms. Lowe, it's just me." Luce, cool as a cucumber, slid onto the bed, lazily arranging himself, on the opposite side of where she lay on the cool cotton sheets. She was closest to the edge of the bed and, unfortunately for her nerves, also the nearest to the freakish nightlight. She just couldn't get used to the thing.

"Sorry, I usually don't frighten easy." Calamity blinked up at him, still in protective fetal position. Realizing her silliness, she unfurled and propped up on an elbow. Luce, in turn, had propped his upper body against the headboard, the very definition of languid elegance.

"Shouldn't I dress for bed? You're all comfortable in your nightwear and I'm still wearing jeans and my shirt—"

He sat a book between them, executing a clandestine peek down her cleavage in the soft lighting. "It would probably be better…eh, safer, if you kept your clothes on."

Fair enough, she conceded. Calamity inclined her head towards their reading material, curious, recalling his scandalous genre preferences.

He flipped open the volume and vocalized in a deep, rich timbre. The words flowed, melodic as well as erotic, from one fascinatingly decadent scene to the next, all with romantic but risqué overtones. The characters were sometimes unknown strangers, other times relationshippers stuck in a rut. The setting and circumstances shifted with each new vignette. They always met in the smoky shadows of midnight where the couple explored voyeurism and her lascivious twin exhibitionism in a variety of arousing and visually stimulating motifs. Lulled by the sensual goings-on in the book, Calamity migrated over to pillow her head on his chest. Hearing the words rumbled directly into her ear as he stroked her French-braided hair was beyond soothing. He paused to press a kiss in her hair. Calamity felt much like she imagined Sasha had earlier with Luce stroking her fur. She closed her eyes and let herself veg-out. Had she been capable, she would have purred.

CALAMITY FAIRE

Wednesday came like a thief in the night, Tuesday night. Calamity awoke to find herself, once again, in Luce's bed but this time she was—as she discovered when the sheets fell away–shockingly without her clothes. Good Grief! Lacy pink undies and a matching bra were the only shield protecting her from nudity. More in confusion than anything else Calam eyed her surroundings suspiciously. She was relieved to discover herself alone in the room…save for Luce's yellow-eyed beastie leering weirdly from the nearby desktop.

"Do you *mind*?!" Calamity yanked the sheet up to cover her perky c-cup goodies. That darn cat was a perv as well as a menace!

The other side of the bedding was conspicuously rumpled. Luce had shared the bed with her, that much she deduced. He'd been reading from an erotic anthology entitled *Midnight: Scheherazade's 1001 Delights*. She'd fallen asleep on his chest, dressed in a mullet top and jeans. By process of elimination that only left one conclusion…Luce removed her clothes. She blinked several times, letting the knowledge melt into her mind like butter over a stack of hotcakes. Perhaps she should have been upset, livid even, but the thought of his doing something so intimate and naughty quite curled her toes—which she noted were also bare beneath the sheet.

Casting Sasha a malevolent glance, Calam swung over the edge of the bed, tucking the sheet around herself Grecian style. She arrived at the bathroom door to the sound of running water. He's probably taking a shower. Still, the minx in her hesitated to release the knob. Whilst she contemplated the ifs, ands, and butts—admittedly a bad pun—a knock at another door put the decision out of her hands.

"That better not be Neanderthal Man again." With nary a thought to her state of dress, or rather undress, Calamity stalked towards the living room, crossed it in three strides, stumbling once over the trailing sheet. She peered through the eye-hole, planning to do an about face should Sly be their early-bird visitor. Instead, she spied her mirror image blinking back at her.

"Just a sec." Calam made quick work of the deadbolt and chain. "Hey, what are you doing here?"

Charisma stared at Calamity as she stepped inside, casting a dubious eye over her sister's disheveled appearance; wild hair—but that was a given—no jammies, strategically wrapped sheet, guilty expression. Determined not to jump to conclusions, Charisma calmly handed Calam the small suitcase of clothes she'd packed for her.

"I came to bring you this. You'll be happy to know there's a blow dryer and a flat iron in there. Eh, since when do you sleep in your skivvies, Calamity?"

Before Calam could think of a response, Charisma's gaze shifted minutely to focus on some fixed point behind her head. The baby hairs on her neck stood on end, even before she heard his deep, disturbingly male voice behind her.

"Since she started sleeping with me."

Calam did a one-eighty, stumbling over the tail end of the sheet. The overnight bag Charisma had just handed her took a flying leap and landed with a thump at Luce's bare, still wet, feet. He was the picture of a man just getting out of the shower, with little droplets of water rolling down his neck, arms, chest, and legs. The ridiculously inadequate towel rode lower on his torso than Christina Aguilera's vintage crotch dusters. The split gaped on the side where his hand held it at his hip, and the towel itself ended rather abruptly mid-thigh.

Charisma gawked in fascinated horror when he had the audacity to bend and retrieve the overnight bag with his free hand, causing the side split to part like the Red Sea. Before anything unbridled could swing into view, she averted her eyes to the ceiling. Calamity, not possessed of a similar modesty, gawked unblinking.

Luce straightened without incident and stepped forward to place the bag on the couch.

Charisma regained her tongue first. "Calam, I need a moment please." She inclined her head over her left shoulder towards the kitchen. "Do excuse us, Sa—Mr. Phoenix."

"No problem." He met Calamity's still entranced gaze with a smoldering expression that bespoke of unfinished business and caused Calam once again to stumble clumsily as she pivoted.

Once in the kitchen, Charisma peered around her, watching for the door to the bedroom to close before she deafened her with a shriek of outrage.

"How could you?!"

Calam bounced back, calmly, as she massaged her assaulted eardrum. "How could I *what*?"

"We had a pact, remember."

"Oh, come on." Rolling her eyes, Calam totted over to the frig, having remembered spotting a yogurt cup in the shelf the day before. "Like you never slept with Paul before you two got married. Besides—"

"Well, yeah, but that was completely different." She explained, indignant. "Paul and I dated for two years. We were engaged, committed. And anyways, I still maintain that I was a virgin on my wedding night."

"Yeah, a *non-practicing* virgin." Calamity scoffed. "I thought we were gonna have to tell everyone that Manny was *premature*."

"Well, if it hadn't taken mama *eight months* to plan the wedding we could've waited. But you…You hardly know this guy." Her voice lowered to a frantic whisper. "Calam, he could be using you just for sex."

"Charisma, Lucifer does *not* need to use me for sex. There's a virtual harem of women at work just dying to nail their heel-marks into his ceiling…and another thing, my relationship with him isn't some cheap daytime soap opera, so please take a powder on the theatrics." Calam punctuated her exasperation with a long sigh. "Besides, I don't make a regular habit of…well, there was the one other time, but that hardly counts. Shane and I—"

"Good grief, you did *the nasty* with Shane. *Shane?* The purple Prima-Donna who thinks he's Prince on the half-shell– *that* Shane? He's a chronic miscreant who can't even do his own wife properly. Are you kidding me?"

"HEY!" Righteous indignation flared up like wild fire as Calamity held the cup of strawberry Yoplait and went in search of a spoon. "For your information, Cheryl never proved those impotence allegations. She was just being a bitch. Shane can get it up plenty." Finding the utensil she needed, Calamity bumped the drawer closed and leaned back against the counter contemplating her last statement.

"At least I think he can, we didn't actually do the deed. He was drunk and rambling on about Cheryl. I just sort of figured it would boost his confidence if he thought we did it."

Charisma's expression meandered between relief and frustration. "As ecstatic as I am to be privy to that information, Shane is not my main concern right now. Satan is."

"Relax, Chris, there's nothing to be concerned about."

She paused to down another spoonful of yogurt. "Luce and I didn't do anything last night, but even if we had, what's the big deal. Virtue isn't like wine or war bonds. It doesn't mature with age. It sours."

"But Satan said—"

"He said we slept together, which we did, but not in the *altogether*." She clarified. "I won't be doing the walk of shame this morning, thank you very much."

"Oh." This announcement seemed to take all the wind out of her sister's sails. "Well, eh, how'd he take the news about dinner tonight?"

"What dinner?" Calamity gingerly downed the last of her makeshift breakfast, not quite clicking on what she meant.

"Eh, dinner tonight at our parents? That ring a bell?"

Calam winced. "I forgot. There was a lot going on last night."

"Humph, well you'd better tell him soon. Dinner's on at seven."

"It'll have to wait." Calam waved the thought away. "Right now, I got bigger fish to fry. Can you hang around until after Luce heads to work? We need to discuss–" She lowered her voice to a conspirator's whisper. "Plan B."

"We're activating Plan B? Sweet! Should I call Reese?"

* * *

Rounding the corner two blocks above Ross-Warner, Calamity slipped on a pair of over-sized shades, obscuring the top half of her face. She walked briskly toward the employee's parking garage, clothed in what she hoped was an inconspicuous outfit. She'd chosen the baggy khakis so she'd have somewhere to hide the metallic wire hanger she swiped from Luce's closet. The everyman's t-shirt and Rockets basketball cap pulled over freshly plaited hair topped off her layman's disguise.

She reached her destination with no one the wiser, glad

to get from under the scorching afternoon sun. It wasn't difficult to locate his car, if it could still be called that. With its rusty shades of faded blue and fender dents the size of meteoroid craters, she'd recognize the roadside menace anywhere. She crossed over to the blind side so she wouldn't be seen by anyone on the covered pathway to the elevator bay. Calamity didn't dare go any nearer for fear of an all-out police assault courtesy of Houston's Finest.

Sliding the hanger from the waist of her khakis, she deformed the wire into a flat grasping claw. Wishful thinking had her humming the musical theme to Mission Impossible as it took her five tries and a broken thumbnail to successfully jimmy the lock. Once inside she deposited the note on the dashboard and got the hell out of dodge.

* * *

If Calamity had been harboring any ill-fated hopes that the indelible Ms. Heyes would be less intimidating the second go around, they quickly evaporated. The woman was a walking, talking testament to poise and professionalism…razor-sharp business suit, attractive no-fuss hair, expressionless face, and brisk manner. And of course, she spoke textbook English.

Their brief meeting took place at Tea Time, a café style restaurant ten minutes' drive from Ross-Warner. That morning when she'd called Ms. Heyes back and explained the delicacy of her situation, she'd been nervous as hell thinking the restraining order would somehow taint her complaint process or at the very least sway the pristine investigator against her. Instead, Ms. Heyes had calmly informed her that one had nothing to do with the other and then succinctly suggested they meet for lunch a safe distance away from the office.

"I will be direct, Ms. Lowe, yours is not the first complaint we have received concerning Mr. Perkins." She elucidated. "However, during the course of investigating yours, I have become privy to extremely unsettling implications and in some cases significant evidence that Mr. Perkins' sexually inappropriate conduct is far more wide-spread, egregious and frequent than originally thought."

Calamity practically licked her lips. "So what you're saying is, he's a habitual offender?"

"In a word, yes."

"So, what does that mean, in terms of my complaint?"

"It is my recommendation that Ross-Warner, in particular the Employee Relations division of Ross-Warner, is not equipped to handle what I feel has the potential to become a very far-reaching investigation. I have made out my report stating as such and further recommended that all evidence be immediately turned over to the municipal authorities and that an in-house attorney be assigned to jointly represent any and all persons wishing to come forward and file criminal charges. Of course, you always have the option of retaining individual representation. Either way, all relative evidence collected by Employee Relations will be made available."

"What about Perkins?"

"A formal decision has not been made regarding Mr. Perkins' status at Ross-Warner. You will be notified. Now, I understand you have submitted your resignation and given two-weeks notice. The decision is yours of course, but the firm would hate to lose you. I hope you will reconsider."

"What about—I mean, I have this lawyer friend of mine…"

"Certainly, contact your legal counsel and give him or her the full account but I would ask that you use discretion until such time as a decision is made."

Apprehension still knitted Calamity's brow. "But what if my lawyer friend works for Ross-Warner too?" Calam nearly winced at the stark disapproval that greeted her inquiry.

"In that case, I would have to advise you against discussing these proceedings until after the decision. These are just my recommendations, the powers that be have the last say, and they may choose to protect their own...his privacy anyway."

The shrill whine of a cellular thankfully bridged the awkward gap in conversation. "Mine. Excuse me please." Calamity rushed to haul her purse into her lap so she could dig for the phone, finding it after what seemed like a million rings. A quick glance at the display, and she saw her sister's work number flashing impatiently. "Hello?"

"Well, have you told him yet?"

"In a manner of speaking, yes." Knowing she had a very delicate audience, Calamity evaded a direct answer. "Look, I'll have to call you back. I'm right in the middle of an important meeting."

"Sheila Heyes?"

"Yes. So, I'll talk to you later."

"Ok, but you better call me back!" With that, the phone clicked.

Calamity's gaze shifted apologetically back to the woman across the table. "Sorry about that Mrs. Heyes. And please rest assured, I'll be the soul of discretion."

Seemingly satisfied with the solemn promise, Mrs. Heyes thanked her and their meeting ended. Calamity let out the proverbial breath she hadn't realized she'd been holding. The emotional energy she expended being worried and nervous left her literally tired with relief.

Perkins' days might be numbered! All was right with her world again. No need for plan B after all. Now, there was only tonight's impromptu meet-the-boyfriend dinner to be endured. "Ugh."

* * *

Lucifer toyed with the palm-sized dinner invitation for the umpteenth time since discovering it a half-hour ago.

His initial confusion had morphed into brief amusement, then annoyance, and finally worry. Did the woman ever do anything normal? Did she know the meaning of the phrase, 'low profile'? Flicking the card to the passenger's seat Luce concluded that the answer to both questions was a resounding 'no'.

When he arrived at his apartment, and discovered it devoid of life, he waspishly considered having his makeshift roomie fitted with a dog and pony leash to keep her out of trouble. No doubt she was already at the appointed address, thus not leaving him the option of taking a rain check on the mysterious event. She hadn't given many details, merely the time, date, address, and dress code. 'Dressy casual', the invite said, which he took to mean slacks and a nice shirt.

Though he'd been anticipating an eating establishment, Luce wasn't overly shocked when he pulled up in front of a nondescript two-story house. Sharing close quarters with Calamity must have either burned out his ability to be surprised or strengthened his mental shock absorbers. Regardless, when he got the little minx alone, he'd give her a good talking-to.

H-TOWN CONFIDENTIAL

Avoiding her sister's disapproving expression, Calamity leaned forward over the back of a chair to straighten the plastic fruit centerpiece.

"You left him a note? As in, Psst...give-this-to-Jaime-during-recess." Charisma glared at her across their parent's meticulously set dining room table. "How on earth do we know he's coming? Did he RSVP by pony express?"

"Oh, you got jokes now."

"Hell no, I'm serious. He could be at home right now with a TV dinner in his lap. Meanwhile, mama is in the kitchen cooking up a feast of dishes so elaborate that I can't even pronounce half of them. She's sent Pike to the store three times."

"Well, it wasn't *just* a note." Calamity reasoned.

"A singing telegram then?"

"Don't be silly. It was a formal invitation. And in my own defense I did try to reach him at work but Stella said he was in negotiations all day. I couldn't very well leave the message with her. It'd have been all over Ross-Warner by the end of the day. Besides, by not giving him an opportunity to agree I also didn't give him the opportunity to refuse either. Shrewd huh?"

"I can think of another word for it." Charisma rolled her eyes as she heard her name bellowed from the kitchen. "Pike must be back with the wine."

Of course, he's coming, Calamity assured herself, after Charisma disappeared through the swinging door. How could he *not* come?

As if on cue, the doorbell rang. Awash with renewed enthusiasm, Calamity skittered into the living room on three-inch heels...resembling a giddy fairy. She paused at the sofa to check the hors d'oeuvre set out on the coffee table. She didn't know what any of the bite-sized morsels were, but she was satisfied just so long as the tray was colorful and attractive. If it turned out they tasted like swill, Luce would just have to swallow and think of England. Heck, that's what she did every year at the office Christmas party.

Taking one last breath to compose herself, Calam flung the door open wide. Lucifer stood as tall as an oak, decked out in black slacks, collared blue-grey shirt and a foreboding expression. His coal black eyes stared a hole into her. He hadn't bothered to scrape away the five o'clock shadow that she normally found sexier than a wet naked Denzel. Tonight though, the combination of dark attire, soul-less eyes, and shadowed jaw sent the air crackling with dangerous vibes. Calamity took a nervous step back, of a mind to turn tail and run for the hills.

"Good evening, Ms. Lowe." The greeting embodied the sort of mock warmth and gaiety one would expect of the Grim Reaper.

Luce had come prepared to wear his annoyance like a boy scout patch, but the instant he saw her he knew he wouldn't last ten minutes. She'd done something different with her hair; it bounced around her face in soft curls, barely brushed her chin and exposed her neck completely. The dress was a throw back from the twenties. Sparkly black spaghetti straps, bodice-hugging gathers down to her thighs where it ended in loose fringes that swayed and shimmered with every movement.

"Ms. Lowe?" He lifted an inky brow in question.

"Yes, of course." Calam turned, wobbled in her shoes and endeavored to ignore the heated gaze warming her shoulder blades. The heat as it happened wasn't all imagination—in the riskier portions of her mind it was—anticipation. As she stepped nearer the coffee table to offer him an appetizer, the unmistakable press of his lips against the nape of her neck shot reverberating tingles down her spine. His sizzling exhale of breath followed...scattering a few extra curls forward.

"Luce—" She pivoted, intending to admonish him about being naughty in her parent's house, but instead tilted herself off-kilter. She wavered on the edge of her heels, reaching out for something to grab. How Luce managed to catch her before she tumbled backward onto the coffee table was beyond what her feeble, desire-crazed mind could comprehend. Perhaps, he had feline reflexes to match his vexatious Spidey senses?

All she knew for sure was that when she opened her eyes...he was holding her in a diagonal dip, one arm around her waist, one hand lost in her hair. His mouth hovered inches from her ruby-red lips. Very dramatic, like the pivotal scene in a Meg-Ryan movie–though Calam supposed she was more a Bridget-Jones type. Maybe just one quick kiss...

"A-hem!"

Lovely. Calam felt fifteen again, as she turned her head towards the dining area to see her family congregated by the dinner table a la English servants lined up to meet the new master. Her father Isaac was all polite interest; Pike comic surprise; Marian matronly disapproval. Meanwhile, her traitorous twin stifled a giggle behind a hastily plastered smile.

"Aren't you going to introduce us?" Her mother prompted, looking from one to the other.

"Yes." She whipped back to face the man still holding

her dangling precariously over the hors d'oeuvre tray and gave him a pointed squint and a whack on the arm. "Luce, let me up please."

He waited an extra beat before pulling her upright to stand beside him, deliberately, she suspected, knowing it would rattle her. She jabbed her elbow into his rib as they took the short walk to join the others in the dining area. School-yard rules, buddy. He smirked, devilishly at the minor assault.

Her father, a man of only average height, rested his hands on her mother's slightly shorter shoulders. Pike and Luce stood like sequoias over the others, both six foot plus. Pike was a sturdy yet gangly giant while Luce resembled a solid steel tree-trunk.

"Mama, Daddy...this is Lucifer Phoenix, my–" How to complete the sentence without offending or outraging anyone, that was the ten-thousand-dollar question. "–eh, friend from work. Luce, my parents, Isaac and Marian Lowe...and of course, you already know Pike and Chrissy."

Luce shook her parent's hands and inclined his brows at the other two. "Yes, Pike, I met at the police station. Charisma, I believe, asked us out on our first date."

Marian's jaw dropped to scrape the floor. "Excuse me?"

Calamity groaned. Pike eyed Charisma rather oddly. In a clear show of acceptance, Isaac leaned closer and slapped Luce—with exaggerated congratulations—on the back. "Welcome to the family, Son."

Calamity and Luce sat side by side with Charisma and Pike opposite and a parental unit at each end of the table. Dinner wasn't quite the catastrophe she'd been conjuring in her overactive imagination. The food, a virtual buffet of inarticulate names, was delicious. Mercifully, the conversation veered around anything too personal. After side-stepping a few explosive innuendoes about the nature of their relationship, Luce eased into his usual charm-the-skin-off-a-snake self.

A smooth joke here, a suave compliment there and he had Marian extolling his praises like a Jehovah's Witness on a road-trip. Her father too, fell victim to Luce's charm. The common link bonding them was a love—fanatical, in Calam's opinion—of Houston Rockets' basketball and an equally fervent hatred of the Rocket's coaching staff. Luce and Pike seemed to get on the best of all. In a family over-balanced by whimsical and wacky females, Pike, laid-back, well-grounded and self-aware had found in Luce, a testosterone-toting realist who also just happened to have comparable tastes in art and music. This was right up his ally, Pike being a unique blend of alpha male and social butterfly. He, like Luce, was comfortable in any situation, could discuss an amazing range of topics with intelligence and aplomb and yet not too uppity to come home and snake his own toilet.

By the time dessert and drinks rolled around, Luce had separate outings planned with three of her four family members and a standing invitation to dinner at the Lowe's. Calamity was almost jealous.

* * *

They pulled away from the curb in Luce's dilapidated death wish. "I like your parents. Your brother too, he's got a level head and an interesting take on things."

She smiled in response. "So, you had a good time."

"Yeah, I did."

"And you're glad I invited you."

"Yes."

"And—"

"Don't press your luck, Ms. Lowe." The cool warning in his voice came out of nowhere. And, the dreaded *Ms. Lowe* was back. "Pushing the envelope may seem like fun now, but if you get caught violating a restraining order, the police will come take you to jail. And no amount of wit, charm, or finesse on my part or yours will get you out. No more stunts. *Behave.*"

Luce watched her stare uncomfortably at fidgeting fingers in her lap, anything to avoid a lecture, he thought. "I need a verbal response, Ms. Lowe. Are. We. Clear?"

Her reply was so low he had to bend sideways to hear it. "Crystal."

"Good. So, how did your meeting with Sheila Heyes go?"

"Fine."

She's pouting, he realized, amused. Well, he'd just see about that. "Where is your car?"

"I left it at your place."

"How'd you get here?"

"Charisma. I was too nervous to drive, plus…" she trailed off and gazed out the window, in petulant protest he assumed.

"Plus what?"

"I figured you'd be mad…about me violating the restraining order and ambushing you with a family dinner. I left my car so I'd have a reason to ride home with you and we could make up."

Luce smirked at her warped female logic. If she'd only told him about dinner in the first place, then there wouldn't be a reason for him to be mad…not that he still was. The present tension in the car as they drove down the darkened residential streets emanated exclusively from her direction and as such, he felt it his duty to put it to rest.

With just that thought in mind, Luce pulled to the side of the street, adjacent a flickering street light. He switched off the engine and slid across the seat, traversing several foaming orange fissures in the sad leather upholstery. He forced her stiff, uncompromising body into the circle of his arms, but still found himself staring down at the top of her head. She could be a stubborn little thing, when she took a fancy to it.

"Calamity, look at me."

She complied, following a reluctant silence.

Luce smiled, shaking his head at her crocodile tears. "Quit crying before you dehydrate. You were wrong, and I told you so. That's the end of it. Now, let's make up…that *was* part of the plan, wasn't it?" He sent her a teasing grin.

Calam parted her lips with a mind to admonish him for making fun of her but he swooped in and silenced her with his mouth. All other thoughts were forgotten at the first startling nibble of his teeth on her bottom lip. She sighed, surrendering her pride gladly in return for the tingling sensations she felt stirring in her stomach at the teasing invasion of tongue. Before she could regain her composure, he swept her atop his lap in an awkward heap. The point of her left heel jabbed a rib, she was sure.

One thing Luce had realized, she wasn't stingy with her emotions. She kissed exactly how she did everything else…with reckless abandon, no holding back. He felt the instant the tension ebb from her shoulders and neck. She came alive in his arms under his tender administrations. Damn, she felt good pressed up against his body, her hands clutching at his shirt, her mouth as hot and eager as his. He could even forgive her for nearly impaling him with those knife-point shoes.

She made him feel free and alive and excited about life in a way that he hadn't been for a very long time. The future, his career path, had always been about duty, responsibility, and financial security. With Calamity in his life and presently on his lap, everyday was an adventure, both at work and at home. As crazy and chaotic as things were at the moment, he realized he was having fun…probably a little too much fun to be having inside a parked car five minutes from her parent's house.

Calamity fell forward on the seat when Luce pulled back abruptly from their fast-escalating embrace. "Wha—" She stammered in bewildered surprise, pushing herself up with her palms against the seat. "Luce?"

Heaven save him when she stared up at him with her

doe brown eyes, confused with just a twinge of disappointment, her lips still half-puckered. She looked so adorably kissed. He just couldn't resist leaning back in for a parting peck and a quick jostle of her bobbing curls.

"Crying shame to waste this outfit. Billie Holiday meets Ella Fitzgerald, very bluesy. Listen, I know a place downtown that plays midnight jazz. You game?"

In the process of righting herself, and checking her hair in the rear-view, Calam nodded. "Sure, sounds like a riot."

* * *

Reese stood outside the door, kicking herself. What had she been thinking? Dropping by Satan's lair uninvited, unannounced…and unprepared for the eventuality of Satan and Calam being out for the evening.

"Serves me right for sticking my nose in where it doesn't belong." Bangles clanking together like so many jingle bells, Reese turned to retreat back to her car. The crack of the door stopped her.

"Yeah?"

Reese made an about-face and found herself locking gazes with a man, but not *just* a man…an eye-pleasing man…dark haired, and dreamy-eyed. Ok, his eyes were more sleepy than dreamy, but his admiring expression kicked them up a notch in her book. A little scruffy around the edges she admitted but hey, she could work with 'scruffy' any day. The wrinkled shirt and low-riding jeans would need to be revised. First things first though, she parked her baser instincts in neutral for the moment. "Uh, I must have the wrong place."

"That depends on who you are and what you want?" The paragon of masculine slacker-dom, inquired, whilst he propped his T-shirt-clad shoulder against the door's frame and finger-combed unruly tufts of black with the opposite hand.

"I'm looking for my friend Calamity."

"Figures." Recognition flickered across his face. "You as crazy as her?"

"Oh, the two of you've met then?"

"Yeah, eh, me and Insanity go way back."

"Well, she's supposed to be staying with a mutual friend from work and—"

"That'd be my cousin, Luce." This revelation came on the heels of an appreciative full-body scan of her God-given gifts. Reese noted with some satisfaction that his eyes widened and took a notable pause at her bosom.

"They ain't here right now, but ah...you're welcome to keep me company till one of 'em turns up. I housesit whenever Luce is out doin' his thang. Never can be too careful." His wicked grin radiated subliminal come-hither suggestions on just the right wavelength.

"I shouldn't..." She hesitated, if only for dramatic effect. Can't give in too easy. "I've got a million things to do and they weren't expecting me anyway—"

"Come on, at least can I get your name or something? You know, so I can tell Insanity you dropped by."

"Reese Martin, but please don't mention I stopped by. Just a whim of mine."

He straightened, stepped to the side and held the door wide in invitation. "Well, Reese, I'm Sly and any friend of Insanity's is a friend of mine."

* * *

If Houston had what Calamity termed a 'red-light district', then the smattering of clubs and after-hours bars in and around downtown would be the spot. At the center of it all was The Phat Cat Café, identifiable by the tubby neon feline blowing blue notes on tenor sax above the threshold of an otherwise austere building face. They waited in line outside, sandwiched between an X-rated Ken and Barbie going at it like rabbits and a fat-cow thin-rail couple that resembled a walking number ten. The faint buzzing vibes provided beat enough to set Calam swaying in anticipation of velvety syncopated jazz tunes. Her mind flashed to a motley crew of musicians and imagined blue notes bouncing off raw wood walls like O'Malley and his band of ally cats as they crooned the scat rhythm "Ev'rybody Wants to Be a Cat".

"I like this place already." She found herself smiling unbidden at Luce, suddenly glad for the opportunity to unwind some of the tension that had built up in her life of late.

"I thought you would."

Luce guided her with a hand at the small of her back. The Phat Cat's inner atmosphere did not disappoint. The instant she traversed the midnight blue silk curtain serving as the doorway, Calamity felt as if she'd stepped through a vortex leading to the past. The place was a tribute to, no, a *mecca of* nineteen twenties decadence. Big band swing tunes permeated the air. To the left was a dimly lit foyer, which housed numerous clothes racks manned by black-n-white attired hat-check girls; an homage to Classic Hollywood. Voluminous velvet drapes, a rich shade of violet, ran the length of every wall from ceiling to floor. The central space was sprinkled with tables, and less liberally with alcoves on the fringes of the room that allowed a more intimate venue. Patrons, gal-pal foursomes and paired couples occupied over half the tables, while meandering wait-staff, bedecked in black-n-white cocktail outfits similar to those worn by the hat-checkers, took orders and served prepared drinks.

Luce and Calam slid into a booth near the back of the café and were approached by a pretty waitress sporting perfect make-up, a welcoming smile, and two menus.

"Hi, I'm Holly. I'll be your server for the evening."

Before Calam could utter a word, Luce declined the menus with a quick shake of his head. "Nah, I'll have a Black Velvet and get the lady a..." He paused for her to fill in the blank.

"Rum and coke." She supplied, without hesitation.

"Word to the wise, Hon. Small sips, it's a twenties rum and coke."

"Eh, what's that?"

She leaned over to whisper, "Its just *rum*."

"Thanks for the warning. I think I'll have an Appletini instead." Calam chuckled in good humor, as she eyed the naked dance floor and abandoned instruments littering the empty circular platform. "Say, where's the band? I thought I heard live music when we were waiting outside."

"Oh, they're taking a break. They'll be back...probably by the time Tony finishes mixing your drinks."

With a parting smile, she shuffled off to put in their order. Calamity settled in besides Luce, burrowing under his wing.

* * *

Sly interrupted her mid-sentence, "Ok, hold up, let me get this straight."

She straightened from leaning back against the kitchen counter top, and took a swig of her lemon-lime wine cooler.

"This guy grabs his secretary's ass, then *he* accuses *her* of assault? That's messed up."

"Well, after *the grab*, Calam drop-kicked his shin and gave him a black eye to match."

Thinking back to the first time he'd met the lady in question, Sly nodded emphatically as he too raised his cooler to take a drink. "Yeah, I can believe that. She tried some of that kung fu yin-yang on me and I had to set her ass straight. Still, it ain't right the boss man puttin' his hands on her like that. Guys like him give us all a bad rap."

"Now you understand why she's living here temporarily. Perkins got a restraining order and the judge wouldn't release her unless Satan agreed to take legal responsibility."

"Whoa, Luce lets you call him *Satan*?!"

"Not really." She confessed. "I think he just puts up with me because I'm Calam's friend. See, I was in on the plan with the nanny cams until—"

"Oh, lemme guess…" Sly finished his cooler with a manly gulp. "Luce found out, went ballistic, and decided for the both of you that it'd be better to bust what's his face the old-fashioned legal way?"

She nodded, sitting the bottle down on the counter behind her. "That's basically how it went, yeah. Except now, his plan has kinda gone south too and we're—if you'll pardon the expression—shit outta luck. That's actually why I'm here. I think Calam's ready to return to our original idea, on the down low of course."

"I'm with you. Say, why'd you guys let him railroad you into doing things his way in the first place?"

"Eh, panic. Damage control." She hunched her shoulders with casual acceptance. "Self-preservation. Blind lust. Take your pick. Calam caved, not me, and ultimately it was *her* ass that got grabbed which made it her call. I *can* tell you this though, if Satan hadn't gotten involved, we'd be a lot closer to nailing Perkins than we are now."

"I say nail him any which way you can. Luce, he's my cuz and all, but he's a slave to the system. What he doesn't realize is that you can't play fair when everyone else is cheating. That's not how you win."

A WRINKLE IN CRIME

Luce stifled a yawn on the circuitous walk from the elevator bay to his office. He hadn't gotten much sleep the previous evening, having only arrived home three hours before his usual wake-up time. He didn't make a habit of visiting after-hour haunts on weeknights, but Calamity had him doing a good many things that he wasn't in the habit of doing. He'd left her asleep in his bed with Sasha sharing her pillow. The cat, like himself, had taken quite a liking to their makeshift roomy. Although from what Luce could see, Calamity's feelings for Sasha were of a prickly nature.

The Phat Cat Café, a great nightspot on the neo-bourgeoisie side of downtown, had proven to be very mellowing; good drinks, heartbeat music, speakeasy ambience. On the whole, lounging in a dimly lit booth over cocktails while some hepcat whined the blues wasn't a bad end to a hectic day. A fleeting smile touched Luce's mouth but he banished it in the next instant when he crossed the threshold of Stella's cube and stepped smoothly back into his legal persona...all thoughts of jazz and liquor stowed away.

First thing, he ran down his mental to-do list: check phone messages and email, talk to Perkins and tell him no deal, prod Stella, review case studies and formulate a legal strategy, and lastly he had mediation at two o'clock...which was bound to cap off the day, he predicted.

Stella wasn't at her desk so he went straight to his office, parked behind his desk and reached for the telephone. He had three messages on his voicemail, one from Perkins in regards to Ms. Lowe, a second from his brother, and a third from Employee Relations. He'd deal with Perkins first.

Calamity's office was the same as always, except she wasn't in it. She'd been replaced with a sort of life-size female drone that radiated the exact pitch of perky and proficient that grated on his nerves.

"Ms. Ames, I need a moment. Is he busy?" Luce gestured to the inner door, curiously ajar. He inclined his head to the side, getting a glimpse of Charlie's compact body standing still as a statue at the corner edge of his desk. Gone was his usual oily self-assurance, instead he seemed to be brooding...worried almost. His haphazardly-groomed hair looked more frazzled than normal. The document he held aloft must be a humdinger to have rattled his poise.

"Let me just check for you, Mr. Phoenix." The temp stood up, a thick fleshy woman of medium height, with thin features and wire-rimmed spectacles perched on the bridge of her nose. She crossed the carpet, and stepped inside the inner office.

"What is it, Brenda?" Perkins' voice was muffled, but still stung like a hard slap.

"My name is *Belinda*, sir, I—"

"Well, have it changed to Brenda. You're not worth wasting three syllables on."

"Yes, sir. There is a Mr. Phoenix here to see you. Shall I—"

"Fine. Show him in."

"Yes, sir."

The temp reappeared in the outer office no worse for wear despite the insult she'd endured. "Mr. Perkins will see you now."

Seeing a rare opportunity to catch his nemesis operating at less than a hundred percent, Lucifer moved into Perkins' domain with the stalking grace of a great cat. His height and strength advantage, he wielded to intimidate by closing in on the much smaller man's personal space.

"Charlie." Luce nodded a greeting, hands tucked in his pockets.

"Phoenix." Still clutching the paper in one hand, Perkins was forced to tilt his head back. "I take this little visit to mean that we have a deal. As such, I expect that lying twit to retract her complaint before the end of the day. When I get the official—"

"On the contrary, Charlie, I discussed your proposition with Ms. Lowe and she has decided to decline. She feels that it does not represent a fair compromise, and I happen to agree with her." Luce noted that the unexpected outcome of their mediation caused the hand clutching the document to tighten, partially crumpling the paper.

Perkins' jaw clenched, and he gave the paper in his hand several distracted glances. He half-turned, knocking over a pencil-holder on the corner of his desk. Pencils and pens splashed out and rolled around unnoticed on the carpet.

"She can't do this."

Luce's brows knitted together. The man before him was acutely disturbed, scared even, and becoming more so by the second. Nothing he'd said should have caused this level of anxiety. "Guess I missed the punchline." He commented, blasé.

"Not to me...She can't do this. That lying bitch! She can't do this to me!" Perkins whirled back around, arms flailing erratically as if fending off an enemy; even wilder eyes flashed bloody murder. "I'll—"

181

"Who? Can't do what?" Luce asked, his curiosity getting the better of him. Something else was going on here.

Perkins crumpled the paper into an angry ball and tossed it uncaringly in his general direction. It bounced off his washboard abs and landed at his feet. Luce bent to retrieve the wad of paper, unwrinkled it as much as possible and scanned the contents. The paper was in fact a hand-written blackmail note stating something to the effect that if Perkins didn't pony up to the proper authorities there would be some pretty graphic photos of his extra-marital activities released to the media. There was also the implication that his soon-to-be ex-wife could use such documentation to drive up her already hefty divorce settlement. The letter was signed, 'I'll be in touch'.

"A girlfriend of yours?"

Perkins mouth twisted into a sneer. "*Or* that lying bitch assistant of mine...the same one you've unwisely chosen to ally yourself with. She's going down for this, and I'll make damn sure you fry with her!"

Luce retained his outward calm. "The obvious, and implied, culprit here is your latest squeeze or any number of ex-paramours with the forethought to bag some photographic rainy-day insurance. Ms. Lowe, however outmatched in her present battle would not stoop to such measures...leastwise not without informing me first." Inwardly, his unease mushroomed. He couldn't help but recall Calamity's eerily similar plan to blackmail her boss.

Perkins stomped to the other side of his desk, shoving the chair aside and seized the phone with lethal venom. "We'll just see about that. I think this is a job for the police, don't you, Phoenix?"

Luce opened his mouth but never got the chance to speak. The harried voice of Ms. Ames drifting in from the outer office distracted him and stilled Perkins in mid-phone call.

"Get out of my way, Woman! I came hear to see

Charlie Perkins and that's just what I intend to do." A loud thump jostled the closed doorframe violently; the accompanying voice grew more insistent. "Appointment my ass! Did he need an appointment to put his hands on my wife?!"

Luce eyed a now shaky Perkins who still hovered over the desk, telephone receiver in hand.

When the outer door rattled opened, it did so with such force that the knob hit the back wall and reverberated. A tallish, heavyset Latino man filled the threshold, eyeing the occupants with malicious intent.

"Which of you is Charlie Perkins?" His thick neck twisted from side to side, trying to decide, swishing a ponytail of graying jet hair.

"Security!" Perkins shouted to no one in particular.

Luce, more amused than alarmed, rubbed his stubble-studded jaw and smiled. Recognizing the avenging husband from the photos on Stella's desk, he pointed to Charlie as if he'd been asked in which direction the restrooms lay. "That's him."

Seeing that the situation was fast getting out of his immediate control, Perkins hollered over the man's shoulder to his temp. "Brenda, call the police! NOW!"

"Who are you then?" The Hispanic man asked, suspicious.

"Lucifer Phoenix. Your wife works for me."

"Oh, you're ok then." He turned his attention back to his quarry, and advanced in that direction. "Excusa, Mr. Phoenix. Charlie here and I have a few things to discuss."

"Be my guest." Ignoring Perkins' frantic outcries with a shrug, Luce turned to exit.

"Phoenix! Come back here you bastard. You can't leave me here with a mad man! Phoenix! PHOENIX!" Luce closed the door on his name and gingerly made his way back to his office.

* * *

183

Calamity stepped out of the bathroom fully dressed and refreshed, with pony-tailed hair full of messy slept-on curls from the previous evening...more kink than curl, if she was honest. She shuffled to the kitchen, trailed noisily by Sasha, got the cat chow out of the bottom cabinet next to the sink and poured food for the mewling feline.

"Alright, already, don't knock me over." She hastily moved aside, and headed for the frig to find her own breakfast. "Luce ought to put you on a diet anyway. That caboose of yours makes Beyoncé look like a stick-figure."

Ten minutes later, armed with peach Yoplait and a plain bagel double-toasted, Calamity slipped into the living room, and plopped down on the end of the couch closest to the telephone table. Balancing the bagel on her lap, she managed to hit the speaker option on the phone's voicemail.

Two messages from Reese; the first reporting for active duty on plan B. The second one gave no details. There was naturally one from her mother calling to tell her what a nice young man Lucifer was. Chrissy called to get the lowdown on what happened after she and Luce left the Lowe house. Lastly, and most exhilarating, was Stella's message telling Luce that she had reconsidered after all and decided to file a complaint against Mr. Perkins.

Calamity finished her breakfast in a blur, so agog with relief and elation that she nearly choked twice. Everything was falling into place perfectly, she beamed. Time to pull the plug on plan B and get rid of the Nanny-cams once and for all. No more guilt. No more anxiety. No more fear that Luce would find out she lied about taking them down.

And the Stella thing was some good news she could share, unlike the Sheila Heyes news which she was forced to keep under her hat...well from everyone except Chrissy. She tried Reese at her work number first, but got a recording. Damn! Reese's cell went straight to voicemail, too. Next she called Luce's office, strike two. She couldn't try his cell because he hadn't gotten a new one yet.

Disappointed and a mite frustrated, she tried her sister at work.

"Charisma?"

"Yeah, it's me. What's up? Everything ok with you and Satan?"

Calamity's mind went blank for a moment, until it donned on her that Luce *had* been a bit miffed with her the previous evening. "Oh, fine. No biggie. He wasn't that pissed. Forget about that, I've got great news."

"*Great* as in nudie pics of Vin Diesel on the internet or *great* as in free ice cream at Baskin Robins?"

Calamity frowned, "I'm confused. Which one is supposed to be better? For me it would have to be the pictures, but you're pregnant so it could be the ice cream."

"Oh never mind, just tell me!"

"There was a message on the machine this morning from Stella. Luce got her to change her mind! We have back-up now; that in conjunction with Sheila Heyes' findings and we're sitting pretty. Perkins is going to fry and I get to keep my job and my integrity."

"Ohh! That *is* great news. Have you told Satan yet?"

"No, I couldn't get him at work. I just wish I could tell him the Sheila Heyes news. It's seriously burning a hole in my stomach."

Charisma sighed into the phone. "You never could keep a secret."

* * *

Luce paused at the entrance to his assistant's cube. Her prolonged truancy set his mind to thinking. Stella was not one to dawdle at the water-cooler or take unscheduled breaks. Knitted together with her estranged husband's visceral presence, Luce concluded that Stella had decided to file a complaint and was probably upstairs in Employee Relations making her statement. The realization lifted his spirits a notch, but not enough to soothe his unease. One problem solved, his focus shifted to the new one just emerging... Perkins' blackmailer.

Glancing around his assistant's domain, Luce flashed back to a week ago. Running down the events in his mind. Calamity had been crouched down before the very desk he stood in front of now, attempting to install a covert surveillance device—which he'd later learn—for the purpose of catching her boss with his hand 'in the cookie jar' and from there blackmail him into confessing. An identical scenario, in fact, that Perkins' blackmail note detailed. He'd confronted her with the flawed logic in her plan and forced her to remove the cameras. He'd accompanied her first to Stella's cube, then the file room, and finally her own office, collected the cams and returned them himself.

Calamity *couldn't* be the blackmailer; they'd taken down all the surveillance equipment, unless...Impossible, he thought, as his brain seized upon an entirely plausible explanation. He didn't want to consider it, but couldn't shake his habit of 'worst case scenario' thinking. If she *had* been clever enough to leave a few of the cameras up, which he wouldn't put past her, then maybe he could find and remove them before someone else did.

His overactive survival instincts screamed at him to cut his losses and turn her in to protect himself from any and all liability. Luce shoved them aside for the first time in his life and allowed his heart to make the decision. Suddenly, he was at Stella's desk, methodically rifling through her knickknacks in search of anything that struck him as odd or could be doubling as a nanny-cam. He'd finished with the desk and the tops of the file cabinets and was working his way to the small three-tiered bookshelf behind the desk when the interruption came.

"Mr. Phoenix?"

Luce froze for a moment, conjuring and rejecting plausible rationales for his present activities until he came up with a satisfactory explanation.

"Stella, good morning." He didn't betray his trademark calm as he straightened from his knees, took a breather to brush the dust off his trousers, and pivoted to face his assistant. "You weren't in and I needed to look up a bit of information. Only, I wasn't aware your system was so complex."

Stella shrugged, accepting the explanation without question or suspicion. Her manner was more distracted than usual. "If you tell me what you need...actually, Mr. Phoenix, there's something I ought to tell you. I left a message on your voicemail but—"

"If you're speaking of your decision to file a complaint, I already know. And let me say, thank you. I know the risks you're taking and I appreciate your confidence in me."

She seemed surprised, so much so that her brows united over a queer expression. "Oh, you got my message? I didn't realize...I mean, I left it after eight so I assumed you wouldn't have gotten—"

Seeing her direction, Luce headed her off at the pass. "No, I wouldn't have. I didn't...haven't, yet. The reason I know is that your husband paid Charlie a visit this morning. Actually, he's still in Charlie's office right now, unless of course the temp has managed to contact the police to eject him." Luce steepled his hands and shot his assistant a questioning expression. "He seemed annoyed."

"Oh." Stella flushed a deep crimson rivaling her dyed-red hair. "Yes, Eli and I are...ahem, no longer separated. I needed some advice so I told him about what happened and he...*we* agreed that it was better if Mr. Perkins didn't get away with it. I had no idea of his coming to confront— eh, I'd better go make sure he doesn't get arrested."

"A good idea." He waited until she was gone to resume his search. After checking Stella's cube, his next stop was the file room. He concentrated on the areas where he'd once caught sight of Calamity dangling precariously from an upper shelf and worked his way around to the outer rim of shelves. He even fiddled with the smoke detector and the exit light, just to make sure that neither served a duel purpose. He came up empty, and decided to check the conference room and the break area, each high traffic areas of office interaction.

Two hours later, having discovered no damning evidence he was left with nothing but his gut feeling. The most obvious place to look, Perkins' office was unavailable. The police had finally come, whether in response to the Eli situation or to the blackmail note Luce couldn't be sure. Either way, he needed to touch base with Calamity. Perhaps he'd overreacted, perhaps not.

At the elevator bay, Luce found himself standing along side Calamity's bangled BFF. "Taking an early lunch, Ms. Martin?" He afforded her a mild nod in the way of greeting.

"Mr. Phoenix." Reese's wrists jangled like wind chimes in the breeze. "How's Calam doing? I haven't heard from her lately. Her sister told me she was having it rough what with the charges and everything. I just wondered—"

"Ms. Lowe is hardly a wilting flower." His voice came out sounding gruffer than he'd intended. If his gut feeling turned out to be right, then here in front of him was Calamity's partner in crime. The elevator door chose that moment of strained silence to open. "After you, Ms. Martin."

She stepped on the elevator jerky and glanced over her shoulder at the towering predator behind her. "I just asked because... I...well, I saw the police in her office. What happened? I mean, you do know what's going on, don't you?"

The elevator door slid closed like the ominous gates to hell, and the ornately decorated yet claustrophobic box started its smooth descent. "Why assume I know?"

"No reason."

Luce noticed her voice jittered and she drifted as far away from him as possible. "If you're honest with me, Ms.

Martin, I may just return the favor."

She pulled a face. "Ok, fine. Belinda may have mentioned that you were by there earlier."

He spoke without preamble. "Stella's husband objected to a few of Charlie's overtures. I imagine the police were contacted to prevent the incident from escalating. Charlie appears to be the kind of man who inspires in others the desire to do him physical harm…among other things."

"Oh."

Luce continued to watch her with discerning eyes until the elevator doors slid open and both stepped out and went their separate ways.

"Well, uh, tell Calam I said 'hi' ok."

"Certainly, Ms. Martin."

MIDDAY RENDEZVOUS

Calamity half-sat half-lay on the couch, reclining against the armrest at one end, surrounded by junk food in various stages of consumption. Sasha snuggled atop her bare feet, purring contentedly. Calamity tried twice to shake the clinging barnacle off but to no avail. Apparently, she'd made a friend for life simply by feeding the beast. She supposed it wasn't so bad having a live foot-warmer. Could come in handy during the cold season, though winter in Houston only amounted to a few scattered days in January when it dipped below sixty.

The commercial break came to an abrupt end causing Calam to almost knock the bowl of popcorn off her lap in a mad rush to unmute the TV. When sound once again accompanied the picture, Susan Lucci, daytime's premier diva, was vamping on some poor flustered handyman in an attempt to stir her main squeeze into a jealous frenzy. No one played the game of love with more cunning and style than Lucci's Erica Kane. Just as she leaned over the kneeling handyman to blow in his ear, the sound of keys jingling outside the apartment drew Calamity's attention. Before she could move her stash of food and get to the front door, Luce was inside and he'd flicked the TV's off-switch.

"I didn't know you were coming home for lunch." Calamity shook off Sasha, shifted the popcorn to the floor, and laid the variety bag of Jolly Ranchers on the coffee table.

"We need to talk."

Well that sounds ominous. She watched him advance in her direction, running both hands over his golden stubble-sprinkled scalp. He came to a halt in the center of the room and just stared down at her for the longest time.

Seeing as he appeared to have no plans to sit, she stood, brushing away crumbs and candy wrappers. When she looked up again, he was more composed, though his hot-ink expression was no less intense.

"What happened?" She broached, tentatively. "Oh, I know, you're here to give me the good news about Stella. I already know. She left a message on the—"

"Are you blackmailing Charlie?"

This soft-spoken, yet blunt question threw her. She stumbled over Sasha, who prompted pitched a hissing fit and ran off. "I eh...Am I...what?!"

"I need to know, Calamity." His stark expression as she spoke and the bald way he studied her clued her in. Something was seriously wrong.

"No games and no plans. Tell me the absolute truth, right here, right now...while we can still do damage control. Are you blackmailing Charlie Perkins?"

"No. Whatever made you think—"

"What about your sister, could she have done this maybe without telling you?"

"Certainly not." She informed him, indignant. "Charisma would never alter one of my plans without checking with me first. Not her style." Her voice trailed off as it dawned on her. If he was here, in the middle of the day demanding to know if she was blackmailing her boss that could mean one of two things. Either her boss had discovered one of the nanny-cams and guessed their purpose or someone else had a bone to pick with Perkins. Both possibilities put her on edge because in either case the police would be called. Even if the camera in her boss's office hadn't already been found, the police would eventually search and find it.

"Someone's blackmailing Perkins?"

"I read the note myself." Luce confirmed. "It claimed that there would be some pretty graphic footage of him released to the public if he didn't come clean...by come clean I assumed you—or whoever—meant come clean about the harassment, but since you're not the one, it may actually mean something else."

Afraid guilt would emote through her nervousness Calamity turned her back on Luce and took a few shaky steps to compose herself. She'd have to dump the cameras straightaway, ideally that very night...if she could arrange it.

She forced herself to ask. "The police?"

"They were in the office when I left."

"Ok, that's it, I'm screwed."

"Calamity?" Luce closed the short space separating them and rested his hands on her shoulders. "If neither you nor your sister are behind this then there's nothing to worry about."

"Like hell! The police will still think I did it." She partook of a cleansing breath to stabilize her churning panic.

"No they won't."

"Oh, really. Why not?" She whirled around and out of his grasp. Her eyes spit fire like two angry snapdragons. "*You* obviously did."

Luce winced as if she'd slapped him.

"Don't waste your breath trying to convince me I have nothing to worry about because I know better. I'm tailor-made to take the fall for this. I assaulted him. Lest you forget, there are criminal charges pending. I have a record of misfit behavior. Hell, *you* actually caught me planting cameras all over the place. Oh, and let's don't leave off that little matter of the restraining order. The police are bound to ask questions and fingering me as the blackmailer solves his problem. Look me in the eye and tell me I'm wrong."

He couldn't lie. She was partially right. She would be a suspect by virtue of circumstance. "I'll be honest, that's exactly what he was up to when I left, but remember the cameras are all gone. No one knows about them except you, your sister, and me. Because of the investigation in progress, they will likely question you about the blackmail note but accusations without proof are not going to hold water with the police."

"Don't forget Reese. She knows." Calam recalled as a sickening feeling gripped the pit of her stomach. *Reese!* Surely she wouldn't have done anything so reckless as to...

"Yes, and Ms. Martin. The point is that no one else is going to find out about your past exploits into executive espionage. His current fling has as good a blackmail motive as any, not to mention his other victims, and any ex-lovers that departed on bad terms. That's a half-dozen possibilities, at least, each with the knowledge to threaten him with the prospect of driving up his wife's divorce settlement. It's even mentioned in the note."

"That's true. Yeah...you're right. Its nothing to go postal about. As long as there's no evidence, they can't prove anything." Calamity nodded, spiting out the jargon he wanted to hear while a plausible countermeasure coalesced in her mind. Reese and Charisma would have to slip into Ross-Warner pretty darn quick, adiós the last three nanny-cams *and* chuck the receiving equipment at Reese's place. "I'm fine now, thank you for talking me back down to Earth."

She felt him relax at her sudden composure. Disaster averted. "C'mere." She went into his arms without missing a beat. They stood in the middle of his living room, lost in a comforting embrace. Who moved first or how solace gave way to desire she didn't know, but suddenly her palms gripped his dress shirt on either side of his waist and his mouth found hers in a feverish invasion. She received his hot, possessive caresses with unrestrained passion. His fingers threaded through her hair, making mincemeat of it, and tugging her head back. From there he had easy access to plunder her mouth with his own...

She yelped in shock when Luce's hands impatiently left her hair, and instead gripped under her arms and hauled her up his body.

"Wrap yourself around me." His voice reduced to a hoarse rasp.

Calamity rode high on his torso and had a clear shot at his delicious-looking Adam's apple. He held her up by her bottom, walked them to the nearest wall and pressed her up against it to brace them. Calamity had the top buttons of his shirt open and was busy devouring his neck with a swarm of little biting kisses.

A garbled moan escaped him, and he tightened his already vice grip on her hips, pressing her closer. "This isn't a good idea, Ms. Lowe."

"Why?" She gasped between kisses and divesting his shirt of more buttons. "Is Sasha watching? That cat is a total perv."

Calamity felt his throaty chuckle against her body.

"Ms. Lowe—"

"You only say *Ms. Lowe* when you're..." She switched targets and went for his left ear, nibbling wickedly at the lobe. "...trying to talk some sense into me."

"Lunch hour is over." He reminded her, already easing off the wall and prying her away from kissing him. "Not enough time for...*this*."

Calamity groaned her displeasure when he took hold of her face in his hands. "Please don't believe it's because I don't want to. Nothing could be further from the truth, but..."

His apologetic ebony eyes sobered her, like cold water

thrown into the face of a drunk. Oh Gawd. He probably thought her a sex-crazed harpy. Panicky and fast becoming embarrassed, she tried to turn away. Luce held fast. "Don't do that. Look at me, Calamity."

"Put me down first." She begged in a small voice.

"No. Open your eyes." But she refused and only closed them tighter, in the manner of a stubborn child. "Ok, we'll compromise." His hands slipped down to her hips, fingers sprayed out, he stepped to the couch and sat down with her in his lap. He stroked her back, leaning in to whisper near her ear...only he spoke not in English but in something Calamity first mistook as Spanish.

Her lashes snapped open in a flash and she pulled back to stare at him, shocked out of her embarrassment. "You speak Italian. You never told me you speak Italian."

He grinned a brilliant black-eyed smile. "You never asked."

She sighed. His beautifully thick and sensual lips begged to be kissed.

"Tonight?" That single word contained devilish promise and a hopeful question.

Calamity knew what he was asking and nodded a fervent 'yes'.

* * *

Calam still reeled from the implications twenty minutes after Luce had departed. Before the next sunrise, she and Luce would be *intimate*. Entwined. Connected as she'd never been with anyone else. Shivers of both anxiousness and anticipation reverberated through her mind...and body. The hairs at the back of her neck tingled. She knew there were a millions things she should be doing but instead, her head whirled with images...beguiling flashes of her and Luce tangled together, a mesh of limbs, amid his white cotton sheets, oblivious to anything but each other, consumed by a haze of desire, sensations, and...she blanked, not sure what to expect, much less how to imagine it in her affection-starved psyche. They'd have to lock Sasha in the bathroom of course.

Her daydream shattered at the blaring whine of her cell phone. She went in search of her purse and found it between the cushions of the couch and dug deep to fish it out. Reese's number flashed in the digital display window.

"Hey, Reese, where you been? I tried to call you yesterday *and* this morning."

"Yeah, I got the messages. Actually, last night, I came by to talk to you but instead, I got to meet Satan's wingman."

"Whoops, I thought Chrissy told you? Me and Luce were at my parent's last night and after that, well..."

"She told me about the dinner thing, but I didn't know when it was...wait a minute, *after that,* what?"

"Luce took me to this cool after-hours jazz spot downtown. I'll give you the scoop later, for now I want to know what went on with you and Neanderthal Man."

Reese snorted. "His name is *Sly*, thank you very much. And just so you know he's got an equally quaint nickname for you too. But moving right along...He's definitely my type, and I think he was really into me too because—"

Calam rolled her eyes, switching the cell to her other ear. "Reese, get a grip. We're not on the Love Boat. I *meant*, what, if anything, did you tell him about the plan."

"Oh. Eh. Right. Nothing, nothing at all. Didn't think you'd want me divulging this Perkins business with a total stranger, cousin or no cousin. I hung out a while, waiting for you. We flirted, traded digits, and he asked me out. I may have mentioned a few insignificant tidbits, but that's it." Calam noted that her friend's voice wavered, as if distracted or worried. "Calam...eh, not to change the subject, but the police are in yours' and Pervins' office, sniffing around."

"Yeah, I know. Luce came home for lunch." Calamity contemplated. Was her friend twitchy because she feared they might chance upon one of the nanny-cams or because she'd gone rogue with a runaway blackmail scheme?

"What else did Satan tell you? I couldn't get any details out of that tight-assed temp. I ran into him in the elevator and he said that Stella's husband turned up to give Perkins a piece of his mind, but I don't buy that. Something else is going on."

Calamity decided to play it straight and feel her out. "Someone sent him a blackmail letter. Luce assumed it was me and came home to rake me over the coals about it."

"He *accused you* of blackmailing Perkins?"

"Why is that shocking?" Calam rolled Reese's response around in her head...outraged, incredulous perhaps, but not guilt-ridden, "It's the exact same plan I hatched and attempted to carry out in the not-so-distant-past. The fact that someone else is running the same game at the exact moment that I'm trying to get the monkey off my back is a very unhappy accident."

"Wait, what are you talking about?" Came her friend's confused reply. "I thought we were full steam ahead."

"We were...but I caught a lucky break. That's actually what I was originally calling to tell you but it's a moot point now. Bottom-line is...I think we better take plan B out into the woods and shoot it, don't you? Either someone is bluffing or they've gotten wind of what we're up to and they're using it to threaten Perkins into submission. Either way, we need to do collateral manage *tonight*...before the police find the cameras and swivel their heads in our direction."

"Yeah, yeah I'm with you on this one." Reese agreed.

Too readily? Calam mused. Beware the over-eager.

"Are we meeting at my place or yours?"

"Neither. Luce expects me at home." *In bed*, her mind flashed to lascivious thoughts. "Plus it'll be better if you and Chrissy do the actual plug-pulling. I'd rather not risk violating the restraining order again."

"*Again?* Stop the press. Did I miss something juicy?"

Calam snorted at the unsavory interest peppering her friend's voice. "Yeah, we really need to swap stories. Let's do the Daiquiri Shack Friday night, and we'll dish the dirt. Listen, I need to touch base with Charisma and let her know what's cooking. You just play it cool until the end of the day."

"Wait, what'll we do with the stuff after we pull the plug?"

"Keep it at your place, and leave the key under the mat. I'll swing by tomorrow while Luce is at work and clean house. With a little luck this whole nightmare will be history by happy hour and we'll really have something to celebrate."

"I love it when a plan comes together."

* * *

Officer-in-training Burton had moved Perkins over to the far side of the office, and instructed him to sit on one of the deep-cushion twin chairs. "Sir, Mr. Cruz has already been ejected from the building and is no longer of concern. You're going to have to calm down and answer some questions or we won't be able to help you very much."

Not so easily placated, Perkins' spine remained rigid even as he sat. "I want to know why that wild man isn't in jail! He storms into my office without an appointment and manhandles my secretary, threatens *my* health, and all the police can do is escort him out of the building. Just what the hell are my tax dollars paying for?!"

"Sir, Ms. Ames maintains that the gentlemen in question did not assault her. He merely elucidated his wish to speak with you. She further maintains that a Mr. Phoenix was present at the time of his entry into your office and no physical violence ensued. When Sergeant Willis and I arrived, Mr. Cruz's wife was present and the two of them were across the room from you. We have since questioned Mr. Phoenix and he substantiates her story. The only thing that Mr. Cruz appears to have done is come into your office uninvited, which is rude perhaps but not against the law. This is a public place of business that accepts walk-in clientele. But as per your request, he was asked to vacate the premises and he did so voluntarily."

"But he threatened me, I tell you…with bodily harm."

"He threatened you how, verbally? Physically? Or are you suggesting that Mr. Cruz, in addition to the *alleged* assault, is also the author of this?" Burton held up the now infamous blackmail note. "A minute ago it was Ms. Lowe blackmailing you."

"No, dammit! That's not what I'm saying. I mean, yes…no…the one has nothing to do with the other." Realizing the histrionics were doing him more harm than good, he paused to take several breaths. After which, he seemed to regain a measure of confidence and self-control. "Mr. Cruz verbally threatened me, right over there while I stood behind my desk."

Behind the desk in question, Sergeant Willis was giving the area a general look-over, poking around, and taking notes. He looked up from his task to address Mr. Perkins. "Was there anyone else present at the time these alleged threats were made?"

"No, we were alone."

Willis continued his line of questions, reasonably and somewhat absently as he poked through the desk drawers and nearby bookshelves. "Did Mr. Cruz—described by you as a wild man—grab you? Hit you? Bellow obscenities?"

"No, not exactly."

"Then what was the *exact* nature of his threats, Mr. Perkins?"

"He told me in a menacing tone that I was to—and these are *his* words not mine—stick to paid companions and keep my filthy tentacles off his wife."

"Or what?" The Sergeant prodded.

"Or nothing, that's it."

"So, how was he menacing?"

"It was implied in his tone."

"I see." The Sergeant nodded with causal indifference as he jotted down something on his pad. "That's when the wife showed up?"

"Yes. She came to put the leash back on the brute, thank goodness."

"And have you received many menacing requests from other husbands to keep your tentacles off their wives?"

"I beg your pardon, Sergeant?" Perkins shot up from his seat, righteous indignation reddened his face. "I've been assaulted, threatened, and blackmailed all within the space of a week and you have the audacity to imply there's been some ill-conduct on my part."

The Sergeant gestured with his writing hand, an almost sarcastic air about him. "I just find all this a rather fantastic coincidence. First, Ms. Lowe assaults you unprovoked. Then Mr. Cruz threatens you away from his wife...again, for no apparent reason. Now, some mysterious person blackmails you. Makes me think maybe the reason so many bad things happen to you is because you're just not a very nice person. I'm old school, you see. In my experience, where there's smoke, there's fire." Oblivious to the mounting tension in the office, Sergeant Willis directed his attention to something aloft.

"Say, what the devil are you looking for anyway?!" Perkins snapped, glancing up at the spot that had captivated the Sergeant.

"Burton, give me a hand over here."

The junior officer traversed the room, and together they stared up at the smoke detector. "What does that look like to you, Burton?"

"A smoke detector, Sir."

"Perhaps, but do me a favor and let's find out for sure."

The officer obliged by pulling back the leather desk chair and using it as a step ladder. Resting one foot on the chair and the other on the desktop, Burton spanned the distance of vertical space and caught hold of detector, twisted it sharply until the outer shell came off in his hand.

Meanwhile, Perkins stood watching the activities of the two, his previous indignation set-aside for the moment.

Burton, holding the circular plastic shell of the smoke detector in one hand, stepped down to the floor. "How'd you know?"

The sergeant shrugged matter-of-factly. "The note warned of embarrassing footage, right? This is the only vantage point in the room to get a good look at the whole office."

"What? What is it?" Perkins walked over to the officers, curious as to what they'd found.

Burton inclined his head heavenward, while the sergeant quirked a brow. "You're being watched, Mr. Perkins. Any idea who would do such a thing to so upstanding a citizen as yourself?"

DOUBLE 'O' DAMES

Reese ambled toward the pounding of her front door, sluggish. Her blonde ponytail hung askew and the ever-present bangle bracelets rattled like alarm bells.

"Justa minute!" She traversed the darkened obstacle course that was her living room, arrived at the door swearing and hastily massaging a bruised ankle.

She flung the door open to find a black-spandex-clad Charisma angled against the threshold, tapping her foot impatiently. "About time, I was growing roots in the asphalt." Charisma took note of the bedraggled woman before her. Definitely a Bette Midler day. "Wow. Rough time at work, huh?"

"Oh, no rougher than usual when the police turn up to question me about my best friend's possible involvement in a blackmail scheme…and yours?"

Charisma rolled her eyes and stepped past the taller woman. "No need to get snippy. You know, rhetorical question and all that."

Reese closed the door, flipped on the overhead, and followed her to the couch. "So, how'd dinner go with the folks. Satan and Pike come to blows?"

"Not even close."

"What's the damage, then?"

"You're not going to believe this. Hell, *I* don't believe it. Pike has a new best friend. Him and Satan rub together better than peanut butter and jelly."

"Whoa, didn't see *that* coming. You serious?"

Charisma nodded for emphasis. "As a heart attack. Him, Pike and daddy are going to a Rockets game in a coupla weeks. Pike gets free tickets."

"It's not basketball season. You must mean a 'Stros game."

"Rockets, Astros, Oilers…it's all the same to me."

"The Oilers left Houston years ago, Charisma. We're the Texans now."

"Whatever."

"Ok, *not* a fantasy football fan." She muttered.

"Say, speaking of PB&J, you got any snack food around here. I'm hungry."

"Jeez, you're *always* hungry." Reese pulled a face and inclined her head towards the kitchen. "Check the frig if you want fruit. Or, there's some oatmeal cookies in the jar on the table."

When Charisma got up to head for the kitchen Reese eyed her outfit. "I see you're decked out in the latest B-N-E fashion."

"Yeah, as *you* should be." Over her shoulder, Charisma eyed Reese's rumpled Capri pants and matching iridescent top, that had 'Beware: Bad Mood Rising' scrawled diagonal across the bust in fuchsia bling. "Calam is counting on us. I'd advise putting on something less…blinding …and don't even *think* of stepping out of here with those cowbells around your wrists."

"Nag, nag, nag…" Reese loped off the couch like a lazy coyote. "Do me a favor, will ya, look under the sink and grab a couple of flashlights while I change. And I hope you have a tote bag or something to put the junk in cause I don't."

"My Prada backpack is in the car. It's a lightweight

special for the shoplifter on-the-go. Tre' chic."

"I bet."

Ten minutes later Reese re-emerged, shroud in black hip-huggers, matching black stretch-knit T, and bangle-less wrists. "Do we have time for coffee? I was up late last night."

Charisma stood, her face full of cookie. "Yeah, there's a Starbucks on the way. Let's go."

"Right behind you."

"You think I could get a muffin or something there?"

* * *

"This is a waste of time." Burton stood alongside his training officer, Sergeant Willis. Together they gave the office building housing Ross-Warner Attorneys at Law a quick walk-around. "If I may be so bold…eh."

"By all means, enlighten me." Willis gestured graciously. He had the look of man giving his lesser cohort the opportunity and the length of rope to hang himself.

"Sir, I think our time would be better spent questioning the most probable suspect, Ms. Lowe. By now, she knows we're investigating and she's a smart woman. Why would she turn up here tonight and give herself away?"

"Burton…"

"Sir?"

Willis shook his head on a deep sigh. "Burton, I like you. So, I'm gonna be nice enough to point out the flaw in your theory before you go embarrassing yourself in front of anyone else."

"Thank you, Sir. Appreciate it."

"First thing, never jump at the lure that's given you. The most-likely suspect is not necessarily the guilty party so it's important to keep an open mind. But you are right about one thing, by now it's gotten back to whoever wrote the letter that we've been making the rounds. But what he or she doesn't know is that we found the camera in the victim's office this afternoon. Now, if *you* were the blackmailer and you knew the cops were poking around in the vicinity where you'd illegally hidden a surveillance camera, what would be your first thought?"

"To get rid of it before...ahem, Sir, I see your point."

"I thought you would."

"So, we're staking out the building to see who shows up to take down the cameras?"

"Exactly. I sent Nate and Sterling to screen the probables."

"Good plan, Sir."

"So glad you finally approve."

* * *

Lucifer leaned over the simmering pots on the stove, tossing a pinch of oregano in one, sniffing the aroma of another, and turning the burner down low on a third. He always managed to keep his cool, whether it be slaving over an elaborate meal in the kitchen or fending off legal lotharios at the office. Meanwhile, Calamity idled around the apartment, nerves frayed like the fringes of a cardigan she'd tried on at the Shabby Chic Boutique. It just wasn't fair that he could be so calm while she narrowly restrained herself from clawing the furniture.

She'd already tripped over Sasha twice, and changed clothes three times. Still, she couldn't relax. After the third outfit, she called it quits, rationalizing that since she would be naked soon it really didn't matter too much which outfit she wore. She sported a knee-length fitted skirt and a billowy button-down blouse that was business in the front and a sheer party in the back. She'd been too keyed up to deal with her hair, so she'd simply parted it down the middle and done a French braid on each side.

"So..." Calam traipsed over to the kitchen and peered in at the feast he prepared. "What are we having tonight...eh, besides sex, that is."

The corners of his mouth rounded in a fond smile. "Nervous?"

"No, not at all. Whatever gave you that impression?"

He turned on her with elevated brows. "Calamity, if you've changed your mind—"

"NO! Eh…no, it's not that." She averted her eyes to the floor, watching Sasha twirl around her ankles purring.

Luce, clad in a sexy all-black ensemble, stepped away from the stove. "Well something's got you jumpy. Maybe we should talk about it."

"It's not something I care to discuss." This she stated in stiff declaration, a tone easily mistaken for haughtiness.

"Calamity." He frowned down at the top of her head and brushed passed her into the dining room to check the place-settings on the table. "Just what is it you think is going to happen tonight? I mean, other than the standard mechanics."

She hunched up her shoulders without looking up at him. "How should I know? I've never slept with you before."

"I wouldn't go so far as to say that." He turned briefly from his task to flash her a devilish grin. "Nothing's happened other than sleep before."

"Ahem, you know what I mean." She gestured with impatience and resumed walking until she met the couch and sat down. This, however, did little to relieve her jitters. "Quit making fun, you knew what I meant."

Luce frowned again. "Hey, don't pick a fight with me just because you're–" He paused to study her tense body language and sensed the seriousness of the situation for the first time. There was more amiss than her usual 'calamitous' brand of neurotics. She wasn't nervous, she was scared…of him. Dinner forgotten, he made a beeline for the couch and sat next to her. "Hold up, why *are* you so panicky?"

In a conspicuous jittery movement, Calam shifted over to put some space between them. "Why shouldn't I be—"

Not letting her distance herself from him, Luce shifted over to close the gap. "Look, I know I'm a large man, and you're a small woman, but you and I both would be hard-pressed to find significant others comparable to our respective sizes. *This* can work. We'll just have to be careful, that's all. I promise, I won't hurt you."

"It's not *that*." She shrugged off the idea like an ill-fitting dress, but then thought better of it. "Well, maybe it is a little, but—"

"Will it help to know that there haven't been so many before you that you need to worry about your performance level...if that's what's got you twisted up in knots?"

"No...well now that you mention it, *yes*...and no...uh...not that..."

As she struggled for two coherent words to rub together, sudden enlightenment struck him. "Calamity, you *have* done this before, haven't you?"

Righteously indignant, she shifted away from him again, this time all the way to the edge of the couch and shot up to her full five foot two inches. "Yes! Of course I have."

Luce followed her movements with considering eyes, closing the gap so that he sat just adjacent of where she now stood beside the sofa. He caught both of her hands in his much larger ones keeping his hold firm but not painful. But, there was little chance of escape. "It wouldn't take much to prove that you're lying...*if* you were lying, that is."

"Are you calling me a liar, Mr. Phoenix?"

"I said *if*, Ms. Lowe."

"It was a very dubious *if*."

He arched a brow at her. "This is a very *iffy* conversation....and despite the fact of it leading to the postponement of certain activities, I can't help but be intrigued by the possibility."

"Let go." Not quite liking or trusting him at the moment, Calamity made a move to extricate herself from her makeshift prison when he tugged her forward sharply enough to topple her against himself.

"Lucifer!"

"In for a penny, in for a pound." Before she realized what he intended, Calamity found herself atop his lap in a very compromising position. He purposely situated her astride him so that he had shockingly easy access to her eh...inner self. To Calamity's further annoyance, she felt hands meandering along her thigh, bunching her skirt upward. Arresting his probing digits with hers, she made a point of digging her nails into his skin. She glared up at Luce's mischievous mien.

"Try it and you'll get a knee to the groin that you won't soon forget." She threatened.

"I will consider myself warned."

Calamity wasn't quite sure herself if her threat was serious or not. It felt like a game perhaps designed to put her at ease, an ice-breaker before Luce forced her to discuss the serious business of her virtue. She didn't kid herself. Now that he suspected the truth, he'd want to hash out all the angles. Luce never glazed over important issues, no matter how embarrassing or complicated they were. There would be a talk and he wouldn't take her to bed until he was satisfied the matter had been resolved.

As it happened, he never got a chance to defy her challenge or initiate the talk. A knock on the door brought their antics to an abrupt halt.

Saved by the bell. Calamity exhaled a deep sigh, not quite sure if she was relived or disappointed. Perhaps a little of both.

Luce extricated himself from the couch and stood for a moment to straighten his clothes. Between the time it took him to right himself and cross the living room to the front door, a swifter, more forceful knock sounded. With his hand on the knob, he turned just his head around and mouthed 'To be continued'. The words, though not vocal, rang with a certain promise that their previous interlude would not go unfinished.

Their visitors, two uniformed police officers, effectively nailed the coffin lid on the moment. Calamity stiffened.

Luce addressed the twosome. "May I help you?"

"Lucifer Phoenix?"

"That's correct."

"I'm Officer Sterling. We need to speak with a Calamity Jones Lowe. She is living at this address, is she not?"

"Yes, Ms. Lowe is a friend and co-worker of mine. I'm also acting as her legal counsel. What is it you wish to speak with her about?"

"The attempted blackmail of Charlie Perkins. We understand that Mr. Perkins has recently accused Ms. Lowe of a physical assault."

Luce waved the officers inside, shut the door and came round to stand next to Calam who was too nervous to do anything but remain seated on the couch. The officers stood a few feet away just beyond the coffee table, one with what looked to be a standard letter-sized writing pad tucked under his arm.

"Is Ms. Lowe under investigation gentleman?"

Officer Sterling shrugged in a non-committal gesture. "Not exclusively. Just standard operating procedure." He then addressed her. "Ms. Lowe I understand that you are under a restraining order that legally forbids you to come within a hundred feet of your boss' person, property, or place of work. Have you in a way violated that order in the past twenty-four hours?"

Calamity glanced up at Luce. He nodded without hesitation, giving her the go-ahead to answer. "No, I've been here all day today."

"And yesterday?"

"I eh, was out and about a little. I had some errands to run."

"What kinds of errands?"

"Average errands. Post office, drug store, trip to my

parent's house, that kind of thing."

"Can you give us a schedule of your movements?"

The silent nameless officer unfolded his arms for the first time and bent to sit the blank pad in front of her.

Agitated, Calamity eyed the paper but made no move to comply. Instead, she ran her hands over her hair. "Look, you might as well know, I can't account for every single second of yesterday. I went a lot of places, made stops, and whatnot. My nerves are a little frazzled lately. You're just going to have to take my word for it. Yes, I have motive and probably opportunity too, but that doesn't mean I did it."

"Fair enough but let me ask you this, Ms. Lowe…would you be willing to provide us with a sample of your handwriting? I'll be straight with you and admit that's what we had in mind anyway. It's completely voluntary and it would be the quickest and easiest way to eliminate you as a possible suspect."

"The note was handwritten?" Calam again shifted her gaze to Luce, who nodded.

"If you're innocent, it'd be a cinch to clear you through handwriting analysis. Just write what I tell you on the pad. We'll take it back to the lab, have it analyzed and clear this whole thing up in a day or so."

Luce spoke for the first time since the 'questioning' started. "We'll want to see a certified report from the hand-writing expert, of course."

"Of course." Sterling assured them, nudging his partner to do the same. The mute officer, nodded, and slid the pad closer in her direction. He further extracted a pen from his pocket and extended it to her as if it were a peace offering between long-bitter enemies.

Calamity eyeballed the pen, then took a turn sizing up the man who held it. His blank slate expression aroused her suspicions. In fact, Calamity couldn't think of ever having seen a face that inspired less trust than his did. She forced herself to extend a hand and accept the pen from him, all the while battling an irrational fear that the simple act somehow equipped the enemy with more ammunition to fire against her. "Ok, sounds simple enough. What'll I write?"

* * *

"No, take a right." Reese re-directed her partner-in-crime with a brisk tilt of her head.

"This place is like a maze. All these hallways look exactly the same." Charisma complained. "I don't see how anyone finds their way around."

"I know. I've been working here for two years and I still make a wrong turn every once in a while."

They fell into a comfortable silence and continued down the corridor. The charcoal-tinged marble walls and dim lighting lent a palpable tomb-like quality to the silence. Charisma paused to cast an apprehensive glance over her shoulder. She eyed the empty hallway and darkened office suites looming on either side, shifting the tote to her opposite arm.

"What?"

"Nothing." Charisma shook off the feeling and quickened her pace. "Let's just hurry up so we can ditch this joint. It's totally creepy at night."

"You're thinking about it all wrong." Reese chatted, with a flip of her bangle-less wrists. "You have to learn to accentuate the positive. We're not creeping around a labyrinthine office building in the dead of night. Think stylish secret agents…on a difficult case…one that requires crack-shot timing, nerves of steel, and a kicking wardrobe designed exclusively by Italy's finest. Of course, we've teamed up with a couple of gorgeous leading men in a joint task force. They're completing their leg of the mission and they'll meet back up with us at the rendezvous point."

Charisma warmed to the picture the taller woman

painted, anything to calm her nerves. "What are our aliases? If we're secret agents, then we have to have cool names."

As they turned the last corner and approached the door leading to Calamity's office, Reese pondered the possibilities. "How about you be Emily O'Hara and I'll be Chase Bourne?"

"Eh, they sound like a bad sketch on Saturday Night Live."

"Yeah well, it's hard to be creative under pressure. You think you can do any better, knock yourself out." Reese unlocked the office and the two slipped inside, flipping the light switch as they crossed the threshold.

"What about something with more of a menacing tone, like... Torch and Blade."

Reese shook her head. "May I suggest something a little more 'double oh seven' and a little less 'South Central LA'."

"Whatever you say, *Chase*."

Reese opened her mouth to retort just as her hand reached out to grab at the now empty space on the third shelve of the bookcase situated behind the main desk in her friend's office. "What the hell, where is it?"

Charisma crowded in behind her, "It's not there?" She scanned the area, the remaining shelves on the bookcase and the surrounding floor. She even pulled back the desk chair to peer underneath. She straightened to find Reese staring at her with incredulous eyes.

"Unless you see something I don't, the picture frame is gone, and with it the camera hidden inside."

Charisma held up her flattened palm, giving much attitude. "Don't give me that look. I was just checking every possibility. The cleaning crew could have knocked it off the shelf or it could have fallen and gotten kicked under the desk while they vacuumed the carpet. Rule number four: Exhaust all avenues."

"Maybe let's go check the smoke detector in Perkins

office." Reese suggested.

A few minutes later, in the inner office, as the two stood on either side of Perkins' desk staring up at the circular remnant of double sided foam adhesive on the ceiling Reese asked in a distant voice, "So, can we panic now or did you want to browse underneath the desk first?"

"Alrighty then, damage control." Charisma swung into action, pulling a frozen-in-panic Reese with her through the two offices and back into the corridor. "First thing we need to do is get the heck outta Dodge. Then we need to touch base with Calamity. There could still be a rational explanation for this."

"Really?" Reese clung to hope. "You think so?"

"Of course not. We're totally screwed, but it helps with the panic reflex if you hover at the edge of denial. Trick of the trade." Charisma headed back the way they'd come at a mild jog, dragging along her sister's friend in one hand and her Prada bag containing the lone nanny cam they'd been able to locate. She skidded to a halt at a turn.

"Reese! A little help here. Which way to the main foyer?"

The other girl mutely pointed left, and they took off in that direction. Minutes later, they stood in the elevator on their way to the ground floor.

"Hey, bangle girl. Snap out of it. We got things to do and if you'll pardon the cliché...time is of the essence. Make yourself useful please and get Calam on the phone while I think of a place to dump this camera. Rule five: shred the evidence."

Reese nodded, embracing the instruction like a lost child. "Of course, good idea." She hit the elevator button for B2. "There's a dumpster on the basement level, several actually, that they empty the paper shredders into for disposal of sensitive information." She whipped her cell phone from her waist clip. "I can't get a dial tone on this darn thing. Must be the elevator. We'll have to wait 'till we get outside."

Charisma shuddered. The basement probably doubled as a set for slasher movies. "No time. One of us *really* needs to warn Calamity that her plan has gone sideways."

"*Or*, you know what we *could* do?" Reese shrugged as she continued to tinker with her cell. "Toss the junk in the lobby trash can and floor it outta here. As soon as we hit the door, I'll try Calam again."

"Yeah, let's do that." Charisma hit the ground floor button to forestall their descent. When the doors opened on to the main lobby, the two darted out at a jogger's pace. Charisma reached her free hand into the bag, extracted the nanny cam and stuffed it in the covered grey trashcan without breaking stride. Meanwhile, Reese was beside her gingerly checking her cell for a dial tone. They rounded a corner, gunning it for the grey double doors they'd entered through some twenty minutes before.

"Uh-Oh." Charisma started at the sight of two of Houston's Finest standing on the outside of the doors. Reese slammed into her back, dropping the cell phone. Belated, Charisma heard her gasp.

"Calamity Lowe?" One officer asked as both advanced on their quarry.

"*Charisma?*" Reese whispered, urgent, pulling none-too-gently on the back of her shirt. "What now?"

"Rule six." Charisma recognized them as the same two who'd paid her a visit at Calamity's apartment. "Deny everything."

* * *

Luce put away the last dish in the drain board, and wiped damp hands on a nearby towel. Across in the living room, Calamity stared out the curtained window on the wall adjacent to the couch upon which she sat. Dinner was a silent awkward affair, made even more so by the pink elephant sashaying around the room in a blinking neon tutu. Calamity ate but only in a perfunctory effort to avoid hunger later. The food, while expertly prepared, withered in her mouth like sawdust. Now that the meal was over, she knew it was time to face the music.

"Don't make this any more difficult than it has to be." Luce stalked straight for her, tossing aside the towel. "You know we have to discuss it. We would be irresponsible if we didn't."

"Yeah, I know." Calamity's shoulders sank as she dropped her head to stare at her hands. "I intended to tell you."

"When?" Luce closed the distance between them in three long strides and sat beside her on the couch.

"C'mere." He exhaled a long-suffering sigh when she didn't response. He picked her up and cradled her in his lap like she'd seen him do with Sasha.

"When were you planning to drop this little bomb on me? Hmm?" He stroked her back with one hand and lifted her chin with the other. His piercing obsidian eyes bore into hers like bolts into a two by four. She relaxed into the soothing warmth of his roaming hand. "When were you going to tell me, Shorty?"

"When it was too late, of course."

His hands dropped to his sides, and he collapsed back against the sofa and swore...first in English, then he trailed off in a string of Italian expletives or so she assumed from his tone as the words spewed forth. Calam didn't dare move or speak. After a moment, he ran a hand over his face and seemed to regain some poise. His arms encircled her again, resting at her waist and he held her gaze.

"Listen to me. I don't know what nonsense is rolling around in that duplicitous little brain of yours, but let's just get one thing straight. This is not a game. This is *us*, Calamity! Two people trying to get together...and we can't do that if we're not in sync on certain things. Do you hear me? I could have seriously hurt you!"

Calamity shivered at the force of his words, sensing that they were at a very important impasse. She felt as if she stood on the edge of a precipice and any movement she made or word she uttered would send her tumbling head first into an unknown abyss. Whether the freefall was one of pain or pleasure she couldn't discern. Shaky and uncertain, she gazed up at him, her hands toying with the edges of his shirt.

"What are you saying?" Her voice squeaked.

"That you've got to start telling me these little secrets of yours. If it affects *both* of us, its important. I prefer knowing versus not knowing."

Her hands crept up from the bottom edge of his shirt and rested flat on his chest. She could feel the muffled throb of his heart. The smoldering heat...radiating off his body just beneath the lightweight, cotton called to her. She yearned for the conversation to end. "What is it you want to know?"

"Anything. Everything." Luce shifted her closer, forcing her hands to fall away as his came up to rest just under her arms. The thumbs of each hand branded her skin through the sheer fabric of her blouse. He skimmed the pads of his thumbs back and forth over the sides of her torso just under her arms. "Start with 'why'."

Calamity sucked in a hiss of breath, distracted by the lazy stroke of his fingers...Oy! She paused to consider, not so much deciding what to tell him as she was contemplating his reaction. "Why have I been living like a nun or why I didn't tell you about it?"

"Both. I'm an inquisitive guy."

"Well...my eh, *inexperience* is nothing to do with my Christian beliefs, or the pact that Charisma and I made when we were sixteen." She broke off when Luce leaned in to nuzzle her neck, his five o'clock shadow brushing against her skin...the brawny scent of his cologne filling her nostrils. "Oh...al-although...I am, eh...was raised Baptist."

"Go on, I'm listening." He whispered near her ear, just before sliding a hand up the column of her neck to tilt her head further back. He exerted the tiniest pressure to arch her back in a pose so suggestive that it reminded her of one those Calvin Kline Cologne commercials with frolicking lovers cavorting about. A gasp escaped her as he nibbled at her neck and shoulder with little biting kisses and licks. Her hands came up of their own fruition, and caged his head against her.

"Its...not fear of physical intimacy or lack of emotional commitment or...any of those tired catch phrases Oprah and Dr. Phil...go on and on about. It's eh..." she hesitated, wondering if she could truly trust him with her deepest confession, a secret she hadn't even told her twin.

"It's...what?" He prompted, as he went to work on the buttons of her blouse.

"I've....I never actually... *wanted* to sleep with anyone before I met you. I... I thought...I worried that maybe there was something wrong with me. I mean, I'm twenty-sex...eh, seven, twenty-seven." She finished the last sentence in a haze, her train of thought wavered more with each delicious brush of his lips, each possessive graze of his fingertips, and burn of stubble...

The kisses stalled out just above the now gaping vee of her blouse. She glanced down at it, her mind a bit fogged over. "Luce..." She raised her head, bemused.

He found and held her face in both hands. His intense ebony peepers melted into a devil's smile. "You worry about the oddest things. C'mere."

Calamity leaned forward shyly, her mouth meeting his in a promise of passion. Her eyes drifted closed as she surrendered to the primal lure of his heat.

* * *

Calam had no idea if she did everything right...but Luce certainly had. Her first experience far exceeded the jumble of superficial expectations she'd collected over the years from cheesy soap operas and silly romance novels. She lay

217

atop him, cheek pillowed on his chest, body nestled under his wing. She couldn't quite wrap her mind around the experience.

She should be happy...weren't people happy *after*? Luce had been so hot and sensual, possessive yet also careful, touching her, gentle but searing and relentless...until at last he was everywhere at once...not just her body, but inside her heart, her mind, and her thoughts.

It was...*dangerous*—was the word that popped unbidden into her mind. Being with him consumed her body and mind. For the short time they'd been joined, she dissolved a little, felt possessed, like she no longer owned herself. But what if he didn't feel the same? He'd had other women, probably countless others. She could be one among a *herd*...unremarkable to him, indistinguishable from *them*.

Calam's world had shifted on its axis. The moment they joined and he caressed her face as if she were the only person in his world...whispering to her as he moved...some in English, some in Italian...soothing words, endearments, sexy compliments when she did something he liked. He ruined her...for any other man. Lucifer branded his mark on her, she was his, now and forever. Gawd, this is dangerous. What if...

"Lucifer?" Calam wiggled against him, her thoughts midways between bliss and panic, her fingertips a-tap on his chest.

"Hmmm. Yeah." He rumbled low and groggy.

"Exactly how many heel marks do you have in your ceiling?"

He tipped his head up to impale her with a 'What-the-hell' stare, one brow jacked aloft. "Excuse me?" The unexpected question jarred him fully awake.

Uh-oh, flag on the play! Lighten it up, quick. The last thing she wanted was another airing of her thoughts. One *heart-to-heart* was enough for the night.

"No details please. Just the number will suffice." She

backpedaled, kissing his chest. "It's only fair."

He shrugged, wrapped one sinewy arm around her, and snuggled back down. "Three. Including you."

No way. He *has* to be lying, right? Calamity shot up, taking the sheet with her. "Is that the actual number or are you low-balling it to pacify me?"

Luce reclined back against the headboard, unabashed by his own nudity. He tracked her through slit lids, wondering if she realized that the idea of pealing away the wrapped sheet from her petite little frame aroused him almost as much as their previous loveplay. She reminded him of his cat Sasha, the way she'd purred and keened beneath him.

"I prefer quality, not quantity." He growled, "C'mere."

HOT MESS ON A PLATTER

Charisma seethed in the back seat of the police car, hands cuffed in front of her, fingers a' tap on her pants leg. She glared at the backs of the two officers through the inch-thick partition.

"I am *soooo* going to sue."

A bangle-less Reese riding shotgun hastened to hush up her irate mutterings. "Shhh! If we tick them off, things could get a lot worse."

"Easy for *you* to say." She spewed back, unrepentant. "You're not trussed up like a downed-calf on cowboy night at the rodeo."

"Whoa, back up off the attitude." Reese held up a reproachful hand. "I'm also not the one who opted to leave my ID at home."

Charisma retorted through clenched teeth. "Given our agenda for the evening, I thought it best to travel light. Do you think Bonnie and Clyde had a carry-on?"

Reese cocked a brow askew. "Eh, would this be the same Bonnie and Clyde who died in a hail of gunfire?"

"Everyone's a comedian." She scoffed, under her breath. "Travel light. That's all I'm saying."

"Oooh, is that rule number seven?" Reese retorted.

Her tone, wired with barbs.

"No, smart-ass, just common sense."

The big-haired blonde opened her mouth to response, only to hesitate. "Hmm."

Charisma's tight expression relaxed a bit. "What?"

"*Is* there a rule seven?"

"Yeah." She admitted with a good-natured snort. "Lawyer-up."

Despite their being in the back of a police car with incarceration staring them in the face, Reese grinned. "Seriously, are you making these up as we go along?"

"No. These are the actual tenets that my sister, the conspirator, lives by." Spent, Charisma's exasperation faded. Instead, a frown creased her brow as worry set in like a hovering cloud. "What are we gonna do?"

Reese's expression mirrored her own. "Do you think if we called up Satan he'd represent us? I mean, it is kind of a conflict of interest seeing as we got nicked breaking into the firm he works for, but he has a soft spot for you and Calam."

Charisma cringed. If they pulled Luce in, that would mean throwing her sister under the bus. Of course, once the police realized their mistake, they'd be knocking at Satan's door next anyway. "Luce is the only lawyer I know. And since the three of us are about to be in a whole lotta trouble either way, I say we invite him to join the party."

"Excellent idea. I concur."

* * *

Calamity inhaled a steadying breath. She was having a devil of a time trying to slip out of bed without disturbing Luce or his pudgy calico cat. Her royal highness had chosen to nestle against Calamity's torso after they'd fallen asleep. She'd have to take the beast with her, she supposed or risk the cat bellowing out a protesting meow. She eased Sasha into the crook of her arm and slid them towards the edge of the bed. Calam landed with a thump, paused, listened, and then glanced back to double-check. Still good.

Yikes...a wintry blast of air wafted over her bare essentials. Calam forced herself not to reach for the sheet. She couldn't take the risk of waking Luce, so she tiptoed into the living room, furball on board, in her birthday suit. Sasha yawned a lazy stretch and re-nestled into the crook of her arm, burrowing talon-like claws deep into the soft flesh of Calamity's side. Agggghhhh! She bit the inside of her mouth, screaming silently. Sheesh, Calamity thought, the things I do for love.

She scanned the darkened room and spotted a shadowy shape that resembled her purse. It sat atop the coffee table, half-covered by discarded clothes. Bingo. Her cell should still be clipped to the side pocket. Next up, cat-detach surgery. She pried the right claw loose and then the left. After much grimacing and a low growl of protest, she shook the furball loose. Ever the fickle feline, Sasha gave her the cold shoulder and curled up on the far end of the couch.

Anxious to hear good news from Reese and Charisma, Calam dove a hand into the pile on the table, fishing around for her cell. She snapped it off the side of her purse and used the penlight app to illuminate her surroundings enough so she could find...ah, that'll do. She grabbed Luce's discarded shirt with one hand and dialed with the other, struggling to get the massive dump of fabric over her head. Being naked in bed was one thing, but lounging around the living room like a nudist was quite another.

Her sister's phone rang and rang...*and rang*. Crap! She left a message and tried Reese, batting away the overlong sleeves impeding her progress. Again, a long series of rings...no answer. She groaned, as she left a second message. Where were they? Why hadn't one of them texted her? Surely, they were done taking down the cameras by now. She eyed the time on her phone. It was almost one o'clock in the morning!

As if in answer, the landline broke the silence with its shrill ring. The second shrill brought with it the telltale rustle of sheets from the bedroom. Damn. Luce was either awake or soon would be. As the phone rang a third and a fourth time, she stalled, not sure if she should answer it…or not. She was, after all, a guest. Then, her suspicious female mind took over. *Who* would be calling him at one in the morning anyway?

"Calamity?!" He barked her name, and she heard more rustling. The bedroom light switched on just before he appeared in the doorframe wrapped in a sheet. His gaze settled on her. She just did make out his perplexed frown in the dim light leeching in from the bedroom.

"Calamity? What are you doing sitting here in the dark? And why didn't you answer the phone?"

"I…" don't know…she almost admitted. She didn't know what do to…what to say…how she was supposed to be, react. She was scared and confused after what they had just shared and why the hell was someone calling him at one in the morning?! Relax. She needed to relax, she told herself. She could ill afford an emotional meltdown right now.

The landline screamed again.

She winced, "I…eh, was just about to get that."

Luce didn't wait for an explanation but treaded over to palm the phone. "Hello? Yes…Yes, I'll speak with her…I assume Ms. Lowe's sister is there too?"

"Is that Reese and Charisma?" Calamity scampered over, hovering as he spoke.

Something's wrong, she thought. His tone morphed into the brisk, borg-like calm she recognized as his 'damage control' voice. He asked an increasingly alarming string of questions, and she rushed to hand him a pen and pad when he gestured as if writing.

"Calm down, Ms. Martin, I think you're jumping the

gun...That is unfortunate but no one's been convicted of anything just yet...Put Mrs. Tate on the phone will you please? Mrs. Tate, tell me what happened...Just give me the short version."

"Convicted?" Calamity mouthed, horrified. Her eyes shifted back and forth as a handful of dire scenarios flashed across her mind.

Luce's focus didn't waver. "Don't say anything else. I mean it, nothing. And please impress upon Ms. Martin the need to keep her wits about her. Even though she wasn't arrested, the police still reserve the right to do so if she should say anything incriminating. The sergeant cannot compel a suspect to answer any questions until he or she has proper legal counsel...I'll be down there as soon as I can...Certainly, I will tell her."

"Tell me what?" Calamity demanded the second he hung up the phone. "What's happened? Where are they?"

Luce delayed his answer long enough to jot down a few more details on the note pad. When he did acknowledge her inquires, it was in his most impassive of tones. "The police have arrested your sister and are holding your friend for questioning. The two of them called to enlist my legal services. Incidentally, they also told me to warn you that there is, at present, a warrant out for your arrest or there soon will be as soon as I can prove that the police have the wrong twin."

Calamity cringed, but replied with all the dignity she could dredge up under the circumstances. "Those Rat Bastards! Jail is no place for a woman in her delicate condition. Chrissy's not having more nausea, is she? Did she say?"

Luce shook his head. He wasn't impressed by her stall tactics. "That makes *twice* this week that you've been wanted by the police. Tell me, how does such a little woman manage to keep up so much trouble in such a short space of time?"

"And why do you just assume that all this is my fault?"

She demanded, peeved.

"I've seen you in action, Calamity. You flirt with disaster the way other women flirt with a second dessert. And I'm not willing to bet my career on the odds that you're *not* mixed up in this latest legal nightmare. Your sister and your best friend were discovered on the premises of Ross-Warner, after hours–" She squirmed as he ran down their predicament. Geez, she hoped it wasn't as bad as he made it sound.

"–They have no reasonable explanation for their presence, or so I assume since they were detained. Your sister was not only detained but arrested, on suspicion of criminal intent as she is identical in appearance to a woman not allowed within a hundred feet of the property line."

She backed away, not quite meeting his eye...rationalizing. "So. What does that prove? Reese could be working on some sensitive material and Chrissy is *not* me. If the police knew that—the second I tell them, I mean—they're gonna drop this nonsense and let her go."

"Oh, did I forget to mention that the police discovered two hidden cameras on the premises? Coincidentally, one in *your* office and the second in Perkins' office. And the crime lab is probably dusting them for prints as we speak."

She winced and turned her back to him. She took several agitated steps seeking an escape from the nasty truth. It would probably take an act of congress to get them out of this mess. "I didn't mean for it to end up like this. Please understand—"

"Spare me, Calamity." He snatched the sheet away from his body and tossed it aside as he stalked to the bedroom, a panic-driven Calamity hot on his heels.

"Luce! Luce wait!" She launched herself at his arm in a futile effort to stop his progress, but it was like trying to stop a stampeding elephant. "What are you going to do? Lucifer, please don't. I forbid it!"

Her words hit a brick wall and bounced off without a scratch. Scared and desperate to regain control of the situation, Calamity grasp at the first thought that popped into her mind. "You're fired! Do you hear me? You're not my lawyer anymore."

Luce came up short at the closet and turned. Frightened and teary-eyed, she stared up at him a silent plea on her trembling lips. Don't take it out on them! Please.

"You didn't take all the camera's down, did you? You've been lying since day one. What are you so afraid of that you can't trust me? You, who would take me into your body but not your confidence." As if remembering the smoldering encounter they'd just shared, he swore.

Sniffling and wiping tears, she took a deep breath to collect herself. "I meant what I just said. I don't want you involved anymore. Reese and Charisma are my responsibility. I can handle this."

"Don't change the subject. You could have and should have damn well told me the truth! Anytime during the last two weeks, you could have come clean, including during our conversation about secrets and clearing the air. What the hell are we doing *here* if you don't trust me? Calam, why wouldn't you let me help you *my way*?"

For the first time since their argument began, Calamity noticed his nakedness. His most private asset had risen with his temper. In spite of the tension rending the air, her emotional upset and her worry at her sister's predicament, Calam was perversely amused by the knowledge that he could still want her even in the midst of his rage. Who knew spatting with one's significant other could be good for the sex drive. Now, she understood the concept behind 'make-up sex'…if bickering was a turn-on, her mind boggled at how a heart-felt apology might affect him.

"Ahem, you should get dressed." Calamity gestured to the flag already at half-mast.

"Answer my question." But he wasn't letting her off the hook that easy.

"Fine. Charisma's my sister and Reese is my best

friend. You're just...you're..." She fumbled over the words. Her voice wobbled, deserting her. He was *everything* to her...and the knowledge frightened her half out of her wits. "You're not *my* anything, not really. Neither of us is *vested* enough yet to trust each other."

"What the *fuck* are you talking about?! I just *di-vested* you of your virginity!" He roared, flailing a thick sinewy arm towards the still-rumpled scene of the crime. "I think that's about as *vested* as you can get."

"Rewind two weeks. Put yourself in my shoes. I didn't know you that well. You're a lawyer, and ultimately you were trying to get into my pants."

"I was trying to have a relationship with you. I do not make a habit of 'getting into anyone's pants'." He spat out the words as if they were abhorrent to him. "Like I said, I prefer quality not quantity."

"Fine." She conceded. "But tell me this...If the situation was reversed, would *you* have trusted *me* to help you *my way*?"

"*Hell* no. But I wouldn't have lied about it either. I also wouldn't have dragged my sister and my best friend into some illegal, cock-eyed scheme to get even. And I sure as hell wouldn't have taken you to bed with all that unfinished business hanging over my head." His voice tapered down some. His intense sable eyes bore into her, disheartened. "I wouldn't have wanted to ruin things between us that way."

Damn! She'd really hurt him. "I didn't lie exactly—" Calamity hastened to clarify, wiping a straight tear in the process.

"Yeah, you did."

"Have I...really ruined things between us?"

She watched him...holding her breath.

He sighed, running a hand over his sexy stubble-studded scalp. "From where I'm standing right now...I don't know."

She sniffled, bleary eyed, not sure what more she could

say. "What about Reese and Chrissy, what are you going to do?"

"I thought I was fired?" He titled his head, his tone a dangerous calm. When she opened her mouth to speak, he cut her off. "Shit. Never mind. I'm going to do my best to get the three of you out of this mess. Then you and I will sit down and have a long talk. After that if things don't work out, we'll go our separate ways. I suspect you will soon be relieved of your position at Ross-Warner, so I don't think we'll be forced into an awkward post-sex friendship. Now, get dressed and don't even think of feigning modesty…never again." He gave her a once over. As if to remind her that there was little he hadn't already seen and lavishly enjoyed.

* * *

Calamity sat in the passenger's seat, clothed in a gray-tone t-shirt and jeggings. The car ride was like the Gulf of Mexico the night before a record-breaking storm. Calm, but ominous.

Heavy in regrets and what-ifs, Calamity hadn't noticed the direction they were headed. In her mind, they were speeding towards the police station to trade herself for her sister and her friend. Instead, Luce pulled up under a flickering streetlight outside a shabby mobile home set far back from the street behind an even shabbier house. She took a long, pained glance around the neighborhood… emphasis on '*hood*'.

It resembled a subdivision of sorts, that is, if by subdivision one meant two-dozen or so dilapidated shotgun houses crowded together on minuscule lots with little grass, no yard space, and about four thugged-out hoopties per driveway.

"Where are we…Hell?"

Luce exited the car and came 'round to open her door. "I want you to stay put while I handle things with your sister." He explained, as he led her from the car towards the mobile home.

"I will not." Calamity snatched herself away from his leading hand. "I'm going to the station with you."

"No, you're not."

"*Yes*...I am, and you can't stop me." She challenged.

As if to prove her wrong, he easily swung her up and over his shoulder like a sack of feed. This time she launched a full-scale attack, kneeing him first in the stomach and then kicking a foot to his groin. He stooped in pain only a moment before he managed to nab her again on her flight back to the car. He gripped her by the shoulders and spun her around.

"Let go before I hurt you." She threatened.

"Calamity, what do you think the police will do once they realize their mistake?"

Breathing deep, she tossed her head and eyed his hands on either side of her with spiteful intent. "They'll let Reese and Chrissy go and they'll arrest me."

"No. They'll arrest you and probably Ms. Martin too just for good measure. The three of you will spend several nights in jail while they shift through the evidence to see which charges sticks to whom."

"That could happen." She admitted, reluctant.

"It's the most logical scenario under the circumstances." He reiterated, exhaling. "Do you really want to roll the dice?"

No, she didn't. As much as she would like to negate his logic, it sounded plausible and he was more familiar with the legal system than she. But she didn't have to like it.

"Calamity, please don't fight me on this. Martyring yourself is a mistake."

"Fine, whatever." She snapped, relaxing her stance.

Feeling the tension ease from her, he loosed his grip.

"Look at me." He waited for her to obey. "And promise me, you'll stay put?"

She rolled her eyes up at him, "Forget it. I'll steer clear

of the police station but I'm not promising anything else until I know who lives in this hell hole."

"My cousin." He started towards the trailer again, dragging her by the wrist.

A family member was probably safe, she thought, but then she remembered she'd already met one too many of Lucifer's cousins. "Wait, which cousin…"

As they mounted the steps to the dinky, mildew-covered trailer home, the door-like orifice in the face of the structure flung open.

"Yo, Luce, my man!" Sly halted when he spied his cousin's companion. "Aw shit, what'd you bring *her* for?"

Calamity's jaw dropped, horror-struck. "Oh, *hell* no."

* * *

"I'm going to get him for this." She muttered, waspish. Perched atop a rickety tan love seat, Calamity tried to exude indifference and dignity whilst a brown, flop-eared rabbit nibbled at her shoestrings.

There were two of the little misfits. While Neanderthal Man traipsed around the smallish living-room-area picking up, tidying, and organizing, a second, spotted-grey rabbit dogged his heels. The stalker rabbit gazed at its master, euphoric. Oh man, and she thought Sasha was bad. Sheesh. Calamity watched the flurry of movement, wondering at the neat-freak routine.

"Excuse me, Mr. Clean or whatever your last name is because I refuse to call you 'Sly' and risk being struck by lightening, but could you please pull Bunnicula here off me before he eats through my shoe."

Her host didn't look up from shoving the books upright on the makeshift bookshelf. "You ask nicely and I just might think about it. By the way, their names are Spike and Buffy. Spike is the one—"

"Gunning for a smackdown?" She shot Spike a warning eye. Calamity could see she would get no help from his master. The cretin. Who on earth kept house rabbits anyway? She scooped up Spike, walked him over to the kitchenette, and dropped him on the tile. "Look, it's been real, but I think I hear my cab outside."

"Why don't you just relax for a while." He picked up Buffy, deposited him on the shelf and moved toward her. "Luce is gonna be pissed if you bounce."

"Sorry Gilligan, but that ship has sailed. Luce is already pissed."

"Correction. He's already pissed *at you*. Me and him are square...unless he gets back here and finds out you pulled a Houdini."

Calamity tensed, on guard in case he had it in his mind to stop her leaving. "Try it. I could use the exercise."

"Whoa, calm the hell down." Anxiety laced his voice. Calamity watched in amusement as he cupped his hands over the family jewels and pivoted his hip out of the line of fire. "I got a date later. I need jimmy and the boys in mint condition."

"A date, huh." Calamity couldn't quite keep the giggles from bubbling up. "How on earth did you manage to lure some poor unsuspecting girl into letting you seduce her out of her virtue? I assume that's what this whirlwind cleaning spree and the oh-so-sensitive love bunnies are all about."

Sly snorted, and stepped away to pick up Spike, who had migrated from the kitchen to the living area. "For your information, I rescued Spike and Buffy from an abusive animal shelter. And that's some way to talk about your friend." He cuddled Spike in the crevice between his chin and shoulder, stroking the bunny fur, like a protective parent. "Maybe they should've named you 'Jaded' instead of 'Chlamydia'."

"My friend?"—what on earth did he mean by that? She racked her brain to remember the something that was nagging at the corner of her mind. The only friend she had at present...Good Grief! Calamity's jaw hit the ground like a safe as she realized the 'poor unsuspecting girl' coming over to meet 'jimmy and the boys' was her Bangle-d Blonde friend. With all that had happened in the past twenty-four hours she'd forgotten about Reese's flirtation——with disaster as Calamity saw it.

When she regained her powers of speech, Calamity gestured to his nether regions. "Well I'm sorry to bust up the party, but you might want to ice down the fellas because they won't be hitting a homer into the nappy dugout tonight."

"And *you*, the all-seeing oracle, would know this *how*?" He shot her a skeptical glance.

Calamity took delicious pleasure in bringing him up to speed. "As we speak, Luce is on his way downtown to spring your date out of lock-up. Man, and I thought *my* night sucked." She smiled wide and phony before strolling over to snag her purse. "Now, if you'll excuse me, my exile to Hell is over."

* * *

Lucifer shifted for the umpteenth time, trying not to upend the cut-rate metal table in front of him. He'd cramped his oak-tree frame into the minuscule metal chair and folded his legs at an awkward angle only half beneath the table. Here, he seethed for the past half-hour. The second he stepped into the windowless room the twosome had erupted into explanation, throwing chunks of information at him with little care for timeline or details. It didn't help that they weaved in and out of each other's narration like drunk monkeys swinging from tree to tree. He courted a migraine trying to follow the retelling. When they finished—her friend with a sigh of relief, her sister an infuriated huff—he abandoned the torturous chair and took a calming turn about the cinderblock room.

On the business end of one anxious look and a second impatient one, Luce addressed the pair of dunderheads.

"I'll have you out of here in under two hours."

Her sister stared up at him, hopeful yet also skeptical. "Just like that."

"How?" Reese wanted to know.

Luce graced them with one of his best reassuring smiles. "Calamity has a record, which means her prints are on file. The police also took yours when they processed you. A comparison of the two will be more than enough to prove that you are not your sister. I had a chat with the sergeant on my way in here."

"But we're identical." She protested.

"Forensics 101. No two people share the same fingerprints. Not even identical twins."

"Oh." Charisma blinked, owlish. "Why didn't I know that?"

Reese eyed her. "Yeah, why didn't you know that? You obviously have a criminal mind."

"Don't go getting high and mighty." The shorter woman warned. "Sergeant Willis grilled us both. You were about one twitchy answer away from trading in your bangles for manacles."

"Almost doesn't count." Reese argued, lofty.

"Ladies, please. Let's keep it friendly." Luce scolded. "First things first. I want to know everything the police don't, starting with whose idea it was to leave the cameras up."

Luce watched as the two women glanced to one another, conspiring via subliminal message no doubt. Gawd, how could he have been so stupid...so trusting.

"Calamity didn't tell you?" Her sister asked him.

"I want to hear it from you two. As your attorney, it's my job to consider all the evidence before I can plan an adequate defense."

"She doesn't need defending. You said you'd have us out of here in less than two hours."

Luce countered. "True enough, if violation of the restraining order is the only thing they've got on her. While we're on the subject, who's prints are they going to find on those cameras?"

Her sister spoke up. "Well, since you put it that way. Only Calamity's, I think. She did most of the, eh, placement planning."

"Are there any more still up?"

"All the cameras are down as far as I know. The police found two of them and Reese and I trashed the last one."

Luce turned and addressed the blonde. "Where is the receiving equipment set up? It's not—"

Reese smiled, apologetic. "Eh, is that bad?"

He groaned as a new set of problems dropped in his lap. "The police might think to get a search warrant, seeing as it's around the corner from Ross-Warner and the most logical place to look."

Charisma closed her eyes. "So, just to be clear, are we *totally* screwed?"

"They may not think of it."

"You did." Reese pointed out. "Plus, the sergeant is extra motivated to nail us since Charisma tossed her cookies all over—"

"Don't bring *that* up." Charisma snapped.

"*It* already came up." Reese quipped, with a snort. "All over the back of his squad car."

"Well, *obviously*, I'll refrain from any more rum-raisin muffins."

Luce didn't know whether to laugh or cry. "O…k. Let's all just relax. They may not have time to get a warrant and execute it before I spring you and Cell-Block Sally here. Assuming we get lucky, the first thing on your agenda is to head for home." He paused to shoot Reese a visual nudge. "As an agent of the law it is illegal and immoral for me to promote the destruction of evidence. *However*, seeing as I haven't passed the bar…yet. I can't technically be disbarred, so I am telling you that you need to do any necessary 'spring cleaning'…*yesterday*. We clear?"

"As crystal. I'm all over it with both hands and a

flashlight."

* * *

"Baby, how's about it? Saturday. You. Me. A steak....and a bottle of something red."

"Saturday's my laundry night, wouldn't you know it." Calamity tossed up her hands in mock disappointment. She gritted her teeth and shuffled a little closer to the passenger side door of the cab. Why had she let the horndog driver talk her into riding shotgun? During the forty-minute drive he had been all hands and cheesy pick-up lines. Only a well-timed shimmy at the last red light enabled her to dodge his upwardly-mobile hand. She felt like a piece of bruised fruit at the supermarket. Thank goodness they were almost there or she might have to give Mr. Wrong the 'Perkins' treatment.

"*Here.*" She exclaimed, spotting the familiar parking lot and anxious to get away from the octopus. "It's this street here."

Calamity hopped out of the car before the wheels stopped rolling. She circled around to the driver's side window just long enough to shove a wad of bills into his philandering hands and bid him a perfunctory thank-you. Purse strapped across her chest, Calamity traversed the shadowy parking lot with a quickness. Experience taught her to be swift and thorough. If Reese and Chrissy got nicked dumping the cameras, then they hadn't had the chance to deep-six the receivers at her apartment. She prayed she was still one step ahead of the law.

* * *

Luce stood in yet another windowless room, with walls the color of putty. A two-way mirror leered from behind whilst Sgt. Willis and Officer Burton pokerfaced him across the dark-wood table.

"Mrs. Tate is free to go and has the department's sincerest apologies for the misunderstanding."

The 'but' threatened like a guillotine poised above. "Let's have all of it." Luce prompted.

"Ms. Martin however must remain pending the results of a search warrant investigation and possible charges being filed. Though, she is not under arrest at the moment."

Not good news. "What was the impetus for the warrant?"

"Partial print found on the camera, ninety-eight percent match."

"She's an employee there. The camera is disguised as...what, a clock-radio or something? Contact with it was incidental."

"That may be so, Mr. Phoenix, but we have to be thorough, you understand. If the search yields nothing, then she'll be free to go."

A FEW GOOD SINS

An orchestra of overzealous crickets sawed their legs raw in the grass-bare backyard as a gyrating shadow took shape a few feet ahead of them. The murky streetlight and the curved sliver of moon fought over who could provide the most deficient lighting.

"Oh...my goodness." Charisma gasped as the undulating shadow hissed at them.

Luce skirted around the orange beast rutting atop a harassed-looking grey tabby. "Mating season." He quipped.

"I still think we should've tried."

"The search warrant was already in play. That's why Willis held her for questioning in the first place. Stalling until they could get a nod to toss the apartment."

Luce traipsed across the devil's prairie with Charisma in tow. He could almost hear the cogs turning in her mind. She must be the more contemplative of the two.

"What are you going to tell Calam?"

"The truth. She's busted. Her and Reese will be co-defendants. I'll try—"

"Stupid idea."

He stopped a few feet away from Sly's trailer. Shaking his head, he turned to eye a woman whom he could probably snap in half without breaking a sweat. "You've known me for what...a week and a half? You're pregnant. It's two in the morning. I've driven you to an area of town your sister mistook as Hell, to a portable shack the back of a rundown house. Aren't you even a little bit curious what my intentions are towards *you*?"

She peered up at him, her confusion half-concealed in shadows. "I assume you're taking me to wherever Calam is."

"Yeah, that sounds about right." He scoffed, about ready to kick himself. "Wanna know something ironic...I think *you* trust me more than she does."

"Which is exactly why we shouldn't tell her the truth."

"And you don't think she'll suspect something when the Boys in Blue turn up with a pair of size one leg irons?"

"It'll be better if it happens that way. Otherwise, she'll hatch another of her *plans*...and trust me, no one wants that. She could be sketching out the particulars of plan C as we speak."

He rolled his eyes. "Why the hell didn't you stop her after plan A hit the skids?"

"You say that as if I could. Calamity is like a force of nature." She shrugged and dropped her head. "Besides, I was bored. Calam's plans are always so much fun...in the beginning."

Gawd, he needed his head examined. "Yeah, I bet. Come on." He pressed a soft hand to the small of her back.

* * *

The relief surprised him. Sly had a major hate-jones for Calamity. Luce would have thought eyeballing her twin for the first time would touch off his gag-reflex. Instead, his cousin sagged against the door-jam.

"Shit, Luce, am I glad to see you. And before you say anything, it wasn't my fault. I don't know none of that kung fu sway." He karate-chopped the air, shooting Charisma a narrowed-eyed glare. "She threatened Spike, too. The woman is *cray*, I tell ya."

Luce felt his left eye twitching. "Sly, make sense and make it fast. My to-do list reads like a Tolstoy novel."

"Insanity." He gestured at Charisma. "She jumped ship. I assume that's why you're here, to bring her back."

Luce murmured a curse. "Sly, meet Charisma. Fate has seen fit to grace the world with a spare, which is lucky for us since you seem to have misplaced the original."

Her gaze bounced from one man to the other and then to the kitchenette over Sly's shoulder. "Eh? Does anybody mind if I have a bite to eat while you two duke it out? I'm starved."

* * *

Calam did one last panoramic sweep of the living room. Her attention fell first to the khaki-colored carpet and stylish sofa set that she'd help Reese pick out courtesy of Furniture Hut. Coffee table, light fixtures, wall sockets...clean. She eyeballed the bedroom and the kitchen as well just to be on the safe side. No wires, cords, chargers, or otherwise incriminating gadgets or gizmos remained. She mopped her brow as she let herself, bottom-first, out the window facing the ripe-for-crime blind ally behind Reese's apartment.

She'd stocked-piled the lot on the dark side of the unit, just under Reese's bedroom window. Now, what to do with it all? She frowned down at the shadowy heap of plugs, wires and recording gizmos. The tangled bundle resembled a creature of doom in a low-budget science fiction movie.

The quickest drop zone was the communal dumpster. Calamity had had enough brushes with the law to veto that option. It was too obvious a place to look. She didn't have her car so long-distance transport was out. She also didn't relish the idea of waiting for another cab. The cabbie was a potential witness, particularly if it was the same one *and* he didn't take rejection well. Pike would come if she called him but she'd rather not have the dubious distinction of getting *both* her siblings arrested in one night.

She walked along the blind ally in back of the complex, trying to reason out a suitable solution. She needed a dark, deserted place within spitting distance, close enough so she could walk carrying a load, but far enough away so that it was outside HPD's search radius.

The best contender, the neighborhood Chevron station. She didn't remember seeing a dumpster but almost all gas station convenience stores had one somewhere. Geez, the place was lit up like a Christmas tree. The price she had to pay for Reese living in a decent neighborhood. She'd incur a certain amount of attention anyway, she supposed, lurking around a closed gas station in the middle of the night with no car.

A siren broke into the medley of cricket-song and mosquito buzz, hailing the approach of Houston's Finest. Her heart seized. A future strewn with mug shots, plea-bargains and parole hearings flashed through her mind. It wasn't until the screaming fire truck and its police car escort flew past the mouth of the ally that her respiratory system rebooted. She bent and shoveled up the first armload of 'toys'. She'd have to make do with the Chevron's dumpster.

The humid breeze made her job all the more miserable. Panting like a race horse, shirt plastered with sweat rings rivaling Saturn, she shuffled down the ally, across the street and slinked around to the dark side of the station's minimart. As she pitched the first load over the side of the dumpster, her nose hairs nearly burned off under the noxious stench.

"One down, two more to go." She turned and hurried

back to get the second load.

* * *

"Where'd she go?" Luce was almost out of patience with his less than intelligent cousin. Sly held Buffy in the crook of his arm, stroking him a la Dr. Evil and Mr. Bigglesworth. He crunched up his shoulders.

"Anywhere but 'ere, let her tell it. How should I know? The bitch bounced up outta here in a cab 'bout an hour ago."

"Sly, I told you to keep her here." Luce groaned. Heaven only knew what lunacy she was up to.

"Yeah, but you didn't tell me *how*." He snapped. "She's yo girl. If *you* can't control her, what the hell makes you think *I* could?"

Damn. He had a point. Luce closed his eyes and let out a sigh.

"Luce?" The tentative female voice distracted his ire.

"Yeah." He opened his eyes to stare down into chocolate brown eyes so like Calamity's until he shook his head to remind himself who he was speaking to. He registered worry in her expression. "What is it?"

"I think I might know where Calam went."

"Where?"

"Reese's place." She cringed as she said it. "To get rid of the evidence."

"Aw shit." He turned to his cousin. "Sly, do you think you can keep *this one* here? She's much more agreeable."

"I'm going with you." Charisma insisted. "I wanna help."

"No. You will stay here even if I have to tie you down. Please. Worrying about you will only split my focus." Luce didn't wait for her answer, but turned back to his cousin.

"Sly, take care of her for me. *Don't* let her leave." He ordered. "She's eating for two, so I'll buy you some more groceries later."

"Yeah, yeah. Sure thing, Luce." He agreed, eager to help. "Whatever you say. Hey, wait, Luce..." He followed his cousin out the door, closing it behind him. "I wanna ask you something."

They stood in the darkness beneath the door's small overhang, on the steps.

"Uh, Sly..." He prompted.

His cousin shifted, uneasy. "Is she ok? I mean, you're gonna get her out, right?"

"Calamity?" Luce's browed lifted.

"Nah, man...her friend, *Reese*." He whispered the name as if national security hinged on no one learning of their conversation. "We sorta...hit it off. We were supposed to hook up tonight. But Insanity said she got nicked and all...I just. Are you gonna shake her loose or what?"

A smile tickled his lips. So, his cousin was crushing on Calamity's BFF? He saw a double date in his future. "Its on my to-do list, Sly. That's all I can promise."

"Ok. Its cool. Do yo thang. For Insanity, too. I mean, we ain't close or nothin'. But, eh, the Boss man playing slap-n-tickle at the office, that shit ain't cool."

"Oh," Luce stared hard at his self-serving, devil-may-care cousin. "I didn't realize you had an opinion about that?"

"Yeah." He ducked his head, sheepish. "Reese, she let some details slip. I ain't trying to pry. Look, handle the shit, however you were plannin' to. I got a vested interest, is all I'm sayin'. So, keep a brotha in the loop, will ya?"

"Sure, Sly." His cousin surprised him, more and more.

* * *

Laden down, Calamity begin her final trudge across the street. She froze mid-step at the muffled sound...knocking, if she wasn't mistaken. Uh-oh. The sound ceased before she could be quite sure of its origins. She waited, still as stone, muscles aching from the weight of her load. More knocking, though more like pounding this time. What were the odds that Reese had company this time of night? Zero. A loud smash and rending commotion confirmed her suspicions. Yep, that'd be Houston's Finest making a house call. She inched back into the ally behind Reese's unit. She'd have to wait them out...and hope she hadn't missed anything.

A half-hour later, she crouched under the bedroom window of Reese's apartment, her back against the wall (literally) with a tangle of surveillance gizmos on either side of her. Her bum was numb against the warm, rough asphalt and her left leg felt as if it were being impaled from the inside out by a crazed acupuncturist. Geez Louise! Its a one-bedroom flop, not a fifty-acre estate. How freaking long could it take to toss the place?

She felt around in her tote, and pulled out her cell. She preferred not to involve anyone else but it was getting late and she didn't relish waiting for another cab...especially if they sent the same over-amorous idiot that dropped her off.

--------------Text message-------------
Wednesday, 1:53 am

Pike, you awake?

---------------Text message-------------
Wednesday, 1:59 am

Am now.

---------------Text message-------------
Wednesday, 2:02 am

Need a favor.

----------------Text message-------------
Wednesday, 2:04 am

@ 2am?

----------------Text message-------------
Wednesday, 2:07 am

yeah…sorry *sheepish*

----------------Text message-------------
Wednesday, 2:09 am

All ears.

----------------Text message-------------
Wednesday, 2:13 am

Reese's place. Circle the block…text me when company leaves.

----------------Text message-------------
Wednesday, 2:16 am

K

* * *

"Mind telling me why I'm driving you to the police station at three in the morning." Her brother asked.

"The less you know….eh, the less you know." Calamity

reminded him. "Rule eight: Spare the innocents."

"That bad, huh. What happened to your lawyer friend?" He commented, disapproval apparent. "Doesn't seem like he's been much help."

"Luce did what he could, but he's restricted by the law."

"Of course, what was I thinking." He scoffed. "Calam, be careful...Ok?"

She waved away his concerns. "Chillax. It's *handled*."

He pulled up in front of the station...but hesitated making the final turn. "And you're sure, you know what you're doing? You don't want me to maybe, hang around. Give you a ride home?"

"Pike, please, just trust me. Everything is under control. Luce will be here soon."

"For the record, I don't like this." He murmured as he shifted the car in gear to turn.

* * *

Luce missed the party at Reese's. He arrived to find a uniformed-sentry standing outside the police-taped door jam of her apartment. The front door hung inside the threshold, half off its hinges. There was no sign of Calamity. The only information he could harangue from the sentry was the name of the investigating officer and the fact that the place was an official crime scene. Luce half-expected to hear the theme song of CSI voiced over in the background.

From Reese's, he made the rounds: Calamity's place, her parents' house, his own apartment...no luck. On the off-chance that she might have done the sensible thing...he even buzzed Sly. No dice, she hadn't returned. He frowned, contemplative. Where could she be? Hmmm...there was *one* other possibility.

* * *

When Pike opened the door, Luce noted that he was awake, dressed and rather blasé. He waved him inside without breaking stride back into the living room. Almost as if he were…expecting him.

"Have a seat." He invited, polite and casual, as if it were tea time. "Want a brew?"

Luce eyeballed the house's interior. Not what he'd expected. The high-end mixture of man cave and Martha Stewart gave off a life-of-leisure type sheen. Her brother didn't cover the tab for this pad with a nine-to-five, Luce concluded. No sign of Calamity though. As curious as he was, he hadn't come for a home tour or a man's night in.

"Another time." Luce, tired and not in a chatty Kathy mood, sped up to the exit ramp. "Where is she?"

"I dropped her off at the police station a little while ago." The younger man picked up a beer off the glass-top coffee table and settled himself on the charcoal grey sectional. "She said you were meeting her there. Guess you didn't get the memo."

Luce braced himself. "What did she do?"

He watched her brother take a long swig of his drink, swallowing the gulp of liquid while he studied his guest. He flicked his wrist, "Sure you don't want one? Hard cider, excellent flavor."

"What. Did. She. Do?" He demanded. Her brother's lackadaisical attitude irritated him.

A brow-rise was all the reaction he got, before Pike turned to the muted wall-sized flat-screen. "I'm pretty sure I'm not supposed to tell you that."

"Did you help her get rid of the surveillance equipment at Ms. Martin's place?"

"I picked up my sister from a friend's apartment. She may have had some luggage with her." He answered, cryptic but telling. "I didn't notice."

Figures, Luce thought. "What'd she do with the luggage?"

Another casual swig. "Its around. I forget where

exactly."

"No questions asked, huh." Luce couldn't help letting a thread of sarcasm and frustration seep into his tone.

Her brother shrugged. "She didn't want me involved. So, I'm not involved."

Ahhh…but he's keeping his eye on the situation in case it becomes necessary to get involved. He didn't say as much, but Luce was beginning to detect a light trace of concern beneath his outward indifference. "Tell me something, Pike."

He inclined his head. "Shoot."

"How far is too far?"

He abandoned the empty bottle on the glass-top and leveled a hard stare at him with eyes the same chocolate brown as his sisters. "If she asked me to hide a body, my only question is where."

Humph. Cradle to the grave devotion, just like her twin. How the devil did the hell-on-wheels woman manage to retain the martyr-esque loyalty he'd witnessed in all her friends and family? The knowledge baffled him. "How can you put such blind faith in anyone as reckless as your sister?"

Something resembling disappointment flickered in the younger man's gaze. "If you have to ask me that, then you don't know her very well." He picked up the remote to flick the sound on to the muted TV. "Shouldn't you be on your way over there to help get her out of the mess that she's gotten you into?"

And just like that, he was dismissed. "Yeah, I guess I should." Luce resigned himself, feeling as if everyone knew a secret and hadn't told him.

* * *

Calamity approached the familiar face, sitting behind his desk in the middle of a sea of similar cubicles.

"Back so soon, Ms. Lowe." Sergeant Willis reclined in

his chair, amused almost. "Sorry about the mix-up with your sister."

"Its cool. So, eh, here I am." She announced, not sure what to do next. "What now? Do you just slap the cuffs on or is there an interrogation and a second mug shot to get through first?"

"Generally, we read you your rights first, but I get the sense you're already familiar with what you can... *and can't* get away with." He gestured in a rather casual, comical way. "After that, there's fingerprinting and mug shots. And all the associated paperwork. 'Perp's allowed to make a phone call or two...lawyer, bail bondsman, priest...or whoever. Then the arresting officer will go over the charges and proceed to interrogate the 'perp."

"So, eh, I'm *the* 'perp in this scenario." Calamity cringed. Geez, didn't they have a less degrading terminology for harmless female suspects?

Willis quirked a brow at her as if reading her mind. "If *alleged* 'perp works better for you, we could go with that."

She shrugged. What did it matter anyway? "Remind me again, what I'm wanted for. I forget."

"Have a seat, Ms. Lowe, and let me get out the Christmas list." He gestured to the empty chair opposite him.

* * *

After exiting the elevator, the uniformed officer announced his intention to escort her to a 'holding cell' and indicated for her to follow him. Despite everything, she hadn't been deemed a significant enough threat to warrant hand-cuffing, thank goodness. She trailed the officer down a short over-bright hallway that ended in a large semi-circular space. He checked her in with the desk sentry, then turned and left the way they'd come. Calam fidgeted, awaiting instructions from her new 'handler'.

The stocky brunette stood and strolled towards one of

a half-dozen steel-grey doors lining the back wall. Calam supposed she should follow. The door the sentry led her to had a miniature window, but try as she might it was too high up for her to peak inside.

Her handler slid the door open and inclined her head. Calamity stepped inside and sighed in relief. Curled up on one of the benches protruding from the side walls lay a familiar face framed by mangled gold frizz...flattened from her usual bouncy blonde curls.

"Reese!"

"Calamity!"

Reese flew at her with gale-force speed. Calam felt as if she hadn't seen her in years. She barely heard the ominous clack of the cell door closing and locking behind her.

Reese broke off the hug and grabbed her by the elbows, pulling her backward onto the bench behind them.

"What are you doing here? I thought he was supposed to get me out, not let them put you in. Where's Charisma? Wait, does Satan know you're in here?" She demanded...then glanced around, lowering her voice to conspiracy level, mischief alit in her elf-green eyes. "What's cookin'?"

Calam wished she had one last trick in her bag. But the damage was collateral and it could not be managed. "I hate to bust your bubble, but *nothing's* cooking. I got arrested without much pomp and circumstance. Chris is fine, she's with Luce. If he doesn't know where I am, I'm sure he'll connect the dots sooner or later."

"Sooner rather than later, let's hope." Reese rolled her eyes. "I'm being held pending charges. What'd they get you for?"

"Oh, the usual...assault, criminal voyeurism, blackmail." Calamity tried for a smile, despite her growing unease. "I'm surprised Willis didn't toss in disturbing the peace just for giggles."

"Blackmail?!" Her friend demanded, irate. "On what evidence? I'm the one who—"

Geez. "Shhh! Please. I *know*, but *they* don't." Calamity eagle-eyed the ten-foot cube to make sure no one was the wiser, even though she was pretty certain their cell was sound proof. "This room could be wired, you know, to capture any incriminating tidbits."

"So." Reese smiled, all smug confidence and puffed chest. "Nothing they tape us saying would be admissible anyway."

"Says who?"

"Grissom on C.S.I." She boasted as if she'd deciphered the Death Sea Scrolls. "The show totally jumped the shark after he left."

"Ree-se." Calamity sighed. Reese was loveable, loyal, and a lot of laughs…but a deep-thinker, she was not.

"Don't give me that *look*." She insisted, explaining with gusto. "Its true. If you go to the Internet Movie Database, it says in the trivia section that his and Catherine's characters were based on real-life criminologists. The majority of the shop talk on the show is accurate. Even the lab equipment is fully functional. They have a guy that does research for each episode to make sure everything is as realistic as possible."

She ended her tale with a 'see, what did I tell you' expression.

"*Realistic*, not real." Calamity groaned. "Never mind. Let's just *not* say anything else that might incriminate you, ok. I'm already fish food. There's no sense in everyone going down with the ship."

"I don't know, Calam. Maybe I should just tell them the truth." Reese frowned, worry darkening her brow for the first time. "I don't mind lying if its to save my own skin, but I won't do it if you have to fry to get me off. I can just explain. Its my first offense, I'll get off easy…well, easier than *you*, anyway. You're a repeat offender."

So, she'd graduated from 'alleged perp' to 'repeat offender'. Calam wondered what folks would be calling her next week…ex-con?

"Just keep quiet. They wouldn't believe you anyway." Calam informed her. Might as well rip the band aid off, she thought. Reese would find out when they released her anyway. "I already confessed to everything. That's why they arrested me."

Reese shot her a 'WTF' look. "Luce told Chris and me to keep our traps shut. Why would you do that?"

"Well, someone had to do *something*, otherwise, we'd all be in here. The police tossed your apartment tonight. But not to worry, I *cleaned* first." Calam paused to ponder. "In fact about it, there's a tiny possibility they could still nail us. Anyway, the point is—"

"What...exactly?" She asked, hands spread in confusion. "I don't get it. I thought the idea was for no one to go to jail or get fired. Charisma is safe. You cleaned my place. No one has a clue about anything...so why confess?"

"Reese, they're having my handwriting analyzed as we speak." She explained. "Whose signature do you think they'll check next, huh?"

"Oh, I don't know...Maybe Perkins' scorned, soon-to-be-rich-off-the-divorce-settlement ex-wife or a bitter mistress, a disgruntled client, any number of other victims, who knows?" She touched her fingertips to her temple and pull at her frizzled curls. "Why would anyone think *I* blackmailed him? Even if the police had found something at my place, the most I can go down for is accessory, having conspired with you and all. At least, that's what Mr. Phoenix told me. The only reason they locked me in here is to buy time so they could do the search. He suspected as much before he left with your sister. Calamity, *you're* the obvious mastermind here and now you've gone and knitted your own noose."

"It not as bad as all that."

"Yes, it is. Unless you can retract your confession...can you?"

"No. I mean, I could but I won't." Calam insisted. She

must stay firm. "It doesn't matter. They won't be able to prove I blackmailed him because I didn't. They'll waste time trying though, and when they can't they'll drop the charges. Time will pass and they'll lose interest. They certainly won't re-start from scratch with a cold trail of dwindling evidence. Trust me, this is the best way to minimized the damage. If we're lucky, the police will conclude that I was just lying to protect you because I thought you did it."

"I *did* do it!" Reese mouthed in a frustrated whisper. "This whole mess is my fault, Calam. I can't let you do this. No way."

Calam patted her friend's hand to reassure her that there was no place for remorse and blame in their friendship. "Look, don't get it twisted. I'm not innocent, here. I did *plan* to blackmail him. You just jumped the gun a little."

Reese cringed. "Yeah, my bad. I should have waited for your ok."

"True. *But* I shouldn't have dragged you—not to mention, Chris and Luce—into my cock-eyed plan. It was selfish and stupid."

"You didn't *drag* me into anything." Reese countered. "Charisma's the one who let the cat out of the bag, and I *offered* to help. None of us are innocent. Well, except maybe Mr. Phoenix."

"There are degrees of innocence."

"And guilt." She reminded her.

"Yeah, well, I started the ball rolling. If someone has to swing, I'd rather it was me."

"Humph." A defiant Reese crossed her arms over her chest, digging her heels in. "I disagree."

"Disagree all you like. Its done."

Calam watched her friend's face crumble a little as the futility of the situation set in. "But, you'll go to jail." She wailed.

"Not necessarily. I'm innocent until proven guilty, and

there's not much definitive proof lying around. Of course, I'll probably be unemployed soon so I won't be able to afford sufficient counsel. And Luce may refuse to represent me after he gets a whiff of the charges and my confession. But, hey, I have pre-paid legal so I'm good."

"Oh geez, do you really think Ross-Warner will fire you?"

Calam gave her the 'Are kidding me?' brow. "Reese. Someone from maintenance is probably chiseling my nameplate off the door panel as we speak. No biggie. I was ready for a change anyway." She dismissed her job with a careless wave. "The most important thing is...you'll be fine. They've got nothing on you."

"Did you ever know that you're my hero?" She asked, deadpan.

Calamity cocked her head to the side. "No, but now that you mention it, you do kind of give off that Bette Midler-vibe."

Reese laughed, green eyes shining, as she leaned forward to pull a grinning Calamity into a hug.

IT'S A WONDERFUL LIE

"Ah...Lucifer Phoenix, legal counsel for Calamity Lowe and Theresa Martin. I need to speak with Sgt. Willis." Luce idled in the foyer of the police station as the officer behind the ballistic glass made a phone call.

"Sign-in, and I'll need to see a picture ID."

Luce scribbled his John Hancock on the ledger as he dug in his back pocket and flipped his wallet open, pressing it against the glass for the officer to examine.

"Have a seat and someone will be out."

Lucifer guessed that was his none-too-subtle way of telling him to moved back a ways. He obliged, but he didn't sit down. He knew from experience the lobby chairs were all form and no function.

The better part of fifteen minutes passed before a loud buzzing sound broke into his thoughts. The interior door popped open.

"Follow me." The uniformed officer led him into the bowels of the station to a familiar salt-n-pepper haired gent seated at his desk, swallowed all around by a sea of similar desks.

"Welcome back, Counselor. What can I do for you?" Willis exuded a mellow casualness that must have taken years to cultivate, Luce guessed.

This time, Luce did sit, opposite the Sergeant. "I was hoping you could help me with a little dilemma I'm having."

The Sergeant gestured in a solicitous manner. "I'm here to help in any way I can."

"I'm wondering why Ms. Martin is still being detained. Is she under arrest?"

"Nope. Just holding her for questioning." He informed him without hesitation. "Matter-of-fact, I believe she's due to be released tomorrow."

"Well, I'm here now. I can take her off your hands."

"Come back tomorrow at noon."

Luce tried a different tact, keeping his voice light and free of inflection. "Anything interesting turn up at her place?"

The Sergeant's relaxed manner ebbed into an alert carefulness. "I'm not at liberty to say."

"Look, Sergeant, let's not dance around the ring. Its been a long night." Abandoning his poker face, Luce gave Willis an exasperated mien. "Ms. Martin has done nothing to deserve spending one more second in a holding cell. You made your play with the search warrant and came up with an empty hand, otherwise, she'd be under arrest. Sure, you can legally hold her for twenty-four to forty-eight hours without filing formal charges, but why would you want to do that? She's probably scared out of her mind. Not to mention, if her employer learns of her detainment, it could jeopardize her position there. Now I am asking you, out of professional curtesy, to release her tonight."

The sergeant gave him a slow, accessing look. Luce wasn't sure what Willis hoped to glean from the scrutiny but he put a cherry on top to sweeten the deal.

"I'll owe you a favor."

That did it. The next moment his chair squeaked as he turned to beckon another officer over. "Burton! Caged bird in 2B needs to fly."

Luce watched the uniformed neophyte shut the filing cabinet, inadvertently knocking the file folders out of his other hand so that papers floated wildly all round him.

"Eh...Sir?" He stuttered.

"Burton, when you get done chasing windmills, cut Ms. Martin loose."

"Yes, sir. Ah, paperwork's gonna take at least-"

"Walk her tonight. The paperwork can wait till morning." Willis swiveled back around to Luce. "We good?"

"Getting there. Now, about Ms. Lowe."

"Not sure I can help you out with that one, Counselor."

"She under arrest?"

"'Fraid so." Willis nodded. "Assault, two counts of criminal voyeurism, blackmail. And such a likeable 'lil lady, too."

"Assault?" Luce gave the Sergeant a skeptical eye. "I think its about time we shot that horse, don't you? A second and *third* victim have come forward and filed complaints alleging workplace harassment. And I don't think he can claim that *they* assaulted him, too."

Willis shrugged his shoulders. "I wouldn't blame them. I wanted to plug 'em one myself."

"Yeah, same here." Luce admitted. "But knowing that, what makes you like Ms. Lowe as both the voyeur and the blackmailer? There's nothing specific linking her to either crime."

His languor went the way of the leisure suit. The good sergeant straightened his spine, to the squeaky protest of his desk chair. "On the contrary, there's a signed confession linking her quite specifically to both crimes."

"Excuse me?" Luce forced himself to maintain his equilibrium. It wouldn't do for him to reach for what he was given.

"Your client waived her right to counsel and signed a full confession. Claims she planted the cameras to gather blackmail material against her boss. We have no reason to refute her confession. She had motive, means, and opportunity."

"I'll want a copy of the waiver and the confession."

"Of course." He beckoned over his shoulder, without turning around.

"It will be interesting to see if the hand-writing analysis supports her claims." Luce measured his words to sound innocuous, however, the minute narrowing of the Sergeant's eyes told him that the dart didn't miss its target. After all, without some corroborating evidence, a confession, however convincing or logical, was just an unproven theory. "In the meanwhile, I'd like to confer with my client."

"I'll have her moved up to one of the interrogation suites."

Just then Burton, who had been laying in wait for a lull in the conversation, came up from behind the Sergeant. "Sir?"

"Burton, show Ms. Lowe to one of the interrogation suites when you spring her co-conspirator."

"*Alleged* co-conspirator, on whom you have no hard evidence." Luce corrected. It seemed the good Sergeant wasn't above firing a passive-aggressive dart of his own.

* * *

"Mr. Phoenix! I'm so glad you're here." Reese came bounding at him like an overzealous street vendor. "You have to get Calam out. They've arrested her."

"Ms. Martin, remember what we discussed." He leveled a quelling eye on her. "The importance of discretion."

She nodded, lowering her voice to a conspirator's whisper. "So, you got this, right?"

"I got this." He assured her, with more confidence than he felt. If he were honest, he didn't have any clue if it was even possible to put this particular genie back in the bottle.

It would depend on the specifics of her confession, what was or rather *wasn't* found at Ms. Martin's apartment, and the outcome of the handwriting analysis. Willis had been a tad too cryptic for Luce to relax. The good sergeant never actually answered his question about the search warrant's findings. Calamity would need to be either a perfect innocent or an impeccable liar. He wasn't quite sure where to place his bet. In either case, her kamikaze friend was one wild card too many.

"Do you have somewhere to go?" He asked, already distracted by the coming challenge.

"Eh, yeah, home."

Luce only half-noticed the questioning stare Ms. Martin gave him, as possible scenarios and plausible legal maneuvers hopped around in his mind like jackrabbits. "Your place is not livable at the moment. I'd prefer you didn't stay there by yourself anyway. Call Sly and tell him to pick you up. You can bunk with him."

"But it's almost four in the morning?"

"He asked about you. He's worried, in fact. Call him." Luce had already started to walk off. "And one of you hit me back with a text, so I know you made it ok."

"Yeah, sure."

"Goodnight, Ms. Martin."

* * *

Calamity paced the length of the coffin-sized room, traversing the bolted-down table and opposing chairs on either side, also bolted. She flinched at the cracked leather straps attached to the table's top, incredulous. Yikes! Why was everything so...hardcore? Just what the devil did they expect her to do anyway? Dismantle the table and beat her lawyer over the head with one of the legs?

"I think I liked the holding cell better." She muttered, pan-scanning the room with weariness.

She wasn't cold, but still, goose bumps dotted along

her forearms. The place gave her the creeps. The impossibly white walls, uninterrupted by windows or even a doorknob. She whipped around, mid-pace, paranoid the walls were sliding closer. Her breaths came a little quicker than usual. Had this place been the backdrop for the making of a 'Women in Prison' movie? Calamity shudder at the thought of being strapped to the table.

"Is there a Blaxploitation movie in my future?" She speculated with nervous sarcasm. Anything, to cut the eerie silence. It was so deafening, until she could hear the buzz of electricity flowing into the light fixtures. At least Reese and Chrissy were safe. The thought brought her some measure of peace.

That left Luce. What was she going to do? To say? She didn't have a plan for him, had meticulously avoided the issue until now. He'd be here soon, if he wasn't already...and then...what? Nothing. Not one viable idea blew through her brain. She was off the reservation, in over her head, up the creek...and a million other euphemisms for screwed. She paused mid-pace, frozen in the throws of a radical idea. Maybe she should tell him the truth?

Could he *handle* the truth? She wondered. Could she handle lying to him... *again*? The thought depressed her. After the closeness they'd shared and his heartfelt disappointment in her earlier, she dreaded another lie. Whereas, two weeks ago, she'd stretched, bent, and mangled the truth with little conscience and even less thought as to the consequences. Now, the mere notion of breaching his trust yet again brought bile to her mouth.

"He probably won't believe me, no matter what I say." She voiced the thought with a humorless, self-derisive chuckle. It was that realization that gave her the final moxie she needed to take the rattler by the tail.

As if on cue, the door's external latching mechanism turned over and the dark angel arrived in all his five-o'clock shadowed glory. Luce dropped the trademark briefcase down on the floor flush with the legs of the table. Perkins carried a briefcase just like it. Did every freaking lawyer in town shop at the same store? Maybe they came with the job and Ross-Warner had them on special order for all the attorneys, Calamity thought acidly. She wasn't sure why the site of the briefcase annoyed her so much. Perhaps she just needed a bit of misplaced anger to give her strength.

Agitated anew, she let her feet do the pacing. Her mind echoed the same restless panic.

"Sit down." Luce ordered.

She didn't even break stride. "I'm good."

He tracked her with his eyes as she darted about like a nervous deer. "I thought you were gonna hang with Sly and let me handle things."

"Changed my mind." The flat statement landed like a brick against cement. No remorse. No inflection. It has to be done. This way, everyone gets off with minimum damage. There's no other way, she fortified herself with that knowledge.

Luce stood behind the bolted chair closest to the door, hands deep in his pockets, a deceptively calm pose, she knew. "You eh...decided to fire me after all, huh."

"Rule nine: Always Have a Plan B."

He nodded, tracking her movements. "Thought you didn't like rules?"

She could feel his eyes boring holes into her. She had to keep moving. If she could just escape his beautiful sable eyes, and not have to witness them as they filled with disillusionment, and anger. The dark ending to their fairy tale that she already saw peeking over the skyline. This would finish them.

"I don't like *other people's* rules. Society's, my parents', Ross-Warner's... *Yours*."

"All I asked you to do was trust me." His voice gentled, into a plea almost. "Couldn't you trust me, just a little?"

She stilled, struck by the glimmer of hope but she

shook it off and kept moving. It wouldn't last...it couldn't. Not after.

"So, what's rule number one?" He asked, soft, but no longer gentle.

"Lie." She let her answer drop like a guillotine.

"Yeah, that definitely sounds like you." His brittle stillness was the perfect counterpoint to her perpetual agitated motion. "Shorty, I have to ask you something. And I need you to think long and hard before you answer. Look at me."

But she didn't. Instead she tracked him out of the corner of her eyes. He'd moved, his stance different...stiff, corded muscles seemed to alternate between gripping and relaxing. As though the composure on display was just that, a display. She'd seen enough of his temper to suspect his real mood bordered on savage...or was in a free-fall hurling in that direction, anyway.

"I'm listening." Please don't ask it, she begged. Oh hell, she couldn't take it. Not when what she really wanted was to leap into his arms, blurt out the truth and let him handle it however he thought best...the legal way.

He stood behind the bolted-down chair leaning forward, his sinew arms taunt. His hands gripped the seat back with tension, as if he were trying to brace himself for what was to come. "This afternoon, ah, yesterday afternoon, actually. When I came home for lunch..."

Her mind shrank away from his words. The last grain of sand drained from the hourglass. Rule ten: Face the Music. Decision time.

"I asked you if you were blackmailing Charlie. Did you stand there...flat-footed, and lie to me? Playing the part of some wronged victim, frightened of being accused of a crime she didn't commit. Anguish, because all the cards were stacked against her. While I *comforted* you."

She shrugged, pretending an indifference she didn't feel. "Well, what was I supposed to say? 'Yeah, Luce, I did it, arrest me.' You certainly wouldn't have gone along with *my* plan, and yours wasn't working worth a damn."

A long moment passed between them. Her in constant motion, him in suspended animation. When he spoke again, there was no warmth or softness...only a frigid calm that she suspected concealed a volcanic spew of pain and rage.

"I think you missed your calling. That was an Oscar-worthy performance."

"Thank you." She injected a note of pride in her voice. If he didn't detest her before, he would now.

"Were you *born*...or *hatched*?" He continued as if she hadn't spoken. Stealing a glance, she flinched at the darkened obsidian pits watching her as if she were a new breed of evil. "A woman without even a nodding acquaintance with the truth. Reckless, irresponsible, unworthy of the infinite loyalty that your family and friends heave at your feet...like pearls before swine."

"Matthew seven and six." She knew it by heart. She stopped pacing and let the wall hold her up while she recited the verse. Her eyes drifted closed. "Give not that which is holy onto the dogs, neither cast ye, your pearls before swine, lest they trample them under their feet and turn again and rend you."

"Lady, you need help. A lot more help than I can give you."

She opened her eyes and turned to face him properly for the first time since he'd entered the room. What she saw caused her breath to skip. Gawd, she'd hurt him. "You should run...just like it says, before I do anymore damage. I got this."

The look he gave her could have turned Medusa to stone. "I would like nothing more than to walk away and pretend this nightmare never happened, but if you think I would leave the future of my legal career to your unscrupulous devices, you really are one short of a six pack." His words cut into her, and cut deep. She squirmed away. "Don't start that walking shit again. Drop your ass in that chair or I will strap you to it."

She obeyed, something in his tone set off alarm bells.

"Don't say another fucking word about anything. If someone asks you what you had for breakfast, you better plead the bloody fifth until I get here. You're stuck in jail for the time being. You're an admitted blackmailer with a prior record. I couldn't get you out, even if I wanted to...and I don't."

"What about bail?" She sighed, weary and ready to have the whole thing done with.

"Forget about it. You can't afford it and I sure as hell am not putting my ass on the line for you again." He bent and retrieved the briefcase, movements careful and robotic. "And if you even think of borrowing bail money from your loyal friend Ms. Martin or your sister, I will rat you out for everything I know."

"I would never do that anyway." She spoke in a quiet, calm voice.

He scoffed. "Lady, I seriously doubt there's anything you *wouldn't* do. Who the hell knows what will turn up at your apartment, which they will go through with black light and a fine-tooth comb, by the way...so I hope you had enough sense not to leave anything incriminating lying around. Ross-Warner will drop you like a safe, if they haven't already. Which is just as well, because after this mess is over, I never want to lay eyes on you again. In the meantime, I'm going to check on your friend and your sister. I'll be back in a couple of days, when the smoke's cleared. They'll arraign you...and we'll know whether they have a case or not. Good day, Ms. Lowe."

He walked to the door and jabbed the button to be let out.

Calam bolted up from the chair, just as the door opened. "Luce?!"

He paused, but didn't turn.

"Don't take this out on Chrissy, when you see her. Ok?"

"I've always been able to tell you two apart." And he continued out the door.

* * *

Noon found Luce at his cousin's front door. He needed a shower, a shave, and a shot–of Jack, straight–with a vodka chaser.

Sly answered, grinning like a loon. "Luce, my man!"

"Dial it down an octave, will you." He ducked his head under the threshold. "I'm running on empty."

Luce turned to find Sly still holding the door open. He rolled his eyes as he watched his confused cousin step over the threshold, and glance around outside.

"Shut the door, Sly."

He complied, rubbernecking for information. "So eh, what's the word? Where's Insanity?"

"At the police station." Luce ambled toward the kitchen, uncaring. "You got any Jack in here?"

"Yeah, cabinet next to the frig." His cousin stared after him. "Wait...what's she doing? Signing release papers or something?"

He killed a fourth of the bottle with the first swig, ignoring his shock-faced audience.

"Eh, there's some *cola* in there, too...and a *glass*."

"I'm good with the bottle." He rolled his shoulders as the whiskey scorched earth down his throat.

"So, Luce, you're joking, *right*? Are we picking her up later? Or did you already drop her off at her place?"

"Humph. I left her ass right where she belongs." He felt his blood boiling back up and tipped the bottle a second time to squelch his rage...and drown out the pain. A throbbing pang in his heart every time his mind contemplated the fact that she'd played him...from the beginning. "She's under arrest, so the Sergeant probably tossed her back in the holding cell."

"And you... *left her there?*"

"Yeah. I. Left. Her. There." He enunciated as if speaking to a five-year old, the half-empty bottle dangling at his side.

"*In jail?* Like, on purpose?" Eyes bugged, mouth ajar, his cousin stood mute, probably for the first time since birth.

A speechless Sly? He never thought he'd see the day. Luce cocked his head back and laughed, a humorless, mean-spirited roar. Sly...silent, at last. He wished he had his camera.

"Shhhhh...Man, keep it down. And give me that—"

"NO!" He snatched away from Sly's shushing, and tightened his hold on the bottleneck. He needed the numbing effect more than he needed to stay sober. "Where are they?"

"Eh...Asleep." Sly answered distracted. "So what happens now...with Insanity—"

"*Nothing.* The DA will make his play. If they have enough to make the charges stick, it'll go to trial."

"That ain't what I meant, and you know it." His cousin made another grab for the Jack, but even in his semi-inebriated state, Luce dodged the lunge. "Dammit, Luce! Knock it off and tell me what's going on. Are you gonna help her out or not?"

"She didn't want my help and she doesn't deserve it."

Sly shook his head, denying the reality of what he was hearing. "This ain't like you, Man. Throwing yo girl to the wolves. Then swigging yourself into oblivion. You're losing cool points fast."

"When I want your opinion...I'll ask for it." Luce sneered at the bend in the conversation. What gave him the right to judge, huh? His *girl* had just drop-kicked him in the face. They should be at a bar, getting wasted together. Band of Brothers, dammit! Ugh, his vision pitched when he tried to lift the bottle again. Half the third swig spilled down his shirt. "What do *you* know anyway."

"Oh *hell* no. I ain't taking that high and mighty shit off

you today, *Cuz*. Not with you weaving like a wino. You ditched–" Sly paused, and took a couple of cautious steps in the direction of the bedroom, listening for sounds of life. Satisfied, he whipped around and continued in a harsh, whisper. "You *ditched* her scared, pregnant twin and her worried best friend at my crib. I been freakin' bragging to them all night, about how my brilliant cousin is the original Philadelphia lawyer. And you bitched out and left her there? What the hell are you doing?! Gimme that!"

His cousin managed to snatch the bottle from him on the third try just as he was about to kill the last swallow.

"Sober the fuck up!"

"Leave off… his–terics… been a loooong night." Luce slurred, bypassed his indignant cousin, and almost collapsed backward onto the couch behind him. "Only reason I'm here is to take the scissor off your hands. The other one is yo headache."

"Shhhh! Don't wake them up." Sly grabbed a handful of his shirt at chest-front. The movement wasn't a violent one, but with his impaired reflexes it took Luce off guard enough so that he had to correct himself from stumbling backward.

"Hey…get yo hands off me." He growled, pushing off. The backward momentum finally did plop him on the couch.

His cousin threw both palms up to show him, no harm, no fowl. "Whoa…What are you gonna say…Huh?! Luce, come on, you're wasted. Her sister's pregnant and worried sick. They don't need to see you like this. Why don't you take the couch…and sleep it off. You guys can hash out some strategy tomorrow. See if we can, maybe, smooth things over with the cops. I mean, we gotta do something. You can't seriously just kick the girl to the curb like this. She doesn't deserve this—"

Luce frowned, bleary, not caring for the way his cousin was painting his portrait. Why was he siding with *her*? "Since when did you start lobbing…lying…lobbying…her

Deefence? You don't…even… lik–…like her.'"

"She stuck her neck out for a friend, so she can't be *all* bad. That'd be Reese in the hot seat, if she hadna swiped those cameras and 'fessed up. Seriously, Luce, listen. You're making a huge mistake, she didn't—"

"Don't wanna her…hear it, Sly. I stuck my neck out for a friend too, an…loo…look where it got me?" He flung his arm out or tried to. His body no longer obeyed him…his arms flailed as they flopped down, awkward-angle to either side of him.

His cousin's gaze raked over his with distaste. "I don't see much damage. No blood. No bullet holes. No balls either. You leave *those* at the police station too?"

"Fuc…yu..ou."

"Take yo act on the road, then." Sly walked back towards the door, and flung it open. "I'll look after them. Since you don't give a damn, anyway…not enough to put your precious career on the line. You think I don't know what this is about? Saving her will somehow trash yo career, right? Same song, different verse. You keep picking yo career over every woman in yo life, you gonna end up alone…and bitter. But not on my couch. Get UP!"

"Sly–" His limbs weighed him down like lead…His thoughts, like his vision blurred together. If he just rested his head for a moment. When the spinning slowed Luce became vaguely aware of something pulling at him. His cousin…Sly was dragging him up from the sofa. After a few tugs, he stumbled forth…barely vertical. He bobbled once or twice before he balanced himself on a delicate teeter. "Sl..Shy—"

"I don't know you, Man. Go sleep it off in the car." His cousin pick-pocketed his keys, and shoved him toward the door. "Face down! I don't wanna have to explain you choking to death to Aunt Bev."

THE DAMAGE

Luce stood at his kitchen counter, inhaling the heavenly scent of his favorite dark roast. His cell phone whined, then did a buzzing dance against the countertop. He abandoned his cup and picked up on the third ring.

"Mr. Phoenix?" A thin female voice inquired.

"Speaking."

"I'm calling on behave of Sergeant Willis. He needs to see you. The arraignment's been set. Also, there are some people here demanding to see your client."

"No visitors. Tell the Sergeant I'll be there in an hour."

"But Mr. Phoenix, her brother and sister—"

"Especially those two." He disconnected, exhaling a half-groan. The last thing he needed was a Lowe family reunion at the police station. Keeping Ms. Lowe out of trouble long enough to erase himself from the equation hinged upon cutting off all potential sources of mischief. And while he admired the love and devotion between the siblings, he'd decided his best course of action was to keep her isolated until after the arraignment. If the three of them hooked up, they'd cook up another catastrophe, for sure. He'd had enough lies, half-truths and half-baked schemes to last him a lifetime.

The sooner he wrapped up this case and showed her the door, the better. Cutting his losses, he told himself for the umpteenth time, was the only rational option. He had his eye on a career as an officer of the court. The woman was chaos in a compact size...like one of those prank cans of peanut brittle that fake snakes sprung from when you popped the top. He fumed. No need for the atom bomb just send Calamity on a mission to search and destroy. He didn't have a place in his well-ordered world for the kind of havoc she wreaked with just a careless bat of her eyelash. He wasn't choosing his career over her, he was making the only sensible choice. The woman was a liar, a manipulator, and a flake...not a good match for him, a complete mix-match, in fact.

So then why did his chest tighten whenever her image drifted into his mind. Had he imagined the minute flash of anguish he witnessed when he aired his opinion of her? An act, of course, or some sort of manipulative plan. It was from the beginning. But then the blazing hot memory of their night together flashed in his mind. She'd given him the gift of herself...a gift she'd given to no one else. That couldn't be an act...could it? No, he dismissed the idea. She was definitely green in the boudoir.

But why take it that far? A woman abstaining for as long as she had...Did she really go to bed with him as part of some plan? And if she was *that* kind of woman, why hadn't she done so before? Any way he twisted it, she didn't make sense. Gawd. He got a headache just thinking about her.

His cell whined again, then danced a gig on the counter, breaking him out of his reverie. He ignored it, opting for another cup of coffee. After a fifteen-minute dance marathon, he switched off the phone and slipped it into his breast pocket.

He was doing the right thing...the only thing.

* * *

Luce turned into the police station just ahead of a roaring ambulance. A fire truck parallel parked outside the main entrance all but obscured the central facade of the building. Just behind it, with the front wheels jacked up on the curb, was a red and white EMT-labeled SUV with whirling lights and a chirping siren. Various officers and emergency medical persons milled around. His hackles rose at the obvious chaos. Who but Calamity could have caused such a scene? Injected with a nervy urgency, Luce abandoned his car in the first available space.

Briefcase in hand, he bee-lined it for the first person he saw, a uniformed female EMT. "What's happened?"

"Woman collapsed."

Luce eyeballed the sea of emergency vehicles and personnel. She must have noticed his incredulous expression because she elaborated. "A *pregnant* woman. Some sort of a ruckus ensued. I didn't get the lowdown-"

Luce bolted for the entrance, only to open the door to a foyer drowning in uniforms, HPD logos, HFD patches and embroidered EMT emblems. A familiar face jumped out at him, a sequoia amid the saplings.

"Pike—" He never got to finish his sentence as the crowd parted to make room for an unconscious, neck-braced Charisma being wheeled out on a stretcher. Pike and a worried copper-skinned gentleman in a business suit trailed alongside. Neither man spared him a glance as the herd brushed by him with a fireman at the helm.

Luce slipped the mobile out of his breast pocket as he caught sight of Burton through the closing door leading to the station's interior. He jolted forward, bumping several people, but he just was able to wedge the tip of his shoe in the doorjamb. "Burton! Where is Sergeant Willis? He's expecting me."

"Ahhh...He's around somewhere." Burton glanced left and right as if expecting Willis to materialize at any moment. "You can wait for him at his desk, I guess."

Luce strolled forth, right-hand dialing on his cell.

"Yeah?" His cousin's deadpan voice greeted him. "Whadda you want?"

"Sly, I need a favor."

"Sorry, I'm fresh out."

"Sly—" But the line went dead.

Ah, hell. He redialed, just as he caught sight of the Sergeant. He signaled him over with a head tilt.

"Whatever it is the answer is *no*." His cousin's ire lost none of its bite the second go around.

"Sly, DON'T hang up. The favor isn't for me."

"Good." His returned, snappish. "'Cause I wouldn't spit on you if your shirt caught fire."

Luce rolled his eyes. "Sly...Ms. Lowe's sister is on her way to the ER."

"Whoa...is she okay?"

"That's what I need you to find out. Is Ms. Martin there?"

"Yeah, why?"

"Take her with you. Try..." He trailed off, looking to the newly-arrived Sergeant. "Where are they taking her?"

"Memorial Hermann Main." The sergeant supplied.

He turned his attention back to the phone. "Memorial Hermann in the medical center. Find out if she's ok and hit me back."

"I'm on it."

Luce slid the cell back into his breast pocket. "You wanted to see me, Sergeant."

"Arraignment's tomorrow morning at ten thirty, Criminal Courthouse on Franklin. Judge Hardin's court." He announced without preamble.

"And?" He prompted. "You didn't call me down here just to give me a personal invite to the arraignment."

"Forensics." The Sergeant brandished a sealed manila envelop. "Thought you'd want a head's up."

Luce took the offering, opened it in as brisk and business-like a manner as he could muster, and scanned the contents. He wasn't quite sure what he expected, damning proof or exonerating evidence.

"Does she know about her sister?" He spoke to distract himself from reacting.

"Not unless she's Wonder Woman. Holding cells are sound proof."

"I'll need to confer with my client." Luce slid the papers neatly back into the envelop.

"Burton will bring her up to one of the interrogation suites."

* * *

"You seem tense." Calamity pronounced, sporting a skittish half-smile. "I mean…not as tense as the last time we spoke, but…you know, more than usual."

Luce stared down at the petite woman leaning on the opposite corner of the bolted-down table. She squirmed under his bald scrutiny. Her nervousness had a sharp edge to it, he noticed. She kept the length of the room between them.

How much should he tell her? The arraignment was tomorrow, and he needed her in the best possible frame of mind. If he told her, she'd be half-mad with worry. Of course, if he didn't tell her and there was something serious going on with her sister or the baby, it would be cruel to have kept it from her. His fury at her manipulations and lies still burned deep in his gut, but it no longer blinded him. Even he couldn't deny the genuine affection that existed between the sisters.

"If I'm royally screwed, you can tell me, you know. I'm not gonna succumb to the vapors. I'm prepared…to lose, I mean."

"Its not about the case." He shifted on his feet. "And I need you to stay calm."

Not surprising, she did the exact opposite. He pinched the bridge of his nose just below his brow, to steady himself and stay his temper.

"Just tell me, already." She demanded, prowling around the room in the same disconcerting manner as she had two days before. "Nothing could be worse than my imagination right now."

"Your sister came to see you earlier. She collapsed upstairs. Pike, and someone I assume is her husband, were on their way to the hospital with her when I arrived."

"Chrissy! The baby." She came at him like a freight train, clutching at his jacketed-arm. "Luce, please, can you get me outta here? I have to make sure she's ok. I'll sign anything you want, I don't care. Please! She needs me."

He ordered himself to stay focused. "Impossible. Your arraignment is not until tomorrow anyway. If you're indicted, bail will be set...We'll talk about it then."

Her eyes darted about. He could almost *see* her mind working, flitting from one radical idea to the next. "Where are they taking her?"

"Memorial Hermann Main, I think."

She stilled, seized on one particular idea. Seeing the cogs of her mind working was like watching a slow-motion train wreck. "What if I were sick? They'd have to take me to the hospital, right? All you'd have to do would be to make sure—"

"I'm going to pretend like I didn't hear that." He scoffed, frustrated, glaring at her as he shook his head. "Still haven't learned your lesson, Ms. Lowe. You're not above the law. No more stunts, not while I'm at the reins. Not with my reputation, my career, and my livelihood on the line. Does it even *touch* you that you could have single-handedly landed us all in jail...your best friend, your brother, your sister, *me*! Has this mess taught you nothing?"

"Apparently not." She dropped her hands, panic still on her face, but she seemed to realize the futility of her situation. He watched her amble over to lean against the wall, distant and trance-like.

"You know, except for her honeymoon trip with Paul, this is the longest we've ever been apart. Even when she went into the hospital to have Manny, I was there. Would you believe my appendix burst the same week?"

"There's *nothing* I wouldn't believe where you're concerned."

Their eyes collided. "I've always been a thoughtless little troublemaker. Old habits die hard, I guess."

"Calamity Jones...Lowe." He mused after a long, charged silence. "Aptly named."

She humphed, letting her eyes slide away. "'Jones' is mama's maiden name. She overheard one of the doctors jokingly call me that, 'Calamity Jones', when I was two hours old."

"Dare I ask why?" He muttered.

"I was born weighing four and a half pounds, via C-section, six weeks early with the umbilical cord wrapped around my neck. We were holding hands, Charisma and I. She grabbed my hand as the docs lifted us out. Got our picture in the paper and everything. Mama still has the clipping."

Luce stared at the woman for a hard minute, unsure of himself for the first time since his teen years. Despite everything, he wavered. No. Not an option. He had to get his head on straight. Damn, but it was difficult to stay angry with her. And yet, equally impossible to forget her duplicity. He wondered, was it possible to both loathe and love someone at the same time?

"I sent Sly and Ms. Martin to check on your sister."

She thanked him in a small, distracted voice...still caught up in her own world.

An unease feeling crept up on him. "Calamity, is your brother left-handed?"

"No, why?" At the mention of Pike her focus sharpened. "Is he ok?"

"Fine. The next time I see him, I'll know to duck to avoid his right hook instead of the left." Luce hedged.

"Listen, I need to tie up some loose ends, but I'll be back. I should have some news for you by then. Don't do anything stupid. If I hear that you've suddenly become sick and had to be rushed to the hospital, I will turn you in myself and to hell with the consequences. Comprendes?"

But, she had already retreated back into her own thoughts. He'd have to be satisfied with the cursory nod of her head.

* * *

Luce noted with unwelcomed irritation that her nameplate had already been removed and replaced with the Temp's, presumably, now the permanent legal assistant.

"Mr. Phoenix, hi. Did you need to speak with Mr. Perkins?"

"Yes, but I'm afraid I don't have an appointment."

"You're fine. He has a conference call in half an hour, but he's free until then." She informed him on the wave of a vapid smile. "Shall I announce you?"

"Please do."

He waited while she slipped into the inner office. She returned a minute later, and gestured for him to enter.

Perkins lounged behind his desk, the picture of an old-world dictator humoring his subject before ordering his execution. "Phoenix, you've got balls to come barking up my tree again." He patronized, "Shouldn't you be off cramming for the Bar exam or something?"

"Why?" Luce met the dig with one of his own. "Did you need a lawyer to represent you? I hear a few of the other associates have followed Ms. Lowe's example. That's what? Three additional workplace complaints and an acrimonious divorce to boot? Employee Relations must be in a tizzy."

His eyes hardened a fraction. "What is it you want?"

"I come bearing news. The assault charges which you

leveled against Ms. Lowe have been dropped, lack of evidence. Likewise, the restraining order is also lining the nearest birdcage since it was predicated on the delusion that an assault had taken place. Thought you'd want to know."

"Thanks for the headline." His pose lost a little of its swagger.

"Let's take it a step further, shall we…Just exactly how acrimonious is your divorce?" Luce let the question hang in the air. A radical Calamity-esque idea blossomed in his mind and for once, he let it linger around and get comfortable. "I wonder how the news of four young women alleging sexual harassment would weigh in with the presiding judge?"

Ah, yeah. He had Charlie's undivided attention now.

"Wh–What are you talking about? The firm has assured me that would be kept under wraps until after my divorce decree is granted." Perkins rubbed at the nape of his neck, uneasy, contemplative, eyes narrowed. "This is *blackmail.*"

"I prefer to think of it as *mediation.*" He dropped down in the chair opposite Perkins. "Ms. Lowe, being newly unemployed, needs a glowing letter of recommendation to help her along to her next position. I want it in my hands by the end of business tomorrow, or I give your wife a chance to triple her settlement. We got a deal?"

"Conniving bastard." He snorted.

"I'll take that as a 'yes'."

* * *

Calamity sat in the courtroom, mute and indifferent to the goings-on around her. The voices of the judge and the district attorney blurred into white noise in the background. Luce stood beside her chair, talking as much with his hands as with his mouth…defending her tarnished honor she imagined, with a passion he no longer felt. He could have been quoting obscure passages from communist propaganda for all she knew. Her central focus riveted to Charisma and the baby. She'd lost any thread of interest she had in her own situation the moment he told her about her sister's collapse.

"Ms. Lowe?"

"Hmm?" She snapped back to the present at the sound of her name. "Yes?"

"The court has declined to pursue an indictment against you."

She glanced around, to find the court's occupants scattered and filing out. "Does that mean I'm free to go?"

"It means all the charges have been dropped." Luce explained. "You'll have to come back to the station with me to sign some paperwork, but after that, yeah...you're free to go."

"Have you heard anything, yet?" She asked, anxiously.

"Fatigue, stress, and indigestion." He spoke with a casualness than hinted at the lack of seriousness of her sister's condition. "She's been ordered to rest for a week. No more running around in the middle of the night, no more getting arrested, and *definitely* no more rum raisin muffins. Doctor's orders."

* * *

Two hours later, as she scribbled an incoherent signature on the last release form and reclaimed her personal effects, Luce stood next to her, still deep in lawyer mode.

"Where are you headed?" He questioned, brisk and businesslike. At her queer glance, he added. "I'll give you a ride."

"No thanks." She declined at once. Since he'd made it abundantly clear he did not wish to resume their relationship, it was high time she started getting along without him.

"I need a word with you." He explained, "And I'd

rather not talk here."

"Ok, but, I can't imagine what we could have to chat about."

He didn't speak again until they were settled in his car, and he turned the engine over. "You never said where you wanted to be dropped."

"Take me to wherever Charisma is." She replied, as she tapped her cell phone against her leg. She must have forgotten to power it off before the police confiscated it. The battery was probably dead by now.

"By the way, you're unemployed. However, your former boss has graciously agreed to provide you with a reference."

Calam gave him the weird side-eye. "Good grief, he's practically a registered sex offender by now." She quipped. "I wouldn't want to work for a company that would hire me based on anything *he* said. Besides, I prefer a clean break, don't you?"

Her words seemed to rend the air between them. The end. It really was happening. Her heart ached at the realization that this would be their last conversation. This stilted tying-up of loose ends.

"Ahh...you left several personal items at my apartment."

"Yes, of course." Naturally, he'd want no trace of her in his life. She wanted to scream, or cry or say something...something more humane or genuine than, "I'll come get my stuff next week. Make it one week from today. Leave the key under the mat and you won't be forced to see me again."

"Calamity." He spoke in a quiet, affecting tone, but his profile gave away nothing of his thoughts.

Surprise muffled her pain. Why, *now*, of all times, would he use her first name over the dreaded 'Ms. Lowe'?

"I wanted to say that...I regret the tone and situation under which I ended our relationship and the way I kept you isolated from your family and friends. It was spiteful and unnecessary and likely facilitated your sister's collapse."

He'd rehearsed, she noted. His words were apologetic, concise, and unemotional. She envied him his reserve. Her thoughts exploded in her mind like gunshots at the shooting range. Her stomach churned with emotional indigestion...her heart writhed with regrets and what ifs.

"Its all good." She lied. "I agreed to let you handle my defense and as I am an admitted blackmailer, a few days in jail were inevitable. You don't owe me an apology."

"I know, but I have standards for my own behavior—"

"Leave it. I certainly don't need a *token* apology." She snapped, ready for the car ride-turned-ordeal to be over with. "You didn't *invent* the nasty break-up. I've had worse, ok."

"That's a lie if ever I heard one." His words cut that time.

"Stop, please!" She was grasping at the bottom rung, one word away from leaping out of the car and taking her chances with on-coming traffic. Couldn't he see that?! "Luce, if you ever cared about me at all, you will let the subject drop."

They rode the rest of the way in silence, with her sitting rigid against the passenger side door, temple resting on the window, eyes closed, breathing slow and deliberate. She clutched her purse-strap as if free-fall awaited her if she let go. How did a girl even begin to exercise a man like Lucifer from her mind? Or more importantly, from her heart?

As the car rolled to a stop on the curb parallel to her parent's house, Calamity breathed her first normal breath in days. She was out of the car and over the curb before he cut the engine. Charisma and Paul's Honda sat in the driveway next to her father's vintage mustang. This she noted with relief.

"Thank you, for the...lift—" She turned, mid-sentence, when she heard the driver's-side door open. He strode forth, as if...surely he didn't mean to come in?! "Wh-what are you doing?"

He didn't spare her a glance nor did he break stride. "I need a word with your parents."

"NO!" She gave chase, but he passed her in three lengths. "Luce, just go. I'll explain."

"Yeah, that's what I'm afraid of." He walked right up to the front door, and waited a beat for her to join him. "I don't like being lied *on* any better than I like being lied *to*."

She idled on the sidewalk, caught, near panic. No, no, no! He can't do this. Couldn't he let her keep at least a little of her dignity? She glanced back at the death-mobile that had brought them here...no help there. Her heckles rose; the next instant she squeaked at the feel of a warm palm at the nape of her neck.

"Come on. Get your purse. I don't have all day." He herded her toward the house, using his firm grip on her nape.

"Please don't humiliate me in front of my family." She begged, grabbing her fallen bag as he propelled her forward. She cringed with each step they took. "I would never do that to you."

"Relax, Ms. Lowe. You can tell them whatever the hell you want about *us*. I'll deal with the legal explanation...which will, of course, be edited-for-television. Do not contradict anything I say or we'll both be embarrassed." His voice held a note of warning.

She croaked out an... "Agreed."...just before they reached the door, which flew open abruptly. Calamity flinched at the foreboding figure before her.

"CALAMITY JONES LOWE!" Marian charged at her with matronly outrage. "How dare you get arrested without telling your mother! What the devil were you thinking?! Do you realize that I've been telling the ladies in the women's circle that you're coming to tea on Sunday? And with your sister just out of the hospital...Heaven help me, between the two of you—"

"Mama—"

Luce cleared his throat. "Mrs. Lowe—"

"Not now, young man, I'm speaking to my daughter." She cut him off, and resumed her worry-fueled tirade. "Have you been convicted of anything? Is that why you're here, to tell us we must begin visiting you downtown. Oh Lawd, Calam, please tell me everything is ok?!"

Before she could answer, her mother launched forward and Calam found herself enveloped in a tight hug. "Mama, I'm fine...really."

Her father came up behind his wife to rest a quelling arm on her shoulder. "Mari, dear, let the young people inside and we'll hear what they have to say."

For a moment, her mother only tightened her hold. When she finally released her vice grip, Calam caught and held her mother's hand as the two of them came inside, followed by Luce.

Once in the living room, Calamity demanded to know... "Where's Chrissy? The Honda's out front."

"Calam! You're here?!" Her sister's muffled digitized voice came out of nowhere.

She stumbled in surprise. "What the heck–Chris. Where are you?"

"Upstairs." Her mother informed her. "She's only allowed out of bed two hours a day for the next seven days. A pre-caution. Oh, and Manny's no longer contagious. He's napping in Pike's room. A lot has happened while you were *incarcerated*."

"Where is Pike?" She asked in the general direction of the speaker-like box sitting on the coffee table.

Marian rolled her eyes heavenward. "Probably eloped to Vegas with a pygmy. No one tells me anything anymore."

Calamity grimaced, and glanced backward at her poker-faced...lawyer? Ex-boyfriend? She wasn't even sure what to call him anymore. "Mama, please. We have a guest, remember."

"We have an uninvited visitor, whom you sprung on us without warning." Her mother corrected, and flowed seamlessly into a smile as she gestured to the coffee table. "Charisma, your sister's friend Mr. Phoenix is here. Say 'hello'."

"Mama." Calam gritted in a warning tone, tightening her grip on her mother's palm. "Be polite."

"I'm nothing if not a gracious host, Calamity." Her mother spewed sweetly. "Perhaps if you had informed your father and I that you were being *paroled* today, I might've prepared coffee and tea cakes to offer everyone. As it is—"

"Hey there, Counselor." Charisma's digitized voice interrupted with cheer. "You'll have to forgive my eh, absence and our general lack of etiquette. Its been a rough week."

"Of course." Luce waved off the apology. "I understand."

"Paul came up with this two-way relay system. Part walkie-talkie, part baby monitor." Their father elaborated, for no apparent reason. An effort to distract her mother, Calam guessed. "Its the only way we could keep her in bed."

"Dr. Miller is over-reacting, Daddy. I only fainted." Charisma complained.

Calamity gave her mother's hand a parting squeeze before she let it go and crossed over to where her father sat down on the sofa. She leaned in and gave him a peck on the cheek. "Everything is fine, Daddy, I promise. Luce will explain. I'm going up to see Chris." She then leaned nearer his ear. "Please make her behave while Luce is here."

Her father smiled and turned to address their guest.

Calamity dared a glance in his direction, only to see him wave her off as he and her father shook hands. Grateful, she made her escape up the stairs.

* * *

"Are you ok?" Charisma pulled back from their hug first, keen eyes scanning her sister's face. "You seem a little...tense."

"I've been incarcerated for the past three days, Charisma. Do the words 'Calgon, take me away' mean anything to you?" Calam eyed the speaker box on the night stand next to the bed. "Shut that thing off. I want to ask you something."

"I unplugged it when you said you were coming up."

"Good." She nodded, distracted. "Where's Pike? I couldn't reach him; my cell is dead."

"He and Paul are off trying to find a legal way to jail-break you."

"Well, call off the dogs. I'm free and clear."

Charisma was already reaching in the night stand's drawer to pull out her mobile. "I'll text, its faster."

Calam plopped down on the bed, weary. "Luce is down there now doing damage control. I've no clue what he's telling them. If mama or daddy mention anything to you, play it by ear and try not to contradict whatever version he's told them."

"I got you, don't worry." A digitized chirping sound signaled the sent text. Charisma laid the phone aside and looked back at her, excited. "Now, I want to hear all the lurid details."

"Aw Chris, the whole thing's been such a hellish nightmare. I was kinda hoping to talk about something else." Calam pled, falling back onto the bed, looking up at the ceiling.

Her sister pulled a face. "Come on, Calam...I'm bed-bound for the next seven days with Mama, Daddy, and a four-year-old as my only outlet. Nuts for the winter, you know. Paul will be at work all day and you'll be—"

"At home, scouring the want-ads." She admitted on a deep exhale.

"What?!" Her sister snapped in surprise.

"I've been quietly relieved of my position at Ross-Warner."

"They fired you... *anyway?*" Calam could almost feel her sister's incredulous stare. "But how can they do that? Didn't another woman come forward and file a complaint?"

"Three others actually, but, that only proves he's guilty. It doesn't mean I'm innocent." She rolled onto her side and shot her sister a sad smile. "No biggie. There are law firms all over town. Shouldn't be too difficult to find one with an opening. Luce even managed to finagle a glowing letter of recommendation from Perkins. Heaven knows how he pulled off that miracle. Hey, that reminds me, can I borrow your grey pin-stripe suit? I think I already have pumps to match."

"Wait, aren't you even going to fight it?" Her brow furrowed, "Calam, can't Luce help?"

"No, he can't. Its done. He's gotten me a recommendation—albeit, a tainted one—and that's all she wrote." She closed her eyes, and rolled over on her back. Avoiding her sister's gaze...a gaze that mirrored her own. Odd, she'd never found it disconcerting until now. A nervous urgency overtook her. She needed to get the conversation going in a different direction.

"Calamity..." her sister stared at her. "Calam, what's wrong?"

"Nothing. Its all good. I'm just tired."

"Ok, we don't have to talk about it, if you'd rather not. Tell me how the arraignment went."

Also not a welcomed topic, Calam grimaced. "Fine, I guess. Whatever Luce said worked, because they dropped all the charges. Honestly, I wasn't paying much attention. I was worried about you." She admitted, gesturing with a weary flutter of her hand. "Luce was kind enough to send Reese and the Neanderthal to check on you. He's really sweet that way. He even gave me a ride over here today.

My car is probably still parked at his place."

"Good grief, did you think he'd make you walk?" She scoffed, giving her a strange look. "Which brings me to another question...Calam, why on earth wouldn't Luce let any of us visit you before the arraignment?"

Calam hunched up her shoulders. "He probably figured if I hooked up with you or Pike, I'd do something stupid." She admitted carelessly. "And who knows, maybe I would have." Calamity knew on some level that her behavior was odd but she couldn't seem to muster up to her usual buoyancy. She tried to smile, but it felt brittle and unreal until even her facial muscles rebelled against the insincerity. Her limbs felt like lead, her heart even heavier. She opened her eyes to spy a worried frown hovering above her. "Would you do me a favor Chris...no questions asked?"

"Name it."

"Just a couple of loose ends that need snipping." Calam inhaled a fortifying breath. "Next week, I might need you to pick up my stuff from Luce's apartment...including my car. I'm not up to it."

"Oh." Charisma sat up a little straighter, sensing the seriousness of the situation. "Calamity, you're talking but you're not making any sense."

"No questions, remember."

"Yes, yes, I know but..." She dismissed her promise without care. "Calam, this is *me*. Please, tell me what's going on."

"There's nothing to tell, really." She forced herself to say in a voice that she hoped didn't sound as dejected to her sister's ears as it did to her own. "Luce is not the right guy for me after all. Its good we found out now before either of us got too attached. No worries. By this time next week—"

"You and Satan broke up?" Calamity felt her sister grab her hands. "When? Why?!"

She tried to shake her off, make light of the situation,

because if she didn't... "Its no big deal. We're still cool. Couples break-up all the time, you know. They say the average millennial goes through five or six relationships a year. Please don't make a thing of it, Chris."

"Ok...its ok. You're right. Luce who?" She nodded, pulling her sister into a hug and patting her shoulders. "No need to make a thing about it. Its all good. You can hang out with me. Honestly, I don't think I can stand a week of Mama hovering anyway, so you'll be doing me a favor. Pike or Paul can go get whatever you need from the apartment."

"Not until next week." Two bear-hugs in one day? Hell, she must really be loosing it, Calam mused.

"Ok, next week then. I'll go myself and take care of it. You can borrow whatever you need from me until then. Hell, in a few weeks I won't be able to wear it anyway."

"Thank you." She rested her head on her sister's shoulder, glad for her support. "I'm tired, Chris...I'm so tired."

"You can sleep here. Plenty of room."

THE TRUTH LURKS

"Mrs. Tate. Come on in." Luce quipped, then stepped aside as the pint-sized woman barreled pass him into his apartment. "I was *just* saying to myself, its been too long."

Luce followed at his leisure, not particularly anxious to hear what promised to be an indignant rant. Sure enough, in the living room, she rounded on him like a rabid Chihuahua. "What the hell did you do to my sister?"

"Nothing." Undaunted, he circled around her and continued his carefree trek to the couch. "She was batting a thousand the last time I saw her."

"Calamity lied to me last week. LIED!" She reiterated, apparently incensed by his lay-about attitude.

"Shocking, really." He regarded her with casual indifference, as he debated the safest method for tossing a pissed-off pregnant woman out of his apartment. "She lied to me on an hourly basis over the past three weeks."

"Yeah, but unlike you, she's never lied to me or Pike in her life."

Luce gave a short, humorless chuckle. "Lady, if you believe *that* then I have a pyramid scheme in Burma that I'd like to interest you in."

Growing angrier by the minute, she advanced on his

prone figure, half tempted to grab the remote off the coffee table and bash him upside the noggin with it. "Tell me what you said to her, dammit!"

"Probably the exact opposite of whatever she told you I said."

"She hasn't *told* me anything!" She snapped, throwing up her hands. "She keeps insisting she's fine and that nothing happened."

He crossed his arms behind his head and relaxed back against the cushions. "What makes you think she's lying? Maybe she *is* fine."

"She's been sharing a bed with me for a week. She doesn't eat. She won't take Reese's calls, and every time Pike or I ask her what's wrong she says 'Nothing, I'm fine'. Trust me, she's *not* fine."

Undaunted, he shrugged. "She's resilient; she'll snap out of it."

"Are you totally cracked?" Charisma tilted her head sideways to glare at him. "Or just a garden-variety idiot? Tell me what you said or did to my sister or I will find a way to make you bleed."

One eyebrow peaked. "Calm down, Mrs. Tate."

"Explanation. *Now.*" She warned. "Or I call for back-up. And trust me, you do *not* want our six-foot-four-inch brother kicking in your door."

"For the record, I've got a quarter-inch on him." Still, he sat up and sobered, elbows resting on knees, hands steepled. "Fine. You want the highlights? She went behind my back and blackmailed Charlie even after she swore to me she wouldn't. On a second...and third occasion when I questioned her about it, she swore to me that she hadn't. When I found out she was pulling my strings, I ended our relationship and everyone went their separate ways. Fade to black."

"When was this exactly?" Charisma narrowed her focus, trying to put together a likely timeline and flow of events that could have led to her sister's depression.

"The day the police came to the office to eject Stella's husband. I just happened to be in Perkins' office when he read the blackmail letter."

"That the night I got arrested?"

He nodded. "The same. I went home for lunch and asked her point blank, and she denied it. She laid it on *real* thick, even went so far as to pretend to panic about being accused of a crime she didn't commit...circumstantial evidence and all that jazz. That night, after we'd had...eh had dinner, we had a frank discussion. She could've come clean then, she didn't."

"You had dinner, huh?" She reiterated, suspicious. He's editing something out. "What happened *after* dinner? What were you two talking about?"

"Us." And that's all he was going to admit, apparently, confirming her suspicion. She should have known.

"This wouldn't happen to have been a *horizontal* chat, would it?" She surmised, giving him a withering look.

"That's privileged information."

"Always the lawyer." She rolled her eyes, disgusted. "The break-up, let's have it. How'd it happen? Paint me a picture please."

To her relief, he complied without further prompting.

"By the time I got down to the station, she'd already signed a confession, and she readily admitted she'd not only lied, but perpetrated this whole convoluted performance of innocence."

"Arrrrgh!" Charisma let out her frustrations in a long, inelegant groan. "You deflowered my sister...*allegedly*, of course...and then ditched her–the next day, I might add– over a lie she didn't even tell?!"

"I'm not at liberty to disclose—"

"Oh shut up! Calamity didn't blackmail him." She announced with weary patience.

"Yeah, she did." He stood, no longer relaxed, but stiff and business-like. "She just got someone else to write the note for her."

"Eh, no, dumb ass, actually, she didn't. Reese blackmailed him."

"Let me show you something." He went into the next room and came back a minute later with a manila envelop in his hand. He tossed it on the coffee table, gauntlet-esque.

"That's how I got her off. Handwriting expert says a left-handed person wrote the letter. She still did it, she just had enough conscience not to let her best friend take the fall. I checked, Ms. Martin is not left-handed."

"I didn't say Reese wrote the note, I said she *blackmailed* him. Your cousin Sly wrote the darn note." She raised her brows, mockingly as she spied a contemplative frown cross his face. "What's the matter? Cat got your tongue?"

"How do you know this?"

"From that night, when Reese and I slept over at Sly's. He told me so himself. I thought you *knew!*" She stared up at him, confused and annoyed all at once. "They both felt guilty that Calamity landed in jail. Sly promised he was going to tell you."

"Eh, I think he tried...But I wasn't in a listening mood." She watched as the briefest flicker of doubt flashed across his face. "Shit."

"A garden-variety idiot then." She surmised.

"It would seem so."

"Well, what are you going to do? You can't leave it like *this*." She walked a few steps toward him. "Look, despite your rather shabby treatment of her I know you still care about my sister. Otherwise, why would you blackmail her boss into giving her a letter of reference."

Taken aback, he humph-ed. "I'm afraid you're mistaken, Mrs. Tate."

"Want to know what I think, Counselor?"

"I'm pretty sure you're going to tell me whether I want to know or not."

Charisma ignore the sarcasm. "I don't think you got Calamity off just to save your own ass."

"Oh really, and why would you think that?" He challenged, his poker face didn't slip an inch. Oh, he's good, she admitted, but he's met his match this time.

"Belinda, our friendly neighborhood temp. She may be as boring as a box of rocks, but she's a live wire of information and only to willing to share. She called Calamity's cell to inquire as to where she wanted her tainted reference forwarded. Since Calam is near-catatonic these days, I answered the phone."

He bent without warning or comment. Charisma twitched in surprised when she felt the tender kiss he placed on her temple. "Thank you."

She frowned at his sudden altered demeanor. "For what?"

"Telling me the truth." He patted the top of her hair, half-smiling.

"What are you going to do?"

He sighed, resigned. "I don't know. Where is she?"

"At our parents, waiting for me to taxi her car so she can get back to her place. I'm worried about her, Luce. She'll be there all by herself. Shane moved out. He finally patched things up with Shelly-belly. I'm going home with Paul and Manny now that I'm up and around again. Pike tried to convince her to crash with him for a while, but she wouldn't."

"Why doesn't she stay where she is?"

Charisma grimaced at the thought. "Bad idea. Mama will only make it worse. She means well, but she doesn't speak Calamity's language."

"I need a minute to get my head together." A quietly spoken admission, that hinted at a much deeper affect. Oh yeah, she smiled to herself. He's sprung.

"Keep an eye on her for me."

"Haven't you been listening? She's refused—"

"Tell her you need help with the kid, and she'll hang close."

"Why, Mr. Phoenix," She gasped, feigning shock. "Are

you suggesting I *lie* to my sister?"

MAKING UP IS HARD TO DO

The hard knock at the door jolted her. She nearly rolled her ankle stepping into her new platform clogs. Who could that be? Maybe Pike decided to pick her up instead of them all meeting over at Chrissy's. Sheesh! He might have warned her first. Bedecked in black jeggings and a thigh-length tunic, purse dangling off her shoulder, Calam tittered across the living room whilst trying to secure her left earring.

"Justa minute!" She faltered to a stop at the front door to finish the job. "There, all done." Looking forward to a fun evening with the fam, and anxious to be off from her tomb-like apartment, she yanked the door open without much thought. "Hey, I didn't know you were picking me up or…"

The Afro-Italian Adonis leaning in her doorjamb uncoiled from his position like a jungle cat scenting prey. His intense sable gaze devoured her in a full-body scan.

"Luce." Her smile withered, while her thought-train derailed in a fourteen car smash-up.

"Calamity, you look good."

Not much had changed, some portion of her mind noted. He looked yummy sporting faded denim and a polo

293

shirt instead of his usual suit and tie. Desire flared like a greasy fire, but was squelched on the heels of a post-traumatic break-up flashback...to their last real conversation and the glower of disgust on his face. She cringed as the horrid rawness of his words churned up. No, don't go there, her mind shouted. Poker-face it and get him outta here PDQ.

"What are you doing here? I thought you hated me."

He winced ever-so-slightly...or so she thought. She wasn't sure she'd actually seen it. He had his game-face on, too. He was a lawyer after all.

"May I come in?" His words, polite and neutral, gave nothing away.

NO! Her mind screamed at her. Remember what happened the last time you let him in? Your heart is still closed for repairs, and your head is a minefield of painful memories.

"Eh, I have plans. Paul and Chrissy are expecting me for dinner." She met his skeptical eye with sober honesty. "Its true. I thought you were Pike coming to pick me up."

He seemed to let the topic drop. "Why did you lie about the blackmail?"

Calam tensed at the question. The spicy whiff of his aftershave played havoc on her senses. She toddled backward, edgy and anxious to be away from him. Her left hand tingled. She wasn't even aware she'd been gripping the knob so tight. She flexed her fingers against her pant-leg as she retreated into the living room. Her heckles rose as she sensed him following her and then heard the door close. Damn.

"I came up with the idea to blackmail him. The rest is just details." She waved a hand, not really seeing the point of the question.

"Yeah, but that's not what you told me...or the police. You confessed, outright. But the handwriting isn't yours. That's how I sprang you. Remember?"

"So what. I know how to fake my handwriting. I'm a

criminal, *remember?*" She stood on the edge of the living room as far away from him as possible. Folding her arms, she rested them on the bar bordering the kitchen, her back to him. She felt his scrutiny, but he kept his distance at least.

"Sly wrote the letter."

Calam couldn't quite quell her surprise. The quick intake of breath and the infinitesimal tensing of her frame gave it away.

"You didn't know that, did you?"

"What difference does it make now?" She shrugged. "Its over. Forget about it."

"It makes a difference to me." He challenged. "Why'd you lie?"

Her shoulders sagged, as she caught his towering form edging closer out of the corner of her eye. "Because I didn't want Reese to get fired or arrested or both. You were right, I should have played it your way. I was reckless and stupid. I could have hurt a lot of people I love...in ways, that 'I'm sorry' just can't fix."

"So, you martyred yourself." He concluded, making a frustrated sound. He ran a hand over his head, wanting to go to her, comfort her, kiss her, shake her. But he held back, knowing he wouldn't be well received. "Dammit, Shorty. I told you *not* to do that. I could've gotten you off, if you'd just trusted me enough to tell me the truth!"

"I know." She whispered, turning around. Luce spied the angst marring her features as she explained. "But what if you got into trouble in the process? You'd already lied to the police. I couldn't let you jeopardize your career. After years of hard work...College, Law School, and who knows how many thousands of dollars in tuition...a prestigious position at Ross-Warner. You could have lost it all. And for what exactly?" A humorless laugh escaped her lips. "A roll in the hay with me."

Luce frowned. "That's not what it was." Her sister was right. She was...different. He didn't like to see her this way, tense and guarded, her normal exuberance squelched, those audacious ideals of hers deflated to the grim acceptance of an unpleasant reality. The Calamity he knew would laugh in the face of any obstacle that stood in her way and then cook up one convoluted scheme after another until she'd gotten the best of whoever or whatever separated her from her goal.

"We were a lot more than a roll in the hay. Why the hell do you think I was so pissed at you?" Black eyes bore into hers with unsettling intensity, daring her to argue with him.

"This is all starting to feel a little too... *relationshippy.*" She snapped, edging away from him again, towards the kitchen. "It's over or don't you remember? I don't have to listen to this anymore."

"Don't belittle us. We were more than a roll in the hay."

"Ok, whatever you say. It was awe-inspiring; the earth moved, really. But, what's done is done." Panicky dread filled her, when Calam saw him advancing on her, she jerked aside a few steps. This is getting too heavy. He wasn't just here for closure or absolution. He wanted something else from her...something she couldn't handle. She squared her shoulders, and hurried past him to the front door. "So, if you'll excuse me..."

"But we're not done."

She ignored him. "Eh, I have to go. I was already late when you got here. Chrissy will be worried. As you can imagine, I haven't been the life of the party lately."

"Call her and cancel." He closed the distance between them in one stride and tried to rest his hands on her shoulders. "Your sister will understand."

"*No.* No, she won't." She flinched away as if she'd been scorched by a flame. "Luce please...I don't want to get into this. Charisma is waiting... *please*...Don't."

"I can't let it go, Calamity." He caught her arm at the elbow and propelled her around to face him.

"Noooo...Dammit!" Calam snatched her arm away and shoved at his chest with all her might, but only succeeded in knocking herself off-balance. Her platforms tilted and she wobbled momentarily before regaining her ground.

He advanced on her despite her trying to ward him off. Her panicked gaze met his determined one.

"Please...you can't...I've just gotten to the point where I think I might be ok and now you—" To her horror, her voice broke. Her eyes, the next to mutiny, blurred over. She swiped at them angrily with the backs of her hands. But once the walls started to crumble, the entire house came tumbling down. "You just show up here, wanting to drag it all back out...and I can't! Don't you understand? I... *can't.*"

"Shorty...Don't cry. C'mere." His arms were around her before she knew what was happening. Cradled tenderly against his solid steel chest, the floodgates broke open. She buried her face in his shirt, hands fisted, still absently 'beating' at him. But all the fight had gone out of her, replaced by stark emotional release. All her pinned up pain, hidden vulnerability, silent anguish, came spilling out in heart-rending tears. Luce picked her up easily, carrying her to the sofa. Her shoes, slipped off her feet along the way, left unnoticed by both of them.

He sat with her on his lap, cheek resting against his shoulder, face burrowed in his neck. He stroked her hair and rubbed her back. He spoke soft words, in English, then Italian. Nothing penetrated the cascade of emotions raining down. After what seemed like hours, the storm died down with a succession of sniffles.

"Shorty?" He tested the sudden silence.

Concerned when she didn't respond, he shifted her in his embrace. Her head lolled back against the crook of his arm. Shoulder-length, two-strand twists spilling around her cheeks and tickled his arm.

"I'll be dammed." He swore, as he stared down at her tear-streaked face. Her eyes twitched under her lids, but she didn't rouse. So he placed her with care on the purple mohair monstrosity, where she instinctively curled into a tight ball.

Luce watched her, fascinated by the small wonder before him. At first, he thought she'd fainted...until he heard the delicate rhythm of her breathing that indicated sleep. He didn't know how long he'd been sitting there, on the floor by the sofa, when a muffled noise broke his concentration.

When it sounded a second time he stood to track its origins. After the fourth sound, he identified the cause. Someone, likely one of her siblings, was calling her cell...which was in her purse from the sounds of it. He collected the forgotten purse and hung it on the rack behind the door. Likewise, he crossed the room, stowed her shoes beneath the coffee table. He slipped his own cell phone from his back pocket to check the time.

* * *

Luce wasn't surprised when a half-hour later, someone started pounding on the front door. That would be either her sister, her sister's husband, her brother, or her best friend. At the moment, he didn't know which one was worse. He dropped a kiss on her cheek, and went to face the music.

He opened the door on her brother's thunderous frown.

"What the hell are *you* doing here?" He demanded without preamble. "Where's Calamity?"

"She's fine. Wait–" Too late, Pike shoved him out of the way and stalked inside like the police scanning the room for evidence of foul play.

"Oh man, you better not be here to rail at her again."

"Pike, relax." Luce backed off, hands raised in surrender. "I'm not here to do any more damage."

His eyes fell on his sister's tiny form, curled up on the

298

sofa. He squatted down to inspect her for himself. His hand rested in her tangle of twists, moving them aside to spy the evidence of recent tears. She didn't stir; her breathing remained deep and regular. Luce watched him dropped a kiss on her temple, evidently satisfied of her physical safety.

Pike remained in a squatted position, but for a man who was equal in height to himself, Luce knew that made him no less dangerous. "Do you have any clue how much damage you've already done. I haven't seen her cry in ten years." His voice was low and angry, his chocolate eyes, accusing.

"What happened ten years ago?" Luce asked, curious what other event had managed to damage her spirit.

"Don't change the subject." He straightened to his full height, walked over, and came eye to eye with Lucifer. "Why's she like that?" He gestured toward the sofa.

"Seeing me upset her." Luce admitted. "She wore herself out crying. I figured it'd be better to let her rest before we talked."

"What the hell went on between you two anyway. I've never seen her so..."

"Hurt?"

"Broken." He corrected, narrowing his eyes. "She's been hurt before, but its never affected her like this. Calam never lets anything or anyone get her down."

Luce tucked that bit of information away in the back of his mind.

"And the worse part is she hasn't said a word against you. Let her tell it...You're a paragon of virtue."

Luce scoffed at this. "Well, that's not true. I made a ton of mistakes. Mine just weren't as blaring as hers."

Her brother eyed him, still suspicious Luce noted, but he seemed willing to be reasonable. "Look, I get that there's some unresolved issues between you two. And I'm happy not to take sides, *but* I am putting you on notice. I want my sister back. So, fix whatever the hell it is you did to her and fix it quick. Because the next time I see her, if she's not back to her old self—"

"Fair enough." Luce held out his hand. After a moment's hesitation, Pike stepped forward, death-gripped it in his own...and used his imprisoned hand to pulled Luce close, so close that their breaths mingled.

"Listen, eh, I'm not trying to get all up in yo Kool-Aid...But if you're not all-in, you need to disappear and stay gone or we're gonna have a *real* problem. She puts on a good show, but Calamity is not as invincible as she pretends. Do you hear what I'm saying?"

"Yeaaah." He nodded, eye to eye, and end-of-the-world serious. "No games. I'm here to stay this time."

"Alright then, 'cause I like you...and I don't want to have this conversation again." He loosened his grip and let his hand fall away.

"Pike, do me a favor. Can you smooth things over with Charisma and Paul? She was supposed to meet them."

His brow quirked. "Who do you think sent me? I'll handle it."

"Thanks man."

* * *

She stretched, full-body, like a lazy house-cat. Her eyes fluttered open as she yawned. She shoved the mop-like hair off her forehead. In the days since the debacle, she'd reverted back to her natural twists. She usually tied them back when she slept, otherwise, they grew fuzzy. Wow, she hadn't slept this good in days. Well, if she ignored the weird dream, that is. She sat up and frowned. Why on earth was she on the sofa...Calam glanced down at herself, and her frown deepened. Fully dressed? What...wait, wasn't she wearing the same outfit in her dream? The one where—

"Hi." The bone-deep voice cut off her thought.

Luce watched her from the arm chair across the room. She blinked several times in rapid succession, seeming surprised to see him. Crumpled shirt, hair sleep-messed, eyes still a bit bleary, but she was a vision of loveliness to him.

"Eh...Hi." Her chocolate eyes held a childlike hesitance, as if she expected to be rebuked at any moment.

"Sorry, if I blind-sided you."

"Its ok."

"Obviously, I should've called first." Luce stood and came forward with caution, trying not to spook her. "But with the way I left it between us...I wasn't sure you'd even pick up, much less agree to see me. I didn't mean to upset you."

"I'm fine." She shrugged, subdued. "No harm, no foul."

Luce studied her as he approached, wondering how he could have ever been fooled. She really was a terrible liar. "Come on, Shorty, don't give me the party line. Tell me the truth."

She blew out a long, tired sigh as her expression reflected weariness. "I can't win with you. First, you're upset because you think I blackmailed Perkins. Now, you're pissed because you found out I *didn't.*"

"See, now, that's where you're wrong. I don't give a damn about Charlie...who blackmailed him or why or any of that other crap. I care that you lied about it."

Sad eyes regarded him. "Well, I can't take it back. So please let's not rehash. Don't you think I feel horrible enough already?" She pleaded, both hands thrown up in a mesh of guilt and frustration. "Gawd, why do you feel the need to talk everything to death? Can't you just...go away and leave it alone. I've already admitted the whole mess was my fault. What else do you want? Am I supposed to grovel for the rest of my life? Take up sack cloth and ashes?"

As he neared the sofa, his heart twisted at her obvious anguish. Anguish he'd caused. "I want you back, Calamity. That's why I'm here." He knelt down in front of her, eye to eye. She flinched away, keeping a certain distance between them. A stiff, awkward distance that bespoke a profound riff between them. He had his work cut out for him. "No one has to grovel."

Chocolate eyes narrowed, alight with a mixture of disbelief and reluctance. "But before you said...uh, that you were done with me and that—"

"Shhh...Forget about before." He cut her off with a swift finality. "I was angry and I behaved badly."

She stared at him for a long moment. Her expression raw, and warring between pain, confusion, and longing. Then she asked the one question he wasn't quite prepared to answer.

"Why should I trust you?" Her voice small, vulnerable...and heartbreaking. Making him feel more and more like a SOB. "You booted me out of your life with all the care and finesse of someone scraping dog doo off their shoe. I know I lied to you but that awful stuff you said...Luce, what happens the next time I do something to make you angry? I'm never going to be the kind of person who blindly follows the rules. And I refuse to tiptoe around, afraid you're going to blow your top and tell me to kiss off every time I do something that you disagree with."

"Then don't." He challenged, wanting to assure her that he wasn't asking her to change who she was. Hell, he'd be lying if he didn't admit that part of the attraction was her recklessness and spontaneity. "I have a temper. That's not going to change either. I can't promise that I won't get angry with you from time to time. But I can promise that I won't let it ruin us again. I'm used to doing things my way, Calamity...And so are you, if you're honest. Given time, we'll learn to compromise."

"I don't know, I–" She left off, having some internal battle with herself. She glanced down, toying with her hands. "Things got serious so fast. Maybe we should've had this conversation before...we, you know. I mean, finding out *now* how incompatible we are, its like... 'ready,

302

shoot, *aim'.*"

"I thought that's the way you liked it." Luce smiled at her shyness, reaching to tilt her chin back up. He relaxed a little when he saw her heart in her eyes. "Leap first, look later. That's how you do everything else."

"Yeah, I know." She admitted, without hesitation. "But this time it's dangerous, Luce. This relationship has got 'Shakespearean tragedy' written all over it."

He caressed her face, tenderly wiping away the crusted remains of her tears with his shirt's tail. "Personally, I think we're more of a modern dramedy."

Eyes timid and fearful, she exhaled a tired sigh, "Maybe we should skip out early and avoid all the drama."

"Damn, you sure picked a hell of a time to act sensible." He countered. At the moment he was hoping to appeal to the wild, risk-taking part of her. He figured he had a better shot with *that* Calamity. "So, is this it, then? Should I cue the violins?"

One corner of her mouth kicked up in a fleeting half-smile. "Luce, be serious."

"Calamity…you know, there's nothing in the rules that says we can't re-write the ending." He pulled her closer, and penned her with his searing gaze. "I want a do-over."

She stared, breathless and transfixed, as if he were a magic trick she couldn't figure out. "A do-over? For what?"

"For *us.*"

"But you haven't done anything wrong."

"Don't hog all the guilt, Shorty." He dropped his hands from her face but he didn't move away. "I let you shoulder most of the blame, but make no mistake, I screwed up too. I don't like being duped, especially by people I trust. And I can be a self-righteous bastard when I think I'm right. I should've taken a timeout to get some perspective. If I had, I would have come to the same conclusion that I've come to now."

"Which is what…exactly?" She inched forward, peering

at him with wide-eyed curiosity.

"That I fell for this zany, fun-loving, mischief-maker, with a reckless sense of justice...and I wouldn't have her any other way."

"You wouldn't?" Her voice held a fragile, uncertain hope.

"I want you just the way you are. We can work this out. All we need are a few house rules—"

She scoffed. "That I will break before the next full moon and then we'll be right back where we started."

He caught her shoulders before she could sag back against the couch...away from him. "Hear me out, Shorty."

"Fine." She tilted her head to the side, with a sardonic lift of her brow. "What kind of rules?"

"Just one. No more lies. Not between us. Not about things that matter...that would threaten us." He shook her shoulders to punctuate the importance of his words. To make her understand his need to have her open up all of herself to him, his need to trust her and be trusted in return. Unable to stop himself, he eased her forward. His hands fell to her hips while he rested his forehead against hers. His voice lowered to a guttural rasp.

"You can lie to anyone else in the world about anything, but tell *me* the truth. I don't care what it is...or how bad. I want...no, I *need* to hear it from you before the police come knocking at my door. I need to know that we're in this together."

Her breath caught. He felt a tremor ripple through her but she didn't pull away. A moment passed before he felt her tiny fingers encroaching upon him, fidgeting with the starched collar of his shirt. "That's all? The truth. That's all you need?"

"Yeah." He whispered, testing the waters with a feather-light touch of his lips to hers.

To his relief, she slid forward, off the sofa. Realizing her intention, he scooped her up against his chest and reversed their positions so he sat on the couch with her wrapped around his torso. Her cheek rested against his shoulder; he felt her sigh as the unnatural stiffness relaxed away. Her warm curves pressed into him, clinging and soft.

"But I'll do crazy things and get into trouble." She confessed in a tiny voice, one hand still toying with his shirt collar. "I can't help it."

"I don't give a damn what you do."

She tensed in his arms, pulling back to gawk at him. "But I thought—"

"Like I said, I'm not trying to change you, just...reign you in a little." He assured her, touching a gentle hand to her hair...careful not to crush the delicate hope blossoming between them. "Be you. Just, eh, let me be a part of the madness too. Give me a chance to danger-proof these plans of yours, or at least help contain the chaos a little bit. Can you promise me that much?"

"But, what if I... *break the law*?" She whispered, with comic angst.

"I'm a lawyer." He whispered back, kissing the tip of her nose. "I can make sure you don't get caught."

"Oh. Ok, cool." She nodded with childish enthusiasm, as if the possibility had never occurred to her before. The woman was damned cute. "No more lies. I promise."

* * *

"Good. That's settled." He stated in a voice that Calam realized meant that he considered the matter closed. "Now, c'mere. I missed you."

In the next instant his mouth found hers, and Calam couldn't say with any great certainly whether the outside world even still existed. All she knew for the moment was the hot, erotic caress of his mouth against hers...more raw and demanding than she remembered. She inhaled the fresh spicy scent of his aftershave, felt the warmth of his body burning through her clothes and moaned. His hands slid up her bare back, beneath the tunic, doing away with her bra strap along the way. He broke away from her mouth and trailed firebrand kisses down her cheek, her jaw and finally around to her earlobe. His hands seemed to be everywhere at once. One gentled her head back, to expose her neck to his mouth. Her mind reeled from one sensation to the next...fast losing all capacity for rational thought.

He spoke in a gravelly, distracted moan against the tender, sensitive skin just below her ear lobe. "I want you, beneath me... *now*."

Calamity's body felt like a hot viscous liquid being consumed in an overheated furnace. Oh, Lawd. Her mind reeled...back to the one other time she'd felt this way. The one night they'd spent together was a sort of tortured bliss, different than she imagined it would be. Even the memory made her shudder. Her initial response had been bliss, but when the afterglow dissipated, she felt awkward, vulnerable, and uncomfortably exposed. It wasn't just the lost of her innocence. He touched her, up close and personal...close enough to do real damage. And the scary part was... now, he *knew* the power he possessed over her. She opened up herself to him...only to be hurt, ridiculed and ultimately rejected less than twenty-four hours later. And he'd witnessed her utter devastation. Oh, Gawd, he *knew*...and he could do it again if he chose. That awful feeling of being naked and exposed, the memory swelled up and with it, panic...the same crazed fear of rejection and ridicule.

"Wait...Please...I can't." She broke away, or at least she tried too. Her intention to flee.

"Na, na, na, nah...Don't run." He relinquished his impassioned assault on her neck and let her retreat...a little, but he caught her before she could escape the circle of his arms. "Shorty? What's wrong?"

He relaxed back against the sofa, taking her with him. Her panting, all frantic eyes, and quaking limbs. He watched her, his breathing even, his eyes so dark and intense bored into hers. Always so calm, so in control, so intimidating. Calam wanted to sink into the floor. She settled for looking away from his probing gaze.

"No, don't hide either." His hand snaked out to capture her chin, forcing her to face him. He whispered, quiet...careful, but determined. "Tell me what's wrong."

Lowering her lashes, she murmured, "I... I'm scared. This, you, us...everything. Its scares me. Its just so...raw and new. Its too much too soon, you know. Those things you said...we ended so...badly–" Her voice broke.

"Aw hell. I'm sorry, Shorty." He leaned in and kissed her forehead...her temple, the tip of her nose, then her cheek. "Shhh...don't cry anymore. I know I hurt you. I promise, I won't speak to you that way again. We'll wait, ok. Its cool. A lot has happened. You're right, we should take a pause. We'll wait." He pulled back, seeking her approval. "Ok?"

She hesitated, her heart bruised but hopeful. "You don't...mind?"

The smile he gave her said he didn't. "Having us back takes precedent over everything else. If we need to slow it down to build a stronger us, I'm all for it."

She reached behind her, beneath her top, fumbling trying to hook her bra back up. Luce caught her fingers, and gently pried them away. "Hmmm...leave it for now. I like your skin. And I don't want anything between us." She let him guide her head back to his shoulder. Where he whispered, "Come home with me tonight. I *need* you there. There's a novella I want to read. Its naughty," He teased. "So I know you'll like it."

She nodded without a moment's hesitation. There they sat, intertwined, his hands stroking the smooth skin of her back beneath the loose tunic. Calamity broke into the oddly comforting silence.

"Luce?"

"Hmmm?"

"I panicked. After we...eh, I panicked a little."

"I know, Shorty. I should have expected it. This is all new for you. I should have taken that into consideration. I just didn't realize it in time. You know, you don't come off as having any sort of weakness, at all."

"I don't?"

"Hell no." He chuckled at the surprise in her voice. "You come off like a pit-bull trapped in a Chihuahua's body. You, eh, made me feel…duped." He admitted, nuzzling her temple as he spoke. "That I could be reduced to a gullible, henpecked fool being led around on a string by a woman half my size. Male pride and all that."

"Oh." She frowned.

"I had no idea anything I said could hurt you this much. Not until I saw how you were today." He confessed. "Pike was right. I don't know you well enough. But we're going to remedy that."

Calamity ducked her head, gathering her courage. "Um, since we're being honest, I should probably clarify something. I didn't lie for the reasons you think. I trust you, just not…not with my friends and family. That's going to take some time." She paused, trying to think of the best way to make him understand her choice…a bad choice as it turned out. "Reese, I know she's a bit cray, but she's a friend. And she's loyal…but you, you're flexible about that kinda stuff. I just didn't trust you with her."

He reared back and gaped at her. "You think I'm looking to double my pleasure?"

She snickered at both the ludicrous suggestion and his cartoonish shock-face. "No, of course not. Silly man. You wouldn't have much luck in that direction, anyway. Reese has the hots for your Neanderthal cousin, remember?"

"So then what's this about your not trusting me with her?"

"Luce, think for a minute. If I had told you the truth, and it turned out you couldn't get *both* of us off, what would you have done?"

"I'd have gotten *you* off. After all, she *did* blackmail

him, so it's not as if—" He paused at the realization. "You knew that. Well, it seems you know me a whole hell of a lot better than I know you."

"Yeah, but that's just because you're logical, predictable. Please understand, I had to come up with a fix for *everyone,* not just me. Lying was simple, quick, and effective. I hated doing it, but it seemed like the best solution at the time. No one got hurt."

He rolled his eyes. "Yeah, no one...but *you.*"

She shrugged. "I'm ok. I always land on my feet."

"Oh? Is that why I found you here...alone, unemployed, and crying on a Saturday evening? Calamity, you're not invincible."

Her fur ruffled at that. "Ok, first off, I have a job interview next week. Second, *you're* the one who made me cry. And I was not *a-lone.* Even before you came I had plans with Paul and Chris—" The memory of her plans brought a crinkle to her forehead, "—who are probably sending out the posse right about now. Let me up, I need to call Chrissy. I'm surprised she hasn't sent Pike to track me down."

His arm tightened around her instead. "She did. He came banging at the door while you were still asleep."

"Yikes." She winced at the thought of the two testosterone giants squaring off...Pike, protective, and Luce, defensive. "How'd *that* go?"

"Let's see. He threatened me with pistols at dawn. It was touch and go for a while there." He teased. "But, yeah, we're square."

"Oh, ok, that's good." Her unease drained away, "Luce, the rules are universal?"

"You bet."

"Can I make one, then?" She smiled at the thought that a moment ago he couldn't bare to let her go, even for a moment, noting with a deep feminine satisfaction when his hands looped around her hips.

"Go for it, Shorty." He gave her an encouraging

squeeze.

"Next time, don't be so quick to think the worse of me." She spoke in a soft but firm voice. "I realize that's a tall order, with *my* track record. But, if our situations had been reversed, I wouldn't have left you. I know you don't believe in my...eh, methods, but please try to believe in *me*."

"Hmm...ok, good point."

"So, it's a deal, then? My rule."

He dipped his head to eye level with her. "From now on, I'm your lawyer, not your judge."

She raised a playful brow. "Eh, can I get that in writing, Counselor?"

"That's my girl." He chucked. "Damn, I missed you. And its not just me. Sasha has fallen into a deep depression since you left. My apartment is a tomb of silent suffering. Even Sly's pissed at me."

"Neanderthal Man? We don't even get along. I figured he'd be dancing a jig at our demise."

"Naw, I think you earned his undying loyalty when you put your neck on the line to spring Reese from the can." He dropped a kiss on top of her head, pulling her close, cuddling her against his chest. "Claims I'm a boring sourpuss without you around to spice things up. Plus, he digs your sister. Him and Reese double-dated with Charisma and Paul, by the way."

"Yeah, I heard about that. Chrissy cleared it with me first. She didn't want me to think she'd gone over to the dark side."

"Heaven forbid." He quipped.

"Eh, Luce?" She broached, tentatively. "About Reese..."

"Its cool, I don't mind." He conceded.

"But you don't even know what I'm going to ask."

"I'd wager it has something to do with us doubling up with Sly and Reese."

Calam shot him a look. "How'd you know that?"

"Are you kidding me?" He quirked a brow. "The two of you are like Romy and Michelle *on crack*. I've been prepared to have my dinner conversation drowned out by those cow-bells ever since your sister asked us out on our first date."

She faked a pout. "Well, once Chris has the baby, she won't be able to hang out much. So its either Reese and Sly or we find a girl for Pike. Hmmm, actually, that's not a half-bad idea."

"Calamity, don't." He warned, making a mental note to give Pike the heads-up.

"What?" She shot him an innocent look. "Everyone needs a project. Trust me, I have a plan."

"Famous last words…"

OTHER BOOKS BY THIS AUTHOR

Dominic's Nemesis

Untitled Sequel to Dominic's Nemesis
(Available Spring/Summer 2017)

D. ALYCE DOMAIN

DOMINIC'S NEMESIS

PROLOGUE

Italy (1800s)

He lay on the pit floor, limbs stiff from lack of movement. The crawl space no longer accommodated his length. With no light to guide him, he planned each movement to avoid scraping against the granite. First, he shuffled his legs, then rolled his shoulders to bring back the circulation. His skin pulled and itched like the devil. The gouges must be scabbing over, he thought.

He hadn't tried to stand in a while, but he knew from the last time that he was almost tall enough to reach the pit's lid. Just a little while longer and he'd try again. He was preserving energy and hoping to be healed enough to try jumping. She would come soon, he knew. For now, the darkness was reassuring. It calmed his mind. As long as he was alone in the dark, nothing hurt him.

He didn't hear her approach. He never did. Light peeked through the pit's lid, casting the iron bars in distorted shadows around him. He trembled and buried his eyes in the bend of his arm. Panicked, he struggled to shove his gangly, pubescent body into a crevice between two outcroppings. If he merged with the granite walls, maybe she wouldn't be able to find him and do more damage.

"Come, come, now, little fiend." Her voice cast a lure like the nectar of a carnivorous flower.

The boy squeezed his eyelids tight despite the arm shield. He knew who awaited him above. He squirmed further into the jagged stone. The taut scabs on his shoulders cracked open and bled. He did not bother to scream or beg. Nothing ever saved him from whatever agony she came to inflict. Instead he prayed, "Help me, God, please. Do not let her see me this time. Hide me."

"Where are you, little fiend?"

He felt her mind rummage around for him like a blind man groping for his cane. Something new, he thought. Didn't she know where he was? Couldn't she see him? The pit was a scant six-foot cube and she waved the candelabra close enough so that hot wax splattered atop his forearms.

"Come here you little fiend!" Her voice turned shrill. "Give me back what's mine!"

Her ham-fisted attempts to locate him left him halfway between fear and confusion. Why couldn't she see him? Or touch him with her mind? By now, he should be frozen, mid-air with tangled clops of hair his only clothing. Fear ebbed into curiosity. He dared to lower his arm and peel his lids open. Even with his head still bowed, the candle-glow forced him to squint.

Here lay the true test, he knew. If his tormentor really couldn't see him or sense him, she wouldn't react to his gaze. He'd learned long ago to avert his eyes in her presence. He hadn't glimpsed his tormentor up close in six years. The boy swallowed the upsurge of fear and snapped his head back before he lost his nerve.

He blinked several times to sharpen his vision. He recoiled, scraping the skin at the point of his hip. Another blink, then he relaxed. Hair. Her obsidian tresses dangled down between the iron grate, seeming to reach for him. Her face was contorted from its cloying perfection, but not in reaction...more from anger or maybe frustration he guessed. He continued to stare, shocked, not sure what to do. How long would her...blindness or whatever it was, last? She started to screech obscenities and jab around with her mind. The violent brush of her mind jerked him from his stillness. He used the jagged wall behind him to pull himself upright. Gaunt, with wobbly knees and a hobbled gait, he crept close enough to fan his hand in front of her eyes.

"Mama?" His voice sounded croaky from non-use.

No reaction.

Then, he caught sight of his arm, the arm that should have been fanning before him. There was only empty space. With a huff of amazement, he glanced around him. His body cast no shadow. It was as if he had faded from existence, become part of the void.

Preview of Untitled Sequel to Dominic's Nemesis

EXCERPT

He had never been troubled with dreams before.

He writhed in his sleep, seeking an escape from his mutinous subconscious. His dark cap of wavy hair chaotic from tossing his head back and forth against the pillow. The dream's thrall crawled into his mind like a poisonous snake slithering along the ground to catch its unsuspecting prey. It was strange in its reality. The in-dream boy lay on his own bed, with his brother sleeping beside him blissfully unaware...just as his waking self and his brother slept most nights. Except, in the dream his small form was wracked by spasms of blinding pain. His very bones felt as if they were being pulled apart.

The boy shifted his shoulder to try to shake off the pain, and felt something snap out of place. He screamed at the horror of the sound more than the pain of the bone's dislocation. The pop of his other shoulder followed suit, but somehow he was still able to move his arms. Sweat glistened off his face, his breaths came in audible gasps. He held up his hands out in front of him. They looked wrong. The skin of his forearms rippled...normally smooth skin bristled with cactus spines...growing, protruding grotesquely from his arms, spreading like a rash to cover the entire surface so that all he saw were spines...elongating...now less like cactus...morphing into

317

porcupine's quills…that blended and weaved together, the quill ends softening into feathers. His arms were no longer discernable, transformed into flapping, wing-like appendages.

Crack. His hip bone crumbled inward, with horrifying suddenness. His legs…he caught sight of them. The boy could see the online of his bones beneath his tan olive skin. His thighs and legs began to retract inward, shortening, while his feet stretched impossibly long, with scaly talons where his toenails had once been. He thrashed around, the foreign parts of his body flopping, and half-formed. He was dying, ebbing away…to give birth to something else, something otherworldly.

He thoughts screamed…but he could make no sense of them. No longer words, or coherent ideas, but more akin to feelings, impressions of reality…instinct and patterns of expression. His mind no longer tried to understand the freakish metamorphosis seizing his body. His mental process struggled instead to survive it. A wavering image of a great bird flickered within his mind, like a candle flame caught in the draft of a swinging door. He couldn't quite hold the image, and some new level of instinct told him that it was imperative that he do so.

The boy, Gabriel, awoke to a beastly sound. He breathed deep. His first thought was of his hands. He brought them up to check himself, flipping his palms over front and back. He sighed. They were normal human hands, his skin also was smooth and normal when he pushed back the nightshirt's sleeves…

"CAHHHH!!"

His head snapped to the source of the half-human sound, midways between the screeching caw of a bird and the panicked scream of a child. His brother was not in bed.

"Giddy!" The boy leaped up, flung the covers aside, and ran around to the opposite side of the bed. What he saw, startled him so that he stumbled. His brother, his twin or at least he thought the freakish creature flailing around on the floor beside the bed was his brother. It shrieked, a malformed beak of sorts where his mouth had been.

He tip-toped toward the half-avian tangle of feathers, talons and dislocated limbs. The boy treaded slowly, not wanting to worsen his

318

brother's already frenzied panic. The oddity of his dream so perfectly mirroring reality wasn't lost on him. The dream boy hadn't been him at all, but Giddy...trapped in the half-bird transformation. The dream was real, a preview of sorts.

"Giddy?"

The flailing paused, and the halfling thing twisted around...a single crazed bird eye caught his.

"Cahhh!"

ABOUT THE AUTHOR

D. Alyce Domain. Is a long-time lover of creative fiction. She learned to read with Dr. Seuss, grew up reading Sweet Valley High, James Howe, and Lois Duncan, and graduated to category romance with Harlequin and Silhouette in her teen years. Ms. Domain started out writing fan-fiction after her favorite fictional characters met with death and cancellation on network television. Inspired by the entertaining, multi-layered storylines created by so many female romance, young adult and television writers, she began to experiment with her own characters. Coupled with her own unique brand of genre-bending romantic fiction, Ms. Domain was able to create a whole new world within the pages of her books.

Ms. Domain was born and raised in Houston, Texas, the youngest daughter of Charles and Eunice Domain. She has one older sister. She earned a BS in Biochemistry and a MS in Biomedical Sciences. She worked in Patient-Based Biological Research before switching careers and opening her own fashion boutique, The Aesthetic Domain. In addition to fashion apparel and accessories, she sells her own original jewelry creations and runs the Boutique & Blog website, which is based in Houston, Texas. Ms. Domain also has avid interests in inspirational music, art/entertainment, and history.